Cocoa, Florida

THE LEGENDS OF SMOKEOVER

THE LEGENDS OF SMOKEOVER

By

LAWRENCE PEARSALL JACKS
(1860 - 1955)

"Now his elder son was in the field: and as he came and drew nigh to the house, he heard musick and dancing."

PARABLE OF THE PRODIGAL SON.

Short Story Index Reprint Series

 BOOKS FOR LIBRARIES PRESS
FREEPORT, NEW YORK

First Published 1921
Reprinted 1970

STANDARD BOOK NUMBER:
8369-3589-6

LIBRARY OF CONGRESS CATALOG CARD NUMBER:
70-125222

PRINTED IN THE UNITED STATES OF AMERICA

THIS BOOK IS DEDICATED
TO
JOHN BUCHAN
IN ADMIRATION FOR HIS WRITINGS
GRAVE AND GAY
AND
IN GRATITUDE FOR WISE COUNSEL
GIVEN IN A FORM
WHICH MULTIPLIED ITS VALUE

CONTENTS

		PAGE
	SMOKEOVER AND ITS SMOKE	11

I THE LEGEND OF RUMBELOW, THE BETTING MAN

CHAPTER
I	THE EVOLUTION OF RUMBELOW	27
II	MR. RUMBELOW'S BUSINESS FROM WITHIN	40
III	RUMBELOW'S FEAST	60

II THE LEGEND OF THE MAD MILLIONAIRE

I	SMOKEOVER GROWS RICH	81
II	THE PROFITEER	94
III	MR. HOOKER'S ADVISERS	115
IV	THE MAD MILLIONAIRE HAS A NEAR SHAVE	128
V	THE TRANSFIGURATION OF A MOUSE	151
VI	MR. HOOKER FACES THE WORST	166
VII	AND DISCOVERS THE UNREAL	171
VIII	AND BEGINS TO MAKE USE OF HIS DISCOVERY	182
IX	MR. HOTBLACK EXPOUNDS THE BEAUTY OF BUSINESS	197
X	AND MR. HOOKER BEHOLDS THE BEAUTY OF WOMEN	209

III THE LEGEND OF MARGARET WOLFSTONE

I	MISS WOLFSTONE BECOMES CLAIRVOYANT	229
II	MISS WOLFSTONE PROVES HERSELF AN ADVENTURESS	244
III	AND EMBARKS FORTHWITH ON A DANGEROUS ADVENTURE	263

CONTENTS

IV THE LEGEND OF PROFESSOR RIPPLEMARK

CHAPTER		PAGE
I	THE EMERGENCE OF PROFESSOR RIPPLEMARK	283
II	MR. HOOKER VERIFIES AN INTUITION	304
III	PROFESSOR RIPPLEMARK IS PUT TO THE QUESTION	323
IV	PROFESSOR RIPPLEMARK IS EXTRICATED FROM A DIFFICULTY	339
V	AND FORTHWITH FINDS HIMSELF IN ANOTHER	357

V THE LEGEND OF THE LEAGUE

I	A DEN OF THIEVES	383
II	"LES BEAUX ESPRITS S'ENTENDENT"	399

PART ONE

The Legend of Rumbelow, the Betting Man

THE LEGENDS OF SMOKEOVER

Smokeover and Its Smoke

THE city of Smokeover is renowned for size, momentum and obscurity. It contains a million inhabitants, not counting those in the cemeteries, who, though they have no votes, are still potent in the common life. There are ninety miles of electric tramways, two thousand public-houses, four hundred schools, three hundred places of worship, five garden suburbs, two square miles of slums, a municipal Art Gallery, a branch of the Society for Ethical Culture, a racecourse, three prisons, a university, a crematorium, and a sewage system which is the wonder of the world. The city government, with a Lord Mayor at its head, is progressive, especially in the matter of raising the rates. Most of the public services have been municipalized. The consumption of coal is enormous, 900,000 tons being carbonized annually in the production of municipal gas alone. The water, brought from a great distance, is pure and abundant, but the light is dim and the air charged with the products of combustion. The odour of burnt petrol pervades the streets at all hours of the day and far into the night.

Smokeover makes all sorts of things; its products are as varied as the merchandise of Tyre, inventoried by the Prophet Ezekiel; the worm that consumes them never dies, and the fire that creates them is never quenched. But the chief product of Smokeover is, of course, itself; or rather its million inhabitants. More than any of its manufactures, more than all of them put together, these men, women and children represent the city's main contribution to the working capital of the universe. What they are worth nobody knows; some holding that they are worth nothing at all, or at least acting upon that assumption, others that their value is immense. On this question hot dispute rages in Smokeover, and a professor of economics in the local university has cynically suggested that the only way to settle the matter would be to turn all the inhabitants, rich and poor, into slaves and sell them for what they would fetch in the open market. But to this, and to all such high-handed methods, the citizens show great aversion, Liberty being one of their watchwords. A few are haunted by a secret fear that they would not fetch much, if put up for auction.

Speaking broadly, one may say that the work that has to be done in Smokeover from day to day is not liked by the majority of those who have to do it. They describe their labour as "laborious," which is far from being a tautology, and consent to it only on condition that the hours are reduced to a minimum and the pay increased to a maximum, reaching the goal of their desires when they have no more of it to do, either because the hour has struck for knocking off, or because they are in a position to "retire." But let no one suppose that the men of Smokeover spend their leisure time in doing nothing.

SMOKEOVER AND ITS SMOKE

They spend it in making demands on the labour of their fellow citizens, thereby creating a vicious circle in the life of the city; since the more leisure one man has the harder another must work to keep the first amused or to prevent him getting into mischief. A few employ their leisure by taking walks into the country and contemplating the beauties of nature; but even this wears out their shoes, which somebody else has to mend. On the whole, the inhabitants are not as anxious to preserve the civilization of their city as they are glad to get away from it. This becomes evident in times of war, when the young men rush to the colours by thousands. Though war in itself is by no means attractive, it often becomes so to the men of Smokeover in comparison with other things—for example, with the Smokeover type of peace.

The city is a hive of contradictions. If you are thinking of the best people who live there, you would pronounce it a model of what such places should be; but if you are thinking of what the best people have to contend against in the worst, you would say that no more wicked city ever existed on this earth. Your impression will vary between extremes, according as you fix attention on the flowers which the tree bears on some of its branches or on the foul juices which feed its roots. Both extremes are reflected in the local oratory, some orators maintaining that Smokeover is progressing towards the earthly paradise, others that it is sliding down an inclined plane towards a dismal catastrophe.

In the suburbs are pleasant houses, thousands of them, with gardens, shady trees, shrubberies, tennis lawns, ponds. Here comfort reigns and beauty is a frequent visitor. As you sit or wander in the gardens you may see the tops of the factory chimneys rising above the tops of the trees and placidly smoking in the distance, and may reflect that, in the economic sense, the gardens are fed by the smoke. When the wind is in the right direction a smell of sulphur will be in the air; you will also observe that the green of the shrubberies is not of the purest; careful old ladies may sometimes be seen wiping the smuts off the laurels with a wet sponge. Here are lithe and beautiful girls, in white frocks, playing tennis, whose joyous faces, light laughter and easy movement will help you to believe in God, and to say "all's right with the world," or at least nothing radically wrong with Smokeover. But down in the slums are women of another type, who fight one another on Saturday nights with hellish outcries and bloody faces, while the men look on. These will help you to believe in the devil, or to fancy that you are in hell already. Which indeed may be the fact, hell most assuredly having no fouler sight to show. Yet all is one. The heaven and the hell, the tennis-playing sylphs and the gin-drinking viragoes—the smoke of Smokeover sustains them both.

Three main interests, the political, the economic and the spiritual, occupy the inhabitants and determine the general form and pressure of their lives. These three make a partnership, an alliance, or, as some are now preferring to say, an entanglement, in which politics are unquestionably predominant.

The political interest of Smokeover covers the fortunes of the world, embracing the whole network of warlike relationships on which the fates of empire depend, and coming to a head at frequent intervals in the policies of rival parties at the elections.

The economic interest, concerned with the production of what the text-books call "wealth" and the Lord's Prayer "daily bread," has to adjust itself as best it may to the political, submitting its accumulations to destruction and contenting itself with what is left over, whenever the politicians go to war.

The spiritual interest, which is popularly known as "Education," comes last, and has to adjust itself to the other two, sometimes to each singly, sometimes to both together, being never allowed to take its place at the common table until the appetites of the more important partners have been satisfied.

Thus the economic interest dances attendance upon the political, and the spiritual on both. The arrangement is accurately reflected in the minds of the inhabitants, which have become so habituated to this order of priority as to be unaware that it exists. A proposal to reverse it would be treated by most of them as unthinkable. "Reverse *what?*" they would ask; and when you told them what you propose to reverse, some would call upon the god of Smokeover to dash you to pieces. All the same, the inhabitants are profoundly restive under the political and economic servitude to which their spiritual interest has been reduced. Not knowing what is the matter with them they blame the government, and can think of no remedy save getting a new one, which is no sooner elected than they become more restive than ever.

THE LEGENDS OF SMOKEOVER

In normal times Smokeover has the appearance of belonging to peace, and of taking little interest in war, either as an occupation or as a spectacle. The city has no fortifications, while the only cannon it contains are mementoes, soiled by the droppings of birds. The barracks are inconspicuous, their very existence unknown to most of the inhabitants. For outward and visible signs of regimentation one looks in vain. The movements of the population, the surging crowds at the stations, the goings to and fro in the busy streets, suggest a fermentation rather than a march; each person appears to be going somewhere, the totality nowhere. Though these people are descendants of a conquering race, citizens of an empire built up by conquest, they have no martial airs, and seldom swagger, save when they are in their cups. But when placed under discipline they soon acquire the manage of arms and the military carriage; the face of the shopman loses its pallor, the shrunken chest of the waiter fills out, the mincing barber comes home to his astonished friends with the robust frame and the hardy countenance of war.

In which particular there is an analogy between the men of Smokeover and the industries by which they earn their daily bread. For, just as these unsoldierly people can on the briefest notice be converted into excellent soldiers, so by a transformation no less rapid the chimneys which to-day are smoking for peace will to-morrow be smoking for war; while, down below, the iron bedsteads are turning into bombs, the ploughshares into gun-barrels, the pruning-hooks into bayonets, and nitro-glycerine is being concocted in the dyeing vat. These sudden trans-

SMOKEOVER AND ITS SMOKE

formations have given rise to the longest of the Smokeover Legends, which will appear in its place.

Indeed, when we closely scrutinize these things our first impression that Smokeover is a peace-made city begins to waver. Beneath the outward semblance of unreadiness for war, and of preoccupation with other things, we discern an inner structure in the life of the city which suggests a very close adjustment to the war-making needs of a militant civilization. Many features of the place which seem at first sight to favour peace, turn out, on closer examination, to favour war. The religion, for example. This is Christianity, which no man construes as a religion of strife. But the God worshipped by the Smokeover Christians has managed somehow to acquire qualities that commend him to the military mind. He rules the universe under a system of inviolable law and punishes mutineers with death, essentially a God of regimentation and discipline in the popular conception of Him, and a hard hitter, easily acclimatized to the atmosphere of the drill ground and ready to become a God of Battles on the turn of a phrase. Of all the vocations and properties of Smokeover none can be converted more swiftly to the uses of war than its religion and its God. So with its morality. This rests on the idea of *duty*, variously interpreted by the philosophers, but recognized at once by the men of Smokeover as that which England expects them all to do when a battle has to be fought. So it comes to pass that whenever a call goes forth for fighting men in Smokeover, religion and morality, the Churches and the Society for Ethical Culture, cry out with one voice to the young men, "Enlist, and we will go with you into the field," the clergy themselves setting the example by becoming military chaplains.

And what shall we say of the "economic system," of the trade, the manufactures, the business, the wage-earning and the profit-making that go on from day to day? These, too, look peaceable enough. But observe the "system" with a closer eye, and what do you find? You find that wealth in Smokeover is so distributed that it can be easiest got at when wanted to furnish the commissariat of war. Which is the easier—to tax and borrow from ten millionaires or from a million men having ten pounds apiece? There are exactly ten millionaires in Smokeover. Is that an accident? And who can fail to see that the distribution of wealth in time of peace is the basis for the distribution of power in time of war? Take the statistics of rich and poor. Lo and behold, they roughly display the proportion of officers and privates contributed by the city to the recent war. Is that an accident either? What a war-making civilization demands is a relatively small class of the rich and well-to-do to furnish the money and the officers, and a relatively large class of the poor to fill the ranks and clean up the mess. Exactly what you will find in Smokeover.

On all grounds therefore we shall err if we take Smokeover at its face value as a peace-made or a peace-making city. In the foreground of the picture are the slums and the suburbs, the chimneys and the tennis lawns, the factories and the mansions, the churches and the taverns, the throng in the street and the crowd at the football match; in the background are marching hosts and bloody battles; and between the two run links of meaning and purpose, which so connect them that foreground and background combine together into one consistent whole. The transition from peace to war in our city is not violent, as some think, but natural and easy. In a war-making world Smokeover stands ready for use at the shortest notice, and with the least possible breach with existing habits of mind. One may compare the inhabitants to a mighty shoal of fishes imprisoned in a far-flung and invisible net, which encloses so vast an area of the ocean that the fishes may swim and disport themselves for hundreds of miles, and reproduce their kind generation after generation, without once discovering that they are in a cruel trap. When war needs the fishes the net is drawn in.

The city has an imposing coat of arms, bearing the legend *Per ardua ad astra;* which means, when translated into the vernacular, "Go ahead." In the local oratory, not the least among the Smokeover products, the stars are sometimes mentioned; but in the popular mind they are objects of little importance, being much obscured by the canopy of smoke which the manifold industries of the place pour into the circumambient sky. To the business men who govern the city—most admirably, so they say—the idea of guiding them either by the stars or to the stars would, if seriously pressed, seem somewhat ridiculous. They read what is written on the coat of arms as a general injunction to Smokeover to widen the streets, to clear insanitary areas, to municipalize gas, electricity and water, to extend the tram-lines into the suburbs and to raise the rates—in short, to go ahead, keeping well abreast of the times. And the city responds, not, however, with a reckless plunge, but with a creeping movement, so slow that the individual inhabitants are not conscious of it until it has carried them a measurable distance, but so irresistible in its momentum that if you get in the way there will be nothing left of you to tell the tale.

But whither is Smokeover going?—that is the question. As we have seen it makes no pretence of going to the stars, in spite of the legend on its coat of arms. But if not to the stars, where else? In the year 1740 George Whitefield, preaching in the Bear Pit, told the inhabitants they were going straight to hell; whereupon there was a panic, attended by many conversions. But those were the days when Smokeover believed in Original Sin and in the book of Genesis, and had, in consequence, a distinct idea of its place in the universe and of yet more dangerous places in the immediate vicinity. But nowadays it has no such idea, mistaken or otherwise. The inhabitants do not bother about the universe, having more important affairs to look after. They know of course their place on the map, know it better than their fathers did in the days when maps were scarce and inaccurate; but in the universe they are completely lost. There is not a soul among them, from the Bishop to the man who empties the dust bins, who could tell the citizens, with a confidence like that of George Whitefield, the exact whereabouts of Smokeover in the general scheme of things. What wonder then that nobody knows whither Smokeover is going? And yet it goes ahead all the time, thinking of the universe, when it thinks at all, as a place where cities cannot go wrong provided they are big enough, produce plenty of smoke and have the right men on the city council.

The momentum of this advance is little understood by those of the citizens who would convert Smokeover into the New Jerusalem. They are apt to deal with the city as though it were a stationary object, ready to be turned in this direction or that by the impact of the Ideal. But when a mass so enormous moves forward, even though the pace be no greater than a snail's, an earthquake is needed to turn it from its course. So it is with the movement of Smokeover. Beneath the changes that take place on the surface, which are important and visible to the eye, there is the invisible urge of the total mass, creeping forward in a path marked out for it by history and by the mental habits of the million inhabitants—a prodigious and terrible force. During the recent war, which was a kind of earthquake, the momentum of the city seemed for once to have met its match; it received a check; conditions looked favourable for a radical change; and the hopes of reconstruction ran high. Had reconstruction begun then and there, a new birth might have happened, and the face of Smokeover definitely turned itself towards the stars. But, alas, the opportunity could not be seized! By common consent reconstruction had to wait till the war was over. Nobody was expected to begin just yet, for plainly nothing could be done until the Germans, who were planning reconstruction on a model of their own, had been thoroughly defeated. The delay was fatal. No sooner was the war at an end than the momentum of the city, which had gathered energy in the interval, resumed its mastery over the lives of the inhabitants. For it was instantly apparent, even to the dullest minds, that unless Smokeover smoked harder than ever there would be a famine in the land. In a moment the radiant dream had vanished, a curtain was drawn over the vision of the stars, and the wise men of the place, having no alternative, were changing their note from the heavenly to the earthly key. The Bishop, the Lord Mayor, the Principal of the University, the President of the Free Church Council, the President of the Ethical Society, the local members of Parliament, the leader of the Labour Party, the Chairmen of the Banks, the Captains of Industry and all the others, domestic and imported, whose mission it was to guide Smokeover to the stars, joined their voices with one accord in urging the city to smoke its hardest, or, as they phrased it, "to produce more." Instead of arresting the monster in his course they found themselves riding on his back, and praising the smoke that went up from his nostrils. They scrubbed him and they cleaned him, they planted trees between his scales, they built garden suburbs behind his ears, they tied bunches of flowers to his lashing tail, they did all they could to make him a presentable monster. But he all the time crept on, taking them whithersoever he would, while the stars shone through the gathering murk with a dimmer light and seemed less important than ever—save perhaps for a brief period when a coal strike extinguished the fires below. In plain speech, Smokeover fell back at a bound into the old smoky ways that had made it what it was, disporting itself as before, and unconscious that it was still held captive in the far-flung net of war. Is not the momentum of this city a prodigious and terrible thing?

All gospels for the reformation of Smokeover, all revolutions for its overthrow, seem doomed to reduce themselves in like manner to the simple formula "Make more smoke." The momentum of the place, which rules the minds as well as the bodies of the inhabitants, will not suffer it to be otherwise. Unless your gospel or your revolution can express itself in smoke-making terms, Smokeover will have none of it. This is the acid test of truth, the standard of righteousness and the canon of practicability. You may borrow your principles from the highest heaven of invention; you may begin in the City of God; no one will *object*; but no one will *believe* until you give these shining things an intelligible, smoke-making application. In all this Smokeover is reaping the fruits of the second of the two great crises in the history of civilization. The first took place when the kingdom of heaven was captured by politics in the age of Constantine; the second when it was captured by economics in the age of Smokeover. Both captures were brought about by the momentum of things.

Towards the end of the war there arose in this city a group of five persons, two women and three men, who, for reasons which the Legends tell, rebelled against these conditions. Rebels in the vulgar sense they were not; for they attacked no government and shot nobody in the back. At the peril of their fortunes, their lives and their reputation for sanity, they resolved to oppose the momentum of Smokeover and to strike for a kingdom not founded on smoke. At first the resolution was taken by each one singly. Later on they found one another out, as loyal spirits are apt to do, and formed a conspiracy, splendid but perhaps quixotic, against the canopy of smoke that hung over their city and hid the light of the stars from their fellow citizens. How they came to find one another out and to lay their plans will be told in these Legends.

They were all great souls; all had drunk the cup of amazement and rubbed elbows with death; and since the psychology of great souls is widely different from that of little ones (a point overlooked in the text-books) some persons may find a difficulty in believing that such beings ever walked the earth, or existed at all. Even the Author himself, who had not created these Legends, but merely collected them in their birthplace, has often wondered at the strange doings he has had to transcribe. On the whole he is inclined to believe that the five conspirators were real people. If so, and if on reading these pages they should recognize themselves under the disguise here assigned to them, he presents them with his apologies for the many lies he has had to tell. It was necessary to tell lies in order to give the public a truthful impression of what these five great souls were after. All legends do this.

That Smokeover should have produced a literature of legend is in itself a sufficiently remarkable fact. As the birthplace of legend no city could have a more unpromising look. When the Author, visiting the city to collect these stories, explained his errand to the wise men of the place, they seemed both astonished and amused, and, after whispering among themselves for some minutes, during which the Author suspected that his reputation for sanity was being canvassed, they informed him with a smile that Smokeover was not Iceland and that he had evidently made a mistake as to his whereabouts. When he replied, with some warmth, that he knew perfectly where he was, and that Smokeover was far too dirty to be mistaken for any other place, and has posed the wise men with a few questions about Iceland and its Sagas which they could not answer, they changed their ground and asked him whether *legends* were really what he wanted, and not rather the plot for a novel. If so, they added, they could supply him with plenty. On this the indignation of the Author broke bounds; it seemed to him an offensive thing that he should be suspected of not knowing the difference between a legend and a novel; and so the parties separated with mutual contempt, the wise men convinced that the Author was mad, the Author convinced that the wise men were fools.

It was only after protracted search that he came upon the first traces of the Smokeover Legends, of which, from certain points in the appearance of the place, he had never doubted the existence. For though to the casual observer Smokeover might seem far too dim a spot to be the home of phantasy, there were, nevertheless, in the hidden parts of its structure, a few features which, closely examined, looked uncommonly like points of contact with an invisible world.

Now it is an invariable rule in the growth of literature that legends originate at the places of transit where ideal things pass over into actualities. They haunt the bridges between the visible world and its heavenly counterpart; they gather at the fords and ferries which carry the traffic of the eternal values across the River of Forgetfulness into the scene of their temporal manifestations. Two or three of these bridges, all in the very heart of Smokeover, the Author was able to find. There he would linger, confident that he would not have long to wait, often averting his eyes or holding his nostrils (for one of the places reeked with sin), but with the listening organ at the utmost tension of expectancy, ready for the smallest voice. Murmurs and whisperings soon began, which grew little by little to the form of intelligible speech. The first Legend to come to the Bridge and become fully articulate was that of Rumbelow the Betting Man. Translated into the vernacular it ran as follows.

CHAPTER ONE

The Evolution of Rumbelow

MR. ARTHUR RUMBELOW, senior partner in the great betting firm of Rumbelow, Stallybrass & Corker, was an incarnation of the gambling spirit and one of the greatest gamesters of any age. He had graduated, with the highest honours, on the Turf, and then, with the Ring as a point of departure, had gradually extended his sphere of operations until it embraced the world. He was ready to lay odds on most events in the heavens above and on the earth beneath. "The things that interest mankind," he was wont to say, "are the things on which you can bet." To great and giddy heights had he come, where, invisible to the gross vision of the multitude, he played his part as the builder-up and the puller-down of human fortunes—the mentor of theologians, the scourge of philosophers, the prompter of the Press, the secret counsellor of kings. The orators declaimed, the parties fought, the voters voted, the cabinets sat, the parliaments made laws, the diplomatists lied; but Mr. Rumbelow pulled invisible strings behind them all. By a nod or a word or a telegram he could upset the plans of the wariest statesman and make monarchs tremble on their thrones—a man mighty in the casting down of strongholds.

Mr. Rumbelow was of unknown parentage. In the back parlours of public-houses, in the smoking-rooms of clubs, at the dinner tables of millionaires, strange stories were told about his father, and yet stranger about his mother; but as these have never been verified and are compromising to the parties concerned they shall not be repeated. So much however may be said: they connected Mr. Rumbelow with one of the noblest families on the earth.

His earliest recollections were of going round to country wakes and fairs with a drunken rascal who kept a Coco-nut Shy, and went by the name of Rumbelow. This man, when he was sober, gave it out that the boy Arthur was his son; but when he was drunk he would tell another tale, which gave rise to the stories aforesaid. *In vino veritas*—to this extent at least that Arthur was, most assuredly, not Rumbelow's son.

The boy's duties were to look after the coco-nuts, to throw them, when knocked off the stands, to the successful competitors, and then to replace them with others, while his master, at the other end of the show, blew a trumpet and took the money.

At the age of ten he began his studies of the Doctrine of Probability, counting up the hits and misses, and recording them each day with a piece of chalk on the sides of the caravan in which he lived with his reputed father. When the sides of the caravan were covered with figures the boy would stare at them for hours in the intervals of business, and finally evolved a formula which he communicated to his master. The result was that the Rumbelow firm was able to offer "shies" at three a penny instead of two—the price hitherto ruling the market. It was the first benefit conferred on the public by the genius of Arthur Rumbelow: he had reduced the price to the consumer. But, of course, it led to bad feeling in the trade. The Rumbelow firm was regarded by the other proprietors as a blackleg or pirate undertaking. There are two methods of making money: the one by selling things dear; the other, far more lucrative, by selling them cheap. From the very beginning Mr. Rumbelow was a convinced believer in the second and the implacable enemy of all who practised the first. The hostility was reciprocal. On one occasion the stand was wrecked by a mob incited for the purpose, and the two Rumbelows grievously pelted with their own coco-nuts, insomuch that all would have been lost had not the young Rumbelow, counter-attacking with inconceivable fury, launched a monster nut full in the face of the leading assailant, who was laid out for dead. After this victory the trade acquiesced in the inevitable, and the price of the sport all over the kingdom was brought down to the Rumbelow level. Cut-throat competition had done its work. Coco-nut shying became more popular, the importation of coco-nuts increased, and the inhabitants of the South Sea Islands began to grow rich. We live in a world where everything is connected with everything else.

The capital needed for starting a Coco-nut Shy is not large. In proportion to the funds invested it probably yields as rich a return as any other line of business known to man. All you require to begin with is ten-shillings' worth of coco-nuts, a dozen props to poise them on, a box of wooden balls, a canvas screen, with your name on it, to arrest the missiles, a trumpet to summon and stimulate the sportsmen, and a hand-barrow to transport the equipment from place to place. For labour, one boy will be enough, an orphan by preference, and of a suitable age to be chastised with a strap without risk of reprisals. You will live in the open air, travel much, see all the wakes and fairs in the country, which are well worth seeing, pay neither rent nor rates, and, if your hobby takes that form, may practise bigamy with small risk of detection. The life will be easy and sporting, the bad debts none and the profits immense. It is to be hoped that when the Social Revolution confiscates private property it will not overlook so flagrant an instance of the vices inherent in a capitalist system. There are Coco-nut Shies that pay over a thousand per centum and scandalously sweat their employees. The young Rumbelow, for instance, who made the fortunes of his master's business, was never paid more than five shillings a week, was cruelly strapped, fed with rotten coco-nuts and compelled to sleep in that corner of the caravan which was fullest of fleas. It was a little out of keeping with all this that Rumbelow the elder was himself a social revolutionary of advanced views and insatiable volubility. He might often be seen, when the show had closed down, on the village green or at the street corner, urging a knot of youths with cigarettes in their mouths and caps stuck on the sides of their heads to rise in mass against their oppressors.

There are many trades which, whether from oversight or favouritism, enjoy a like immunity from the zeal of the reformer. Arthur Rumbelow, having begun life in one of them, was quick to find others of a similar nature. Under the mental discipline afforded by these vocations he developed, as we shall presently see, a brain which was more than a match for all the Finance Ministers of Europe, whether of the conservative or the revolutionary type. At the period of his great prosperity he was wont to say that, however much the community might subtract from his enormous wealth by way of ransom, he would undertake, in six months, to extract from the community twice as much, and that without the least risk of interference by the State. By these means Mr. Rumbelow became, in due course, a most dangerous man; he acquired an art by which he could capture institutions, even the most democratic, for his own ends; and, had it not been for that high moral nature which he inherited from unknown ancestors, there is no telling what desolations he might have wrought on the earth. But we are anticipating.

One night, after a particularly violent speech for social justice, Mr. Rumbelow the elder retired to a neighbouring public-house, drank himself full of fiery spirits and went staggering home with a fixed resolve to strap Arthur, on the ground that he was a sanguinary aristocrat, within an inch of his life. Arrived at the caravan he proceeded to put his plan into execution. But Arthur, who was now sixteen, resisted; there was a scuffle, and the great Coco-nut King fell down dead. In the interior of the caravan was a lady with whom Mr. Rumbelow had just contracted a bigamous alliance. This lady, on seeing the dead body of her lord stretched out at the foot of the caravan steps, fled shrieking into the night and was never heard of again. There was an inquest; a verdict of death from alcohol; a funeral of the fallen hero under the Red Flag; after which, no other heirs or assigns forthcoming, Arthur took possession of the business—goodwill, coco-nuts and all.

His first acts were to burn the contents of the caravan, to fumigate its interior with sulphur and to wash down the walls with boiling water. He then took the money that was in the cash-box, went down town, bought himself a fashionable suit of clothes and a bottle of eau-de-Cologne, had a hot bath, his hair cut and his hands manicured, dined at an expensive restaurant, and was in time to open business when the fair began at half-past seven in the evening. Next day he went to a firm of decorators, where he ordered the repainting of the caravan in black, gold and cream-white, according to a design which he had drawn on a piece of paper, at a cost of £40, half of which he paid on deposit; then to a furniture shop, where he bought some kitchen utensils, a bookshelf, a brass bedstead, an armchair and a water-colour picture; then to a bookshop for Todhunter's Algebra and Shakespeare's works. Lastly to a maker of musical instruments, from whom he ordered a silver bugle, the firm having only brass ones in stock. There was money in the cash-box to pay for all that, and much more.

Hence that dainty caravan which arrests the eye of the artist as he wanders through the country fair; hence that courteous and well-dressed young gentleman who summons you to the sport by the call of a silver bugle, and sometimes plays a merry tune into

THE EVOLUTION OF RUMBELOW

the bargain; hence that sudden outbreak of a craze among the young women, who crowd the Rumbelow stand; hence the roaring business of the reconstituted firm. There are dark looks, of course, and foul words among rival proprietors; there is more sinister talk of cut-throat competition; and in the neighbouring public-houses, towards closing time, mention is frequently made of a fierce dog to be let loose, of a head to be bashed in with a silver bugle, of a so-and-so caravan to be raided and burnt. But all that comes to nothing. For among the purchases of Arthur Rumbelow there is one not mentioned in the list above—a revolver and a box of cartridges. The conspirators know it. They know also that the eyes of Arthur Rumbelow are vigilant and that his long white hands are very quick—a dangerous man even at this early period.

Four years after this Arthur Rumbelow was the owner of twenty-five Coco-nut Shies, and had a well-appointed office in the city of Smokeover. Every month his operations extended and some competitor was absorbed or driven out of the market. Coco-nut shying was fast becoming not only a popular but a fashionable sport; titled ladies and the wives of Cabinet Ministers might sometimes be seen taking their turn with pot-boys and housemaids at the Rumbelow stands. Wherever the great legend, "Rumbelow's Mammoth Coco-nuts" displayed its folds, it was, to the aristocracy, a guarantee of style, and to the proletariate, of good value.

And so it went on until the rumour spread in financial circles that Rumbelow controlled the entire Coco-nut Shying of the United Kingdom. Then the whole country caught the fever and began to resound with the crash of the falling nuts and the shouts of the competitors. The invalid heard them on his couch, the student at his desk, the worshipper in his church. Professors of History compared it to the Dancing Mania of the Middle Ages, and wrote articles in the reviews. A new business sprang into existence under Rumbelow's creative touch—that of providing private "Shies" for country houses, seaside hotels, golf clubs and Atlantic liners. A committee of sporting Members of Parliament, egged on by the wife of a Minister, commissioned Rumbelow to erect a "Shy" in a basement room of the House of Commons, for the refreshment of tired legislators. Bishops ordered them for their palaces to keep the younger clergy out of mischief at ordination times, while a certain Dean, who had become a "dead shot" at the game and a terror to the whole Church, suddenly sprang into fame as one of the foremost theologians of his time. Meanwhile Rumbelow, travelling *en prince* in the South Seas, was buying up every coco-nut plantation he could lay his hands on.

Then one day the news was flashed by cable that Rumbelow has sold the whole concern, Shies, plantations, goodwill and all, to an American syndicate for a million dollars. The news fell like a thunderclap. From that moment the doom of Coco-nut Shying, as a progressive sport, was sealed. Nothing so intensely British could flourish under the Stars and Stripes, and, beyond that, nothing the Americans had to offer could make good the loss of magnetic contact with the master mind of Rumbelow, which had been from first to last the actuating force of the

THE EVOLUTION OF RUMBELOW

whole development. And when later it became known that the American syndicate was composed of persons interested in the manufacture of chewing-gum, and that their object was to develop its export to the British Isles; and when boxes of this odious commodity began to appear on British stands in place of legitimate coco-nuts, the disgust and indignation of the sporting public knew no bounds. Since then all kinds of vile substitutes have been offered, and Coco-nut Shying, as everybody knows, has gone to the dogs. A case is on record of a fair in a north-country town where the objects on the stands were, not even boxes of chewing-gum, but—*nefandum dictu*—frozen sheep's heads from South America! Naturally the Shy in the basement of the House of Commons has been cleared out, and the room is now used for Lost Property. The dainty caravans have been sold to enthusiasts for the Simple Life, and the sweet challenge of the Silver Bugle is heard no more.

On the close of this chapter in his history Rumbelow disappeared entirely from the public view. For five years he remained hidden, and there is nothing but conjecture to fill the gap. Some said that he was lovemaking, a school in which so far he had neither committed errors nor won distinctions. Others that he had retired into the wilderness, that he was meditating great things, and would presently return on the wings of the storm. Others that he was travelling on the Continent and secretly indoctrinating the unconverted nations in the Gospel of Sport. Others that he was studying, under an assumed name, in a foreign university. Others that he had been shipwrecked on an island in the Southern Seas and was married to a dusky bride.

In each and all of these rumours there lurked an element of truth. For certain it is that when the five years were elapsed Rumbelow suddenly reappeared on the Turf, accompanied by a woman of extraordinary beauty, whom he introduced as his wife. It was the great race meeting of the year, and observers noticed that as Rumbelow moved about among the Ambassadors and their wives on the Grand Stand he conversed fluently with each in his own tongue, while they, on their part, seemed to accept the pair as members of their own fraternity. Some thought that the lady was an American, judging by the vivacity of her manner; others that she was a Russian, judging by the brilliance of her beauty; and this seemed to be confirmed when Mr. Rumbelow was heard to converse with the Russian Ambassador in that language.

The next news was that he had purchased the country seat of a nobleman, that a great architect was remodelling its defective features and building in the castle grounds a private chapel or sanctuary in a novel style, which some said was that of a Shinto temple; that immense house parties, in which persons of every class were mingled without social friction, were constantly being entertained; that Rumbelow had made a law that all inmates of the house, whether guests or domestics, should address his wife as "My Lady"; that this was willingly done both by Princes and revolutionaries; and that a member of the Independent Labour Party having once ventured to address her as "Comrade" was promptly ordered to

THE EVOLUTION OF RUMBELOW

pack up his traps. All this gave rise to much speculation, which rose to fever height and spread all over the world when it was noised abroad that the German Emperor was spending a week-end in the Castle, and that the Lord Chancellor was another of the guests.

Meanwhile great things were happening in the neighbouring city of Smokeover, where Mr. Rumbelow still maintained his business headquarters. Here he had entered into partnership with the betting firm of Stallybrass & Corker, of which he quickly made himself the master. It was an active and malign concern, but shamefaced, furtive and obscure, hiding itself away in a back street. Under the magic touch of Rumbelow's genius it underwent a rapid transformation, both as to its inner character and as to its outward manifestation. In a year's time he had installed the business in a magnificent block of offices on the corner site of two main thoroughfares, while a cloud of telegraph wires concentrating on the roof bore witness to world-wide ramifications, and almost shut out the light of the sun, never strong in Smokeover.

What was going on inside? One of the greatest wonders of the age. Have you ever paused in the midst of your scientific preoccupations and trembled before the terrible truth that in human affairs, whether on the large scale or the small, whether in the fate of nations or the state of your own nervous system, no man knows what is going to happen next? On that high mystery Mr. Rumbelow's business was founded. It had been revealed to him, whether by inspiration from above or below no man can say, that horse-racing is only one of a million uncertainties on which men may gamble. He was prepared to gamble methodically on most of them.

For example there was the Department of Politics. Here, if so disposed, you could bet with Mr. Rumbelow on the fate of Ministries in your own or any other country, on the issue of elections, on probable majorities, on the chances of particular statesmen to get into the Cabinet or to be offered this portfolio or that. You could bet on the chances of So-and-so being made a bishop or a Regius Professor, and there was nothing to prevent the candidate backing himself. If a measure was before Parliament you could bet on its passing into law. If a revolution was threatened you could bet on its occurrence; if an agitation was in progress you could bet on its success. Mr. Rumbelow was not only prepared to bet with the public on these and a hundred such-like things, but also to furnish the Press for an adequate fee with accurate and absolutely trustworthy information of the way the public was betting; every night the cloud of telegraph wires was alive with messages recording the daily odds. At the time when Rumbelow was in his glory there was hardly a leader writer in London or the provinces who would have dared to compose his article without a telegram from the great bookmaker at his elbow. In the jargon of the journalists' clubs he was known as "the barometer"; the question "How is the barometer to-night?" meant, "What are Rumbelow's latest odds?" His influence on the Press was immense.

It has been said, by an accomplished student of human nature, that if ever a New Messiah should

THE EVOLUTION OF RUMBELOW

appear in the midst of our confused and aimless civilization, he would be regarded by three-fourths of his contemporaries as an unmitigated scoundrel, and not recognized in his true character until after he had been cast out of the vineyard and killed. From this we cannot argue, in strict logic, that all men whom the world condemns as unmitigated scoundrels are necessarily Messiahs. But it does seem to give a chance to one of them. Was Mr. Rumbelow that one? Perhaps the sequel will show. Certain it is that at the stage of his evolution to which Mr. Rumbelow had now arrived no Churchman of any denomination would have dared to risk his reputation by spending a week-end with the bookmaker in his country house. But he had round him a small band of devoted disciples, some of whom were prepared to maintain that he was the greatest Strategist of his time. They affirmed—with what truth will be seen hereafter—that he had taken in hand the two most powerful forces of existing civilization, which are cupidity and the love of gambling; that he had harnessed them to the sciences, and that in doing this he had betrayed a prescience wholly lacking in those who condemned him.

CHAPTER TWO

Mr. Rumbelow's Business from Within

YOU are, let us suppose, a friend of Mr. Rumbelow, and have received from him a visiting card on which he has written "Show this gentleman over the Office and give him the fullest information. To Heads of Departments. A. R." So, leaving your motor in front of the great entrance, you pass into a spacious hall adorned with pillars of coloured marble, and are accosted by a stately commissionaire to whom you show the card. "Which Department will you see first, sir?" he asks. "Oh," you answer, "the first that comes—any you like." He invites you to enter the lift and stops at the first landing. Over a glass door you see the words inscribed "Political Department." "Wait a moment, sir, while I inform the Head," says the commissionaire, and pointing you to a luxurious arm-chair on the landing he passes into the interior.

While you are waiting several persons come out through the door. The first is a prominent politician whom you know by sight. He enters the lift at once and disappears, a little annoyed at observing that he is recognized. The next is a young man with his hands thrust into his pockets in a manner which slightly over-emphasizes the rearward of his anatomy. He is an Oxford undergraduate: yes, he is one you know. What has he been doing? Well, he has been presenting testimonials from College Dons, and explaining certain ambitions of his to the Head of the Department. He makes no secret of it at all. He is glad to say that his bet has been taken. "Nothing like a bet, sir, for steadying your purpose. It keeps you to it. I've backed myself for fifty. I got the tip from my tutor." In due course he will be a Double First.

Amazed and bewildered by this revelation you now enter the office. Something in the atmosphere instantly warns you to be on your guard. You feel instinctively that the place is full of the subtlest temptations—perhaps a friendly dæmon has whispered it in your ear. "Fortunately," you can say to yourself, "I never bet."

You are received by a courteous and enthusiastic gentleman in gold spectacles—the Head of the Department.

"You have called at a fortunate moment, sir," he says. "Just now we are engaged in launching a number of speculations of unusual interest and great public importance, which I shall take a keen pleasure in explaining, later on, to a personal friend of Mr. Rumbelow. But before we come to particulars it is essential that you should grasp the general principles on which our business is based. Our business, sir, has a philosophic foundation; it is, if I may say so, saturated with the profoundest methaphysics, and is conducted by a mind which is equal to their application, a combination rarely to be found. Ideal aims are here united with business-like method, and the whole is directed by skill, by expert knowledge, by intellect trained under the severest discipline known to man—and behind it all the mind of Mr. Rumbelow, which I verily believe is one of the greatest minds the human race has ever produced."

If you are a Christian you will be inwardly warned by the manager's loyalty to his chief, but if you are a cynic (which is more probable) you will smile rather dryly at his exaggerations.

"How, I wonder, did these great ideas originate in the mind of Mr. Rumbelow?" you will ask.

"By *revelation*," the manager will reply. "But I perceive, sir, that I am overtaxing your credulity at the outset. Pardon the mistake. Let us proceed at once to view the working of the Office. And first we will inspect the brain of the business in actual operation—the great ganglion to which all the nerves converge. I am about to show you our Mathematical Department."

The manager now conducts you to the rear of the vast building, far away from the noise of the thoroughfares in front. You enter a spacious and lofty hall of fine proportions, rectangular in shape, save for the apse which concludes the further end. A gallery approached by stairs from below runs round the walls, and thousands of books of reference, attended by a staff of librarians, are ranged on the shelves above. On the floor of the hall and on either side are rows of small compartments, divided from one another by screens of polished oak, arranged as private studies, fifty or sixty of them, each with a telephone on the table. You can see the occupants, who are of both sexes, bending over their work and constantly putting the telephones to their ears.

MR. RUMBELOW'S BUSINESS

Down the central aisle run long tables to which girl messengers bring papers, which are received and filed, or passed on, after inspection, by automatic delivery to one or other of the compartments. In the apse at the further end, on a dais, sits a solitary figure whom no one approaches; a telephone receiver is attached to his right ear, kept in position by a system of metal bands which encircle his great head in a kind of cage. On the panelled wall behind him hangs a silver bugle, the only decoration, and the mascot of the Firm. The floor is thickly carpeted, the workers wear rubber soles, the silence is profound. The manager at your elbow speaks in the lowest of whispers.

"The pick of the mathematicians of Europe," he says, indicating the workers on either side of the room. "Note the gentleman on the dais opposite. He is our head mathematical expert. His salary is five thousand a year. He has discovered four new kinds of infinite and can work equations in six dimensions; mathematical psychology is his specialty, and the rapidity of his calculations is amazing. Note that young girl in the compartment next but one to the east end. A perfect marvel, sir, a Pole, a great musician, and a mathematical genius. She is at work on the caprices of the Woman's Vote—one of the most puzzling speculations we have had to formulate—and has discovered certain uniformities which, as we shall apply them, will give us control of over a hundred constituencies. Then the young man in the light suit in the compartment opposite. His subject is the Mathematical Logic of Bad Habits —a department from which we expect great moral results. The Head is at this moment correlating his formulæ with those of the Polish lady on the other side. Now turn to the man in the third compartment on the right. He is a Senior Wrangler and can play twenty games of chess blindfold; he has the fate of the Coalition Government this moment in his hands. The man next to him is dealing with the business of Canon Fairtemper, a small but interesting speculation. Lower down observe that elderly gentleman with the white hair—one of the deepest and most delicate minds in the Office. He is studying the intrigues of Lord Stringpuller—you may have seen him leave the office just before you came in—a disreputable adventurer whose political career Mr. Rumbelow has determined to end.

"But the greatest marvel of all, the masterpiece, is not here. It is in a small room beyond, where visitors are not permitted to enter. Seven men, representing seven great nations, sit there immersed in the profoundest investigations. Ah, my dear sir, if you could only see the development of those seven skulls, you would get a new conception of the mental power of the human race! The International Problem is in their hands. They are working out the Chances of War in all ages and have already produced astonishing formulæ, one of which I regret to say indicates that we are on the eve of a terrible conflict. You have heard our latest odds on the European situation? Three to one against peace! We wired the German Emperor to that effect not an hour ago."

The manager now proposes that you should inspect the Department of Capital and Labour. As you thread your way along the carpeted corridors it occurs to you to ask: "What was that affair of Canon Fairtemper's which you mentioned just now in the Hall of Silence?" The manager will reply:

"Canon Fairtemper, sir, has been marked out by Mr. Rumbelow for perferment—a man of the loftiest ideals and a well-equipped theologian. He is heavily backed; but the opposition is also strong. None the less Mr. Rumbelow has determined that he is to be the next Bishop, and has woven a most delicate net round the whole operation—a work of art I assure you, a small thing but a perfect gem. Canon Fairtemper has had to be kept in ignorance of what was going forward, having certain prejudices which seem to me not in keeping with his general broadmindedness. Hence our chief difficulties. But Mr. Rumbelow has overcome them by a veritable masterstroke. The result is as nearly certain as any sporting event can be. It is one of the surest things on our books. And that prompts me to make a suggestion. If you should feel interested in the matter and we could make it known that a man in your position were backing our favourite, it would greatly help us to steady the market, which has been wobbling most unreasonably during the last few days. —You don't bet? I'm sorry to hear it, sir. But here we are at the Department of Capital and Labour and I must hand you over to my colleague, Mr. Hotblack, our leading psychologist."

You will find Mr. Hotblack, the psychologist, somewhat quicker than his predecessor in coming to the point. He is more brusque in his manner and has an unpleasant way of looking you up and down; also, of looking at you out of the corner of his eye.

After a few preliminary explanations he will boldly open out as follows:

"Our present odds against the Social Revolution occurring in England during the next ten years are 2 to 1. We can recommend this speculation as one of the best forms of insurance against the confiscation of private property. The method of procedure is quite simple. You take our odds, 2 to 1, and back the coming of the Social Revolution, say, for $10,000. The Revolution comes; we lose, you win; your other property is confiscated by the revolutionaries, but you receive from us $20,000 cash down—a useful nest-egg for your old age and for your wife and children. I advise you to do it at once."

"But surely," you exclaim, "this won't help me much. The revolutionaries having confiscated my existing property would make short work of the $20,000 I should receive from you?"

"Oh, *would* they?" Mr. Hotblack will reply, breaking into an unpleasant and long-continued fit of laughter. "There, my dear sir, you are mistaken. You are evidently not aware that the mass of the revolutionary party, including all its prominent leaders and thousands of their followers, have secured themselves against the coming of the revolution exactly as I am now advising you to do. They would all be in the same position as yourself; if they touched your winnings they would cut their own throats; believe me they will never dare to do it. Wherever the Red Flag waves, sir, our agents are hard at work. In Russia, at the present moment, we are doing an enormous business—the Chief has already made three visits to the country. Mr. Rumbelow, sir, has the whole movement in the hollow of his hand. At the first move to touch your winnings, or those of anybody else, he would publish the list of his payments to the revolutionaries, a list that would contain thousands of names, from every country in Europe, and a counter-revolution would sweep them out of existence in a day. I will tell you one of the secrets of our trade, sir; for I observe that the Chief wishes you to have the fullest information. A revolutionist is almost invariably a gambler. We study psychology in this Firm, sir."

"Still," you will persist, "I don't quite understand. If the Social Revolution were to come, with your odds 2 to 1 against it, Mr. Rumbelow would lose millions, and would ensure his own ruin at the same time as he insured the revolutionists."

"I am afraid, sir, you don't understand betting," Mr. Hotblack will answer. "The odds on the social revolution vary from country to country, and there are twenty-seven countries on our list. We treat each country exactly as we should treat each horse in a racing event. Mr. Rumbelow has 'made a book,' sir, and the art of making a book is so to adjust the odds against each entry that whatever happens the bookmaker is not only covered against loss but stands to win. That is precisely what Mr. Rumbelow has done. He has treated the problem internationally. He has included the whole field.

"The principles on which we deal with the Social Revolution," he will continue, "are of course of very wide application; several of our leading Departments are based upon them, and it will perhaps save you trouble if I explain at once what they are. Mr.

Rumbelow, sir, has devised a system of Compensation for the Evils of Life, much more effective and business-like than the Compensations provided by Nature, which most people find so unsatisfactory—doubtless you have read about them in Emerson. Our Compensations, sir, are paid in coin of the realm, cash down at a stipulated moment. The principle is that you insure compensation, in money, for any evil you may be afraid of, by betting upon its occurrence within a given time. Take, for example, our Department of Life Insurance. We have reduced Life Insurance to its simplest elements and stripped it of all circumlocution. The evil you fear, in this case, is death. Death is the Summary Evil of Life. Now, sir, judging from your healthy appearance, I should say at a guess that the odds are 5 to 1 that you will live another twenty years. Very well. You back yourself to die within that period—say for £1,000. If you die within that period your heirs receive from us £5,000. If you survive we win and make £1,000 out of the transaction, which you can cover, if you like, by yearly deposits, with us, of £50—to be returned to your estate, of course, along with the £5,000, if you win your bet. In this way you insure a compensation for death, amounting to £5,000, for £50 a year. There is no Insurance Company in the world which can produce anything comparable to this for cheapness and equity.

"Name almost any evil you choose, and you will find that Rumbelow, Stallybrass & Corker are prepared to take you on. You have, let us suppose, a pretty daughter who has many admirers, and you are afraid that she may end by marrying a scoundrel, who will desert her and leave her a burden on your hands. Put the available data before us, and our Detective Department will take the matter up at once. In a few days their reports will come before me as Chief Psychologist, my deductions will be made, passed on to the Mathematical Laboratory, and an hour afterwards the odds will be scientifically determined and telegraphed to you. They may be in your favour or they may be against you; and you will take your own course accordingly. Let us suppose they are 3 to 1 against the dreaded *mésalliance*. You then back the *mésalliance* for £1,000. Your worst fears are realized, your daughter marries the scoundrel, you win your bet, you receive £3,000 from us, which you may now hand over to your deserted daughter or keep for your own Compensation, as you choose. Now, tell me frankly, can Nature provide you with any Compensation comparable to that? Pardon the illustration; it is a particularly good example of our method—a method, sir, which in the opinion of many competent judges is the nearest approach to a *practical* solution of the Problem of Evil so far discovered by the mind of man.

"In all this, the Philosophy of the Firm inclines somewhat, as no doubt you have observed, to the side of William James and Professor Bergson. We trade on the adventures of the universe. Our raw material is the Unexpected, of which the supply is unlimited and immense."

"Well," you reply, "I am no great psychologist, but I imagine the result of this must be to make Mr. Rumbelow an object of equal hatred to all parties. I wonder he is not assassinated. I suppose he is guarded by detectives."

At this Mr. Hotblack the psychologist can hardly contain himself. He roars with laughter and chokes with merriment.

"Ho! ho! ho!" he cries. "Really, my dear sir, you don't understand—you don't understand these things. I protest—you don't! Assassinated! Guarded by detectives! Why, sir, Mr. Rumbelow is the most loved and trusted man in the entire community. He has millions of clients—millions among the working men, tens of thousands among the capitalists, and by one and all he is wellnigh adored. He is the living link between Capital and Labour. Their admiration for his skill is only equalled by their confidence in his integrity. Between him and his clients the bond of loyalty is sacred and reciprocal—a loyalty unique on the face of the earth. Since the days of his boyhood Mr. Rumbelow's name has been a byword for all that is straightforward, honourable and humane. He has never swindled a client out of a halfpenny, nor suffered a client to swindle a halfpenny out of him. There is a halo round the head of the Chief, sir. Assassinated! Guarded by detectives! Why, if a hair of his head were injured the reprisals would be appalling. In twenty-four hours Smokeover would be a heap of smouldering ruins and calcined human bones."

This makes you feel foolish: you have made an absurd *faux pas*. You have little psychology; you have less mathematics; you are not a betting man; but all the same you have no relish for being thought an innocent booby. You are shamefaced and con-

MR. RUMBELOW'S BUSINESS

fused. What are you to do? Your evil genius suggests an answer.

"Mr. Hotblack," you say, "I will back the Social Revolution for ten pounds."

"Your name, sir?" says Mr. Hotblack quickly.

"Tangle," you reply.

Instantly Mr. Hotblack seizes his telephone; makes connection with the Hall of Silence, and cries into the instrument: "Mr. Tangle backs the Social Revolution for ten thousand."

"Stop," you exclaim, "I said ten *pounds*."

"I distinctly heard ten *thousand*," says Mr. Hotblack. "We never allow a client to alter his stakes. Besides, the figures have already been received in the Hall of Silence and passed through twelve mathematical processes while we are talking."

"It is infamous!" you cry; "I am not a client but a visitor, making a little bet as a compliment to the Firm. I shall contest it in a Court of Law."

"You will lose," says Mr. Hotblack.

"I shall write to the *Times*."

"The *Times* will not put it in."

"Then I shall inform Mr. Rumbelow. I am one of his oldest friends."

"Oh, that is another matter," says Mr. Hotblack, and then, speaking through the telephone, "Cancel Mr. Tangle's bet."

You rise from your chair, and bidding Mr. Hotblack a frigid good-morning leave the room.

On your way out you call in at the office of your former guide, the courteous gentleman in gold spectacles. In tones of indignation you tell him what has happened.

"Mr. Hotblack," he will say, "is certainly too precipitate. But he is a devoted servant of the Firm, a great psychologist and a reader of the human mind. I should not be surprised to learn, sir, that your first thought was ten thousand, not ten."

"Well, to tell the truth," you will say, "I did think of ten thousand for a moment. But then I remembered in time that I was not a betting man."

"Ah! I imagined as much. In reading the inner mind of a client I have never known Mr. Hotblack to make a mistake. But now, sir, what are your general impressions of the Firm?"

"That the whole business is risky through and through. At every moment you must face the possibility of enormous losses."

"Unquestionably that danger exists; but we face it with courage and confidence," says the manager. "We have less reason to be nervous than any business firm in the United Kingdom. You forget that every single operation of the Firm involves a synoptic view of the whole business we are then and there transacting. If, for example, you put half a million on the maintenance of European Peace—I would not advise it, though, as a matter of fact, we have such a bet on our books at the present moment—if I say you back Peace for half a million and a boy at the street corner backs a race-horse for half-a-crown, the two bets will be instantly correlated in the Hall of Silence, by an expert in Differential Equations, under a formula which covers the entire operations of the Firm. In addition to which, sir, I must beg you to believe that Rumbelow, Stallybrass & Corker are not altogether without public spirit. We can face losses in a Great Cause; but all, sir, under strict mathematical regulation. If war breaks out, as now seems inevitable—the odds against peace have gone up during the last half-hour—you will see what the Firm can do in a Great Cause. It will cover itself with glory. Mr. Rumbelow, sir, will become immortal. He will tower above the ages, and the British nation will find that it can build no monument high enough to do honour to his memory."

You listen bewildered; not to say repentant. By your own confession you are not a betting-man; but the atmosphere of the place has hypnotized you. You are out of your depth, and had better retreat to the safe ground of general principles. So you say:

"Your remark about the synoptic view struck me as deeply interesting."

"It *is* an interesting point, sir," says the manager. "It's just the point where we cut the knot. I've had many conversations with Mr. Rumbelow about it, and that's *his* way of putting the matter. As a sociologist he attaches great importance to the synoptic point of view. All of us are taught to think synoptically. A year's training in our office Mr. Rumbelow regards as the finest preparation a man could have for public life, and especially for high callings."

But you have had enough. You thank the manager for his courtesy and take your farewell with all the dignity that your recent fall has left intact. Your car is waiting for you outside, and the chauffeur, having smoked all his cigarettes, has gone to sleep.

Such was Mr. Rumbelow's business when at the height of its prosperity. Then came the war.

On the day after war was declared Mr. Rumbelow was at his office at nine in the morning. Summoning the twelve Departmental Managers he gave orders that pending the receipt of further instructions all business was to be stopped. Then, accompanied by Mr. Hotblack the psychologist, the chess-player, and the Head Mathematical Expert, no longer wearing his metal cage, he entered the Inner Chamber, where the seven International Thinkers, undisturbed by war's alarms, were at work in the silence; and until six o'clock in the evening he remained closeted with these Mighty Men. Their deliberations ended, Mr. Rumbelow came forth with a document, countersigned by each of the Mighty Men, in his pocket; passed into the Hall of Silence; took down the silver bugle from its peg behind the Head Mathematician's chair; went home to his Castle and dined alone with his beautiful wife. He laid before her the Rumbelow scheme for winning the war.

Next day he took the first train to London, and in the course of the morning interviewed four members of the Cabinet, all old clients of the Firm. Without circumlocution he informed each of them in turn that if the Government would give him the control of the telegraphs, the cables and the wireless for three days he would stake the entire assets of the Firm on a victorious issue in five weeks, laying the odds at 1,000 to 1. "I will put the enemy in a position," said Mr. Rumbelow, "in which he cannot continue the war. I will shake the morale of his

MR. RUMBELOW'S BUSINESS

civilian population. I will block his sources of supply, I will undermine his governments, I will confuse his plans, I will upset his finance. I will create a state of affairs in which not a cannon can be founded, not a cartridge filled, not a button sewed on a soldier's tunic without my consent. I will paralyze the enemy in every nerve." A distinguished Russian statesman, who accompanied Mr. Rumbelow at these interviews, was urgent that the offer should be accepted without a moment's delay.

What happened next is lost in the impenetrable darkness of Official Secrecy. The future historian will search the Record Office in vain. But students of the numerous private memoirs which have appeared since the war will observe that those who affected to control its conduct were haunted from first to last by the spectre of Something-which-ought-to-have-been-done, but was not done. Was this the Rumbelow Plan? The world will never know.

That the Cabinet, if it ever considered the matter, had good reasons for rejecting Mr. Rumbelow's proposals nobody will doubt. Public opinion would have been outraged. The Party Machine would have been wrecked. The Ministry would have been forced to resign. Hundreds of Members of Parliament would have lost their seats. Labour would have been furious. The Theory of the State would have been fatally compromised. The dignity of our Parliamentary Institutions would have been affronted. The Generals and the Military Correspondents would have been in revolt. The week-end house parties, the dinners, the political luncheons, would have been in confusion. There would have been riots in the West-end Clubs, the wives of Cabinet Ministers would have become unmanageable and the whole fabric of society would have been shaken to its foundations. And what would the Nonconformist conscience have said? That Mr. Rumbelow had laid the odds at 1,000 to 1 that he could win the war in five weeks was not an argument sufficiently strong to set against calamities such as these.

And if these reasonings were not conclusive there was something else; nay, there were two things more. "Have you ever inspected the roof of Mr. Rumbelow's great office in Smokeover?" a friend will say to you. "Well, we have, or rather a friend of ours has, and we can tell you something. The roof is *flat*; it is composed of reinforced concrete seven feet thick, and there are gun emplacements at the four corners. Our friend has seen them. And a friend of his who knows the engineer who installed the electric light can tell you *as a positive fact* that the place has huge cellars which are simply *packed* with big guns and ammunition. *Who is Rumbelow?* Answer that if you can."

And here is another friend who will enlighten you still more explicitly. "My dear sir," he says, leaning over confidentially to your side of the first-class carriage, "if you think that Rumbelow, Stallybrass & Corker are just a gang of mathematicians and chess-players, all I can say is—bless your innocence! *Rumbelow, sir, is a Jew*. He is the head centre of a world-wide Jewish plot against civilization. He is using women as his decoys—his wife runs that part of the business. Hundreds of women in Society are in his toils. One of them told me at dinner last night, in the Prime Minister's presence, how she had discovered the plot in the nick of time. Her sister, who is married to a high official in the German telegraphs, had told her that for weeks past thousands of telegrams to Rumbelow, *from Jew financiers*, had been pouring through Berlin. The code is a racing vernacular, and appears to refer to some north-country races. The Kaiser is implicated—probably as a victim. He wired to Rumbelow three times just before the declaration of war. The scoundrel could do all that he said; he could win the war or lose it at his pleasure; but whichever he did the downfall of Christian civilisation would inevitably follow and the Jews would have their heel on the neck of the whole world. Why on earth doesn't the Government act? All they need do is to send a couple of men down to Smokeover with orders to cut through the wires over Rumbelow's office."

That Mr. Rumbelow's offer was not accepted events have proved; the rest remains in obscurity. It is not until the Government informed him that his premises would be required for the Ministry of Raw Materials that we emerge on to the sure ground of historical fact. The great building was taken over; and those members of the expert staff who were unfit for the field were provided, with a promptitude which gave rise to some suspicions, with War Service at home.

The seven Mighty Men were drafted into the Secret Service, with the exception of the German, who narrowly escaped being shot as a spy and was finally interned. The Polish genius became a censor of Polish correspondence. The twenty-fold chess-player was dressed in khaki and sent to a leather factory in Walsall, where he was employed in tying up straps in bundles of twelve. The Head Mathematical Expert became Controller of Bacon. In this manner the force of the Firm was dissipated and its operations suspended for the time being. Some of its more promising speculations were irretrievably ruined. Canon Fairtemper lost the bishopric. Lord Stringpuller got the portfolio for which he had backed himself, and assisted in bringing about several notable disasters to the British arms.

Under the new régime the magnificent office of Rumbelow, Stallybrass & Corker soon became a very different place. The cloud of wires overhead, so taut and orderly under Mr. Rumbelow's administration, was adjusted to new destinations; they sagged, intermingled and crossed; they seemed to announce the confusion that reigned below. Muddy feet defiled the marble pavements, the patterns faded from the Turkey carpets, the polished columns lost their lustre, the grates were filled with torn paper, ends of cigarettes, remnants of ham sandwiches and buns. Where Science had once whispered her profoundest secrets the fat contractor now chuckled and the indignant manufacturer blasphemed. In the private room once occupied by cool long-headed experts, there now sat bewildered amateurs, who alternately tore their hair and affected knowledge they did not possess. Saddest of all the transformations was that which passed over the Hall of Silence, where the giggling flapper and the anæmic clerk now played at hide-and-seek.

Meanwhile Mr. Rumbelow himself received a

commission in the Guards and went to the front. There his valour and ability soon made themselves felt; insomuch that fond enthusiasts, innocent of the laws of military promotion, began to prophesy that he would become Commander-in-Chief of the British Army. But Destiny had otherwise determined. He had risen no higher than the rank of Major when a dangerous wound, received in the neighbourhood of Delville Wood, ended his military career. The Guards had been heavily attacked, they were cut up and demoralized, when Major Rumbelow, counter-attacking with his old fury, blew a silver bugle, rallied the remnants of his force, hurled the Germans back into their trenches, and fell on the parapet, shot through the body.

Meanwhile "My Lady," with a softened light in her beautiful eyes and a thread or two of grey in her wonderful black hair, sat on high in the Castle, looking out towards the perilous East; often hearing the low thud of the distant artillery borne on the winds of night; and then retiring to her sanctuary, where she would practise those strange exercises of hers which, later on, proved so disconcerting to the theologians.

CHAPTER THREE

Rumbelow's Feast

THE great business of Rumbelow, Stallybrass & Corker remained, during the war, in a State of suspended animation; its stately Office abandoned to the incompetence of the self-important and polluted by multitudes of unsportsmanlike feet—one huge pandemonium of muddle, bad temper and mutual obstruction. Meanwhile the Chief himself, pain-drawn and wasted, was being wheeled up and down the terrace of his Castle, attended by his beautiful wife.

In the spring of 1919, the particular Ministry of Confusion then in possession—the Office had changed hands several times during the war—cleared out, to the immense relief of the old caretaker, who was now in the Smokeover hospital, dying of a broken heart. Next day Mr. Rumbelow's car drew up at the main entrance of the Office, and the Chief, leaning heavily on the arm of his wife and walking slowly, entered the building and inspected the abomination of desolation that reigned within.

The armies of purification and order immediately followed; Mr. Rumbelow seemed to have them at his beck and call; painters, polishers, scrubbers, window-cleaners innumerable; scaffolds, ladders, buckets, ropes, brushes, soap. Powerful hoses with great

RUMBELOW'S FEAST

copper nozzles played right and left; they squirted water by the ton, it ran down the marble stairs in cataracts, it hit you in the face and drenched you to the skin. Every room was fumigated; for the local bacteriologist had informed Mr. Rumbelow "that the whole place had become a Microbe Exchange." The Turkey carpets were taken to be cleaned and disinfected, in wagons; behind the wagons came the sanitary carts of the Smokeover Corporation, lined up in a row, to receive the loads of dust, ashes, torn paper, broken crockery, empty boxes, half-smoked cigarettes, match-tails, mouldy crusts, tea-leaves, chicken bones, hair-pins, scraps of red tape, novelettes, corks, eggshells, and rubbish of every sect and denomination that poured from all parts of the building. From basement to roof the cleansing work went on; and high above the roof, clinging giddily to poles and standards, were men stretching wires and beckoning to one another in mid-air. They were restoring Mr. Rumbelow's lines of communication with every region on the face of the earth.

During the period of suspended animation the great business was not altogether at a standstill; the fires were damped down but not quite extinguished. Even in the darkest days of the war, when the amenities of life were hardest to come at, a sporting gentleman could, on making due inquiries, find the means of lodging a judicious bet with Mr. Rumbelow. Several pirate concerns were started, and thousands of letters were sent through the post bearing the forged signature of the Firm. There was, so they say, a small shop pretending to sell coffee and buns, not far from Victoria Station, where officers and men proceeding to the front could take the odds on their chances of coming back alive; and a yet more secret place, the drawing-room of a fashionable flat in Mayfair, where ladies of uncertain reputation betted on the lives of their "men." Both these concerns broke their banks and vanished; which is sufficient proof that Mr. Rumbelow had nothing to do with them. Mr. Rumbelow never broke his bank, and, though he vanished at the last, it was like Elijah in a chariot of fire.

All this time Mr. Rumbelow kept in touch with his misused experts and knew where every one of them was to be found. Every Christmas during the war he sent them cards, exquisitely drawn and painted by his wife, on which the motto was inscribed, "Watch and be ready. Let your lamps be burning and your loins girded up." And each expert, as he looked upon the words, would heave a sigh of longing for the day when his Master would return.

And now it was coming to pass. The news spread that the great factory that made no smoke, but did more business than any, aye, even than Hooker & Co., the mighty profiteers with the seven belching chimneys, was about to rekindle its fires. And a thrill of expectation ran around the world. But all were not pleased.

Often and often had the question been asked, even in the days before the war, why the arm of the law was not upraised against the malign operations of Rumbelow, Stallybrass & Corker. Most people knew the reason. Some never will.

Why, for example, did the police refrain from interference? Because the policemen, including the

Chief Constable, were clients of Mr. Rumbelow in one or other of his numerous Departments. Why were the magistrates slow to act? For the same reason. Why was it useless to put detectives to watch the doors? Because the detectives all went inside. Why did Members of Parliament take no notice of the appeals of their constituents to bring up the matter in the House? Because the said Members, with an eye to the coming Election, had insured themselves against the treachery of the said constituents by Mr. Rumbelow's arts. Why did great newspapers refuse to take the matter up? Because Mr. Rumbelow's odds were the best index they had to the way the wind was blowing. Why was the Church apathetic? Heaven only knows.

But now that this shop of iniquity was about to reopen, now that this gin-trap of Beelzebub was again set in the public highway, it was clear that somebody must do something. And who or what more fitted to do something than the Smokeover Branch of the Society for Ethical Culture? The Branch resolved to rouse public opinion by a whirlwind campaign.

The first step was to enlist Professor Pawkins' incomparable powers of moral invective. Professor Pawkins, who held the Chair of Moral Science in the local university, had recently become the President of the Society, under circumstances to be described hereafter. The Professor disliked public action, believing that the slow percolation of the ideal was the true method of reform, but was at length induced to draw up a Manifesto, which was duly exhibited on the hoardings of Smokeover, with a whisky advertisement on one side and a stabbing scene from the cinema on the other. In this Manifesto Professor Pawkins, with an eloquence too fervid to concern itself with the niceties of metaphor, called upon Smokeover "to rise in mass to attack the open sore in its midst, which was swallowing up the gains of industry, upsetting economic relations, spreading ruin broadcast and undermining house and home." It was further announced that a Public Meeting would be held in the City Hall on such a date, and that a Monster Petition to both Houses of Parliament would await signatures.

The Public Meeting took place. All the members of the Society were present, many of them on the platform. In addition there were about thirty or forty tramps of both sexes, who were just then enjoying the hospitality of Smokeover, attracted to the meeting by the warmth of the City Hall; for the night was cold, and so was the workhouse. They seated themselves as near as possible to the heating apparatus, where they went to sleep and distributed fleas among the more respectable portion of the audience. And there was one other, to whom the policeman touched his hat as he passed through the door, an honour which he had not bestowed on anybody else. This person entered just after the meeting had begun and sat down at the further end of the Hall, in the shadows under the gallery.

There were seven speakers, domestic and imported; and the proceedings lasted two hours. When all was over, the thunders of the captains and the shoutings, the resolutions and the votes of thanks, and the policeman had hustled the last tramp out of the Hall, the Chairman sent for the Monster Peti-

RUMBELOW'S FEAST

tion, which had been lying in the vestibule, that the signatures might be counted and the extent of the victory ascertained. The name that stood at the head was Arthur Rumbelow, and below that the policeman's. There were no others.

The Whirlwind Campaign was well launched and ably supported; it passed from city to city, and gave occasion for many eloquent speeches. But to rouse the great British public to the point of taking moral action is never an easy thing. And it so happened that at this time nine other Whirlwind Campaigns were sweeping the country against nine different "open sores" on the body public. The organizers of the nine condemned the Anti-Rumbelow campaign as a nuisance, which indeed was their normal attitude towards each other; it got in their way, clashed with their meetings, took up the space in the newspapers that was due to them and, as they said, generally "queered their pitch." With ten Whirlwind Campaigns going on simultaneously about ten "open sores" produced by ten different social diseases, the public naturally became, first, confused, then bored, then contemptuous, and finally cynical. While Smokeover was attacking Mr. Rumbelow, Glasgow would be attacking Whisky, Manchester would be attacking Protection, Birmingham would be attacking Free Trade, London would be attacking the Rates, South Wales would be attacking Capital, Ireland would be attacking the Union, the Opposition would be attacking the Government, and the Garden Cities would be outroaring the carnivora for a Vegetable Diet. For three days the public would attack the first "open sore" presented to them, no matter which; then, with slightly diminished vigour, they would go on to the next; and so on till they came to the last, when the Great Divorce Case or the Great Fight or the arrival of Mr. Charlie Chaplin would furnish a timely diversion, and the whole lot would be forgotten. Meanwhile the Representatives of the People would watch the game from their Olympian seats, and, leaving the ten Whirlwind Campaigns to blow each other to a standstill, would pursue their accustomed way, and quit London as usual on Saturdays, some to ponder their intolerable burdens, some to pray for divine guidance, and some to spend delightful week-ends at country houses, playing golf, tennis, bridge, hide-and-seek and catch-as-catch-can. Needless to say the assault on Mr. Rumbelow came to nothing, though Professor Pawkins expressed himself well satisfied with the launching of the Ideal, which, he said, would slowly percolate into the common, or universal, mind; and he quoted the lines of Emerson:

> "One accent of the Holy Ghost
> The heedless world has never lost."

As to the Monster Petition, the presence of Mr. Rumbelow's signature at the head of a document calling for his own suppression was open to various constructions and had the effect of preventing other people from signing. What was the Society to do? It was a nice point in morality. Was Mr. Rumbelow's signature given in good faith? Some said "yes," others "no." Was the policeman's in order? Should he be reported to the Chief Constable? Some said "yes," others "no." Finally, after long discus-

RUMBELOW'S FEAST

sion, it was decided by a small majority of votes that the signatures were not *ex animo,* and therefore insignificant, except as ink. Both were accordingly obliterated by a patent process which left no mark on the paper. After that signatures were more easily obtainable, though not many, and in due course the document reached its destination and was brought under the notice of the Prime Minister, nine others arriving on the same day. The Prime Minister was just then packing his trunks and his papers for Paris, where, along with three other gentlemen, he was about to decide the fate of a few hundred million human beings; and being in a tremendous whirlwind of his own, of which the public knew nothing and which was carrying him Heaven knows whither, he paid no more attention to the minor whirlwinds than he would to a fly which had settled on his nose.

In the meantime, Mr. Rumbelow, undisturbed by these excursions and alarms, had been rapidly pushing forward his sinister preparations for the reopening of his office. There was no advertisement, no display, no announcement in the press; these adventitious aids to success Mr. Rumbelow needed not; but it was to be a great event, and to be celebrated in a manner worthy of a reunion so happy. To each of his jubilant experts he sent a beautifully illuminated card, the work of the same delicate hand as before, inviting him to a banquet to be held in the Hall of Silence on such a night. And not to the experts alone. To every soul connected with the vast establishment a like invitation was sent; to the Heads of the twelve Departments, to the sub-managers, to the cashiers, to the telephone clerks, to the bookkeepers, to the telegraphists, to the women typists, to the shorthand writers, to the girl messengers, to the tall commissionaires, to the watchmen, to the caretakers and to the very charwomen who scrubbed the office floors. All received the same joyous greeting; all were summoned in the same loving and gracious terms to join in celebrating the Master's return. For the wounded still in hospitals, for the mutilated and crippled men in their homes, the care was individual and minute. It was evident that My Lady knew the name and condition of every one. Mr. Rumbelow's motors, of which he had seven, were to penetrate the suburbs and to wait at the hospital doors: an invalid carriage would bring the boy who had been shot through the back and was paralyzed for life; guides would be sent for the blind; an attendant would feed the man who had no hands; a trained nurse would accompany the devoted old caretaker who was dying of a broken heart. Is the old mother wistful of a gleam of joy before the everlasting silence falls? Bring her, in God's name! Is there a fair enchantress? Is there a winsome daughter whose face you would have us see? Let the bright lassie come; for whom you love do we not love also? Are there children you cannot leave? We are ready for them. Our good Mr. Hotblack has turned his office into a Palace of Delights, and he himself will be there, the Great Magician, with live rabbits and fiery serpents in the crown of his hat, which will chase you round the room and turn into boxes of chocolate under your very nose. Does any need a smart suit of clothes for the festival? Let him go to the tailors and mention Mr.

RUMBELOW'S FEAST

Rumbelow's name. Or a pretty frock? Let her go to the dressmaker and say My Lady has sent her. "Did she wish adornments—a chain round her neck, roses in her hair, shoes with bright buckles on her feet?" "Get them where and as you will; get them in plenty and say: ' 'Tis My Lady's wish.' Let your garments be shining, and your colours fair. For our beloved Master is safe and sound." Thus she wrote, in her own hand, to every one, according to the minute particulars of each.

But not for merriment alone was the feast being prepared. The Master had made it known that he would speak to his loyal followers, that he would tell them the History of the Firm and something of his own life, and then, having gathered the past together and looked to the rock from which they were hewn and the hole of the pit whence they were digged, would plunge into the future and unfold a vision of the glories awaiting them. Then a health would be drunk and the trumpet would sound.

Never was a banquet more nobly decked; majesty and loveliness were the keynote of it. The Master's conservatories had been ransacked, his orchid-houses had been stripped, his beds of violets and lilies had been swept as with a mower's scythe, to furnish the flowers: there was not one too many and not one too few. Along the tables, covered with the whitest of napery, lay fluctuating rivulets of scarlet leaves, tendrils gathered from a precious tree, which broke into graceful curves round the space allotted to every guest. Down the middle ran the flowers, not huddled together, as the manner is with some, but freely spreading on long stems and seeming to fall towards the beholder and beckon him; they were of every hue and their odours filled the air. There were three hundred guests and each had his own particular flower, different in race or in colour from all the rest; no two were alike. There was a white rose for the Head Mathematical Expert; there was a fiery cactus for Mr. Hotblack. The charwoman found before her a rare orchid from Brazil, a marvel of colour, having the wings of an angel white and gold, which flower was by her most tenderly carried home and kept alive in the neck of a bottle for three weeks to the delight and wonder of the street. All knew the hand that had done these things.

At either end was a raised platform and a high table dressed thereon. At the one sat the Master with the Twelve Heads on either side of him; and, lest the curse of thirteen should alight, there was place reserved for another. Wonder at this, O ye curious, for wonder is the beginning of wisdom! Our present discords shall make the sweeter music ere the feast is done.

At the other table sat the Seven Mighty Men, Masters of Adventure, Lords of Contingency, Privy Councillors of the Unforeseen, each beneath the flag of his nation—the British, the American, the French, the Italian, the Russian, the Japanese; aye, and the German too, black, white and red. It faced the Master, his soldier's harness on his back and his wound still aching; he looked upon the flag without abhorrence, honouring the high gifts over which it waved, as a soldier should; nor was there one in that company, mutilated or whole, who would have questioned the fitness of these things. For this also was

RUMBELOW'S FEAST

My Lady's doing, and the seal of beauty was on all her works.

On a stage below were the workers in the Hall of Silence, the Head Mathematical Expert in their midst, each with his high gift burning bright and shining upon his neighbour. Here was far-sighted Calculation with long head and steady eye. Here was the careful face of old Experience. Here was the Beauty of Competence, lithe-handed and alert. Here was a youth stalwart and dexterous; there a girl, like one of the living creatures in Ezekiel's vision, all fire, light, colour, loveliness and velocity.

The mutilated men sat apart. Among them My Lady had gathered her choicest flowers and there was a hundred pounds in money under the plate of every one.

And now the feast has begun and the company is in full cry. Many are the strains of joy and merriment; many the vicissitudes of repartee; now varying with occasion, now prompted by personality; but through them all love for the Master is the fundamental note, softening all voices, purifying all laughter, ennobling all wit. Good it is to see the grave faces of the Seven Mighty Men, transfigured and radiant; or the Head Mathematical Expert, unburdened by the cares of thought, his wit sparkling like a diamond; or the blithe spirits of the Polish Genius glancing darkly under her braided brows; or the comely frocks of the young girls and the lights of love and joy dancing in their bright eyes. Good also to hear the roars of laughter from the Twelve Heads, under the leadership of Mr. Hotblack, as the Master tells them the story of the Monster Petition.

Better still to enter the shadows under the gallery and watch My Lady waiting upon the mutilated men, or bending over the paralyzed boy and promising she will teach him to paint. And best of all to visit the old caretaker, who has hardly turned his gaze from the Master since they brought him forward in his wheeled chair, and to hear him say, in tones which touch the heart and come from it, "Lord, now lettest thou Thy servant depart in peace, for mine eyes have seen Thy salvation."

The feast is ended; the Master has risen in his place; all voices are hushed. Clear, vibrant and solemn are his words:

"Let us reverence the dead!"

There is a rustle of rising figures; a clatter of crutches suddenly seized and planted on the floor; the men in wheeled chairs cover their faces; the paralyzed boy closes his eyes; My Lady, dressed in shining white, kneels by his side. Then Silence, save for a low and continuous humming in the cloud of telegraph wires overhead, which all hear, and each interprets as he will. Suddenly the tension is relieved. A soft note, hardly to be distinguished from the humming overhead, but gradually increasing till it becomes a clarion call, breaks out from some hidden place. It is the Silver Bugle blowing triumphant music.

The last echoes die away; all are expectant and silent; the First Toast is coming and it is My Lady who will speak.

She has taken the vacant place by the Master's side, and stands there, clothed in radiance: her girdle a flaming scarlet, her hair black as the tents of Kedar, a single diamond blazing like a star above her brows—a woman sent from God.

"In all ages," she cries, "men have poured out libations to the Invisible, wine and oil and precious ointments and blood. The powers of the Invisible are with us to-night. They are riding on the wings of the wind that blows over this city. We can hear their still small voices calling to us from above in the humming of the wires. To them I raise my glass. I drink to the city that hath foundations. I drink to the Communion of Saints—the dead, the living, the unborn. I drink to the Church Militant and to the Church Triumphant. I drink to the New Jerusalem coming down from heaven like a bride made ready for her husband. I drink to the universal brotherhood of man."

All bow the head. In the solemn hush that follows the night wind gathers force and the humming of the wires grows louder and more musical. 'Tis the only reply. All hear it, and each interprets as he will.

Next comes the Motto of the Firm, and who but the Master can speak to this? The words of it were his own; the spear-head of his purpose, the arrow of his desire, the winged messenger of his imagination—his call, his slogan, his battle cry, and the prelude to his mighty deeds. This was the Motto:

"IDEAL AIMS, BUSINESSLIKE METHODS, SPORTSMANLIKE PRINCIPLES"

He spoke of the beginning, of the middle and of the end: of the birth of the Firm on a dunghill; of the foul juices that fed its roots; of their translation into life and growth and power; of the metabolism of the spirit; of the spreading of the tree till its roots were beside all waters and its branches covered the earth; of the hour coming swiftly, when the Firm, like the tardy cactus which blossoms after a hundred years and is all thorns and ugliness till then, would cover itself with lordly flowers and astonish the desert places with beauty.

He spoke of the kingdoms of this world, and of their perishable foundations; and then of the deeper foundations of the Firm, of the indefeasible loyalty of its members to one another, of their union in the sportsmanlike spirit, of their co-operation in the businesslike method, of their solidarity in the ideal aim.

He spoke of revolutions: how they revert to the type of that which they destroy and so destroy themselves; how the Firm had no part in these vicious circles, having its eyes set upon a city with foundations, of which the pattern had been shown it in the Mount.

"Great Companions," he cried, raising his hand towards the Seven Mighty Men, "I summon you to a new enterprise—perhaps the last. Concentrate your sciences! Organize your high thoughts! Explore the hidden ways! Meditate on the mighty works of the past, on the triumphs you have won against tremendous odds, on the deeds deemed impossible that you have done, on the mountains you have overturned by the roots, on the sufferings you have embraced as your right and transmuted into joy. It shall be so again. But not scatheless shall we emerge. Death and suffering must mingle with the game. But what then? Think of the heroic dead whose presence has been with us to-night. What matters the worst if we meet it as sportsmen should?"

Then he would have spoken of My Lady, and of her excellence among women—the guardian angel of the Firm. But he was overtaken by a storm. At the sound of her name a divine madness rushed upon the assembly like a mighty wind. The multitude sprang to its feet, wild with joy; some shouted, some sang, some danced, some laughed, some babbled; the mutilated men banged their crutches on the floor till they were weary; the paralyzed boy half raised himself; the Seven Mighty Men cried Ha! Ha! and to end all the player of the Silver Bugle stepped forth from the shadows and blew his gayest music.

What a merrymaking then followed! The spirit of Joy, which builds the soul into a house of many mansions and makes sweet music in every one, held sway over the company like a good priest over his flock, and claimed the humblest guest as a communicant. Dance on, ye happy souls, in the shining meadows of your dreams!

The revels are ended and the guests bestir themselves to depart. By the door stands My Lady; behind her is a bank of greenery, dark myrtles and bright ferns. The last to pass out is the old caretaker, in his chair, wheeled by the nurse. My Lady looks in his face, bends over him, takes a red rose from her girdle and places it in his hand; and her voice as she bids him farewell trembles with love. The old man answers not a word but reverently kisses her hand. Then the nurse fares forward with her charge into the lighted streets.

THE LEGENDS OF SMOKEOVER

The streets are crowded; multitudes are pouring out from the theatre, the cinema, the public-house; the boys are crying the evening papers; the night walkers are plying their trade; the sons of Belial are abroad. Great buses charge along the highway; motors flash hither and thither, emitting their fumes and sounding their horns. The good nurse, piloting her little carriage, must needs walk warily, now pushing it along the pavement, now, when the press is thicker, in the perilous highway; and with quick eyes right and left at the crossing of the streets. But the night is clear and the stars are bright.

And now they reach the hospital, all dangers passed. The nurse, leaving her station behind the chair, steps forward to ring the bell, for it is late. That done, she turns round to look at her charge and to speak of their happy arrival. The old man is dead; his white hands are on the coverlet, one with the fingers extended, the other tightly grasping My Lady's rose.

Here the Legend of Rumbelow the Betting Man came to a close. At first the Voice had spoken clearly, rising at certain points into tones so loud and ringing that all Smokeover, had it been awake, would have heard. But the time was the dead of night, Smokeover was in a deep sleep, and save for the Author, the Bridge was deserted.

At the last, when telling of the old caretaker's death, the Voice had sunk into a low and solemn whisper, almost inaudible, and the Author had much ado to hear what was said. Moreover there was confusion of sounds. Long before the end came, the

RUMBELOW'S FEAST

Author had been aware that several Voices were striving to make themselves heard. He perceived that more Legends than one had come to the Bridge, all connected together and all eager to speak. Once, when the Voice mentioned the name of Hooker, the great profiteer, another narrative began to mingle with the first, so that the Author had difficulty in keeping the two disentangled. This Voice was the most intrusive of all that were striving to speak, and it may be that the Author, in spite of his care to keep the two distinct, has introduced into the first Legend certain matter which belongs to the second. At all events the old caretaker had hardly breathed his last when the Second Voice took up its parable. It announced the Legend of the Mad Millionaire.

PART TWO

The Legend of the Mad Millionaire

CHAPTER ONE

Smokeover Grows Rich

THE great city of Smokeover, judged by the smoky standard, did well out of the war. But beyond the canopy of smoke, now denser than ever, the stars shone down with an angry light.

Both extremes of the community pillaged the State to their hearts' content. They had their excuse; they could hardly help it; for the State encouraged the pillage. The loot was enormous, grotesque, suffocating. The wages of the workers went up by leaps and bounds; they stared at them in amazement; they were drunk with money; they struck for more; and their spending was as foolish as their earning was immense. A riveter's wife would pay £70 for a sealskin coat—a bad one; a moulder would buy a piano which he could not get into his house and had to keep in the back yard; a boy would light his cigarette with a ten-shilling Treasury Bill; the child of a puddler would be sent to school in a pair of gold spectacles, to be broken immediately and replaced by another next day; the miners had their private cars; the jewellers' shops were packed on Saturday nights with working girls. Nobody paused to think that in a year or two all these things would assuredly find their way to the pawnbrokers. The day of the workers had come and they were making the most of it.

Nor were their lords and masters behind them. The same post that brought a man news at his private house that his only son had been blown to bits, or drowned in a submarine, would deliver, at his office, cheques from the Government to the tune of a hundred thousand. He, no less than his employees, was at a loss what to do with his money. To whom was he to leave it, now that his only son was gone? How was he to spend it? He could not pull down his barns and build greater—for the builders were all fighting. He would buy a country seat. He didn't want one, but he would have it all the same, and sell if he got tired of it. Besides, his wife and daughters would like it; perhaps later on somebody would make him a Baronet. Yes, he would subscribe heavily to the Party funds, when the war was over. For the rest he would take up the War Loan. What if the State went bankrupt? He didn't care; the whole world was bankrupt, his own life included. And he felt ashamed of himself when he thought of what was going on at the Front. Making money in heaps while those poor fellows were being slaughtered in heaps and his own flesh and blood was being tortured. In the night he would dream of heaps, of piles, of mountains: mountains of corpses on this side, mountains of money on that. There were times when these men loathed themselves. There were times, again, when they were bored to death by their ever mounting accumulations.

"Do you know," cried one of them as he drank champagne with his companions at the Conservative Club, "do you know what I would thank God for?" "We can't imagine *you* thanking God for anything," was the answer. "Well," he said, "I would thank God for a Capital Levy."

Another said:

"Where's the sense of making money in this way? They just *pitch* it at you. Why, you can't even do 'em in. Last week I quoted 'em my stuff at 30s. a hundred-weight; that's a profit of 200 per cent.; and, by God, I got a letter by return of post offering me 35s. I've sold 'em a thousand tons at that price. I tell you, there's no *sport* in it. It isn't good enough for the kiddies to play at."

"If you want sport," said his companion, "why don't you go in with Rumbelow? He'll give you a run for your money."

"Oh, that's another line altogether. Rumbelow's in Art; I'm only in business. But I'll tell you another thing. They ought to have let Rumbelow run this show. They say he made 'em the offer. He'd have saved the country thousands of millions. Good for us they didn't take him on! If they had, your old Dutch wouldn't be blazin' with diamonds, and me and you wouldn't be swillin' Heidsieck at two guineas a bottle. By the way, how's that lad of yours on the minesweeper?"

"Not heard from him for a month."

"Fishy, ain't it?"

No, for all its roaring wealth and flowing champagne Smokeover was not a cheerful place, seldom visited by the sun at the best of times, and now overshadowed by the black wings of the Angel of Death. That woman who bought the sealskin coat. What was her motive? The love of finery, think you? Hear what she said to her neighbour over the backyard fence. "I've done it, Mrs. Perkins, to spite God. I prayed him awful to spare our Joe. And now he's just been killed. I'm going to get a bit of my own back again out of the old monkey." That girl who has had an illegitimate child. Light-of-love, say you? Her own version is different. "I knew my Bill would never come back. . . . And I wanted him to leave me a remembrance." . . .

Among the many admirable "movements" for which the City of Smokeover was famous, was the Branch of the Society for Ethical Culture already mentioned by the other Voice. In one of the local directories it appeared under the head of "Places of Worship"; in another under the head of "Clubs and Societies." The members of the Branch were divided among themselves as to which of the two was the correct caption for their "movement"; but the discussion of the matter had proved so acrimonious and absorbed so much of the intellectual energy needed for greater things, that finally the question was dropped by common consent and the two directories left to have it their own way. It was a peculiarity of the Ethical Society, at least of its Smokeover Branch, that the members could never agree as to whether their cult was "a religion" or something else.

The Smokeover Ethical Society was active and enlightened; but it was small, and obstinately refused to grow larger. A Society more up-to-date in the programmes it offered to the public you could not imagine; the last thing out in science, politics, philosophy and social reform was always its theme. The members were most excellent people, with a leaning perhaps to the iconoclastic side; several professors of the local university were among them; there was the headmistress of a leading school; the Warden of the Women's Settlement; a radical lawyer; a dentist; a banker's clerk; a male designer of women's frocks; several spiritualists; two labour agitators; three or four argumentative working men; and last, but not least, a beaming champion of the Simple Life, who lived in a caravan, and nourished himself on crushed oats which he ate out of a nose-bag, like a horse, thereby avoiding the use of crockery. His name was Whistlefield.

These persons were intent on a great moral reformation. But, alas, the public at large showed no eagerness to be morally reformed, for it is only the moral who are interested in morality! Lecturers of great ability were brought in from all parts of the country, and sometimes a crowd would be gathered; but next week, when there was local talent on the platform, only the stalwarts of the Society would be present. The stalwarts, moreover, were not all like-minded; they had the fiercest arguments among themselves and the meeting generally broke up without any conclusion being registered.

Then came the war, and with it a breath, or rather a blast, of new life began to stir the Ethical Society. "Reconstruction" was in the air, and at this magic word morality seemed to rise from the dead and to become positively attractive. The Society took up Reconstruction. It began to reconstruct everything in the heavens above and on the earth beneath; and the public was excited. Never before had such pro-

THE LEGENDS OF SMOKEOVER

grammes been offered to Smokeover; never before had such audiences gathered to hear them developed. In one winter the Society reconstructed Religion, Morality, Education, Finance, Government, the Church, Literature, Philosophy, International Politics, Art, Housing, Agriculture, Manners, Dress, Marriage, the Family, Labour, Capital, Diet, the Drink Trade, the Universities and the Elementary Schools. Name anything of importance and the Committee would immediately put it into the hands of an expert reconstructor and announce a public address. For in those days Reconstruction was a roaring lion, seeking what and whom it might devour. It was like the lion in *The French Language Made Easy*, which "ate up the clergyman's boots and my grandmother's inkpot," and presumably the clergyman and my grandmother as well.

One lecturer would reconstruct Smokeover; his successor, next week, would reconstruct the Universe; but nobody asked whether Smokeover as reconstructed by the first gentleman would fit in with the Universe as reconstructed by the second; enough that both were to be pulled to pieces and then put together on a new model. Indeed the most casual inspection of these reconstructions revealed that they were all at sixes and sevens, and that any attempt to carry them out would result in a general *mêlée*. At the time, however, it was as much as your reputation was worth to call attention to this, for the reconstructors were a touchy generation; so the point had to be passed over in silence.

In all this the Society's attitude towards the war was thoroughly patriotic. By way of interlude to the general orgy of Reconstruction, lectures were introduced on "The Fundamental Righteousness of the Allied Cause"; it was proved to the hilt by experts in righteousness; and the point was laid down again and again that, unless "we" won the war, the world would be reconstructed, not by "us," but by the Germans, a calamity not to be thought of. This way of putting things was resented by the pacifists of the Society, and the two Labour agitators resigned.

Yet these things, like many another grotesque phenomenon, were not without their deeper root in the tragic soil of human life. It was a dark and terrible time; Ramah was filled with lamentation, and Rachel was weeping for her children. Beneath the wandering intellect was the broken heart, which is the same whether you live in a slum or a palace, in Smokeover or Essen, in London or Berlin. Everywhere the phenomena were alike and the causes identical. Some would seek their consolation in the mutterings of wizards; some became the neophytes of strange religions; some ran to the Crucifix and embraced it; while others, more numerous than all the rest, turned angrily on the world that had smitten them so cruelly, and would have broken it to pieces. Hence that fever of the public mind which they called Reconstruction. It spoke the language of social science; it was discussed and elaborated by men without emotion; a "Ministry" was formed to carry it on; but within all this lay the agony of a disillusion, the delirium of a broken heart. The Society for Ethical Culture was no exception.

The first President of the Smokeover Branch was Mr. William Hooker, M.A., J.P., a public-spirited citizen, a man of commanding presence and dignified countenance. He was a manufacturer of clocks. The business had been founded by his great-grandfather at the end of the eighteenth century, and passed from father to son until in the year 1895 it came into the hands of William Hooker. It had an unbroken record of prosperity, having moved with the times, as a clock factory should. In 1914 it was in full swing. It employed 500 operatives, who were well paid, and had a yearly output of 5,000 clocks with a high reputation for excellence all over the world. The "works" stood on the very edge of the City, with a slum area on one side and wide open ground on the other.

The average net profit to the firm, after all the costs of production had been paid, was 8$s.$ on each clock; and as all this went into the pocket of Mr. Hooker he had a clear income of £2,000, an amount which maintained a remarkable uniformity from year to year, good times and bad. His clocks found a ready market even when other trades were slack, and they leapt over the tariffs of foreign nations.

Mr. Hooker's friends often urged him to increase the business. But he had no desire to do this; having other pre-occupations. Moreover, his social conscience being tender, he was afraid of becoming over-rich. Even as it was, he would often ask himself uncomfortable questions. But he had made a calculation, and found that were the whole of his profits to be distributed among the work-people their wages would be raised only one shilling and sixpence a week all round. This, he thought, would not make much difference to them, though perhaps the "system" might be wrong which, every year, brought five thousand times eight shillings into the pockets of one man. On the whole, the sum was not excessive as a charge for the management of so large a concern, though he had to confess that the actual labour of management was light, the business having been so well constructed and wound up by his forbears that it ran like one of his own clocks. Mr. Hooker had also read Ruskin. It pleased him, therefore, to think of his good, honest, comely clocks, and of the benefits they conferred upon mankind. "At this moment," he would sometimes reflect, "there are hundreds of thousands faithfully ticking in many lands. They are reminding my fellow men of Time and Eternity, of Duty to be done, of Life and of Death. They are speaking the Truth. They are registering the order of the world and contributing to its maintenance. They are doing moral work." Thus, on the whole, his conscience was at ease.

All that is best in a nation of shopkeepers was represented in the traditions of the Hooker family—brains, rectitude and kindness of heart. The finances of the shop were sound; it was exceptionally clean in its appointments and in its personnel; the goods were of the very best, and the buyer could always count on promptitude, fairness and courtesy. Shopkeeping of this character is apt to develop a certain moral earnestness, which pervades the shop like an atmosphere and descends from father to son. Needless to say the Hooker family were originally Quakers.

Mr. Hooker combined the advantages of a University education with those of a business training.

His father, intending him for the business, had sent him in the 'eighties to Cambridge, where he studied Political Economy and graduated with high distinction in Mental and Moral Science. But his religious beliefs fell away and he ceased to call himself a Quaker, or even a Christian. This, however, only served to increase the moral earnestness which a Christian ancestry had instilled into his blood. His life now presented itself to him as a moral problem, which it was his duty to solve, and to solve moreover in a definite and businesslike way. He would not leave Cambridge, so he resolved, until he had equipped himself with a working philosophy of life. At last he believed that he had found it. Reading widely, and thinking deeply on what he read, he came to this conclusion: that the true and final business of every man is to affirm his own personality, but always in such a way as to help others to affirm theirs; in other words, to treat all men as ends in themselves, and to think evil of no man. With this equipment, which he intended to articulate and develop, he went into business, as a man furnished for the battle of life and ready for all contingencies—a man with Principles.

Refraining from public utterance during his father's life, lest he should break the old man's heart, William Hooker took up the work of the Ethical Society as soon as the way was clear. It became his hobby, his preoccupation, his delight, and above all—his Duty. Fortunately his business, being well wound up, ran of itself. To the conduct of its affairs he gave as much time as was necessary; to philosophical reading, to the preparation of his lectures to the Society and to the work of organizing its propaganda all over the country, he gave as much time as he could. If you called at the factory and asked to see the principal, as likely as not you would be told that he was away on "ethical business," a phrase well understood in the office, though somewhat bewildering to the stranger. It meant that Hooker was attending a fortnight's conference of Ethical Societies in London, or that he was giving a course of lectures at a Settlement, or that he was organizing a new branch in another town. But you would find a most competent manager in charge, who would attend to your affairs and send you away satisfied.

Mr. Hooker had three sons, fine strapping fellows with the excellent Hooker brains—his only children. They went to the war, and after surviving three years of active service without a wound, toward the end all three were killed in rapid succession, one in a manner too horrible to be thought of. These blows cut down to the roots of the clockmaker's life and liberated strange emotions he had never felt before. Then his wife, an excellent woman and devoted mother, went half insane, and took to drink. Whereupon Mr. Hooker became less regular in attending the meetings of the Society; seemed absent-minded whenever he turned up; grew tepid about reconstruction, and had the air of a man who was bored with morality. But of that more anon.

Another incident contributed to the same result. Not long after these calamities had occurred there came down to Smokeover a certain lecturer, whose remarks gave offence to the more enthusiastic of the ethical reformers. He was announced to discourse on "The Perils of Reconstruction." He began by telling his audience that though many things might be changed after the war, the multiplication table would have to remain as it was; a point, he said, that was in some danger of being overlooked. He then launched into figures, intended to show that all the belligerents after the war would be over head and ears in debt and on the verge of bankruptcy. For some time afterwards these debts, he said, would be used as currency and things would be quite lively; but a dark hour would follow when the bills would have to be paid. "Then look out!" he cried; "three years after the war you people will not be reconstructing Society. You will be asking where to-morrow's breakfast is to come from." It was a horrible wet blanket, and in the discussion which followed the lecturer was hotly denounced as a pessimist, a cynic and a traitor to the ideal. Hooker, who was in the chair, felt most unhappy. The last consolation he had for the horrors of the war was being taken away from him, for, in those days, as we have seen, "reconstruction" was the balm in which many hurt minds sought relief. After the lecture, the speaker, a well-known financial expert, went home with him and the two men sat up till the small hours of the morning discussing the situation. The result was that Reconstruction became a word which, even when spelt with a capital letter, did not impress Mr. Hooker; for he was a man of great intelligence. Weary with the burden of his private sorrow he had no heart for the discussions of the Ethical Society; grew impatient with all its definitions of the Supreme

Good; lost interest in the Relation of the Individual to the Social Whole; became sceptical about Progress, and seemed to himself to be living in a world so utterly gone to pieces that it could never be reconstructed by the art of man.

But the greatest of all Mr. Hooker's troubles has yet to be told. He had become immensely rich.

CHAPTER TWO

The Profiteer

AS in a crowded city, where there is no regulation of traffic, men drive their vehicles in fear of collision at the street corners, and the best driver is often at the mercy of the worst, so were the nations of the earth in the troubled times when Mr. Hooker began his adventures as a rich man. Geography showed these nations *fixed* in their places on a map of the world; but history showed them *in movement*, on lines that crossed at a thousand points, in spaces where there was little room to manœuvre and where the rules of the road, if there were any, were not observed. Some of them had set up within their own borders admirable systems of government by consent of the governed, but their plans were being constantly upset by the doings of their neighbours, who drove their vehicles at the international crossings without the least regard to the consent of the others who were coming full tilt round the corner. Self-government is no exception to the rule that the real value of political arrangements is always far less than the face-value. The people in a self-governed country would decide, for example, that their taxes must be reduced, and, after making innumerable speeches, would hold a general election to return a government for that purpose; when, lo and behold, another government, a foreign one, would threaten war upon the first, and the taxes, instead of going down, would go up by leaps and bounds. And strange it was to observe how these people, whose taxes were thus being determined by causes over which they had no control, would cling tenaciously to the belief that they were being taxed only by their own consent, declaring, in grave books of history, that the National Debt had been created by their elected representatives, but forgetting Napoleon who made them create it. There were other delusions of the same kind which added greatly to the general confusion of the world. Behind the order that reigned in the parts was the disorder that reigned in the whole. And of course the disorderliness of the whole was constantly disturbing the orderliness of the parts. Not even in the ages of primitive savagery were the fortunes of mankind more insecure.

In spite of the delusions aforesaid the fact of this general disorder was gradually forcing itself into recognition. For a long time past evidence had been growing that human affairs were out of hand, that however well governed the world might be in parts the huge totality was not governed at all. It was becoming clearer every day that the course of events, both at home and abroad, corresponded neither to the consent of the governed nor to the consent of anybody else. Strictly speaking it represented what nobody wanted. Civilization was not proceeding according to plan. It was taking a line of its own, paying no regard to the desires of the multitudes nor to the programmes of the reformers. Behind the backs of all the Parliaments somebody was playing tricks with the fortunes of mankind.

Were all men philosophers these things would doubtless have been set down to their proper causes. But all men are not philosophers. The instinct which leads the savage to knock off the head of his fetish because his hunting has failed, or a spoilt and passionate child to slap his mother because he is suffering from the toothache, is still strong in human nature and in the crowd. So, in the present instance, the discovery that things were going wrong had the effect, first, of throwing society into an exceptionally bad temper, and, second, of stimulating the search for a culprit upon whose head the common anger might be discharged.

The belief gained ground that *villainy* was abroad, and though no price was officially put on the head of the villain, it was generally understood that his capture would be a signal service to mankind. So everyone was on the alert to detect the author of this strange miscarriage in the world's affairs. In literature, in the press, in the pulpit and in all places of resort or assembly where men take exercise in denouncing the misdeeds of their fellows, the self-constituted detective was at work. Few were so fortunate as not to be suspected of having a hand in the mischief. The air was full of mutual recriminations. Labour said it was Capital. Capital said it was Labour. The revolutionaries said it was the powers-that-be. The powers-that-be said it was the revolutionaries. The Government said it was the Opposition. The Opposition said it was the Government. The women said it was the men, and were burning

THE PROFITEER

houses and haystacks to prove their accusation. The name of the villain was Legion. Some blamed the Churches; some the philosophers; some the schoolmasters; some the newspapers; some the taverns. But few were wise enough to blame themselves. Never had satisfaction with self been more complacent and dissatisfaction with others more threatening. There was still abundance of loving-kindness in the world, but it was mostly out of sight, where the cinematograph operators and the newspaper reporters could hardly be expected to find it.

It is one of the results of free speech, and of democratic institutions in general, that people who think themselves innocent are provided with unlimited facilities for proving other people guilty. Democracy is a system which endows the citizen with the utmost freedom to discharge his responsibilities on to the shoulders of somebody else, and with the widest range in selecting a culprit for whatever goes wrong. There is no kind of freedom men value more highly or of which they make a readier use. The disadvantage of the system is that a world where everybody is free to choose his own culprit is precisely the kind of world where the real culprit is most likely to escape detection. All he has to do is to join in the general hue-and-cry and shout "Stop thief!" a little louder than the rest. The Immortals, who watched these proceedings from their invisible stations, knew well enough who the real culprit was, and would sometimes whisper the secret to an incredulous world.

But these whispers produced no effect save indignation against the Immortals; and in 1914 a position had been reached where every class, interest or party was regarded by some other class, interest or party as guilty of the miscarriage of civilization. To the question "Who is the culprit?" there were, perhaps, a thousand different answers, one or other of which was certain to find you out.

All of a sudden this chaos of angry interactions found vent in a world-wide explosion. In an instant the problem of culpability was simplified; the thousand answers were reduced to two. For the world had split into two groups, each believing that it had found the culprit, the villain, the enemy, the troubler of mankind, in the other. And since there was no arbitrator to judge between them (nor would his award have been accepted if there had been) they fought it out, until, after four and a quarter years of unimaginable bloodshed, one of them was decisively beaten.

The culprit had been found, convicted and sentenced. To all parties the cost had been enormous. Half Europe had been ruined; hundreds of millions of people, who were offensive to each other, had been punished; posterity, on both sides, had been penalized for generations to come; vengeance had slaked her thirst in blood and tears. "And now," said the sanguine, "wrath having burnt itself out, let us begin to love one another."

Alas! the echoes of the guns had hardly ceased to reverberate, and the steam from the blood-soaked battlefields had only just been blown away by the kindly winds, when the old question broke out anew. The culprit was still at large! The parties, the interests, the factions, the groups, the classes, the

THE PROFITEER

nations, faced one another as before, each pointing a minatory finger at one of its neighbours, and crying "Thine is the guilt! But for thee all would be well." And so, once more, the moving circle of Distrust, which whoso enters must play the double part of fugitive and pursuer, resumed its vicious revolution, like a roundabout of wooden horses at a country fair, with a steam organ to grind out devil's music while the senseless chase goes on.

Such was the state of things in the world at large when Mr. Hooker made his *début* as a millionaire in the city of Smokeover. Needless to say, there were not wanting many, both in Smokeover and elsewhere, who were quick to perceive that a promising culprit had appeared upon the scene. The hue-and-cry was immediately at his heels and no mercy was shown him by any of his pursuers. Mr. Hooker's name was soon converted into a synonym for social guilt. Mentioned at a public meeting, or in a newspaper article, it acted as a lightning conductor for all that was fuliginous in the temper of Smokeover. It became a figure of speech in the local vernacular, and was used by revolutionary orators to indicate the most dangerous class of social criminals. They were "the Hookers of industry," "the Hookers of Commerce," "the Hookers of finance," "the Hookers of civilization"—and down with them all! The name itself, the mere sound of it, gave point to the accusation. In the minds of an angry crowd it conjured up images which set the demonstrators booing till they were hoarse. For Mr. Hooker had been freely represented in local caricature: sometimes as a monstrous beast of prey with claws or talons; sometimes as a bloated giant with his grappling hook in the vitals of the working man.

How it came to pass that a man so good found himself in a position so uncomfortable the Legend has now to tell.

When the industries of the country were mobilized for the purposes of war, Smokeover immediately answered the call. Mr. Hooker's clock-factory was among the first to be commandeered. Its operatives were skilled, its machinery was easily adaptable, and the open country on one side of it gave scope for unlimited extensions. Mr. Hooker was told that there were enough clocks in existence to keep the world well informed as to the time of day until the war was over, and that his plant must be converted without a moment's delay for the manufacture on an immense scale of timing mechanism for shells, torpedoes and mines; of hand-grenades, the locks of rifles, the working parts of machine guns and of a hundred other things whose action depended on fine springs and the interlocking of small wheels.

His patriotism assented; it was a righteous cause, and almost before he had realized what was happening the experts were on the scene. Then came the instructors from Woolwich Arsenal, and all day long there were groups of men and women gathered round the machines learning their lessons. The draughtsmen, the architects and the surveyors followed; railway sidings were thrown out on the open fields adjoining; an army of workmen were digging, shovelling and laying tracks. Piles of bricks, stacks of timber, dumps of cement, train-loads of steel girders and building material of every kind began to appear; a thousand hammers were banging day and night; and presently a group of immense buildings rose like an exhalation. "Shells, shells!" the public was shouting, and since the fuses were here, why not make the shells themselves next door? Is not this Smokeover the Mighty with the labour on the spot and the raw material not far off? To be sure, said the Government, and Mr. Hooker nodded assent. And why not explosives and poison gas to fill the shells—Smokeover can do that! To be sure, again said the Government. So up went another group of buildings bigger than the first, and, beyond that, streets of huts, with the flag of the Y.M.C.A. fluttering at intervals, eight canteens, a hospital with doctors and trained nurses in attendance, a recreation ground, a welfare building, a new water main and drainage system, in fact, a town. Eight thousand operatives were assembled, men and women, of whom some lived in the huts while the rest came and went in trainloads every day; and the seventh commandment was none too well kept.

And now "Hooker & Co.," blown out to enormous magnitudes and transformed in a fashion to make its Quaker founders turn in their graves and to paralyze the mainspring of every clock the factory had turned out, was in full blast—one huge stithy of war, sprawling over many acres of "England's green and pleasant land." Viewing the sheds and warehouses from the windows of a passing train you wondered when they would come to an end; you counted the trainloads of shells waiting in the siding; if it was day you watched the great chimneys belching smoke, and suddenly put up the windows to keep out the acrid fumes from the steaming vats; if it was night you saw the sky lit up for miles around with the flames of "Satanic forges" raging below—a steering point for the first Zeppelins that crossed the seas. It was a marvellous transformation, worthy of the Arabian Nights. It was a prodigy. It was used as a text, or object-lesson, to convince incredulous allies of the titanic efforts Great Britain was making to win the war. French statesmen, taken to see it the day after their landing in England, exhausted the dictionary for terms of admiration. Neutrals were staggered. Business experts from America cried, "Great snakes!" and booked orders for a million dollars' worth of machinery on the spot. But none was more amazed that Mr. Hooker himself. Sometimes, as he drove up to the works in his Rolls-Royce, and looked on the scene of what once had been his innocent clock-factory, a thought would cross his mind which made him shudder, and challenged reflection. He shuddered to think of the ease and rapidity with which small wheels made for telling men the time could be converted into enormous mechanism for blowing their souls out of time into eternity.

Sentries walked up and down in front of the gates, or guarded the dumps; detectives prowled about on the watch for German spies. All day long taxi-cabs and private motors would drive up to the entrance, and brisk men in uniform with red and gold on their caps would leap out. Sometimes the detective, after looking in at the window, would respectfully open the door and the sentry would stand to the salute. It was Sir William Robertson, seeing things for him-

THE PROFITEER

self; or it was "our military expert" escorting a duchess and preparing an indictment; or it was the Prime Minister to confer with Mr. Hooker; or "them two—did you see 'em, Bill—that long bloke with the round man in blue—blowed if I don't think it was K. of K. and old Father Joffer."

And the money? The accounts which the head cashier brought Mr. Hooker week by week of the money that was rolling in and the money that was rolling out caused him to gasp. All he knew distinctly was that what rolled in far exceeded what rolled out. The generosity of the Government was amazing. It was perpetually atoning to Mr. Hooker for its own mistakes. If the War Council were all at sixes and sevens, if a disaster occurred in Gallipoli or a hundred thousand men were blotted out in France, the result to Hooker & Co. was that money rolled their way in a more impetuous flood than ever. There was no checking it; there was no controlling it: you had no alternative but to sit at the receipt of custom and rake in the shekels. The thing simply went on. It went on for three years, and at the end of that time Mr. Hooker possessed a fortune of two and a half millions sterling. By common consent he was acclaimed the King of Profiteers.

What was Mr. Hooker going to do with all this wealth? The question was on the lips of many. Everybdy seemed to know what *he* would do with it *if* the money were his, though of the hundreds who gave their views hardly two agreed. Moreover it is one thing to know what you would do with two and a half millions when you haven't got them, and quite another thing if they stand to your credit in the bank. The first is easy as talking; the second difficult as martyrdom—especially if you happen to be President of a Society for Ethical Culture.

Mr. Hooker had asked himself the question long before it had been asked by anybody else; and, what is more, he had answered it. He had not graduated in Ethical and Political Science for nothing; he had not lectured up and down the country for twenty years on the Moral Ideal without meaning what he said. He knew that he was becoming a social danger of the first magnitude, and could have given points to any moralist who had taken him to task on the subject. He had studied the matter from every point of view; he had put his sensitive conscience under the severest cross-examination; and he had made the most damaging comparisons against himself. "Rumbelow's wealth, for example," he had reflected, "is the fruit of his own wickedness. Mine is the fruit of the wickedness of my fellow men—the wickedness which has caused the war. Rumbelow can at least plead that he has earned his by his wits. Mine has been thrust upon me by the force of circumstances with hardly an effort of my own. Which of us two is the greater villain, the more despicable character? Unquestionably myself."

Moreover, sceptic as he was in regard to matters of which other men speak with bated breath, he had an uncomfortable feeling that somewhere in the universe there was a Great Inspector of Motives who might put him to the question; and he had pictured to himself what a sorry figure he would cut at the Day of Judgment if he were asked to state what his motives had been in amassing his millions, and he could only reply, with his thumb in his mouth, "Please, sir, I had no motives at all. I couldn't help it." Nor was his peace of mind increased by the knowledge that his friends in the Ethical Society regarded his position as anomalous and compromising, and that to the public of Smokeover he was becoming an object of dislike and contumely. Once, when his name had been mentioned at a public meeting in the City Hall, loud cries of "humbug" and "hypocrite" had risen from the audience, while the name of Rumbelow, which had been mentioned a moment later, was greeted with thunders of applause.

Tormented by these questions from the first moment the money began to flow in, Mr. Hooker had set himself with his accustomed moral thoroughness to find an answer. It was not long in coming. "I will bide my time and let the thing work out to its conclusion. I will endure these taunts and suspicions in silence. I will let the world think of me what it will. Then, when the war is over, I will use the wealth it has brought me for the purpose of making war impossible for evermore. I will use it, to the last penny, in promoting the cause of Ethical Culture all over the world. I will spread our Society into every town and village and I will make it my residuary legatee. I will establish a great organization, I will set on foot an immense propaganda. I will make an atonement for myself and my fellow men. I will hoist the devil with his own petard."

Such was the firm resolution, and Mr. Hooker, trained by a lifetime of acting on principle, knew that he could trust himself to carry it out. His peace of mind returned to him; his high brows were radiant, and as he sat at the Board Meetings and passed the accounts, a mysterious smile, as of a man who holds a happy secret locked in his breast, would overspread his fine countenance. It is true that a great Rolls-Royce car, of the most expensive equipment, did, somehow, make its appearance; and a country house did, somehow, manage to get itself transferred to Mr. Hooker. But the radiance was not extinguished and the smile was still there. It was all part of the Great Moral Plot. It was all helping to pack explosive into the Monster Petard which was to hoist the devil sky-high. The Rolls-Royce was needed to carry Mr. Hooker to and fro on his weekly visits to the War Office or to his interviews with the Prime Minister. The country house was needed to entertain the Generals and the Admirals, the Controllers of this and the Controllers of that, the Editors and the Correspondents, the Lords and the Ladies, and all the gossiping emissaries of chaos who were constantly travelling between Smokeover and the Capital.

So it went on till the summer of 1918; two millions of high explosive had now been packed into the Great Petard. Morally comfortable as Mr. Hooker had been all this time, humanly he had been ill at ease. A cloud of anxiety for his three splendid sons, dearer to him than all the wealth of Ind, nay, than his own life, had constantly overshadowed him. At first it was wellnigh intolerable, but use and wont had done their work. All three had been at the front from the beginning, they had taken part in many actions, had won decorations and advanced in the Service, so far not one of the three had received the least injury, and at last Mr. Hooker came to take it for granted that they would return safe and sound. Then the lightning fell.

Alec, the second boy, was the first to go. Shot through both legs and with his right hand blown off, he had been taken prisoner at a point where the attack of the Hindenburg line had temporarily failed. He was laid on a stretcher and was about to be taken to the rear by two of his own men when a rain of shells from a British battery fell upon the spot and wiped out the whole party. Before Hooker had recovered from the first shock the news came that George, the youngest, was gone. He had taken part in a bombing raid over Frankfort; his machine, attacked on the return, had been disabled and set on fire; and George had been burned to death in the air. A fortnight later Edward, the eldest, was shattered by a bomb which exploded prematurely in his hand, and died in two days after agonies so dreadful that the doctor who attended him could only speak in generalities. When Hooker heard this news the fountains of the great deep were let loose within him and it seemed to him that his heart would burst.

William Hooker was a strong, wise man, who had long trained himself to treat the ordinary shocks and pains of life as a philosopher should. But, till now, he had been a stranger to the elemental emotions which lie hidden, like chained tempests, in the "abysmal deeps of personality"; he had known nothing of those major agonies which cause the soul to sweat as it were great drops of blood. He had known of course that if his sons were killed he would suffer profoundly, and had often trembled at the thought. But when the thing actually happened it came upon him with an overwhelming cruelty of which his darkest forebodings had given him no hint. His philosophy, far from proving an anodyne or a defence, only served to light up the depth of his desolation and throw into clearer relief the general senselessness of the world. Whether Mr. Hooker had learnt to contemplate his own death with equanimity, as Epicurus teaches, is not certain. But he was far from equanimity in contemplating the death of his three sons.

And a horrible thought was haunting him—the poisoned spear-head of his self-reproaches. That ill-made bomb that had killed Edward? What if it had been made in his own factory? What if *he* had made it? The chances were even so. It was a Mills bomb that had killed his son; and of the total supply of Mills bombs to the army one third came from Hooker's firm. Only three weeks before a complaint had been received from the War Office that some of the bombs supplied by Hooker & Co. were faulty and had caused accidents. And the Government paid him seven shillings apiece for every one! And the seven shillings he had received for the very bomb which had disembowelled Edward and blown off the half of his handsome face was to be used for the promotion of Ethical Culture! O shameful mockery! O infinite turpitude! "What loathsome reptile," he cried aloud, "can compare with me? *Seven shillings!* Judas with your thirty pieces of silver I salute you. Hell itself despises the pair of us!"

THE PROFITEER

Then it was that signs appeared which suggested to those who witnessed them that Mr. Hooker was losing his reason. For thirty years he had never said a prayer; he had no belief in the God to whom men pray. But one day the butler, entering the library, found his master on his knees, his face turned upward and his hands clasped in an attitude of supplication. Was he praying to God? No, no. "O Edward, forgive me! O George and Alec, have pity on your father!" That is what the butler heard him cry.

It may be said that if Mr. Hooker had believed in God, and in His righteous government of the universe, all would have been well. Perhaps it would; but such might-have-beens are difficult to appraise. Believing in God worked differently, in those times, with different people. Some, unquestionably, it helped through their troubles. To others it brought a new trouble, in the form of a doubt, which added greatly to the bitterness of their cup and, in extreme cases, drove them mad. Some, who had lost their sons in the war, lost their God as well, and, feeling *that* as the worse loss of the two, fervently regretted that they had ever believed in God at all—just as they might regret that they had ever begotten and brought up sons, to be shot through the brain or die in agony at the age of twenty. Sometimes the troubles yielded to the belief, and sometimes the belief yielded to the troubles. You could never tell in which of the two ways belief in God was going to work, and this Voice has no wisdom to say whether Mr. Hooker would have belonged to the one class of sufferers or to the other. Perhaps it **may** be counted some mitigation of his lot that with all his manifold distresses he had no trouble about God. But of kindred trouble he had plenty—about himself, whom he despised; about the world, which seemed stupid and cruel; and about morality, which seemed unreal.

Can we wonder, indeed, that Mr. Hooker was not able to talk about morality and that it *hurt* him to hear it talked about? Can we wonder that he found his home, no less than his office, a dreadful place? Can we wonder that he broke down at the Committee of the Society for Ethical Culture? It may be doubted if there were on the earth any Society, ethical or non-ethical, literary, scientific, political or philanthropic, any club, place of worship or other visible institution, quite big enough to hold Mr. Hooker and the immensity of his self-contempt. Not on the earth, most assuredly.

In the month of September 1918, when the German resistance was known to be yielding and the end of the war in sight, the Committee of the Ethical Society met to draw up its programme for the coming session. Thirteen members were present—all the committees of the Society were large in proportion to its total membership—including the two Labour agitators, who had been persuaded to return to the fold, two professors and the headmistress of the High School for Girls, Miss Margaret Wolfstone, a fine looking woman of thirty.

Of Miss Wolfstone another Voice is waiting to speak. Suffice it for the present that she had introduced the practice of smoking cigarettes at the committee meetings, a habit acquired while acting as a nurse during the war; also, that a long white mark, concealed by a thick braid of hair, ran across the upper part of her low, broad brow. It was the scar of a wound caused by a splinter of wood when she was in charge of the cot-cases on a hospital ship, torpedoed by the Germans.

Mr. Hooker began by saying that he would propose to the Committee a line of action for the next session different from that pursued in the last. He doubted if the Society had done full justice to the financial expert. Perhaps that gentleman had needlessly depressed them. Still, there was no denying that the financial outlook was extremely dark, and that the whole edifice of Reconstruction was in grave peril. He would propose that for the next session the Society should confine itself to the question of National Finance, as the foundation of reform, and that a series of experts should be invited to lecture upon the matter.

He had, however, a more startling, though, he believed, a sound proposal to bring forward. He had been informed that Mr. Arthur Rumbelow, who was now recovered from his wounds, had been giving close attention to the question of National Finance during the period of his convalescence. In spite of Mr. Rumbelow's abominable ethics, they all knew that he was a man of great intellectual power; and he had heard that since his wound, which had brought him to the point of death, Mr. Rumbelow's mind had been moving in new directions and that he had been greatly softened by the influence of his wife. He proposed that Mr. Rumbelow be invited to give the Inaugural Address. "There will be an enormous crowd to hear him and we shall have to engage the City Hall."

The dismay of the Committee on hearing this proposal was plain to see; but Miss Wolfstone, her two elbows resting on the table and the cigarette held aloft in her left hand, said quietly:

"I support that proposal. I came to know Mr. Rumbelow when he was a cot-case on the hospital ship, and—well—to believe in him." At which both the Labour agitators said, "Hear, hear."

But the two professors would have nothing to do with it. One of them said, "Finance is outside our province. We are an Ethical Society. Besides which, if this proposal is carried, our work will be ruined. My colleague and I would resign at once. To bring out a man of Mr. Rumbelow's calling under the auspices of this Society would be a scandal to morality."

"Never mind about morality," said one of the agitators. "Get the best man for the job."

After more discussion the proposal was put to the vote, three voting for it and nine against. Mr. Hooker then said:

"I am not surprised that you have rejected my proposal. I am not hurt. Perhaps I ought not to have brought it forward. But the truth is that my interest in our work is not exactly what it was. Not that my ethical convictions have changed in the least. But the events of the war have taught me that our *methods* are futile. We are a mission to the converted. We pipe, but nobody dances. The world is refractory to moral teachings such as we have to offer, always has been so, always will be so. What we are

THE PROFITEER

doing has been attempted a thousand times before by moralists of every school, but it has made little or no impression on the brutishness and stupidity of mankind. If it had, Smokeover and all its villainies would never have come into existence. Smokeover is the symbol of our defeat, which has been overwhelming, though we affect not to see it. We do not touch the essential agony of life. We get nowhere near the centre. The big things escape us. Meanwhile the Rumbelows are masters of the situation. We must change our methods. We must form an alliance with them and all they stand for. We must ask them to teach us our business. Frankly I would make friends, yes, *friends*, with the mammon of unrighteousness; though some of you will think I am not the man to say it. But, as you know, the circumstances of my life have greatly changed."

Here the poor man, who had made an effort to control himself, broke down completely, bowed his head in the fold of the arm which lay on the table, and sobbed aloud. Miss Wolfstone went up to him and putting her hand on his shoulder said, "Let me go home with you, Mr. Hooker."

"No," he answered, recovering himself, "I must finish what I had to say. I can't explain, but those of you who have been hard hit like myself, and I know that some of you have, will understand. I can no longer talk about morality; I can no longer bear to hear it talked of by others. It hurts me: it hurts me cruelly. It gives me a horrible sense that I am in a world of dismal unreality. I must cease to be your President. That is all."

And with that he got up, shook hands with the two

professors who had opposed him, and left the room.

When he was gone all tongues were loosened except Miss Wolfstone's. She remained silent, listening to the others. "He's not the man he was." "I fear his mind is becoming unhinged, like his wife's." "His breaking down was a bad sign." "His proposal about Rumbelow was a worse." "It is better that he should resign." "He was never really rooted in philosophy—always seemed to me to be preaching." "What has upset him is not so much the death of his sons as the money he has made out of the war." This was the talk.

When Miss Wolfstone went out she found Hooker on the steps, toying with the brim of his hat and looking vaguely up and down the street.

"Where are you going?" she asked.

"I don't know. I don't know which way to turn. If I go up the street I go towards my office. If I go down the street I get nearer to my home. Both are dreadful places. For pity's sake, my dear lady, take me somewhere."

She linked her arm in his, drew him to a taxi-stand and bade the driver take him to his home.

CHAPTER THREE

Mr. Hooker's Advisers

MR. HOOKER'S advisers were importunate, numerous and discordant. Every post brought him a heterogeneous pile of begging letters, genuine and fraudulent, pathetic, tragic, comic, cunning, stupid, modest and impudent. Some pleaded broken hearts, some threatened blackmail. Some addressed him in fawning tones as a benefactor sent from heaven; some told him plainly that he was the blackest of villains. In the course of a single day he received ninety-four requests for subscriptions to public objects. All gave him, either openly or by implication, what the writers considered good advice. Had Mr. Hooker yielded to what this crowd of applicants demanded his millions would soon have been dissipated; in which event, no doubt, the advice given him by a cynical correspondent that he should "destroy his wealth" as the safest thing he could do, would have been in large measure carried out. If Mr. Hooker himself could not be justly accused of cupidity, his vast wealth having been thrust upon him by the force of circumstances, he was certainly an active cause of cupidity in other people.

All Smokeover hummed with the question, "What will Mr. Hooker do with his money?" It competed with the League of Nations and with the Great Divorce Case as the chief topic of public interest. Working men shouted it to one another as they raced home on their bicycles at five o'clock. In crowded assemblies, where torture was being endured under the guise of hospitality, people in evening dress screamed it into each other's ears, or breathed it into each other's mouths. It made the week-end house parties more than usually piquant; Cabinet Ministers might be heard discussing it at dinner with be-jewelled women, dressed, or undressed, in the last creations from Paris. It invaded the Common Rooms of our ancient Universities, where many bottles of generous port were consumed without any conclusion coming in sight. A question was raised about it in the House, and the Chancellor of the Exchequer was asked by the Labour Party what action he meant to take: he said the matter was occupying the attention of his department. Women gossiped and agitators thundered. In clubs, in drawing rooms, in railway carriages, at the church door, and sometimes, *sotto voce*, in church itself, the question ran and spread and diffused itself, like an epidemic. Once, if report speaks true, it was debated for more than an hour by four persons dressed in deep black, as they sat in a mourning coach which was following the hearse at a snail's pace to a cemetery five miles off. Boredom found it a relaxation and grief an anodyne.

But neither in the mourning coach nor anywhere else was interest in the question quite so keen as the meetings of the Smokeover Branch of the Society for Ethical Culture.

MR. HOOKER'S ADVISERS

So far as the members knew, nothing of the kind had previously occurred in the history of the Ethical Movement, and they foresaw that the event would have a profound effect on its fortunes. If Hooker turned traitor to the cause and became a vulgar plutocrat, as some said he would, the whole movement would be discredited and set back. If on the other hand he remained true to his principles, consulting his conscience, acting from the highest motives, and applying the Moral Will to the disposition of his money; if, in a word, he used the whole of it to promote the Ethical Revival which was so long overdue, what might one not see? In spite of their preliminary doubts and of appearances to the contrary, it was generally conceded that Hooker would use his money for "doing good"; or at least for Reconstruction. But *what* good would he do? *What* would he reconstruct? That was the question.

The Society felt that the question, involving as it did, a great ethical problem, was one on which it ought to make a definite pronouncement; and so absorbing did the interest become that for the time being the members could hardly concentrate their attention on anything else. Little by little the weekly discussions grew shorter; the definitions of the Supreme Good more perfunctory; the relations of the Individual to the Social Whole more hastily sketched. Even the more contentious members of the group, who formed the majority, began to refrain from making speeches. The truth was that they were all looking forward to the moment when, the meeting over, they would retire to the tea-shop over the way and interchange ideas on "what Mr. Hooker would do with his money."

On one occasion the Committee on Practical Applications was meeting in the dingy little room at the back of the Hall; Professor Giles, the psychologist, was in the chair; and the first topic on the agenda was "Action of the Society in regard to the League of Nations." The programme of action was rapidly drawn up and adopted almost without argument. "And now," said a member, "the next step will be to approach Mr. Hooker for a large donation to the League Propaganda Fund."

"You forget," said another, "that Mr. Hooker is losing faith in Reconstruction."

"Yes," said the Chairman, pushing his agenda aside, "and that raises the whole question of what he is going to do with his money. The more I think of it the more convinced I am that he is in an impossible position. If Hooker were an ordinary man of business we all know what he would do. He would do like all the rest. Perhaps a little better, but essentially the same. But he is not an ordinary man of business. Handling money is not his line. He is a student, a thinker, and a man with an extraordinarily sensitive conscience. He knows too much about ethics to be able to make up his mind in a matter of such complexity. He will be another Hamlet. It would not surprise me in the least if he were to commit suicide. Besides, the deaths of his three sons have broken him, and I hear terrible stories about his wife."

"I hope," said one of the working men, "that he

MR. HOOKER'S ADVISERS

will pull down the east end of the town and rebuild it."

"I wonder, Giles," said Professor Smith—his subject was History—"I wonder what *you* would do, if you were placed in a similar position."

"Put that question to yourself," snapped the psychologist, "and mind you answer it."

"If the money were mine," said the dentist, "I should give the whole of it for the alleviation of physical pain, which is the only real evil in the universe."

"I know what *I* should do," said the designer of women's frocks. "I should go to the dogs."

"I suspect that a good many of us would do that," interposed the Warden of the Women's Settlement; though what precisely she meant was not clear, for she was seventy years of age.

Here Miss Wolfstone blew a ring of smoke. "For my part," she said, "I should do an infinite number of things. All of them quite *small*."

"I wish," said a gentleman with a red tie, "that Hooker would hand the money over to me."

"Then we should see something *big*," said Miss Wolfstone.

"Yes, and you'd soon find out what it was. We should want your school as a hospital for the wounded." This was spoken with some asperity.

"I think," said the Professor of Ethics, "we ought to appoint a special sub-committee to deal with the question and draw up a joint resolution to be submitted to Mr. Hooker in the name of the Society. It is a matter on which the Society ought to speak with united voice."

"Had we not better ask Mr. Hooker first whether our advice would be welcome to him?" asked Miss Wolfstone.

"Welcome or not, it ought to be given," said the Professor.

"But do you think we should agree?"

"The issue is perfectly simple," said the Professor —his name was Pawkins—"unless we can agree on a plain practical matter of this kind what prospect is there of our agreeing about anything?"

"None," said the designer of women's frocks. "All the same we shall not agree about this."

After further discussion the idea of a joint resolution was abandoned. Professor Pawkins, defeated on this point, but still insistent on the "duty" of the Society, now suggested that the members of the Committee should write as individuals to Mr. Hooker, leaving him to infer the general trend of the Society's judgment from the separate opinions. In any event he intended to do so himself. This led to further dissensions, Miss Wolfstone affirming that she, for her part, would not write to Mr. Hooker unless he definitely asked for her advice. Finally an understanding was reached to send him a carefully worded letter inquiring whether, in view of his long connection with the Society, he would be willing to receive individual opinions from the members on a matter so nearly concerning himself and them.

A week later it was reported to the Committee that Mr. Hooker had written a letter of thanks to the Secretary for the kind interest the Society had shown in his affairs, and said that, far from taking it amiss,

MR. HOOKER'S ADVISERS

he would be profoundly grateful to any member of the Committee who could throw the least light on the very difficult position in which he found himself.

In the month that followed Mr. Hooker received at intervals a dozen letters in all. The following are summaries of the most important. Let us take the Professors' first.

Professor Giles wrote that he realized the difficulty in which Mr. Hooker was placed. But to put himself in Mr. Hooker's position was a psychological impossibility. Then followed a long explanation of why this was so. In the last paragraph he advised the millionaire to do nothing definite for the present; to take his time; to watch the course of events and to act only when ripe reflection coincided with clear opportunity. He added, that times of confusion like the present were not favourable to men who had far-reaching decisions to make. "Wait therefore till the atmosphere has cleared. The things that are clamouring most loudly for money now are not those that will need it most three years hence."

Mr. Hooker thought it a sensible letter, but wondered how long it would be before "ripe reflection coincided with clear opportunity," and whether he would be able to recognize the exact moment when it came.

Professor Marchbanks, the Economist, wanted to know in what capacity he was expected to speak. If as a Political Economist, he would gladly give his opinion as to the economic consequences of any course of action Mr. Hooker might choose for himself, but he would not take the responsibility of guiding his conscience.

Professor Smith, of the History Department, plumped for a large endowment of Eugenics.

Professor Pawkins wrote a letter of sixteen pages, which meant, when reduced to its essence, that he didn't know what ought to be done. He developed twelve hypothetical methods of dealing with the money, and invited Mr. Hooker to balance their respective advantages. On the whole he was inclined to think that the question was one of casuistry, which, he said, was a dangerous subject.

The designer of women's frocks came next. His vein was light-hearted and a trifle impertinent—for the designer, in spite of his long association with the Ethical Movement, was not, it must be confessed, exactly a gentleman. He said he was very sorry for Mr. Hooker; that, obviously, the sum of money in question was much too large for any one man to handle, and that it ought to be broken up. He suggested, therefore, that it should be distributed in twelve equal portions among the members of the Committee, each of whom would then be left responsible for its right application. And he added some rather good remarks on the duty of distributing excessive responsibilities, reminding Mr. Hooker, jocosely, of a lecture he had once given on the subject. This was the smartest reply Mr. Hooker received, but it was also the most unkind.

The Warden of the Women's Settlement, who was a disciple of Herbert Spencer, said that Mr. Hooker's duty was perfectly clear and simple. He must devote the money, without reserve, to promoting Altruistic Evolution.

The dentist implored Mr. Hooker not to disperse his benefactions, but to concentrate on a single point, perhaps a minute one, and strike a telling blow. He instanced physical pain. If Mr. Hooker preferred Hospitals, rather than Anæsthetics pure and simple, he knew of many that were in need of funds; and he wrote out a long list of them.

The two labour agitators were brief and precise. They said, in terms so nearly identical as to suggest collaboration, that if they were in Mr. Hooker's position they would hand over the millions to the strike chests of the Trades Unions.

The radical lawyer told Mr. Hooker that he had a chance to do the biggest thing of his time. Let him devote his fortune to the revival of the Old Liberal Party, with Peace and Retrenchment for its motto. "Start a first-class Liberal newspaper with ample funds in every large town. Get Asquith back and send Lloyd George and his practitioners to the rightabout."

One of the working-men, not an agitator, suggested the foundation of "a Moral College for Labour." That, he said, had been his dream for many years, and he only wished he were in Mr. Hooker's shoes.

Four of the letters came from the obsessed. One said that he would give every penny of the money to the suppression of vivisection; the second that he would do the same for launching Prohibition propaganda on an enormous scale. The third proposed a colossal foundation for enabling bereaved persons to get into communication with the departed. Mr. Whistlefield, the Champion of the Simple Life, counselled the millionaire to buy up agricultural land and cultivate oats, which, he said, eaten dry, were the finest brain food in the world and highly conductive to moral elevation.

Miss Wolfstone wrote as follows:

"My dear Mr. Hooker,

"I have no true place in the Ethical Society now that you are going. I shall leave with you.

"I joined it, for reasons that you can imagine, when I was groping, before the war. It was no light burden that I carried. But one and another would dose me with what they called 'salvation by character'—a shallow and profane conception, which I abhor. It hurt me cruelly.

"But I stayed on. Why? Because in the first place I was strongly attracted by the ideas you were continually enforcing. Then, from the time when the Ministry of Munitions requisitioned your works, I foresaw that a tragedy would overtake you, and I wished to be there when the blow fell. For the rest there was a fascination in studying those queer types of character, so different from one another, which formed our little band, I myself being probably the queerest of the lot. All this was a woman's weakness, and I confess that I succumbed to it. But it has taught me much.

"May I beg you to leave the atmosphere of the Society, to take yourself out of it altogether? The members, excellent people as they are, cannot help you. They will merely pester you with generalities and so leave you more bewildered than ever. Your problem is far out of their range. They think it is easy. It is, as you know well, immensely difficult.

"One of the bitterest trials you have to encounter is that you will be driven, in spite of yourself, to suspect the motives of everyone who approaches you —you, who have trained yourself for years to think evil of no man. Fearing that they would be suspected, those who could help you most will keep aloof from you; and that will increase your loneliness, and leave you exposed to sycophants, conspirators and toadies. I hardly dare approach you myself. Every word in this letter is open to misconstruction— and would be instantly misconstrued by a censorious world. But you and I know one another pretty well, and I take my risk."

There remained two more letters. Both came from outsiders; which showed that the members of the Committee on Applications had been talking more freely than they ought. The first was signed "Cynic," and ran thus:

"MY DEAR MAN,

"Your problem is insoluble, and the sooner you recognize this the better. There is no mode of disposing of this money that will not do more harm than good. Whatever you do with it, you will wish you had done something else, and you will be right. It is essentially a poison. Don't flatter yourself that you are going to promote the good of society, for there is no good in society as it now exists that is worth promoting. Damn society. It is the mother of quarrels—*societas mater discordiarum*. Leave it to quarrel itself to death, as it soon will, and as your money, dispose of it as you may, will help it to do. Therefore I counsel you to *destroy* all this wealth. *Destroy it*, Hooker; wipe it out of existence as soon as you can! Don't *give* it, don't *leave* it to anybody! Above all don't spend it on yourself. Destroy it, destroy it, and again I say, destroy it! You will find that no easy thing to do. But write to me, Poste Restante, Southampton Row, London, and I will tell you how, without doing harm to anybody, you can make this wealth to be as though it had never been. I am an expert in the destruction of wealth."

The last letter to arrive was written in a schoolboy's hand. Looking at the address Hooker recognized the handwriting of his little friend, Billie Smith, son of Professor Smith, one of his pupils in the Moral Education Class.

"Dear Mr. Hooker,

"I heard Father tell Mother last night that you didn't know what to do with all your money. Ted and I talked about it in bed till half-past twelve and made a plan and got an awful rowing from Father this morning for not going to sleep. We want you please sir to bury the money in an island under a palm tree and make one of those funny maps with the murdered man's blood, and don't forget to put the skeleton on the top of the chest bearing two points North by East from the ship so that we shall know exactly where it is. Then Ted and I are going to be pirates and we will find the treasure and do lots of good with it and make all the poor people happy. Oh do please sir it will be such fun and you can have

MR. HOOKER'S ADVISERS

as much of the money back as you like when we get it and then we can write a book and you shall be the man with a wooden leg and one eye. We promise to do *right* sir Ted is such a good boy and I am not a cruel one and follow our consciences just as you said we ought when you used to take us in the Moral Class and we won't kill anybody unless it is in self defence and we'll spare all the passengers and be ever so polite to the ladies and allow no bad language and make anybody walk the plank that tells lies. Oh do please, we both promise. You are always so kind to boys. Our cat had seven kittens yesterday and one has no tail.
"Your loving friend,
"BILLIE SMITH.

"P.S.—We think Socrates and Buddha would be ever so pleased if you do what we say.

"P.S.—You needn't murder the man unless you like. He might fall from the masthead or something like that which would make him bloody."

The effect of these letters on the mind of Mr. Hooker was fourfold: first, to cause him to remember that Billie Smith's birthday occurred next week, and to order a microscope to be delivered at Billie's address on the morning of the great day; second, to raise his high regard for Miss Wolfstone, whom he resolved to take more fully into his confidence; third, to increase his antipathy to meddlesome moralists; fourth, to convince him that if his problem were ever solved at all it would have to be solved by himself and by nobody else. The solution, he saw, would never be *found*. It must be *created*, and, save himself, there was no man living who could create it.

CHAPTER FOUR

The Mad Millionaire Has a Near Shave

THE impression left by Mr. Hooker, at this time, on the minds of those who knew him was that of a "broken" man. Many of them fell into the habit of referring to him as "poor Hooker!" sometimes checking themselves as though the adjective were not appropriate, but inevitably recurring to it later on. His co-directors found his presence at the weekly Board meetings troublesome and dangerous. He would constantly intervene with some highflown proposal which was not "business"; he would press it with obstinacy and pour out moral indignation on any who opposed him. On one occasion he told the Board to its face that it was "a den of thieves"; on another he invoked the fate of Sodom and Gomorrah on the whole undertaking. They agreed that he was impossible, and must be got out of the Chair at all costs. They implored him to go away "for a long rest"; one of them offered the use of his villa on the Riviera—which suggestion was ill-received. They wrote to Mr. Polycarp, solicitor to the Firm, urging him to use his influence and if necessary to "take steps."

The Ethical Society was emphatic in the same sense. "Poor Hooker," said Professor Giles, "is done for. As a moral force he may be written off.

THE MAD MILLIONAIRE

Yesterday he stopped me in the street and said, with the strangest manner, 'Giles, when is that talking shop of yours going to put up its shutters?' I'm afraid he will discredit the Movement."

His domestics had no doubt about the matter. Said Robert, the butler, to Jenkins, the chauffeur, "Between you and me, Jenk, the old man's goin' dotty. I told you about me catchin' him sayin' his prayers. Well, this morning at breakfast blowed if he didn't empty his coffee into his porridge plate and eat it with a spoon."

"And I'll tell you a worse thing than that," said Jenkins. "He's taken against petrol. *Smells* it everywhere! He's always stopping the Rolls-Royce and saying there's something wrong with the car. When we were in London yesterday he calls through the speakin' tube and says, 'Jenkins,' says he, 'what's wrong with the car?' Right in the middle of the traffic it was. So I pulls up and I says, 'Nothing, sir.' 'It stinks of burnt petrol,' says he. 'It comes from these 'ere motor buses,' says I. 'It's the characteristic odour of civilization, and I hate it,' says he —them were his very words. I tell you the old man's breaking up. And a good 'eart, too."

And what did Mr. Polycarp, the lawyer, think? Mr. Polycarp, whose office in Bedford Row was panelled with black boxes bearing on their outsides the legend "Hooker & Co.," or "William Hooker, Esqre," thought it a very bad business and anticipated serious trouble. For Mr. Hooker, having shaken off the dust of his feet against the Ethical Society, had determined to make a new Will, but without any clear plan, or notion how to make it. Two or three times a week the agitated millionaire would fly up to London on this errand with proposals which Mr. Polycarp could not understand, still less apply. For example, he would commission the lawyer to draw up a Will "for the general purpose of financing the Moral Ideal," and then ask if it would be ready next week. Or he would launch into Kant's doctrine of the "Good Will," and tell Mr. Polycarp to make one. Or he would break out into invectives against the State, which, he said, was an immoral institution and the perpetrator of innumerable crimes against its subjects, and implore Mr. Polycarp to save his wealth from the predatory designs of "the Great Leviathan." The lawyer interpreted all this as evidence of mental disarray, and when his client left the office he would find himself at his wits' end and fling himself back in his chair. Then, after ejaculating "Poor Hooker!" several times, he would put his mouth to the speaking tube and call to his managing clerk:

"If Mr. Hooker should come in when I am out, see that he transacts no business and does not commit himself in any way."

Most assuredly the millionaire was "breaking up." And the humour of it increased the curiosity of the public as to what would become of his vast acquisitions—a curiosity which reflected the bewilderment of the millionaire himself.

But the breaking up process had gone deeper than the gossips were aware of, or than Mr. Polycarp could divine. It had penetrated to the hidden foundations of Mr. Hooker's orderly life, and, shattering these, had let loose the imprisoned forces from below, things as yet without form, which later on would grow accustomed to the light and clothe themselves in ideas. There was confusion, of course, but through it all something definite, though dimly apprehended, was struggling for expression, and Mr. Hooker, baffled by the half-formed thought within him, was turning to this friend and that, in a vain appeal for the liberating word.

After one of these interviews at his lawyer's office, Mr. Hooker found himself awaiting his return train at a London terminus. The platform was crowded with soldiers returning from the occupied territories. One group in particular caught his attention. It was gathered round a tall man in civilian clothes and appeared to be engaged in eager discussion.

Mr. Hooker went forward, and finding a first-class compartment empty took his seat, lit a cigar and fell into a deep introspection. As he mused the confusion seemed to abate; the thoughts that jostled in his mind lost their sharp edges; anxiety vanished and a profound calm descended upon his troubled spirit.

Suddenly he was startled from his reverie by hearing, or seeming to hear, the strains of a melody, extraordinarily sweet and penetrating, coming from somewhere above his head, and accompanied by the patter of light feet and the sound of laughing voices. It lasted for several minutes and then abruptly ceased.

He sprang from his seat and called to the guard, who was passing the window:

"Guard," he said, "where did that music come from?"

"What music, sir?" said the guard.

"I distinctly heard music and dancing a moment ago."

The man shook his head, and Hooker, greatly wondering, went back to his corner. Had he been asleep and dreaming? Or was it some frolic of the soldiers on the platform? He never knew. A moment later the whistle was blown for departure.

The train was already on the move when the guard, running along the platform, flung open the door and thrust into the carriage the tall civilian whom Hooker had seen surrounded by soldiers.

"Thank you, guard," cried the man. "See me at the other end. Is the lady in?"

"Yes, sir," shouted the guard, "in the next coach forward."

It was Rumbelow. Occupied for a moment in arranging some packages on the rack he did not notice his companion; but Hooker had recognized him at once, and had time to study him.

The bookmaker was a man in the prime of life. There was nothing in his appearance to reveal his calling or to suggest a monster or a shark. On the contrary, he had the air of a prince and a soldier; his features were strongly marked, but open: the eye clear and of a deep blue, the nose finely cut and very long, the ear small, the hand white, delicate and long fingered. If there was anything saturnine about the face it was in the mouth, the corners of which were slightly drawn down.

Rumbelow turned round. "Mr. Hooker, I believe," he said. "I am glad to see you about again, sir. We heard you were ill."

Mr. Hooker extended his hand, and Rumbelow, who seemed for a moment surprised, returned the grasp.

"It was kind of you," said Hooker, "to make inquiries about me the other day. I was touched by it. Indeed I went so far as to write to you last night hoping that you and Mrs. Rumbelow——"

"Call her 'My Lady,' " said Rumbelow.

Hooker, who had heard of this foible, went on: "Hoping that you and My Lady would dine with me."

"That most assuredly we will do, Mr. Hooker. Thank you; I have long wished that you and I might be better acquainted. I believe we have much in common. But beware, sir. My Lady and I are compromising acquaintances for a man in your position and with your connexions."

"You are thinking of the Ethical Society," said Hooker. "I have left it. And as to being compromised, I am no longer solicitous about that."

Rumbelow was silent for a few moments, thinking what this might mean. Then suddenly came the question, "What, Mr. Hooker, are your views on gambling?"

"All my life long," replied Hooker; "I have had a horror of gambling. It is, I believe, the cause of incalculable harm. I regard it as one of the most terrible scourges of society."

"You hit me hard," said Rumbelow, "and you hit me on a sensitive spot. As to my calling—if I may be equally frank—there seems not much to choose between yours and mine. I am a bookmaker; you are a profiteer. Chance has made us both what we are. Only, with me, chance has been scientifically handled. I have worked much harder for my fortune, Mr. Hooker, than you have for yours. Perhaps for that reason the moralists think me the greater villain. Anyhow, I doubt if either of us can afford to throw stones. Don't you think we might treat one another—well, as *neighbours?*"

"In strict justice," said Hooker, "neither of us has one jot or tittle of right to his fortune."

"And which of us," said the other, "has one jot or tittle of right to be alive?"

"What do you mean?"

"Only that the larger chances of life include the lesser. There's a kind of gamble, Mr. Hooker, at the root of human life. Our very existence depends upon the turning of a hair, the flutter of a butterfly's wing. If you trace out the web of life you will find that the origin of every human individual hangs upon some contingency fine as a gossamer thread. What does your philosopsy make of *that?*"

"Nothing," said Hooker. "It is the most inexplicable thing in the universe. No philosophy can face it."

"I believe," the bookmaker continued, "that all events are guided and controlled by invisible powers. Our meeting to-night, for example, was unquestionably prearranged, and I have little doubt that it will lead on by some unsearchable path to issues of the greatest importance. As a gambler and a student of gambling, I find the invisible world constantly in my thought as a very close reality. A fine estimation of odds is the nearest approach the human intellect can make to the secret of destiny. The secret itself we can never penetrate, but in some of the higher operations of our Firm we come very near to it—surprisingly near, I assure you, so that one feels that another step would carry the mind clean over the boundary which separates the visible from the invisible world—which is much the more real of the two, sir."

Mr. Hooker sat astonished, not only at what the other was saying, but at the intensity and conviction of his manner. The gravity of a thinker sat upon his brow and the fervour of a devotee was in his voice. He remembered his interview with Polycarp, and how aloof he had seemed to be from his interlocutor. But with this man he seemed to be standing on his own level, and strangely at home, even though the language spoken was one he could not understand.

"I don't follow you," he said. "In my view of things chance has no place and no meaning. We are under the reign of law, and everything happens as it must."

"Perfectly true of natural forces," said Rumbelow, "but perfectly futile in the affairs of men. Is it not strange, Mr. Hooker, that with all we have learnt about the uniformity of nature and the reign of law, the future of the human race, the thing that concerns us most, was never so dark and inscrutable as it is as the present hour. But come to our Office; ask almost any question you choose about an important event in which men are interested, and we will give you the odds on its happening as closely determined as human knowledge can make them."

"And the end of it all is," said Hooker, "that

thousands of men and women are being morally ruined. If we learnt that a clerk in our Firm had been betting with yours we should turn him off at a moment's notice."

"I am not blind to that side of the matter," said the bookmaker. "But look facts in the face. You cannot suppress the gambling spirit; it belongs to the nature of life. It is one of the most powerful forces in human society, and will always remain so. The war has enormously increased its power: war and gambling are twin brothers. The soldier has been a gambler since the first wars were made. You saw those men on the platform before the train started. They were men of the battalion I served with at the front—all betting-mad and clamouring for the odds on this and on that. But what are you going to do? It must be taken in hand, controlled, converted to higher uses—the way of all sound reforms. If only men like yourself would cease denouncing the thing, and come over to our side and help us to turn this tremendous force into the right channel, instead of wasting your fine intellects on moral propaganda that interest nobody but yourselves, we should soon have the situation in hand and the world would see a real instance of the union of ideal aims with businesslike methods, and——"

"Stop!" cried Hooker; "your words arrest me. 'The union of ideal aims and businesslike methods' —I've been searching for that phrase for weeks. It says what I was trying to say to my lawyer this afternoon—exactly expresses what I mean. Where did you get it?"

"'Tis the motto of our Firm," said Rumbelow.

"But you have not heard the whole of it. 'The union of ideal aims with businesslike methods and sportsmanlike principles.'"

"I don't understand the last," said Hooker. "'Sportsmanlike principles!' I didn't know there were such things. And, if there are, what have they to do with ideal aims?"

"Everything. It's the crowning touch; the growing point of the whole enterprise; the jumping-off place for the next great undertaking of the Firm. The three things, sir—ideal aims, businesslike methods, sportsmanlike principles—form the strongest confederation of spiritual forces ever introduced into human affairs. None of the three is anything without the others. In combination they are irresistible."

Rumbelow spoke rapidly and his eyes flashed. Said Mr. Hooker:

"I get no further than the 'businesslike methods.' This afternoon I dropped a phrase at my lawyer's which brought him to the same point. I said that I meant to finance the Moral Ideal."

"Bravo!" cried Rumbelow.

"But he answered that the Moral Ideal had no business organization; and it was plain that he treated it as the hare-brained notion of a fool."

"He was a fool to think so," said the other. "It is a perfectly sound proposition—provided you add the sportsmanlike principles. That, sir, is the mission of our Firm; and we intend to carry it into the highest regions of human interest—yes, into religion itself."

"Mr. Hooker," he went on, "you know something

of my history. You think of me doubtless as a man who has had an evil education. 'Tis a mistake. Every stage of my education has been exquisitely adapted to the purpose of my life. Every step has been guided. In no other way could I have learnt what is needed for the carrying out of my designs. In no other way could I have gained control of the forces I am going to employ. In no other way could I have discovered the means of mobilizing wealth for spiritual ends and countering the imbeciles who now misgovern the world. I have done harm, you say. Doubtless. But not one thousandth part of the harm inflicted on mankind by the powers that made you a multimillionaire. The men who wield those powers are gamblers, sir—with this difference between them and me, that they pretend to be something else. They are bunglers at their own game. They handle forces they can't control. Their science is beneath contempt. They practise arts which would cause a man in my profession to be instantly expelled from the Turf. I tell you, sir, that Newmarket will go into the Kingdom of Heaven before Westminster and Washington."

"It is strange," said Mr. Hooker, "that in all this you seem to be saying what I was trying to say to my lawyer this afternoon. I told him, for example, that all States are, fundamentally, war-making institutions."

"Conducted by politicians and diners-out who know nothing about war," added Rumbelow. "War, Mr. Hooker, is the supreme gamble in which all the forces of our civilization come to their inevitable issue. Until that is understood wars will never cease.

And the tragedy is that the men who run the gamble—the politicians and the diners-out—have neither ideal aim, businesslike method, nor sportsmanlike principle. Your own fortune, sir, is neither more nor less than a by-product of a huge, clumsy, stupid gambling transaction set on foot by gamblers of the most incompetent type—the German Emperor, for example: men who do not understand the bare rudiments of the business. You and I ought to be friends. Gambling has enriched you by chance; me by method."

"You cannot make me more ashamed of myself than I am," said Hooker. "But all this does not reconcile me to gambling."

"Then you must go deeper. The business that I conduct is saturated in metaphysics. It rests on the truth that the whole universe is in essence a sporting event. A sportsmanlike principle is interwoven with the very stuff of reality. Life itself, Mr. Hooker, if you study its origin, was a win against enormous odds—hence all the greater virtues of mankind, courage, magnanimity, loyalty and love. In the beginning was the wager! The losses have been colossal, unimaginable! Only a Divine universe would have dared to back itself against such odds—or escaped bankruptcy so long. What better proof could you have that the universe is Divine?"

As the ex-president of the Ethical Society listened to this outburst, half hypnotized by the intense animation of his companion, two feelings alternated in his mind and strove for the mastery. Now it was a feeling of profound relief, as though the heavy burden of his life were falling from his shoulders and the problem that had baffled him so long on the point of being solved. Now it was a feeling of dream-like bewilderment, as though the occasion, the place, the objects in the carriage, the man before him, were all unreal and about to vanish.

And so they did, but not by the touch of a spirit hand.

As Rumbelow was concluding his last sentence Mr. Hooker heard in the far distance a prolonged whistle. It grew rapidly louder and was answered by another near at hand. Rumbelow flung open the window and, leaning far out, peered ahead.

There was a violent jar; a screech of suddenly arrested wheels; the light thickened; the air grew foul with dust. Then a terrific crash and total darkness.

It was as if all the violence in the world had been suddenly let loose upon the millionaire. He was hurled from side to side, struck in the face, twisted, compressed, suffocated, drenched with water, and at last flung headlong with his mouth in the dust. There he was held tight; he could not move nor see nor speak. But consciousness was alive—the consciousness of the unendurable.

What had happened? He knew not. He remembered afterwards how his agony had framed itself into a question, and how he had halted between two opinions. Was he in this world or the next? The next, assuredly; and survival, then, was a fact. He was sorry. Why should his mouth be full of dirt? Why should he be held fast in a vice? Was it to be always so? Or was this only the beginning of the resurrection? Ha! things were improving already! The weight on his body was growing lighter—he could move his leg. There was air in his face. And surely that was a voice he knew. It was saying: "Lay him on the embankment and put that cushion under his head. Hand me the crowbar—quick! There's another yet." So it was this world after all.

Time in these things cannot be reckoned: it does not go by the clock. There came a moment, perhaps soon, when Hooker, roused by a sense of new danger, found himself on his feet, trembling and dazed. Not far off a fierce fire was raging, the flames were blowing his way and the hot sparks were stinging him. Close at his feet lay a little girl with broken legs, shrieking with terror and pain. He stooped down, and taking hold of the child by its arms, for he could not lift it, dragged it along with him a little further from the flames.

He hardly knew where he was. He gazed vacantly around him, noting the sights, but indifferent to their meaning. Screams, imprecations and horrible cries rent the air and seemed to break out in chorus. Somebody was yelling out the words of the Lord's Prayer; another was calling on Jesus Christ and mingling his name with obscenities. He was aware of figures running hither and thither in the glare and shouting to one another. "Quick with the buckets!" "There's water in the engine!" "Helpers to the rear of the train!" "Shovels and picks this way!" These were the shouts. But there was one sound that fixed his attention more than all the rest. It was the voice of a child calling, "Mother, mother."

Unable to stand longer he sank down into the

seat of a first-class carriage which had been split in two, trying to collect himself, to piece things together. Vague memories of his conversation with Rumbelow haunted him. But what next? The gambling losses of the universe, the great virtues of mankind, loyalty and love, and then—the light goes out, a shock, agony, a resurrection, the next world and then—this world again. There was no intelligible sequence. He closed his eyes, and as he did so the truth began to dawn upon him.

There was a hand on his shoulder and he heard a voice. He opened his eyes and saw in front of him the dark figure of a woman, her hat gone and her hair hanging in disorder over her shoulders.

She stood for a moment looking into his face, and then kneeling down gave him a drink of brandy out of a flask. Hooker eagerly swallowed the draught. As he drank there rose before him with visual clearness, and perfect in every detail, a scene from his boyhood, when he had fallen from a horse and his mother kneeling beside him was holding brandy to his lips, exactly as this woman was doing. "Surely she is my mother," he thought; and in a moment his arm was round her neck, he drew her head down to his, kissed her fervently and said, "God bless you, dearest mother"; and he held the woman's face close to his.

In a moment the illusion broke, his wits returned and he knew where he was and what he had done. "Forgive me," he said, releasing his arm. "The shock had bereft me of my senses. I was in a dream. I thought you were my mother."

"It was a lovely thing to happen in a hell like

this," she said. "I shall not forget it." And without another word she went away.

Hooker, greatly revived by the brandy, got upon his feet and followed in the direction the woman had taken, resolved to help if he could. Presently a man, running in the opposite direction, crossed the line to intercept him. It was Rumbelow, wrapped in a steaming wet blanket and with the hair burnt off one side of his head. "Ah, that's good, Mr. Hooker! You had a near shave. The whole mass collapsed the moment after we got you out. We've had a terrible struggle at the burning coach, and only saved three. But now, if you can do anything, follow me to the rear of the train. There are soldiers under the wreckage."

Hooker followed as best he could, miserably conscious that he was too sick and unsteady to be of any use. He made his way with difficulty, falling once or twice over obstacles. By the time he reached the end of the train he could stand no longer, and sat down, helpless, on a lady's cabin trunk. In front of him was a third-class coach, tilted on its side and partly telescoped by the one behind it; cries were coming from beneath. Near by two men, dreadfully crushed, lay on the track; they were shrieking and writhing about. Another was brought out by the soldiers, and died almost immediately under his eyes. Rumbelow, with four or five others, passed before him, carrying a broken rail to be used as a lever. The rail was placed in position and a dozen men, hanging their weight upon it, strove in vain to move some huge obstacle. Presently they desisted, and one of them said, "We'll never get him out, sir. There's tons on top of him." Another said, "He's dead already. He's stopped groaning." Then, to belie the last speaker, the voice of the imprisoned man, distinct and piteous. "Is the Major there? Oh, God, I want to speak to the Major."

"I'm here, sergeant," cried Rumbelow, peering under the wreckage. "Keep up, man. We'll have you out yet."

The voice replied as before, "Oh, God, I want to speak to the Major," and repeated the words again and again.

A guard's lamp had been placed on the ground, and by the light of it the top of the man's head could be plainly seen behind a tangle of wheels and timbers. Above the head were his two hands caught between boards and hanging from the broken wrists, like the hands of a man in the pillory.

Rumbelow flung himself on the ground, and began to worm his way in. He advanced a few feet, but could get no further. Then he tried at another point, and had nearly reached his object when a piece of wreckage in front of him sank down and the passage was blocked. Again he came out, and starting from the other side made a third attempt. A doctor who was standing by put something into his hand.

As Rumbelow worked his way in he could hear the man from time to time repeating his cry in a fainter voice. At last, despairing of getting further, he called out, "Now, sergeant, what is it? I can't come any nearer."

The man gave a reply, but the voice had become a whisper and the words were lost. Then Rumbelow began to pull at the objects in front of him, and one of them yielding a little he was able to force his shoulders forward and to bring his head almost into contact with the man's. Immediately above him hung the crushed body of a dog, and its feet, dangling down, brushed the back of his neck.

"The dog's dead, sir," gasped the man. "Bought it for my missus. She's main fond of a dog."

"I'll buy her another."

"And send it to Wigan, sir, please. A fox terrier."

"I will."

"Put your hand in the front pocket of my tunic, sir. There's forty pound."

"I have it."

"And put it on the Blue Bird, sir. And if we win, send the money to the old woman."

"Sure thing, sergeant."

"Thank God," said the man; and after a few incoherent mutterings he sank into his last sleep.

When Rumbelow emerged from the wreckage he had the appearance of a man who had been rolled in blood. He had been lying in a pool of it, while the blood of the suspended dog, dripping on to his head and shoulders, had done the rest. A cheer greeted him from the group of soldiers, and the doctor began asking him questions.

"I'm not hurt," said Rumbelow, "only filthy and sick. I must sit down. And here's your opium. It wasn't needed. The man's dead."

Then his eye fell upon Hooker, seated on the cabin trunk a few yards off. As he crossed the line he said to the guard, who was holding the lamp, "Go down the train and try to find My Lady. She has some brandy." Then he sat down beside Hooker on the cabin trunk.

For some minutes the two millionaires sat thus in silence side by side, Rumbelow unable to speak. Presently the guard stood in front of them with a flask of brandy in his hand. "My Lady will be here directly, sir," he said. "She's helping a doctor. I told her you weren't hurt."

"This gentleman first," said Rumbelow, as the guard handed him the brandy. And for a moment the two men, feeble as they were, seemed inclined to dispute. The guard decided the quarrel. Holding the brandy to Rumbelow's lips he forced him to drink; and the other drank after him.

"And now, if you can, tell me what happened," said Hooker.

"I took a bet," said the bookmaker, "and I have been very near to the invisible world. The man's dead."

Hooker replied: "I want to say one thing, and to say it while I can. I have heard of many heroic deeds, but have never seen one before. The one I have just seen has made a deeper impression than the thousands I have heard about."

"I tell you," said the other, "I was making a bet. It was all in the way of business." And he told what had happened.

Another voice interrupted him. "You're sure you are not hurt, dearest?" it said. And Hooker, looking up, saw with astonishment the woman who had given him the brandy, bending over the bloody figure of Rumbelow.

"Not at all," was the answer. "Only my old

wound hurts a bit. But let me present a companion in distress."

"Oh," she cried, "we are friends already! Mr. Hooker presented himself just now in the most beautiful way imaginable. He shall tell you about it himself. But not now. Come along, both of you. The relief train is up, and we can do nothing more." And the three moved off in silence down the line.

As they were going a soldier ran after them. "Excuse me, sir," he said, addressing Rumbelow, "but all of us in our carriage were backing the same 'oss as the sergeant."

"How many?" asked the bookmaker.

"Well, sir, there was thirteen of us to begin with—unlucky number, sir—but three, that's includin' the sergeant, are killed; there's six safe, and the rest casualties. Two can't speak."

"Ten in all, then. Write out your bets and post them to the office."

"What about them two as can't speak, sir?"

"Put them in along with the rest. I'll be responsible."

"And what about the dead men, sir. One of 'em leaves a widow and five children."

"Double their stakes. I'll be responsible for them too."

"Thank you, sir; if ever there was a real sportsman livin', it's you, sir, though pardon the liberty."

The soldier left them. The woman, linking her arm in her husband's, said, "That, dearest, is not business."

"Good enough for this hell," said Rumbelow.

And what was Mr. Hooker thinking as he listened

to these things? Perhaps he was not thinking at all, but exercising some deeper faculty which the experts have not yet named.

One might suppose that with such an exhibition of violence under his eyes, he would at all events have been in no doubt as to the reality of an external world. The actual effect was precisely opposite. Things visible and material seemed not to have established, but to have destroyed themselves. To his own consciousness at that moment he was a broken thing in a broken world, where logic had exploded in the general shock, and where everything that happened was incredible. All that he saw about him, all that he heard, all that he felt even, seemed unconvincing and unimportant. The wrecked train, the horrible mess, the clouds of dust and steam were signs of a universal collapse in which his own personality had broken up along with everything else. The voices of Rumbelow and the soldiers were dream voices; their proceedings fantastic and irrational. The pains that shot through his body, the faintness, the nausea, the laboured breadth, the dizzy brain—at one moment he would feel these things as his own, at the next he would observe them from a centre of complete indifference, as though they were the miseries of another person in whom he had no interest. Then it would seem to him that what had happened did not matter in the least, and if the skies had fallen in upon the ruin it would have made no difference.

Rumbelow and My Lady were walking on in front, the man leaning heavily on the frailer form of the woman. Hooker followed close behind, supporting his steps with a broken umbrella he had picked up on the line, and aware that he might fall at any moment. As he watched the two in front there came over him the sense of a cruel and inequitable contrast. "Here is this man," he thought, "leaning on a woman who belongs to him, and here am I leaning on an umbrella that belong to somebody else. The universe is fundamentally unjust."

He struggled on, full of contempt for the umbrella and hungry to share the strong support he saw in front. "If only I could lay hold of that woman's arm," his thought went on, "I should know where I was. I should stagger no more; I should rest upon the only firm and solid thing that is left in the world. Why should Rumbelow have it all?"

His resources were coming to an end. Making a desperate effort to hurry forward and overtake the object of his desire, his limbs suddenly gave way beneath him and he fell heavily on the line. As he fell he clutched at the woman's skirts, and words came to his lips which he had used to another woman a few days before.

"For pity's sake, my dear lady, take me somewhere. I am completely lost."

In the relief train the three were separated. Hooker was laid on a stretcher and placed with many others in the guard's van. As he lay there his mind wandered among confused and terrible images, finding no rest.

Little by little his thought took definite form and concentrated upon a point. "Had not Rumbelow saved my life," it ran, "those accursed millions would now belong to the Society for Ethical Culture. I have yet to make my Will."

He was greatly troubled. Now the trouble would seem to expand and blow itself out to immense proportions until it lost its outlines in the realms of nonsense. Now it would contract again and return to a burning focus in the problem of his Will. And along with this a conviction that there was only one way of escape. He must throw away his broken umbrella and get a firm grip on the woman's arm. The guard, standing over him, noticed that from time to time he would fling out his hands and clutch at something that seemed to be eluding his grasp.

CHAPTER FIVE

The Transfiguration of a Mouse

MIDNIGHT had passed on the day of the accident when the millionaire, in complete collapse, his clothes torn, his face covered with dirt, was delivered by the driver of an ambulance into the hands of his chauffeur and head gardener, who had been anxiously awaiting their master's arrival. By them he was carried upstairs on the stretcher and deposited upon his bed; the housekeeper was then roused and a consultation held. Should Mrs. Hooker be summoned? The suggestion was immediately negatived by a decisive shake of the head from Mr. Hooker. An hour later a doctor was in attendance, and shortly after a trained nurse. Matters, so said the doctor, looked serious.

In the days that followed Mr. Hooker gained for the first time in his long life a direct, experimental knowledge of the disagreeable process of dying. Most men who pass through the penultimate stage of death go on to the last, and so leave no witness behind them. But it had been ordained for the millionaire that, as yet, he was not to die, but only to make a very close acquaintance with death as a positive factor in life. Hitherto he had treated it as negative, as a thing or a no-thing which must not be suffered to trouble the thoughts of a wise man. According to the admirable philosophy on which his conduct of life had been founded, we must continue our efforts to improve the world, without reference to the certainty that the more we improve it the more men lose when they die. With death as a fact of daily occurrence, Mr. Hooker was, of course, thoroughly familiar; but neither its normal ravages in times of peace nor its abnormal ravages during the war had undone his conviction that it should be treated as a negligible or negative thing. It is true that the death of his three sons had shaken him at that point, giving him a vague sense that there was something out of perspective in his picture of life. From the philosophical point of view, however, all that was a mere weakness, to be rebuked by the well-known saying of Spinoza. He knew by heart all the tunes which philosophers whistle to keep up their courage when passing the cemetery.

But now he was making his approach to death on the ground of personal experience, which, philosophers may be reminded, is a very different thing from speculation about it. Death, like most abstractions, is presumably unreal, but dying has a distinct savour of reality. Mr. Hooker began in fact to die, and so rapidly as to leave in those about him little hope of his recovery. It was, to him, a poignant experience. The physical shock, supervening on a period of mental tension which had long been taxing his vitality, brought him down, by no primrose path, to the very gates of the grave, salting him with fire at every step of the way, both in body and in mind. That permanent possibility of pain which physiologists call the nervous system had been centrally attacked; and, through the broken barriers and the open gates, the imprisoned fury poured into his field of consciousness like an inundation. Storms of pain overtook him at intervals; they would engulf him; they would blot out his awareness of everything else, turning his whole being into an impersonal sea of agony, with no meaning save that which was expressed in the moaning of its waves. The pain over, he would fall into a lassitude so extreme that he wondered if he were not already dead; the objects about him would become insubstantial, the light a mere attenuated darkness. There were nights of fever, when he would struggle for long hours to break away from his self-consciousness, battling with it as with a nightmare; and these would be followed by days of depression, when the thin blood, propelled by a feeble pulse, was hardly vitalized enough to maintain the sense of his identity. And sometimes, when depression was at its lowest, there would suddenly occur moments of elation, of strange and delightful discoveries, of illumination and peace—perhaps due to the action of an opiate, perhaps the work of the Holy Ghost. On these occasions he would become acutely conscious that he was in the near presence of death; he would wonder what was coming next, intensely curious, as though the romance of his life were about to begin.

Through all the phases of this experience there ran a ground tissue, sometimes reduced to a mere thread, which connected everything else with the scenes of the accident. From that point the images in his mind seemed to originate, and to that, however far they might have wandered afield, they would always come back at last. Around this imagery he would weave all kinds of queer philosophical problems and wrestle with them in his nightmare dreams. They would haunt him in the daytime and return with a variation next night. "Is life worth the fuss we make about it?" "Why does the world break our bones when we are trying to leave it a little better than we found it?" "Whence comes the splendour that breaks out of things when they are at their very worst?" "Why does the universe listen indifferently to the lectures of the Ethical Society about the Supreme Good, and to the screams of women enduring the Supreme Evil in a burning coach?" "Where can I find a ship manned by great souls, that I may sail off with them into the everlasting Silence?" These were some of the problems afterwards remembered and noted down.

The last returned again and again. Sometimes he would see a ship, now a great one with spreading sails, now a boat manned with oars; it was moored a little distance from the shore; on the deck stood the bloody figure of Rumbelow, with his hair burnt off, and beside him his wife holding a brandy flask and beckoning him to come on board. These two were always there, but they were never alone. Behind them stood others, more dimly seen, who would vary and change into each other—Miss Wolfstone, his three sons, the nurse who attended him, and a little boy dressed as a pirate. He would take a great leap towards them, hoping to alight on the ship, and would find himself falling, falling, into a bottomless abyss.

Often as he lay awake during the daytime the

things about him would seem half real, thinning themselves down into shadows, into ghosts. The wall opposite looked like a mass of suspended grey, and once when the doctor leaned against it he wondered why he did not fall through. The dream world and the waking world would change places. He spent long hours in a vain effort to determine which was which, but always came back to the conviction that the room about him was *not* real, and that the being who lay outstretched on the bed was *not* himself.

Though the proximate causes of all this lay, no doubt, in bodily conditions and in the immediate train of events which had led up to them, there were remoter causes with a far deeper root in Mr. Hooker's life. A man's nightmares, like his daydreams, are not unrelated to his character, and often betray, when closely scrutinized, the preparations of a lifetime. One of his experiences, which he recorded with particular care as soon as he was able to write, and passed on to a few intimate friends, clearly presupposes a distinct atmosphere, and could hardly have occurred save to one whose nature had long been nourished by dealings with the moral ideal. It happened a few days after the worst was over, Hooker being then in the first stage of his return journey from the gates of death.

The only person in whose presence he had taken any interest during his illness was one of the two nurses, a woman of fifty—thoughtful, intelligent and, as Mr. Hooker was quick to perceive, highly conscientious. With her he would from time to time exchange such scraps of conversation as the intermittent lucidity of his mind permitted him to maintain. He found her sympathetic, and felt instinctively that her skill was merely a fine form in which natural kindness expressed itself. With that strange insight which leads the heavy-laden to find one another out, he divined that she, too, had received more than her share of the burden of life; and once, acting on his intuition, he said to her quite suddenly, "Nurse, is there no one to deliver us from this intolerable load?" The woman paused in her work, as though her own thought had been uttered, and he knew from the way she looked at him that he had spoken home.

Some hours afterwards, the time being then about ten at night, a strong desire to be left alone came over him, and he asked the nurse accordingly to turn out the lights and leave him. This she did, the room being still partly illuminated by the bright fire burning in the grate.

When she was gone and the room silent, the queer thought suddenly took possession of Hooker that the silence was *the sound of his own life*. It seemed to him a wonderful thing, and he sat up in bed to listen to it. Presently the sound of the silence was broken into by another, very faint. It was the gentle gnawing of a mouse behind the wainscot. Of this, after a time, he became acutely conscious—not in irritation, but in expectancy, as though it presaged the coming of some great event. Very slowly the new sound seemed to enlarge and multiply; at first almost inaudible and then increasing by continuous change within itself until the silence was full of it. It was the *evenness* of the crescendo which fascinated

TRANSFIGURATION OF A MOUSE

the listener; and this also he found wonderful and amazing.

Then the gnawing ceased, and Hooker, intensely alert, fixed his eyes on the corner of the room from which it had come. A moment later the mouse itself appeared on the floor, a tiny apparition born from nowhere in particular, now creeping warily in search of fallen crumbs, now darting with incredible velocity from point to point, now vanishing in a flash at the sound of a footstep outside. It was here, it was there; it came and it went; it was and it was not. As for Hooker, no marvel he had ever seen or heard of could compare with the gorgeous mystery of the self-originated movements of this little beast.

At last the creature came to a pause, sat upon its hind legs, turned towards Hooker, and lifting its forefeet began demurely to clean its face. The effect on the millionaire was overwhelming. In an instant it was as though all the values in the universe had inverted themselves and become concentrated in the being of the mouse. What importance, what adequacy, what completeness! It seemed a focus of intense but calm luminosity, where all forces, problems, agitations came to rest; the centre of a universe radiating perfection upon all its surroundings till they became transfigured; the minute growing point of a renovated world. Such was the vision, if vision it was. As Hooker gazed upon the astonishing thing and felt the room and all the objects in it reverberating with the splendours that streamed from the central point, the whole burden of life fell from him; his problems seemed to solve themselves; or rather they mattered not at all; they were empty phantoms. But this was real; and the conviction seized him that the essence of things was altogether lovely and lovable, that the ultimates were secure, and that he himself would be kindly dealt with at the last. Till that moment he had never known, or even dreamed, what happiness really is.

And now the nurse had entered the room. Again it was her *movement* that attracted him. It was an astonishment, a delight, a pageant of beauty beyond utterance. Whithersoever the spirit went, she went, impelled by self-actuated forces, which seemed to link her with all nature, with the rolling tides and the flowing winds and the courses of the everlasting stars and the rivers of eternal life. She walked in glory; her nurse's garments made music as she passed; her plain and patient features were no more; it was an angel from Paradise that was offering him food.

"Nurse," he said quietly, as she bent over him, "you are a radiant and wonderful being!"

She gazed at him in astonishment, in alarm. An hour earlier she had left him a wasted, weary man looking ten years older than he was. Now he was ten years younger, perfectly calm and self-possessed, but every feature in his face aglow.

"You are wonderfully better, sir," she said.

"I feel a new life in me," he answered. "The truth is I have just made a great discovery, in which you, and everything, seem to participate. This world is a queer place, nurse."

"Some people would give it a worse name than that," she answered.

"They are wrong," said Hooker with decision; "they should give it a better."

"But what was the great discovery, Mr. Hooker?"

"Promise," he said with a smile, "that you will not report me to the doctors to-morrow for being out of my mind, and I will tell you."

"I promise," she answered.

"Well, then—*I have just seen a mouse as it really is*. And I can tell you that it really is something ten thousand times more wonderful than it seems to be. So are you. So is everything in the world."

The nurse, sorely puzzled and not knowing what to say, went away from the bedside and stood gazing into the fire. After a little she turned to Mr. Hooker and said:

"You may remember that Jesus Christ used to see the flowers as they really are;" and she quoted the words about the lilies of the field.

"Ha!" he cried, "that rings true! But I had forgotten it. Thirty years ago I dismissed all that from my life, because I abhorred the use that has been made of it. Since then I have hardly opened the New Testament except to find a quotation now and then. Perhaps I have been wrong. I must read it again. Perhaps to-morrow."

"If you will allow me," she said, "I will read it aloud to you."

That night Hooker slept well. Next day the doctor was jubilant at the change. Before leaving he drew the nurse aside.

"Anything peculiar last night?" he asked. "Any more queer fancies?"

"Not a trace," she answered. "He was perfectly

self-collected, and talked in the most sensible manner imaginable."

"He is distinctly better," said the doctor.

"I am sure he is," said the nurse.

For more than a week the readings from the New Testament went on, Mr. Hooker steadily recovering day by day. At the end of that time they had read through the Four Gospels, the major Epistles of St. Paul, the Epistles of St. John and the Book of Revelation, Hooker making no comments meanwhile, but promising the nurse to give her his impressions when they had finished.

"I think," he said at length, "what I have thought and often said during the last thirty years, that the least Christian thing in the world is Christianity—not, of course, as it exists in simple lives, but as men have set it out in books and creeds and churches. But I had no idea till now that the original was so good, so penetrating, so powerful and so generous. The misconceptions about Jesus Christ are really scandalous. It is a terrible misfortune that the churches and the chapels have captured him. I imagine that the real man was about as unlike the current conceptions of him as two things could possibly be to one another. But perhaps I offend you?"

"Far from it," said the nurse; "I have often thought these things but never dared to say them."

"Coming to it all afresh after so long an interval," he went on, "it makes a surprising impression—an impression of something the flat opposite of the mournful thing that passes current as Christianity, with its funeral airs and its incubus of a God. It seems to me, now, as though it were the proclamation of a great holiday for the spirit of man. Essentially a festive thing—a song, not a sermon. Those closing discourses of St. John, for instance, are full of high spirits—simply exuberant; there is nothing there in the minor key; and then that passage about drinking wine in the Father's Kingdom, and most of all the Parable of the Prodigal Son, which culminates in a merry-making. And the lilies of the field that make a mock of Solomon and all his glories; and the sparrows, not one of which is forgotten before God! The infinite importance of the particular! The vision of the hidden beauty of the world! It all bears upon that. Why, nurse, if Jesus of Nazareth were to walk into this room, he would tell you, as I did, that you are a radiant and wonderful woman."

"Perhaps if *he* were to tell me so, I should believe it," said the nurse.

"You touch on an interesting point," he answered. "When you were reading I was constantly struck by the extraordinary power he had over women. They were always about him and were deeply implicated in his life. Some of his finest sayings come out in conversation with them. With the Woman of Samaria, for example, he reaches his very highest point. He seems to have required their presence as an incentive to his genius—a thing I have often observed in men of exceptionally fine nature. I find him joyous and even romantic—as unlike as possible to the hortatory personage he is commonly supposed to have been. But I must not go on."

"Oh, do," she replied. "I have been longing to hear this for twenty years."

"I suspect," said Hooker, "that if women had drawn up the creeds of the Church they would have given a very different version of the Christian religion from the horrible travesty men have made of it. At least they wouldn't have lost the keynote, as men have done. After all, the Magdalen understood him far better than St. Peter. I wish she had written a Gospel."

"Don't you think," asked the nurse, "that some of her memories have been preserved?"

"Renan thought so. In several of the passages you read I was conscious of a woman's touch. In the stories about children, for example, I seemed to be in direct contact with a woman's mind. I wonder that people are not aware of it. Probably they are blinded by the Church and Chapel conventions that have been woven round the whole subject. What a pity!"

"Yes, indeed," said the nurse. "But you seem to have forgotten the Cross, Mr. Hooker. Does that belong to the festival?"

"There is something strange about that, which I can't quite penetrate yet, and must think over. But while you were reading that part of the story it seemed to link itself on, in a very remarkable manner, to the impression I got of you a few days ago, and that still lingers with me. Does the Cross mean anything to *you*?"

"It is the part of Christianity that I am best acquainted with," said the nurse, and the tears swam in her eyes.

"I thought so," said Hooker; "and there, I imagine, we have something in common."

TRANSFIGURATION OF A MOUSE

Not many days afterwards, nothing to the purpose having been said in the meantime, Hooker again returned to the subject.

"That was a strange experience of mine the other night," he said. "It still goes on reverberating, though the echoes are growing fainter every day. I was like a man going down into a dark chasm until I reached at last the central blackness of the pit. Then I took one step more, and came out, to my immense surprise, into the most radiant and joyous surroundings. I have been asking myself whether it was an abnormal occurrence or whether it may not be after all a natural sequence in the order of the world—the best and the worst meeting, so to speak, at their extremities."

"I think it was natural," said the nurse; "things often turn out like that."

"I am glad you think so," said Hooker. "I should be sorry if the experience were morbid or unnatural. But now it is passing off and the world grows almost as grey as ever. I wish I could capture that moment and retain the spirit of it."

"You should do a good deed," said the nurse. "You should give somebody a cup of cold water."

"I have thought of that, too," replied the millionaire; "but the trouble is that I can't think of any deed good enough for the purpose."

"A very little thing would do it," she answered.

"Have you—have you found that so yourself?"

"It's my profession," said the nurse; "what I am paid for and earn my living by."

"Then I shall turn the tables on you," said Hooker, and a smile came into his face which seemed to betoken that the joyous experience had not altogether passed away.

She looked at him in surprise. "What do you mean?" she asked.

"As I said," he went on, "I have been thinking about a deed to commemorate the occasion and to capture the spirit of it. And I have hit upon one which springs naturally out of the circumstances—not good enough, but good as far as it goes. When I recover, one of my first acts will be to place you in a position of complete independence."

"Impossible!" she cried. "No, no—you don't understand, Mr. Hooker. Nothing in this world would induce me to give up my profession. *I should be selling the Cross.*"

"I expected you to say something of the kind, though not to put it in that way," said Hooker. "But you needn't give up your profession. I shall merely place you in a position where you can choose for yourself whether you will give it up or not."

She seemed bewildered, and Hooker went on.

"Whenever a gift is in question two wills are involved—the will of the giver and the will of the receiver. I cannot give unless you consent to receive. I ask your will to co-operate with mine in doing the very thing you said I ought to do. You cannot refuse."

"But it will be misunderstood," said the nurse.

"Doubtless," replied Hooker. "But for my part I am long past the point where I could attach the least importance to the misunderstandings of the world. And so, I imagine, are you."

Once again tears swam in the woman's eyes, and

TRANSFIGURATION OF A MOUSE

from the way she thanked him Hooker knew that he was doing a good deed. And the conviction was so reassuring and so pleasant as to leave no doubt in his mind that he had caught the very spirit he wished to commemorate. For the first time a light seemed to dawn on the problem which had so long been haunting him. He had, in fact, embarked upon a road on which he was to travel far. It was as though his dream was beginning to come true; as though, at last, after his many fallings into the abyss, he was actually on board "the Ship of Great Souls," with whom he was destined to sail away into the silence.

CHAPTER SIX

Mr. Hooker Faces the Worst

MR. HOOKER, as we have told, had trained himself to "systematize" his conduct under a unitary law of action. But when he asked himself, as he presently did, how far his promise to the nurse conformed to his Great Principle of "so affirming his own personality as to help others to affirm theirs," he became involved in some mental confusion. He found that if he made certain large assumptions about the nurse, and about himself, and looked at the matter from a carefully chosen angle of vision, the action and the Principle seemed in tolerable accord. But if he dropped the assumptions and changed the angle of vision, and imagined certain contingencies, there was no making the two fit one another. From one point of view, which he was unconsciously determined not to take, the action looked extremely rash. It might be fraught with disastrous consequences to the personality of the nurse and of other people, including his own. And he began to wonder whether, after all, there might not be some truth in the doctrine of the Will-to-believe. But that question did not disturb his fundamental serenity of mind.

At an earlier time these theoretical difficulties would have given Mr. Hooker an uneasy conscience, would have worried him during the daytime, kept him awake at night, and led him into many long and inconclusive arguments with his friends in the Society for Ethical Culture. But now, though he was fully aware of the existence of these conundrums, they seemed to him of no weight. The promise that he had just given to this woman, of whom he knew little, sprang so naturally out of the circumstances, was so entirely in keeping with the joyous tone and the radiant atmosphere of his recent experience, and so exactly expressed the spirit he wished to commemorate, as to give him an inner assurance that he was doing right—an assurance without which he was incapable of undertaking any deliberate action. To tell the truth, he was a little astonished at himself; but it was a pleasing astonishment, such as a man may feel when he makes an interesting discovery. And the pleasure was further enhanced on finding that Mr. Polycarp, an extremely critical man of the world, after a few professional hesitations, gave the business his emphatic approval and promptly began his part of it. Doubtless Mr. Polycarp had been making inquiries, but had he known how far Mr. Hooker, once started on this new track, was destined to go, he would have expressed himself differently.

Mr. Hooker's illness, and the experiences which attended it, had for the time being taken him out of the atmosphere of the insoluble problems that were haunting his life. But, as he had told the nurse, the world about him was now losing this fleeting radiance, and sinking back again into its customary grey; which meant that his problems were returning.

They were the problems of a high-principled man whose principles were no match for his circumstances, and which, as a matter of fact, he could not apply. It had fallen to his lot to summarize in his own person the essential conditions of the harassed and aimless civilization into which he had been born, a civilization which has set itself to heap up riches without knowing who should gather them, or for what purpose they ought to be gathered. To the ungoverned forces of this social maelstrom he owed the position in which he found himself; they had thrust his wealth upon him, they had slain his sons, they had ruined his life. By creating the war they had created his problems, which had been tossed up as it were out of the boiling confusion of the world, and assigned to him for solution. Why to *him* rather than to anybody else? As well might we ask why Simon of Cyrene was suddenly pounced upon by the Roman legionaries, haled out of the crowd, and compelled to bear the cross of Jesus Christ.

Of all Mr. Hooker's burdens, by far the heaviest and the ugliest, but the least spoken of, waited for him daily in his own home—his wife! Under the shock of a grief greater than her affectionate nature could bear, an hereditary taint had suddenly declared itself; the imprisoned thing, once at large, worked havoc; and in six months she had become a terrible wreck—her mind unhinged by an irresistible craving for alcohol, and constantly infuriated by a violent antipathy towards her husband. A set of apartments in the vast and gloomy mansion had been allotted to her; there she lived almost a prisoner, guarded by two trained attendants. All that science could sug-

MR. HOOKER FACES THE WORST

gest, every influence, every entreaty that could be thought of, had been tried in vain.

Day and night this dreadful thing kept its watch over Hooker's life. What was he to do? How apply his Great Principle to a situation like that? At this point, as at so many others, Hooker felt that he was no longer steering his ship by chart and compass, but battling for life in a hungry and merciless sea. And who would pity a multimillionaire? Who imagine that he was not the most enviable of mankind? Great God, if they had only known!

One day, when convalescence was well advanced, Mr. Hooker, who so far had spoken no word about his wife, directed the nurse to inquire whether it was possible for her to see him. He was well aware that if this had been possible before, it would have been done; and her continued absence had told him all he needed to know. It was a thing of which he could not bring himself to speak.

The nurse left the room and presently returned with the report that Mrs. Hooker was too ill to see him that day. He knew what that meant, and his countenance fell.

A moment later the door was thrown violently open, and Mrs. Hooker, maddened with drink, her hair dishevelled, her clothes wet and torn, flung herself into the room—an appalling apparition. Standing at the foot of the bed and grasping the brass rail with both hands, so that force would be needed to remove her, she poured out a flood of accusations.

"Where are my sons, you villain?" she cried. "Where is George? Where is Edward? Where is Alec? They are mine, not yours! I brought them into the world! I went down into the valley of death three times for their sakes! *You* didn't! You have sold them! You have sold my property! Millions have been paid you for their blood! To hell with you and your money! Judas!"

The dreadful scene lasted but a few seconds. The attendant from whom she had escaped in the night was quickly on the spot and the poor woman was taken away. This was the last time that Hooker saw his wife. When she was gone he lay for hours thinking of what she had once been and of what she now was. He was drinking the very dregs of his cup:

> "Nessun maggior dolore
> Che recordisi del tempo felice
> Nella miseria."

A week later her superhuman cunning again defeated the vigilance of her guardians. For a day and a night no trace could be found of her. On the second day her dead body was discovered in an outhouse of the home farm, where she had secreted a store of champagne under a heap of straw, by what means no one knew. She had evidently determined to destroy herself in this manner. In the neck of one of the empty bottles that lay around her she had inserted a scrap of paper, on which she had scrawled directions as to where and how she wished to be buried, adding at the end: "George, Edward, Alec: Glory, Glory, Hallelujah!"

When the news was broken to Hooker he merely remarked: "I shall attend her funeral." The rest of the day he spent alone.

CHAPTER SEVEN

And Discovers the Unreal

IN our dreams we are all familiar with the broken sequence, the interrupted continuity, the irrational new start. It is this perhaps that most distinguishes dreams from waking experience. A train of images will maintain its coherence up to a certain point, and then suddenly slide off into another which has no connection with what has gone before. You are in a railway carriage conversing with an intimate friend; a moment later, without any noticeable transition, you are in a wood fighting a duel with an unknown antagonist. You are outside Salisbury Cathedral admiring its beauties; you enter and find yourself without the least surprise inside the Albert Hall listening to a political speech. You are at the side of a river, looking at the opposite bank and wondering how you can get across; then without making any passage you *are* across, looking at the bank you have just left. In the waking world there are natural transitions from point to point, in the dream-world the transitions are either unnatural or wanting altogether; and for that reason, chiefly, our dreams seem unreal and meaningless.

Extreme suddenness, occurring at important points of life, has the same effect in our waking experience. A poor man opening his letters one morning learns that a relative in Australia, whose existence he has forgotten, has left him heir to half a million. For a long time afterwards he will declare, quite truly, that "it all seems like a dream!" The sudden death of one whose life was interfused with the current of our own affects us in a similar manner. The wife whose husband has been killed in an accident or fallen down dead in a fit of heart failure will seem to herself to be in a world of unrealities, and will tell you, as before, "she is in a dream." Even when death is not physically sudden, the interruption of sequence in the moral world is so violent, especially when the broken relationship is a vital one, that it often leaves the survivor in a dreamlike atmosphere for many days.

This was the atmosphere which Mr. Hooker was breathing, and breathing deep, in the days that followed the death of his wife. As he gave his evidence at the inquest, which he did without betraying the least emotion, so that people wondered at his indifference; as he interviewed the undertaker and the clergyman, and showed to the latter the pathetic scrap of paper on which the suicide had written her wishes; as he viewed for the last time the dead body of the woman who had been for long years the centre of his beautiful family life; as he sat alone in his library pondering the train of events which had culminated in this manner—his feeling was not only that the events themselves, but that the whole scheme of things to which they belonged, was phantasmal, and that he himself would presently awake to find it so. It was all catastrophic, unexpected, irrational; a world of violent and illogical changes, where the reasons of things, if they had any, only disclosed themselves after the event, and where in consequence it was impossible to prepare oneself for what was coming next. Had some infallible messenger of truth appeared upon the scene and assured Mr. Hooker there and then that the war was a dream; that its strange consequences to himself had never taken place; that his wealth and his bewilderment, his sorrows and his philosophy were fictions; that the railway accident was a nightmare; that Rumbelow was the ghost of his fancy; and he himself the inhabitant of another sphere of which all these things were the distorted shadows—Mr. Hooker would have found in the words of that messenger a mere echo of his own mind, not, perhaps, of its articulated thought, but most assuredly of its *tone*.

In the midst of these dreamlike inconsistencies and dim suspicions there was, however, one point which obstinately asserted itself as having solid value and harbouring no illusion. Whenever Mr. Hooker's mind turned back to his deed of kindness towards the nurse he seemed to get an anchorage in the firm ground of reality; there was nothing dreamlike about that. His thoughts in these days often turned in that direction, not for any pleasure he might have in contemplating his own benevolence, but because he found there a resting place for his mind, as though it were the one bit of genuine substance in the sea of fluctuating shadows by which he was surrounded. His only regret about the matter lay in the feeling that the deed was *too small*, that it needed enlarging; and this feeling finally took shape in a resolution to increase the scale on which he had originally intended to endow the nurse.

On the day preceding his wife's funeral, to which he seemed quite indifferent, he spent a long time with his lawyer arranging the details of this matter, his mind keenly interested and alert. Mr. Polycarp, who had approved of the deed in the form Mr. Hooker had first presented it, was amazed on learning in full what his client intended to do, using every argument he could think of to bring him to reason, and plainly telling him the mildest construction to be placed on his action was that he was out of his mind. But he could make no impression at all on the millionaire's resolution. He gave the nurse £30,000.

Mr. Polycarp went away from the interview with the gloomiest forebodings. "This man," he said to himself, "will fall under the influence of women and will end by perpetrating some gigantic folly."

Nor would his fears have been diminished had he been able to read Mr. Hooker's mind. He felt complete satisfaction in what he had done. He half fancied he could hear a voice crying, "Do it again, Hooker; do it again!" "I wish I had made it £50,000," he said aloud, as he paced his library on the day of the funeral. "But, thank Heaven, there are others. I must find them out—these noble women. There is Miss Wolfstone. She shall be the next;" and his face beamed with joy.

At that moment the undertaker entered the room and informed Mr. Hooker that his wife's coffin had been placed in the hearse and that the funeral was ready to start.

Mrs. Hooker had been the only child of a clerk

in the original clock factory. Her mother had died when she was three years old, under circumstances not dissimilar to those which had attended her own death, a fact which had been concealed, and only discovered when the experts who were treating Mrs. Hooker began to make inquiries. Till the time of her marriage she had kept her father's house, a girl of fine character and a devoted daughter. The directions she had scrawled on the scrap of paper were that she was to be buried in her father's grave, and she had also named the clergyman who was to conduct the service.

Besides Mr. Hooker, the doctor and some of the servants there were only three mourners at the funeral—two women in dingy black whom Mr. Hooker had never seen before, and a little boy with a bad cold.

Mechanically following the undertaker, like a man walking in his sleep, the bereaved husband took his seat in the car beside the doctor, the hearse immediately preceding. The doctor was instantly struck by his absent-mindedness. He made no allusion to his wife, showed no signs of grief, and seemed to attach not the least importance to what was going forward. Twice the doctor tried to engage his attention by some commonplace remark. "It was unfortunate the weather was so bad." No reply. "After all, they ought to be glad that Mrs. Hooker's life had not been prolonged?" Whereupon Mr. Hooker turned upon him sharply: "Don't talk to me about that," he said; *"it bores me."* After which the doctor held his peace, while Mr. Hooker, with a look of intense preoccupation on his face, seemed to be oblivious of the other's existence. He was constructing plans in the real world he had just discovered. What could he do for Miss Wolfstone? How was he to set about the task of creating for her some sphere of action where she would find full scope for her great powers of mind and character? Principles were beginning to count for less in the mind of the millionaire, and persons for more—a dangerous point of transition.

Arrived at the cemetery gates the official in charge of the place put a telegram into his hand. He was about to thrust it in his pocket when the doctor persuaded him to open it. The telegram came from the clergyman who was to conduct the funeral. 'He had been taken suddenly ill, but the cemetery chaplain was on the spot and would take his place.' Hooker merely remarked, "What does it matter? The thing has no meaning, anyhow. Go on."

Presently the chaplain, without his robes, appeared on the scene. The man had evidently been drinking—we will suppose for charity's sake that he had not expected to be on duty that afternoon—and at once began to bluster about the sacrilege of burying a suicide. For some time an altercation went on between him and the superintendent of the cemetery, which ended in the chaplain assuming his robes and leading the way to the mortuary chapel. As to what went on inside, the less said the better.

The abomination over, the mourners wound their way to the grave, the swaying chaplain at their head. It was raining heavily, and they had a long way to go, to a part of the cemetery now almost disused. At last the little party, under dripping umbrellas, ar-

AND DISCOVERS THE UNREAL

rived at a spot where a rectangular pit had been dug among the crowded tombstones. The chaplain was already half through the committal service, which he was gabbling in the falsetto voice of official piety, occasionally losing his place and lapsing into incoherence. He was standing at the head of the grave, steadying himself against a tombstone, on the top of which there was an angel blowing a trumpet. The undertakers' men now raised the coffin, and were about to lower it, when one of them slipped on the wet clay, the men at the other end lurched forward, and the head of the coffin fell heavily on the chaplain's foot. "Damn and blast you," he roared out, "what are you doing?" Whereupon one of the women in black, who had been restrained with difficulty from making a scene in the mortuary chapel, threw down her dripping umbrella, stepped over the open grave and struck the drunken chaplain a violent blow in the face. Let a veil be drawn over the rest.

Had Mr. Hooker's senses, and their attendant sensibilities, which were finer than most men's, been in full commission the shock of this hideous thing would have been overwhelming. But, mercifully, he was still in a dream, or at least but half awake. As they walked away he linked his arm in the doctor's and for the first time his tongue was unloosed.

"We are arrived at last!" he said.

"Arrived at what?" asked the doctor.

"At the unreal end of things. At the vanishing point of all significance. At the point where every bit of sense and reality has been strained out and nothing but nonsense and illusion remains. That scene we have just witnessed represents it. Some people would say that you touch reality when you come to these brutal elements. You don't. You touch nonsense and nothingness."

"It gave me a pretty violent shock," said the doctor. "I can't help thinking there was something in it."

"*Something*, yes. But *how much?* Just as little as there possibly can be. If not absolute nothing, then just as near to nothing as you can get."

He paused for a space and then went on:

"You may know that for many years I have been a student of philosophy, combining the study of it with a business life and with ethical propaganda—a queer combination, as it now appears to me. Till lately I was President of the Society for Ethical Culture, the members of which, with one notable exception, thought I was beside myself. That is now a closed chapter, though I may tell you that had it not been for the man who saved my life in the accident, and then for the care of the good nurse who has just left me, the Ethical Society would have inherited the whole of my fortune. I don't care who knows it and am quite indifferent to what people may say. Well, most of the philosophers I have studied embark on what they call the 'quest for reality.' *The Pathway to Reality* is the title of a famous book. They should do the exact opposite—start from the other end. Reality is given in the fact that they are interested in finding it. Starting from that they should make it their business to discover the Unreal, to expose it for what it is, or rather for what it isn't. They would find the Unreal in the general life of the civilization that is going on around them, in the sickness and miseries of an acquisitive society, in the murk and sordidness of things, in Smokeover Cemetery, and in all that it stands for—though I imagine that some of them would have to be crucified and rise again the third day before the truth began to dawn upon their minds. The whole question needs to be turned round and set up on its other end. It came to me in this way during my illness, with something of the force of a revelation."

"I don't follow your meaning," said the doctor.

"Of course not. To follow my meaning you would have to follow my experience during the last few days; and your bitterest enemy would not wish you that. Step by step it has brought me down to the point where we are now arrived—the unreal end of things. Between that and the real end there is an immense interval. In less than a fortnight I have traversed every step of the way—to find myself *here!* This cemetery, the gloom of it, the hideous tombstones, the rotting flowers, the funeral service, the chaplain, drunk or sober, represent the world with the values gone out of it. There's next to nothing in the whole place! As a specimen of reality it is beneath contempt—a province in the Void, a bit of the universe that doesn't matter. Death has dominion over it all, funeral service included. Ghosts, doctor, ghosts! As to what we have just witnessed, take it as an episode in a nightmare, nothing more. The thing is too bad to be true."

"I am afraid," said the doctor, "that what you are saying is too *good* to be true."

For some time they had been in the car, returning to the house, Hooker apparently in high spirits and the doctor both amazed and alarmed. Hooker went on with his parable.

"I have something else to say which you as a medical man ought to know. There are hidden powers in human life which when once they are liberated work astonishing transformations. But the process of liberating them is terrible to the last degree, and may easily kill the strongest man. Indeed, it may be that death is the natural mode by which they are liberated in all men. It seemed so to me when I was on the point of dying. I was conscious of the beginning of an immense enlargement. But beware, doctor, how you tamper with those powers. They are high explosives."

"I have heard of such things," said the doctor. "But they wither on contact with the brutal facts of life."

"You are mistaken," said Hooker. "It is the brutal facts of life that wither on contact with them. They linger on and hold their ground against all comers. They are the only key we have to the meaning of this otherwise abominable world. To-day has been the witness of it. From first to last I have stood above it all, yes, superior to it, completely master of it. At this moment I feel myself immeasurably strong. Forces have been helping me: I know not what they are, or who they are, and am not anxious to know. Perhaps they are great souls still inhabiting the flesh—one of them has been in my thoughts for many hours. Perhaps they are the spirits of the departed. Perhaps they are the ultimates of the universe. But they are *real*, doctor, they are *real*, and what else matters?"

AND DISCOVERS THE UNREAL

The doctor listened to all this without comprehension, but with a grave doubt lurking in the background of his mind. He was reflecting that Hooker on returning home would be alone for the rest of the day, both the nurses having departed; and he saw danger ahead. He resolved that he would spend the night in the house. Hooker had no difficulty in divining his thought. His perceptions just then were abnormally acute.

"Doctor," he said, "your manner betrays you. You are alarmed—I see it in your face. I know what you are afraid of, and I don't wonder. If anyone six months ago had spoken to me as I have just spoken to you I should have drawn exactly the inference that is troubling you. Yesterday my lawyer informed me that I was out of my mind, and now you are thinking the same thing—which is unfortunate for me at a moment when important business has to be transacted. But spend the night in the house, and tell me frankly to-morrow whether or no you can certify me as sane. I have a reason for asking it."

CHAPTER EIGHT

And Begins to Make Use of His Discovery

MR. HOOKER'S accession to vast fortune had been so rapid that sufficient time had not yet elapsed to gather round him that permanent retinue of friends, admirers and hangers-on whose mission it is to attend the sorrows, feast at the tables and occupy the bedrooms of the rich. Hence it was that the doctor, seated next morning at his solitary breakfast in the great dining-room, had the impression of being in a deserted house. Without was the murk of a winter's day; a dirty mist hung in the air; a sullen rain was falling; the smoke-stained laurels growing by the window dripped and shivered under the downpour. Within was silence and a deeper gloom. The butler, dressed in a new suit of black, who had introduced him to his victuals and then left him to help himself, might have been the only living inmate of the house; and even he seemed only half alive.

Twice, in answer to questions as to Mr. Hooker's whereabouts—Was he in his bedroom? Was he in the library?—the butler had replied with a whispered "No, sir." These were the only words he spoke, uttered in a tone of immense responsibility, and after a pause for deliberation, as though the negative were the final secret of the universe, revealed to the servants' hall by the funeral of yesterday, and embodied in his new suit of black. The whole house seemed to echo the whisper; it was the voice of the place; the voice of the Everlasting No, Sir; the walls passed it on to the furniture, the weather took it up outside, and the trees, slowly shaking their heads under the weight of the rain, confirmed it. As the doctor looked round the dining-room, with its sumptuous appointments and unnecessary array of chairs, a presentiment came over him that he, too, had arrived at the unreal end of things. He ate his breakfast without appetite. His boiled egg was a negative thing—tasteless, phantasmal and difficult to swallow.

His breakfast over, the doctor took a turn through the rooms, hoping to encounter Mr. Hooker here or there. All was chill, melancholy, sepulchral. At certain points he detected an odour of oak varnish, as though a new-made coffin was, or had recently been, in the house. No one was about; the very servants seemed to be hiding themselves. The doctor listened for indications; he could hear nothing but the drip and rustle of the rain. The thick-carpeted floors were a mockery, for the only footsteps in the place, if any, were the footsteps of ghosts.

At length he found the millionaire standing alone by a great window in the drawing-room, looking out upon the rain, his hands behind his back. At one end of the room were the arum lilies and azaleas which yesterday had formed a screen for the bier of the dead woman. In neither of the two grates, which were of burnished steel, after the mid-Victorian fashion, was there any fire. The room was cold and the odour of coffin furniture was unmistakable.

That Mr. Hooker was suffering under a severe reaction was obvious to the doctor at a glance. All traces of yesterday's exaltation had vanished. The eyes were dull and tired, the face pale and drawn, the powerful shoulders tilted forward, and the great domed head seemed to have shrunken. But the mouth was firm and the square-set obstinacy of the Hooker breed sat upon every feature. As he turned to greet the doctor he drew himself erect. He was a big man and seemed all the bigger in his loneliness.

"My dear sir," said the doctor in a sufficiently formidable tone of authority, "you need rest and change. Both are imperative. A voyage round the world, for example, or a yachting cruise in the Mediterranean. I advise the Mediterranean, with a medical man in attendance. You must quit Smokeover without delay. Sea air and sunshine will make another man of you."

Mr. Hooker made a gesture of impatience.

"No, sir!" he said, with the emphasis of a man not to be trifled with; "no, sir! Such things are not worth discussing. They are irrelevancies—the conventional disguises of medical ignorance—shallow stratagems for getting patients out of the way and escaping further responsibility. Tell these things to the feeble-minded."

Had this rebuff been administered by a poorer patient there is no telling what the doctor would have replied. He was certainly nettled, but, setting the answer down to the morbid irritability consequent upon a sleepless night, he contented himself with a mild rebuke.

"I see you have no high opinion of medical science. Is not that a little ungrateful in the circumstances?"

"You mean," said Mr. Hooker, "that medical science has just saved my life. But, before that, it was saved by Mr. Rumbelow; and before that his was saved by Miss Wolfstone. The hospital ship on which he was returning after his wound was torpedoed, and Miss Wolfstone, who was the nurse in charge, rescued him at great peril to herself. But of course you know the story."

"Everyone knows it," said the doctor. "At this moment Miss Wolfstone is the talk of Smokeover."

Mr. Hooker turned a searching glance on his companion's face. "What are they saying?" he asked sharply.

"They are talking about her connection with Rumbelow. The circumstances are extraordinary, and speculation is active."

"Is her name being coupled with mine, as well as with Rumbelow's?" asked Mr. Hooker.

"Since you ask—yes."

A look of grim determination came into the face of Mr. Hooker, and, almost as though he was talking to himself, he said:

"In future they will couple it still more closely than they are doing now. But go on, doctor. Is this talk—are these rumours—discreditable to the persons in question?"

"Gossip is seldom otherwise," said the doctor, who was growing uncomfortable under the directness of Mr. Hooker's interrogation. He was casting about for a change of subject, but the other gave him no time.

"At what point do I, personally, stand affected? What inferences are being drawn? Are people saying that I am out of my mind?"

The doctor had been dreading this. But there was no going back now.

"Well, sir," he said, "the fact cannot be disguised that you are causing a good deal of perplexity to many of your friends. In particular, your action in regard to the nurse, which has become public property, lends colour to——"

He hesitated for the next phrase. But Mr. Hooker did not wait for it.

"What has that to do with Miss Wolfstone?" he asked.

"Only this—people are inclined to think that when a man has done one anomalous thing he will probably do another."

"They show extraordinary prescience," said Mr. Hooker, "and I shall not disappoint them. But these unfavourable constructions that you speak of—are they countenanced by the medical profession? What do they think of what I have done?"

"They condemn it."

"On what grounds?"

"As indefensible from every point of view."

"Name one of them."

Here the doctor saw an opportunity to relieve himself of something he had on his mind and at the same time to bring the conversation to a safe distance from the point of danger at which it now stood.

"I have heard your munificence to the nurse described as a false emphasis," he said. "We doctors naturally think of alternatives. You are probably aware, for example, that the medical side of our local university is sorely in need of funds. Had you given an equal sum to that object, you would not only have conferred a real benefit on the community, but expressed the gratitude you owe to medical science for your recovery. For, after all, Mr. Hooker, it was not the nurse who saved your life."

"You have entirely mistaken my motives," said the millionaire. "Nothing was further from my intention than to express gratitude for my recovery; nor to confer benefits on the community. My reasons are my own, and to me absolutely conclusive. As between you and me, as between me and any doctor in Smokeover, they are probably incommunicable. But to carry them into effect, as I am fully resolved to do, it is essential that my soundness of mind should be attested. I see an obstacle in my way and am under no illusions as to its gravity. You understand that I am about to make my Will. Are you prepared to certify that I am competent to do so?"

"Mr. Hooker," said the doctor, "you have challenged plain speech, and I shall use it in answering your question. At this moment I doubt if any medical man of standing in Smokeover would do what you require. The matter is complicated, professional feeling runs high, and the unfavourable impression of which I spoke has gone deep."

"But your own opinion is what?" asked Mr. Hooker.

"I decline to give it. The matter is one for an independent specialist. You place me in a difficult position, sir, and under the circumstances the only possible answer is what I have just given. So long as this strange action of yours stands unrevoked, with the possibility of others of a like nature to follow, you will not get a favourable verdict in Smokeover. May I implore you, if there is yet time, to revoke it, and to reconsider the whole course of action to which, as you say, it is leading up."

"Never!" cried Mr. Hooker. "My resolution is irrevocably taken. The reasons you bring against it are no doubt irrefragable when taken by themselves—I know them by heart. But they are not to be taken by themselves. They are part of a larger system of ideas and of customary habits of thought which, in its totality, is pernicious and false. In human affairs, doctor, whatever is irrefragable is likely to be untrue—and let the fact that I have said so be remembered when the question of my sanity is finally determined. For the rest, I shall take the choice of a specialist into my own hands. To-night I am expecting my lawyer, and I shall be glad if you will meet him here and tell him all you know. And the specialist will, if possible, arrive to-morrow."

The doctor was at the end of his resources. All through the conversation he had felt himself helpless against the impregnable rock before him. As a last effort he returned to his original method of attack.

"All I have heard from you to-day, Mr. Hooker," he said, "confirms what I said at the first. In Heaven's name, take yourself in hand. Circumstances have thrown you back on yourself. Leave Smokeover at once. Get out of this atmosphere.

AND USES HIS DISCOVERY

There is no other means to break up your self-centredness. As to the nurse——"

"Leave her aside," said Mr. Hooker, in tones that intimated the end of the interview, "and leave me to break up my self-centredness in my own way."

The doctor left the house with mixed feelings, not pleasant on the whole. On the one hand he was glad to have escaped a breach with his wealthiest patient, which at one moment had seemed imminent. But he resented the high-handedness with which Mr. Hooker had conducted the interview. He had the uncomfortable and even humiliating sense of being in the grip of a will far stronger than his own, and against which he could make no professional headway. But remembering that Mr. Hooker was a multimillionaire, he frankly forgave him all. Was he mad? If so, who was sane? The doctor looked back at the gloomy mansion, and the genius of the place seemed to answer "Nobody."

Within an hour of these occurrences new and yet more sinister rumours had begun to circulate in Smokeover. They started in the main street, spread rapidly through the business quarter, penetrated the Clubs, and were telephoned thence to the suburbs. The rumours were that Mr. Hooker's car had been seen to draw up before the portals of Rumbelow, Stallybrass & Corker, and that a massive gentleman in a fur coat, who was unquestionably Mr. Hooker himself, ex-president of the Society of Ethical Culture, and sole surviving representative of a venerated family of Quakers, had passed into the interior of that flagitious establishment—drawn thither by what attraction who can say? Curiosity was a-tiptoe and cynicism was in its glory. Who now could doubt that Mr. Hooker was mad? Only those who believed him wicked—of whom by this time there were many.

At this point the Author again found himself in difficulties with the competing Voices at the Bridgehead. There were at least three of them uttering discordant versions of what happened next. The Author waited for the competition to subside, and in this he had the help of a passing thunderstorm, which drowned the Voices and compelled him to seek shelter under one of the arches of the Bridge. Here he passed the time in watching the River of Forgetfulness, whose swift and gloomy waters, swirling in majestic eddies, fascinated his gaze and even tempted him, more than once, to plunge in and make an end. When he returned to his post the Voices seemed to have chosen their spokesman. One only was audible. In note and accent it was different from that which had spoken before. The mode of utterance was more rapid, and a further peculiarity was that now and then it would suddenly stop short, as though to reflect on the matter in hand, sometimes indulging in a quiet laugh over what it had just narrated—much to the annoyance of the Author, whose fingers were numb with the cold of the night, and growing tired with their long exercise. He was impatient, moreover, for a definite answer to the question—what did Mr. Hooker do with his money? But the Voice went on:

Mr. Hooker passes through the great swing-door of the Office, and perceiving in front of him a tall

AND USES HIS DISCOVERY

official in uniform presents his card, with the inquiry, "Is Mr. Rumbelow within?"

Mr. Rumbelow is not within, but the Heads of Departments are all at their posts, and Mr. Hooker is assured that the mention of his name will instantly place any one of them at his service.

Mr. Hooker pauses to reflect. As yet his acquaintance with the organization of the Firm, and with the personnel of the staff, is imperfect, but he knows enough to make an intelligent suggestion.

"I believe," he says, "that one of the Heads is a famous psychologist?"

"You mean Mr. Hotblack, sir," replies the official, "the Head of the Psychological Department. Certainly, sir. Your card shall be sent in to him at once."

Five minutes later Mr. Hooker, comfortably seated in an arm-chair and by the side of a cheerful fire, is confronting Mr. Hotblack, in the private office of that highly strung but ingenious gentleman, whose keen and radiant eyes are examining the millionaire as though they would anticipate his secret thoughts. Mr. Hooker's face presents the contrast of a benignant placidity, and meets the penetrating gaze of the psychologist with an expression which seems to say, "All the psychology in the world will not divert me one hair's-breadth from my purpose."

"I am come in search of an item of information which I believe you are in a position to give me," says Mr. Hooker.

"The resources of the Firm are at your command, sir," replies Mr. Hotblack, "and I can assure you that in the matter of information they are immense.

But before we proceed to business may I say that it gives me peculiar pleasure to meet you? Your name, Mr. Hooker, is honoured in this Office. The Chief himself has mentioned it in terms of veneration. He rejoices that he was permitted to be an instrument in preserving your life. The Chief, sir, attaches great importance to such things."

To this Mr. Hooker makes no reply, and Mr. Hotblack, mentally noting his silence, goes on:

"May I be permitted to offer you the congratulations of the Firm, though doubtless they would come more fittingly from Mr. Rumbelow himself? We have heard—who has not?—of your recent munificence to the nurse. From the point of view of the Firm, sir, you have done a most significant deed— ideal in aim, sportsmanlike in principle, and, I have no doubt, thoroughly businesslike in method."

A shade of annoyance, as of a man who dislikes to be praised, passes over the countenance of Mr. Hooker.

"I do not understand you," he says.

"There are two types of morality," replies Mr. Hotblack, "the legalistic and the sportsmanlike. The legalistic begins with the highest principles, which deteriorate in application and become progressively impure the further they advance from their point of origin—you may see a remarkable example of this in the efforts that are now being made by purists and physiologists to deal with the problem of sexual relations, not to speak of the Ten Commandments themselves. The sportsmanlike begins in the common soil of human nature, improves with each fresh application, and finally establishes itself on the

AND USES HIS DISCOVERY

ground of absolute validity. Your action in regard to the nurse, sir, belongs to this type. It was a creative deed, and contains within it the promise of a splendid progeny."

At these words Mr. Hooker's countenance brightens, annoyance gives place to eagerness, and he is about to follow up Mr. Hotblack's remarks with a yet more pregnant observation of his own when he suddenly recollects himself and says:

"The action of mine to which you refer is not unconnected with the business which brings me here to-day."

"Let us proceed to that at once," says Mr. Hotblack.

"I have heard," says Mr. Hooker, "that the Firm has frequent occasion to investigate the mental condition of its clients, and that you employ experts for the purpose."

"We employ many," returns Mr. Hotblack. "Indeed they constitute the most important section of our External Staff. In the cabinet behind you, Mr. Hooker, there are at this moment thousands of tabulated reports, in a dozen languages, on the mental condition of our clients. All the most notable persons, both in Europe and America, have been put under investigation. They are investigated as individuals and as groups. And I may tell you, as a point of psychological interest, that groups composed of perfectly sane individuals are often condemned by our experts as hopelessly insane in their corporate mentality. The Reports, I assure you, make sad reading. In one of those drawers, sir, there is a long list of lunatic groups—it is the Black List of the

Firm. Indeed, sir, of all the problems for which I, as chief psychologist, am responsible, this is by far the most delicate and momentous. A matter on which the Firm has enormous experience."

"Then perhaps," says Mr. Hooker, "you can furnish me with the name of an expert, of a specialist, whom I can summon immediately to decide in a difficult case."

Here the sharp eyes of Mr. Hotblack become arrow-points of thought, and Mr. Hooker can almost feel them darting through and through the cortex of his brain.

"I conjecture," says the psychologist, speaking with great rapidity, "that the case to be decided upon is your own; that your munificence to the nurse has caused doubts of your sanity among the ignorant; that, nevertheless, you are determined to follow it up with other deeds conceived in the same sportsman-like spirit; and that the way is blocked for the moment by the menace of a legal difficulty."

"So far you are right."

"Then I have no hesitation in recommending you to place yourself in the hands of Sir William Timbertree."

"I have heard of him."

"A telephone message from the Firm will bring him down from London by the first possible train. His fee is four hundred guineas for patients introduced by the Firm, five hundred for others."

"I shall summon him without introduction," says Mr. Hooker, "if you can assure me of his qualifications."

"His record attests them," says Mr. Hotblack.

AND USES HIS DISCOVERY

"You may remember, sir, that when the war broke out, the Chief laid before the Cabinet a plan which would infallibly have ended it in five weeks. The Cabinet dismissed it as the scheme of a madman. Whereupon Sir William, at the risk of his great reputation, publicly took up cudgels for the Chief, and declared from his seat in the House of Commons that the collective mind of the Cabinet, judged by the standard of Mr. Rumbelow's intellectual powers, was on a level of imbecility; adding that on strictly scientific grounds he would refuse to certify the collective sanity of any Government in the world."

"It is enough," says Mr. Hooker.

"But I must warn you," continues Mr. Hotblack, "that Sir William's personal characteristics may offend you. In private life he is an avowed atheist, a reputed loose-liver, a user of foul language and intolerably vulgar in his manners. Professionally he is a mystic, a Puritan, and fanatically devoted to the interests of his patients. He never begins an operation on the brain or the spinal cord without invoking the Divine blessing on the knife and compelling his assistants to join him in prayer."

"Give me his address," says Mr. Hooker.

As the millionaire places the slip of paper in his pocketbook and rises to leave, Mr. Hotblack takes out his watch.

"I perceive it is one o'clock," he says. "May I suggest, sir, that we lunch together at the Club?"

To which Mr. Hooker assents and, having sent off a telegram in his own name to Sir William Timbertree, presently walks out of the office in company with Mr. Hotblack.

And now the tongues of rumour are again let loose. First they report that Mr. Hooker and Mr. Hotblack are lunching together in the Club at a table for two; next, that they have retired to a quiet corner in the smoking-room and are closely engaged in conversation. What, in Heaven's name, are they saying? The sequel will show.

CHAPTER NINE

Mr. Hotblack Expounds the Beauty of Business

"NO legislation." Mr. Hotblack was saying, "no social system that the wit of man can devise, will prove effective in preventing the accumulation of wealth by individuals. Whatever measures society may invent for checking the profiteer can always be evaded by minds endowed with certain faculties, and not only evaded, sir, but captured and made use of for defeating the very purpose they are intended to serve. A daring and creative mind, like Mr. Rumbelow's for example, is always more than a match for any system of repression that may be directed against it. The Chief knows this; he has proved it over and over again. If a set contest were to take place between 'the will of society'—though I doubt if such a thing exists—between 'the will of society' and the will of Mr. Rumbelow, I should not hesitate, as a psychologist, to lay the odds at 10 to 1 on the Chief. It is a fortunate thing for the world, sir, that the Head of the Firm is a friend of man; were it otherwise one might well tremble for the future of the human race."

"One trembles in any event," said Mr. Hooker.

"Rightly so," answered Mr. Hotblack. "The future of mankind is by no means assured, and I may tell you, in confidence, that the Firm has periods of pessimism, when even the Chief himself wears a look of trouble. This morning, for example, we have received a Report from the Seven Mighty Men, endorsed by the Head Mathematician, which indicates that the odds, at the moment, are in favour of impending catastrophe to civilization. But Mr. Rumbelow, sir, has not quailed. Immediately after reading the Report he issued a general instruction to the Heads of Departments informing them that the entire resources of the Firm were to be staked, with the odds against us, on averting the threatened calamity. How great the calamity is you may imagine when I tell you that it involves the destruction of Mr. Rumbelow himself and of all that he stands for. He is under no illusion in these matters. He is fully prepared for the fate which has been meted out to all the greatest benefactors of mankind. Of course he is aware that by throwing the resources of the Firm into the lighter scale the conditions will be altered; but even so, the odds remain heavily against us."

"The spirit of all this," said Mr. Hooker, speaking with some emotion, "the spirit of all this moves me deeply. I have seen with my own eyes the self-devotion of which Mr. Rumbelow is capable when the odds are against him; indeed I owe my life to it. If only I knew more of the operations the Firm is engaged in, and were convinced that their nature was such that I could support them, I would throw in my lot with Mr. Rumbelow to-morrow."

"It would be a splendid consummation to a noble life," cried Mr. Hotblack, raising his voice and dropping his cigar in his excitement. "But I must

MR. HOTBLACK EXPOUNDS

warn you, Mr. Hooker, that you would be facing the odds of financial ruin. They are two to one against us."

"If they were twenty thousand to one I would face them," answered Mr. Hooker with equal enthusiasm, "provided I stood upon honourable ground."

"Which proves that you are a sportsman at heart," replied Mr. Hotblack.

At this point of the conversation there was a noticeable stir among the other gentlemen in the smoking-room. They had already drawn their chairs as near as they decently could to the corner where the millionaire and the psychologist were holding their debate. At the words "twenty thousand" the newspapers they were pretending to read were simultaneously lowered, and the smokers looked at one another, as who would say, "Just what we expected."

Mr. Hotblack noticed the movement, and pushing his chair into a position which brought him close to Mr. Hooker's ear, said, "We must speak lower. These men are listening. One of them has just gone out, and, unless I am much mistaken his version of what we have been saying is already on the telephone. I shall indulge him a little further when he comes back. But to the point, Mr. Hooker. Before explaining the operations of the Firm, may I ask a question? Your action in summoning Sir William Timbertree—the question of your soundness of mind—does it turn on certain views you hold as to the capacity of women to be entrusted with the disposition of wealth?"

"I have said as much already," answered Mr. Hooker.

"Thank you. I wished to be clear on the point. For it so happens—and it is important in connexion with what I am about to tell you—that the views of Mr. Rumbelow as to the functions of women in the coming age are extremely precise. He holds that their greatest achievements will be more in the economic than in the political sphere. As earners, or producers, of wealth they will always play a minor part; but as spenders of it, as directors of the ends and uses for which wealth is employed—the unsolved problem of the industrial age—their power and influence will continually increase. Mr. Rumbelow is backing this tendency to the uttermost. At this moment he has in the Office a list of all the most capable women in Smokeover, in the preparation of which I have had the honour of assisting him. You would be surprised to learn what a large number remains, even after the most rigorous sifting out."

"On the contrary," replied Mr. Hooker, "I should not be surprised in the least."

"Ha!" exclaimed Mr. Hotblack, and for a moment he looked out of the window, with the air of a man who is putting this and that together. Then, checking his meditations, he broke off to a general observation.

"In the scale of moral values, Mr. Hooker, as well as in that of efficiency, women have a greater range than men, both upward and downward. The types are more varied and the degrees more numerous. A bad woman is far worse than a bad man; at the common level she is still his inferior; but above that she outstrips him and reaches a summit which no man can attain, until at the highest she becomes the master-work of the creative mind. A spiritual religion should worship a goddess, not a god."

"A spiritual religion should worship the spirit," interrupted Mr. Hooker.

" 'Tis the same thing," replied Mr. Hotblack.

"I agree," said Mr. Hooker. "But we are wandering from the point. Tell me—is the name of Miss Wolfstone on Mr. Rumbelow's list of capable women?"

"It stands next to My Lady's," said the psychologist. "Apart from the special reason Mr. Rumbelow has for honouring Miss Wolfstone—for, as you know, she saved his life—he regards her as a woman of exceptional power, and destined to leave her mark on the world. Mr. Hooker, I am about to declare to you one of the secrets of the Firm, which I have good reason to believe will be safe in your keeping. The Chief has determined to do for Miss Wolfstone that which has never yet been done for any woman."

"Perhaps I shall anticipate him," said the millionaire.

The psychologist turned upon his companion a glance full of intelligence. When the conversation was resumed the cigars of both men had become appreciably shorter. It was Mr. Hotblack who broke the silence.

"Assuming, sir, that you have settled the disposition of your fortune after your death, the problem remains of dealing with it during the remainder of your life. If I may venture a bold suggestion, I would advise you, earnestly and solemnly, to consult Mr. Rumbelow."

"I have thought of it," replied the millionaire. "But you must understand, Mr. Hotblack, that in this matter I intend to act upon my own initiative. I shall adopt no man's ideas. I shall avoid all customary modes of dealing with wealth, which, I am persuaded, are based on a profound ignorance. Custom, as Carlyle says, makes dotards of us all, and in this matter more than in any other."

"An act of will has no value unless it is self-originated," said the psychologist; "in fact, is not an act of will at all. Do I correctly interpret you?"

"You do."

"Then let me assure you that by consulting Mr. Rumbelow you will not impair the independence of your own decision. You will reinforce it. The more so if My Lady's influence is added to his. Seek her out, Mr. Hooker; seek her out, I implore you! Whatever you undertake she will transform into music, into beauty, into joy."

As he spoke these words a visible change passed over the countenance of Mr. Hotblack. It was as though a mask had fallen off. The features softened, they shone with an inner light, and the penetrating eyes seemed to be gazing at some object a long way off. Then, to the astonishment of Mr. Hooker, the psychologist leaned back in his chair and slowly recited the following verses:

"O Lady! we receive but what we give,
  And in our life alone does Nature live:
    Ours is her wedding-garment, ours her shroud!
    And would we aught behold, of higher worth
  Than that inanimate cold world allowed

MR. HOTBLACK EXPOUNDS

To the poor loveless, ever-anxious crowd,
    Ah! from the soul itself must issue forth
A light, a glory, a fair luminous cloud
    Enveloping the Earth—
And from the soul itself must there be sent
    A sweet and potent voice, of its own birth,
Of all sweet sounds the life and element!

"O pure of heart! thou need'st not ask of me
What this strong music in the soul may be!
What, and wherein it doth exist,
This light, this glory, this fair luminous mist,
This beautiful and beauty-making power.
    Joy, virtuous Lady! Joy that ne'er was given,
Save to the pure, and in their purest hour,

"Life, and Life's effluence, cloud at once and shower,
Joy, Lady! is the spirit and the power
Which, wedding Nature, to us gives in dower
    A new Earth and new Heaven,
Undreamt of by the sensual and the proud—
Joy is the sweet voice, Joy the luminous cloud—
We in ourselves rejoice!
And thence flows all that charms or ear or sight,
    All melodies the echoes of that voice.
All colours a suffusion from that light."

"I congratulate you on the rendering," said Mr. Hooker. "Your training as a man of business has left you with a fine sense of poetic values."

"A business training," replied Mr. Hotblack, "separates us from the poets only when it is incomplete. But when business has her perfect work, she brings us back again to poetry and to the other arts. In the same way, sir, the present age of commercialism, in which the great singers have hung up their harps, will lead on, when its issues are complete, to a revival of poetry. The businesslike method, sir, is a *beautiful* thing."

"You surprise me," said Mr. Hooker. "I have heard it said that the relationship of business to the fine arts is not affinity, but repulsion."

"It is a profound error," answered the psychologist, "and could only originate in minds which understand neither business nor art."

"You would not allow then," pursued Mr. Hooker, "that the general ugliness of Smokeover, of which we can see a glimpse out of that window, accurately reflects the nature of business?"

"I will not allow it for a moment," replied the other. "Smokeover, sir, is unquestionably an ugly creation. But it is the ugliness of a caterpillar waiting to be changed into a gorgeous butterfly. When Mr. Rumbelow has completed his work, Smokeover will emerge as glorious as Athens; not, mark you, by abandoning business, but by becoming thoroughly businesslike."

"Then is she not thoroughly businesslike at the present moment?"

"Far from it, sir; far from it!"

Here Mr. Hotblack paused to choose his words. His face wore an air of perplexity, as though he found it difficult to make intelligible what he wanted to say next.

"The truth is," he resumed, "that business, as Smokeover carries it on, is under alien domination.

MR. HOTBLACK EXPOUNDS

It dances attendance on the unsportsmanlike principles, the mean aims, the unbusinesslike methods, which characterize the general misgovernment of the world. Our business life has never been free to develop according to its own genius. It has been suffered to develop only into such forms as were convenient to the blind and wicked deities which for ages past have filled the earth with strife, bloodshed and confusion. Smokeover, sir, is an unconscious accessory to deeds of darkness that are perpetrated beyond its ken. The ugliness of those deeds is reflected in the ugliness we see out of that window. This sprawling city, with its foul congestions, the ill-built streets, the squalid slums, the dismal cemetery, the tawdry palaces, the hideous statues, the vitiated atmosphere, the darkened skies, the dirt, the noise, the shabbiness—what is it all but a faithful image of the international muddle whose begotten offspring it is? Now, sir, Mr. Rumbelow has determined that the business of Smokeover shall be liberated from those pernicious entanglements, set upon its own feet, and placed under the control of enlightened business men. When that has been accomplished the caterpillar will slough off its ugliness and emerge into beauty."

It is probable that Mr. Hooker would have received all this with complete incredulity, had not his mind been prepared for new ideas by recent transactions in his inner experience. Even as it was, a certain measure of incredulity asserted itself. His eye glanced round the room, resting first upon one and then upon another of the gentlemen occupying the arm-chairs. Among them were some of the leading business men in Smokeover, and these were of many types. One, who was different from all the others, had the face of a wolf. Indicating this gentleman by a slight movement of his eyelid, Mr. Hooker asked:

"Is *that* the type that will rule the future?"

"No, sir," answered Mr. Hotblack with great energy, "it is not! The business man of the future will not be a devourer of widows' houses! He will be an artist, an evoker of human harmonies, a prophet of the ideal bargain, a servant of his own particular muse! And for that very reason he will be all the more a business man. Twenty thousand times more, sir—to quote your own figures! And the odds will be heavily in his favour."

In delivering the last two sentences Mr. Hotblack had raised his voice from an energetic whisper to a kind of shout. He repeated the words several times, somewhat to Mr. Hooker's surprise. Finally he brought his fist down on the table, exclaiming at the same time, "Twenty thousand, no less!" Having said which he relapsed into one of his pensive moods.

Mr. Hooker was puzzled to read the expression on the psychologist's face; for while, as always, deep thought sat upon his brow, a certain slyness seemed to be dancing at the corners of his mouth. And the mystery was only deepened when Mr. Hotblack suddenly broke the silence by repeating three lines of the poem he had just quoted, and that, too, in a manner most peculiar. Mr. Hooker noticed that the first two words of the quotation were pronounced in a voice loud enough to be heard by the whole

MR. HOTBLACK EXPOUNDS

room, while the rest was murmured in tones so low as to be nearly inaudible.

"*Joy, Lady!* is the spirit and the power
  Which, wedding Nature, to us gives in dower
  A new Earth and new Heaven."

His recitation ended, Mr. Hotblack glanced round the room and became aware that the gentleman of the lupine countenance, with an untouched whisky-and-soda on the table before him and the *Sporting Times* held in front of his face, was closely watching him out of the corner of his eye. Meeting the scrutiny of the wolf with a glance of scorn, and leaning towards his guest, Mr. Hotblack said in a yet lower voice:

"I perceive, Mr. Hooker, that we are surrounded by fools—by men, I mean, to whom all poetry is a dead letter or a nuisance. The atmosphere of this place is depressing; already I feel it impeding the cerebral circulation, and clear thought is becoming impossible. We are overheard, sir. Let us return to the Office immediately. I have still to explain the operations of the Firm. It would be a desecration to speak of them in the presence of men such as that."

When they had passed out of the room, which broke into a buzz of conversation the moment the door was closed, Mr. Hotblack remarked:

"Have you ever observed, sir, that in these days it is wellnigh impossible to quote a dozen lines of first-rate poetry without mentioning the name of a popular race-horse?"

Mr. Hooker confessed that he had not observed it. But ten minutes later a score of telephones were distributing the news that Mr. Hooker, on the advice of Rumbelow, Stallybrass & Corker, had backed Joy Lady, a runner in the Grand National, for twenty thousand pounds.

CHAPTER TEN

And Mr. Hooker Beholds the Beauty of Woman

ON returning to Mr. Hotblack's private office, they were confronted by an agitated clerk with a sheaf of telegrams in his hand. The psychologist glanced through them.

"They must wait," said he, "till my interview with Mr. Hooker is concluded. Meanwhile inform the Staff that we shall all be working overtime to-day—probably till midnight."

When the clerk was gone Mr. Hooker said:

"You are evidently busy, Mr. Hotblack. I fear I am wasting your time."

"Have the goodness to remain, sir," said Mr. Hotblack. "Nothing can be more important to the Firm than that you and I should understand one another. It is true that since reopening after the war we have been doing an enormous business. At the moment we are overwhelmed. We must increase our capital and double the Staff. But now permit we to explain the nature of the business on which we are engaged."

"That is what I am anxious to learn," said Mr. Hooker.

"You will be surprised when you hear it," replied Mr. Hotblack. "But let me prepare you by saying that the sportsmanlike principle which guides our operations is essentially creative. Its nature is to transform the material in which it works and continually to surpass itself. If you have read the works of Professor Bergson you will need no further explanation."

"I understand what you mean."

"Then the road is clear," said Mr. Hotblack; "you shall learn at once what the operation is on which Mr. Rumbelow has determined to stake the entire resources of the Firm, with the odds against him at two to one. Last week he summoned the Heads of Departments, and the Seven International Experts, who are to formulate in detail the plan of our strategy, and gave us the general idea of the new campaign. Permit me to read what he said, as it was taken down in shorthand from his own lips."

"You will have an attentive listener," said Mr. Hooker.

Whereupon Mr. Hotblack opened a locked drawer in one of his cabinets, drew from it a type-written document and without further delay read as follows:

" 'The modern political State, gentlemen, is a fighting institution, an instrument in the struggle for power. Beneath its mask of industrialism, which has deceived many, it remains in essence what it was in the days of the feudal dynasties, a war-made and war-making mechanism, the only difference being that, now, it makes war on a scale and by methods that are an outrage to the fighting instinct itself, inherent as this is in human nature, and one of its noblest elements. As the ultimate function the State is designed to perform, all else in the long run must give way to the necessities of war, its inner conditions, social, economic and political, having gradually adapted themselves to this purpose in the course of the war-making centuries.

"'In its character of war-maker the State has control of the entire economic resources of its subjects, destroying them at intervals in conflicts with its neighbours. No reforms of a decisively beneficent character are possible so long as that control exists. Both in the production and in the distribution of wealth everything now hinges on the need of maintaining its easy convertibility to the uses of war. Every sixpence in Smokeover is a potential cartridge, placed where it can be easiest impounded by those who would turn it into one. Smokeover itself, unknown to its inhabitants, has always been a munitions factory in germ, ready to be converted at a moment's notice into an implement of the war-making power. The process by which some of its citizens have recently grown suddenly rich and others suddenly poor is a mere back-wash from the general flood which in four years has wiped out half the wealth of the world. All that is characteristic of our civilization, its vices and miseries, as well as its efficiency, has its origin in these conditions.

"'Gentlemen, it has now become the mission of Rumbelow, Stallybrass & Corker to liberate the economic resources of mankind from subservience to the caprices and imbecilities of foreign policy—to place the wealth of the world in an impregnable position, when it is no longer exposed to capture and destruction in the interests of war and of the irresponsible powers which cause and make it. In other words, we shall break the domination of the political over the economic interest; and we shall do this as a first step towards liberating the spiritual interest from both.

"'Modern war depends in the last resort upon financial conditions. Whoever controls the strings of international finance controls the forces which govern the origin of war and its maintenance. Gentlemen, we shall remove that control from the hands of the politicians and from the malign mechanism of which they are the unconscious agents. We shall do this by no revolutionary methods, but by a series of businesslike operations which will leave the political state intact for other purposes, but incapable of making war.

"'Step by step we shall build up an independent system, on an international basis, for the organization of the commerce of the world and of its attendant finance, avoiding all political entanglements and allowing no professional politician to have any part in the direction of our affairs.

"'We shall establish the method of collective bargaining between nation and nation, so that the exchange of goods between them, instead of being conducted by thousands of confused and disconnected transactions, as it now is, will be effected in a comparatively small number. Our Mathematical Department has already worked out a complete scheme for this purpose, which could be put into operation to-morrow.

"'Involved in this is the establishment of an international bank and of an international currency. The bank will cover the whole network of our operations with an adequate system of credit scientifically controlled. The currency will be valid for all transactions conducted under the seal of the Firm; it will gradually supersede the confused and debased currencies now in use; and by correlation with the system of collective bargaining will abolish the whole problem of monetary exchange.

" 'As collective bargaining, carried on by international currency and backed by international credit, gradually extends, the Customs barriers set up between nations will fall down, and universal free trade will follow automatically.

" 'Such is our general plan of campaign. But our attack upon the problem of international finance will have for its immediate objective a point in direct line with the historical character of the Firm.

" 'Our first operation, the growing point of the whole undertaking, will consist in the application of the gambling method in its most highly developed and scientific form—that, namely, of Insurance against Risk. Our Insurance Department, on which the finest talent in the Firm has long been concentrated, will, so to speak, lead the attack. We shall underpin the entire structure of industrial civilization with an elastic but infrangible system of Mutual Insurance, in which the interests of all nations will be so co-ordinated but no injury can be inflicted on any part without being shared by the organism as a whole. To the citizens of the twenty-seven countries where our Branches are already established we shall offer the means of insuring themselves against the dangers inherent in the war-making State. They will insure their cities against bombardment from land, sea or air; their commerce against blockade; their mercantile marine against destruction; their goods against confiscation, whether by taxation or loan; their lives and their sons' lives against death or mutilation in battle. In addition to that they will insure against the capricious violence of nature—against earthquakes, famine, pestilence, storm and other catastrophes.

"'Before many years have elapsed we shall have accumulated a vast and stable fund, under international trusteeship, administered in the name of Rumbelow, Stallybrass & Corker. In this fund the interests of all nations will be so combined that not a life can be sacrificed, a house bombarded, a ship sunk, a sovereign spent on powder and shot without the entire comity of nations becoming jointly responsible for the damage. Needless to say war will be impossible.

"'During the transition period, when economic control is gradually passing from the war-making powers into the hands of the Firm, there will be dangers to be guarded against. The International Fund will have to be protected from pillage, in whole or in part, by any predatory State that may covet its vast resources. To meet this danger our assets will be given the utmost mobility, so that they can be rapidly transferred from threatened points to places of safety. They will be so distributed over a world-wide field of investment, or capable of being so distributed, as to be virtually inaccessible to the government of any single state. Any cupboard that may be attacked will be automatically emptied the moment the burglars appear upon the scene.

MR. HOOKER BEHOLDS BEAUTY OF WOMAN

" 'These, gentlemen, are the problems on which you will now proceed to concentrate your high gifts, both in severalty and in combination. When your plans are complete, the entire organization of the Firm, with its world-wide ramifications, its immense resources of brain power and expert knowledge, will be flung unreservedly upon the hazard, in the fervour of that sportsmanlike tradition which is at once our glory and our inspiration.' "

Mr. Hooker listened to all this, as he had promised, with a profound and rapt attention. More than once he had been on the point of interrupting the reader, and could hardly restrain himself, at a certain passage, from starting from his chair; interjecting, however, an emphatic approval which Mr. Hotblack had not overlooked.

When the reading was over he remained for some minutes immersed in thought, and then, like a man weighing his words, said slowly:

"Mr. Hotblack, the man who could show us how the economic and the spiritual interests of mankind may be freed from their present entanglement with the political system would be the greatest benefactor the world has seen for many ages. First he must disentangle them; but then, mark you, he must show how the three interests are to be co-ordinated in a new synthesis."

"Mr. Rumbelow will do both!" cried Mr. Hotblack.

"I have often reflected on these things," continued Mr. Hooker. "I have been reflecting upon them for years. And this is the conclusion I have reached: that the double task I have just mentioned was beyond the wit of man, and that nothing short of some immense catastrophe would detach the spiritual and the economic interest from their present dependence on war-making conditions. At one time it seemed likely that the recent war was the catastrophe in question. But things have turned out far otherwise. The chains which bind the spiritual and the economic interests to the dangerous wheels of the political machine have not been broken but riveted anew. For ages to come the chief task of industrial civilization will be to pay off the debts of the last war and to maintain the system which will inevitably lead to another. There was a time when I believed, in common with many others, that the establishment of universal free trade would achieve the end in view. Since then I have learnt to my sorrow that political idols, to which everything else has to be sacrificed, will not suffer it to be. But for this I would devote my entire fortune, at this moment, to a world-wide propaganda in favour of universal free trade."

"Would it interest you, sir," asked Mr. Hotblack, "to learn Mr. Rumbelow's views on this subject?"

"It would," said Mr. Hooker, "for I have not altogether lost the hope I once had in this direction. You must remember, Mr. Hotblack, that among the Quakers, from whom I come, Free Trade is a tradition. My great-grandfather discussed it with Dr. Johnson. My grandfather was mobbed in Bristol for advocating it after the Napoleonic wars. My father was one of Cobden's earliest friends. When I studied economic science in Cambridge years ago my father was terrified lest I should be led astray,

MR. HOOKER BEHOLDS BEAUTY OF WOMAN

and gave me a solemn charge, shortly before his death, never to betray the cause. 'It will draw the dragon's teeth,' he said; 'it will make wars impossible.' But let me hear Mr. Rumbelow's views."

"They coincide with your own," replied Mr. Hotblack. "You must know, sir, that whenever the Chief offers an opinion on an important subject, I make a note of his very words. Here they are."

Taking a note-book from his pocket, Mr. Hotblack consulted the lettered index, found the place and began to read:

" '*The Quakers have been essentially right in most things———*' Pardon me, sir, this is the wrong passage."

"Go on, I pray you," said Mr. Hooker; "I wish to hear the rest of it."

" '*The Quakers have been essentially right in most things. They have preserved the original impulse of the Christian religion, for which they have paid the price in becoming one of the smallest of the sects. In trade especially they have proved themselves genuine sportsmen, always giving the other party to the bargain a fair run for his money. My Lady and I have often been tempted to join them.*' "

As Mr. Hotblack read this out a dark suspicion flung its shadow across the mind of the millionaire. Was the man before him an artful villain? He remembered how he had once asked himself the same question about Rumbelow, and that an hour later the bookmaker had saved his life. In an instant his generous soul dismissed the thought; and Mr. Hotblack went on:

"Here is the passage about Free Trade. I find,

after all, that it runs continuously with what I have just read about the Quakers.

"*'If the politicians who made the recent peace had struck decisively for universal free trade, they might have put the rest of their damned treaty'*—observe the careful choice of language, Mr. Hooker—*'the rest of their damned treaty on the fire. But nothing decisively beneficent will ever originate in that quarter.'*"

"The politicians do their best with the machinery they have to work," said Mr. Hooker, "and I greatly dislike the harsh judgments that are directed against them. But, if this is what Mr. Rumbelow means, I, too, believe that the machinery itself is radically unfit for serving the major interests of mankind. The political bottle, Mr. Hotblack, is not made for the wine of moral idealism. It bursts under the pressure.

"Permit me, as a psychologist, to amend the figure," replied Mr. Hotblack. "The political bottle, sir, is made of the skin of a highly pachydermatous animal; it does not burst, but blows the idealism back into the face of the unfortunate idealist. Anyhow, men are losing faith in it. The worship of the Bottle, which, as you know well, Mr. Hooker, has displaced all other forms of religion in our Western civilization, is rapidly becoming a discredited cult. Consider what is happening in Smokeover itself. Here are the politicians urging us in accents of desperation to 'produce more,' as the only alternative to economic ruin. But Smokeover will not respond. Production steadily falls off. Why? Well, sir, for fifty years before the war Smokeover had been 'producing more.' But what has become of 'the more' it produced? Most of it has been blown up on the battlefield and the rest has made fortunes for men like yourself. What motive can men have for supporting a system which disposes of the fruits of their toil in this manner?"

As Mr. Hotblack, incautiously yielding to the current of his ideas, pronounced the last sentences, Mr. Hooker winced visibly; and the psychologist was casting about for an effective mode of making amends when the door opened, and Mr. Rumbelow, accompanied by My Lady, walked into the office.

There was a moment of surprise, of tension, of tentative adjustment to new conditions, as when the blinds are thrown up in a darkened room, or the mist breaks on a mountain top, or an army is ordered to take a new front, or a sailor losing his landmark has suddenly to find his bearing by the stars, or as when a soul released from the body is wondering what has happened and where it is.

In a few seconds the transition was effected, the four figures standing motionless and silent meanwhile; each keenly conscious of the other's presence, but unconscious of itself: My Lady wonderful, radiant, self-luminous, a pure essence diffused through the room; at her side the Chief, a princely, superstitious adventurer, a leader in attack; before him Mr. Hooker, erect, Quaker-like, responsible, an image of moral worth, a master of men; behind him the psychologist, alert, sagacious, loyal; and, around them all, the office furniture, the desks, the cabinets, the pigeon-holes, the shelves, the typewriter, and the telephone—the mechanism of business, the apparatus of finance.

Once before Mr. Hooker had seen My Lady's face, but not clearly nor in the light of day. Now, too, she was dimly seen; for the moment he beheld her a mist gathered in his eyes. Joy and pain ran together into one experience: the joy of beholding an immortal thing, the pain of a poignant contrast between the immortal presence and its corruptible setting; the two interpenetrating one another and forming in their union a third emotion for which there is no name. It was an astonishment, nay, a shock.

My Lady was the first to speak, and as she spoke the tension was released, the difficulty removed, the transition completed and a way opened for free intercourse.

"Dear Mr. Hooker," she said, "you have been in great tribulation. We wish you to know that you have friends who love you."

The mist in his eyes became great drops and these, rolling down, were the only answer he made to My Lady's words. He turned to the Chief.

"Let me thank you for saving my life. There was a link forged between us that night. It will last. I am glad to have lived if only to hear what My Lady has just said."

Mr. Rumbelow grasped the hand of the millionaire, but the reply came from My Lady.

"Have not we three stood together at the point where life joins hands with death and the worst passes into the best?"

With a dignity that became him well, Mr. Hooker

lifted the fine hand of My Lady and kissed it like a courtier of old.

She turned upon him a smile that was all radiance. "We began well," she said.

"We shall end better," he replied.

Mr. Hotblack was standing in the background, deep in thought. "This," he was reflecting, "is both a beginning and an end. Were all revealed that the present moment contains, were the promise of it suddenly expanded into the fulfilment, no one would ask any more what Mr. Hooker will do with his money. His problem is solved."

Up to the last word spoken the Voice of the Legend had shown no signs of weariness or failure, rather gathering strength as it went along. But now it abruptly stopped. Was the Legend at an end? Or was the Voice merely pausing as it had done so often, to reflect upon the last turn of its story? The Author was in doubt. He rubbed his cold and stiffened fingers, musing deeply the while on what he had just heard; and as he did so certain memories were awakened which moved him greatly. An ejaculation must have escaped him, or perhaps it was a sigh, or it may have been a tear. But whatever it was the Voice seemed to observe it, and suddenly went on, not rapidly as before, but slowly, as the manner of the Immortals is when speaking of their own business.

Mr. Hooker's well-spent life had been devoted, in essentials, to the pursuit of the True and to the service of the Good. With Beauty, the third of the immortal Sisters, his acquaintance hitherto was limited and incidental. Born in an age which looks upon Beauty as an adornment, and in no sense a necessity of existence, and in a land where those who accord it divine honours are apt to be made a mock of, he so far shared the characteristics of his generation as to be untroubled by the presence of the ugly. Like many another rich man in Smokeover, he lived in an exceptionally ugly house, and was indifferent to its ugliness. The Ethical Society over which he had presided did, indeed, from time to time offer lectures to the public on the relation of Art to this, to that and to the other; but not all the gentlemen who gave these lectures were either lovers of the Beautiful themselves or causes of its being loved by other people. Mr. Hooker, who listened to the lectures with great attention, was roused by one of them to buy a large number of pictures, a thing which had hardly occurred to him before; but they were not very good, he seldom looked at them, his attention being preoccupied by what most men consider the weightier matters of the law. He was one of those who can live without beauty or the love of it, unaware that under these conditions things are only half seen, life only half lived, deeds only half done. He knew of course that it was better to hear the lark sing than the mouse squeak; better to walk in a forest of trees than in a forest of chimneys, better to inhale the fragrance of roses in his garden than the stench of burning lubricants and the fumes of petrol in the Smokeover streets. But the difference between the ugly and the beautiful was not vital: it touched no essential value, and was by no means to be compared to the difference between right and wrong.

There is, however, one manifestation of the Beautiful, and that a supreme one, to which mankind, even in ages the most sordid, has never been indifferent. Whether writers on "Æsthetics" have ever noticed the fact or not, and most of them seem to have overlooked it, there is little doubt that the highest and purest form of Beauty revealed to the eye of sense is that which may be seen in the face of a beautiful woman. Here the soul of Beauty becomes incarnate and displays its power, mightier than death, more terrible than the sword. In this form, at all events, Beauty is still acknowledged as a necessity of human life and not as a mere adornment whose presence or absence makes no vital difference. Provided everybody were given his "rights," a world without Art would present no great difficulty to the mass of your voters, agitators and electioneering politicians, nor would it be a nightmare to some of your moralists; and a world cut up into half-acre allotments, canopied by smoke, where the hooting of motors never ceased and the glare of their headlights was never extinguished, where the larks were all served up on toast and the birds of Paradise all killed for their feathers, could be borne by most of you—if only the Clubs were comfortable, the newspapers piquant, the cinemas attractive, the public-houses well warmed and the beer good. But a world without beautiful women would be intolerable to everybody, and most intolerable to the women themselves. The presence of beauty in this form is never treated as a mere addendum to the values of life, but always as part of their essential constitution.

Do you say that this solitary exception to the general indifference cannot be set down to a love of the Beautiful for its own sake? The point is doubtful, but may be granted for the sake of argument. The beauty of women is assuredly one of the chief perils that beset your pilgrimage through time. It marks the point where the road to heaven intersects the road to hell, but without any clear intimation or legible finger-post set up at the parting of the ways to determine which is which; and many there be that go astray when they come to it. Yet to keep the love of beauty alive on any terms, in a world where so many forces are conspiring to destroy it, is something gained; and were this all you owed to women you would still owe them much. As Dante bore witness, the beauty of a woman may become, to the beholder whose vision is uncorrupted, the passport into a world of absolute and eternal values. Such a vision, unmingled with carnal desire, is a spiritual experience, as pure, as profound, as long lasting as any that is accorded to the soul of man.

It had come to Mr. Hooker. Like the lightning which shines from the one part of heaven to the other, at an hour when no man expects it, Beauty had suddenly unveiled herself, and Mr. Hooker, gazing upon her face, saw his past interpreted and knew beyond gainsaying that all was well.

A dim light was breaking over Smokeover, the dawn was coming and the Voice grew faint. For some time longer it continued to mutter, but the

MR. HOOKER BEHOLDS BEAUTY OF WOMAN

Author could catch only brief and broken fragments of what it said. He heard the name of Margaret Wolfstone repeated several times, of Billie Smith, and of another person, a Professor, the rest of whose name the Voice seemed unable to pronounce. He is not sure that the Voice which spoke these names was that which had told him the Legend of the Mad Millionaire. It may have been another. The stir of Smokeover rousing itself for the day's work was making it hard to distinguish these subtler sounds, and the Author was on the point of closing his book, with a disappointed sense that the Legends were incomplete, when a third Voice, different from any he had heard before, said quite distinctly:

"Try the other Bridges."

Next night the Author posted himself at another Bridge, hard by the spot where the Smokeover High School for Girls overlooks a winding in the River of Forgetfulness. He found it a good Bridge for his purpose. What he heard there shall be told in due course.

PART THREE
The Legend of Margaret Wolfstone

CHAPTER ONE

Miss Wolfstone Becomes Clairvoyant

MISS MARGARET WOLFSTONE, of Girton College, ex-nurse of the Red Cross and now headmistress of the Smokeover High School for Girls, was notable among women for a fine presence and for a winsome and beautiful articulation of the mother tongue. Her manner was vigorous, but under restraint; her address buoyant and charming; her laughter musical, timely, and not infrequent. She looked you straight in the eyes and grasped you firmly by the hand. If you tried to draw her portrait from memory you would get into difficulties and end by falling into a passion with yourself. Now you would draw her features too masculine in their strength, now too womanly in their tenderness. You would probably begin by making her the handsome but rather domineering matron of a hospital, which you would instantly rub out. At the next attempt she would emerge as a Raphael Madonna, which clearly wouldn't do; but you would only make matters worse by putting in Mona Lisa's smile. Then you would begin again: you would sit down, change your pencils and think; and, sure you had her this time, would produce an excellent study of Lady Macbeth. Worse then ever! And now for a last effort: you will abandon yourself to "inspiration," and let your pencil draw what it will. It draws Lady Hamilton as a laughing Mænad. Then you give it up. A most elusive woman!

Why Miss Wolfstone had remained unmarried was a problem to be thought on, for a woman more fitted to be the mother of the Gracchi would be hard to find. Yet the reasons were simple: first, that fathers for the Gracchi are none too plentiful; second, that Miss Wolfstone was hard to please; third, that she was devoted to her profession as a teacher. Most assuredly opportunities were not lacking. Had an instrument been constructed for recording emotional disturbances among Miss Wolfstone's male friends, the needle would often have trembled, and sometimes with violence. It trembled every month when the Council of the Girls' High School interviewed their headmistress: it trembled at the meetings of the Society for Ethical Culture, especially when Miss Wolfstone was smoking cigarettes. There was a credible report that she had received eight offers of marriage when acting as a nurse; and even now there was a gallant officer with one arm who had more business in Smokeover than his War Office duties could account for. She liked him all the better for having only one arm, and told him so; but she was sorry he had so few ideas.

Miss Wolfstone was a most accomplished and original teacher of the young; her school was filled to overflowing. The girls loved her, and it was a common saying among them that "you could not tell her a lie; no, not if you tried *ever so*." She had developed a method of dramatizing the teacher's work and was training her assistants in the use of it. When a problem had to be solved, even in geometry or in grammar, she would represent the elements of it as actors in a drama, set them in movement one against another, sketch a situation and bring on a crisis. Experts in education would come down to Smokeover to study her work.

She would carry the same gift, sometimes with disconcerting effect, into the discussions of the Ethical Society. She would remind the disputants that in every case of "doing good" there are two wills to be considered: the will of the person who "does" the good, and the will of the person to whom the good is "done." Then she would construct a dialogue between the two sides and end up by telling the angry philosophers that the whole was a marionette show, of which they themselves had been secretly pulling the strings. Had this been done by anybody else it would have been resented; but the grace and good humour, not to say the good looks, of Miss Wolfstone carried it off. Though formidable she was not aggressive.

And that was not the end of her dramatizings. Every Christmas the girls of the High School acted a play written by the headmistress. A public hall was engaged for the performance; all of Smokeover that possessed evening dress turned out to see it; and once a dramatic critic came down from London. He reminded his readers next morning that no woman had ever been a great dramatist, but admitted that Miss Wolfstone unquestionably had "talent."

The girls at the High School always knew when Miss Wolfstone's play was in preparation. They knew it by the peals of laughter that would suddenly break out towards midnight from Miss Wolfstone's little study on the second floor. When Miss Wolfstone was in the schoolroom she often laughed under due restraint; but when she was writing her plays, and alone in her study, she sometimes let herself go—a point to be considered by those philosophers who teach that solitude and laughter are incompatible. Not that her emotions in the study were all of comic origin. There were others; but these were inaudible.

One dismal afternoon in winter, at the very hour when Mr. Hooker was discoursing to the doctor on the Unreal End of things, Miss Wolfstone was standing at the window of her study looking out into the great playground that lay beneath. Had the day been fine she would have been playing hockey with the senior girls. But the weather was vile, and Smokeover had put on its filthiest attire. So, playground games being out of the question, she sent the girls to the gymnasium and resolved to profit by a quiet hour to finish the scene in her play at which she had been working last night.

Before her was the playground, the surface dimly visible through the mist as a pool of water, and beyond that the gloom of the great city, the sound of its traffic now sunk to a growl. Standing at the window, her mind's eye pictured the scene beyond: the cold and foggy streets, the dirty pavements, the thoroughfares sweating black mud, the macintoshes and the umbrellas, the crowded and mephitic trams, the condensed moisture running down their windows in streams. She thought of the great chimneys and of their smoke pouring downwards under pressure of the drizzle, and of how the air outside would be full of smuts. From this her mind passed to the enormous wealth which had been rolling into the city during the last years. A moment later she was thinking of Mr. Hooker and of his perplexities and of his recent escape from a violent death.

Then she turned to her table and took up a card that was lying there. It announced a lecture by a celebrated Pessimist for five o'clock that day, under the auspices of the Society for Ethical Culture. The subject was "The Putrefaction of Modern Art—illustrated by lantern-slides of the tombstones in the Smokeover Cemetery." Miss Wolfstone laughed. So Modern Art was not only defunct but putrefying. What next? At the same time she felt sorry for those who had to bury their dead in the Smokeover Cemetery on a day like this.

The Smokeover Cemetery! The words seemed to grip her consciousness with a sudden mastery; thought came after, pointing a finger; and her imagination, always quick to follow when thought was pointing the way, was instantly at work, flitting hither and thither over the melancholy scene. She saw the hideous tombstones, massed together in every combination of ugliness; she watched the funeral processions passing through the iron gates and winding their way to the open graves; she was inside the mortuary chapel listening to the dreadful service of the Church of England and to the sobs of the women in black. With great rapidity the facts became concrete and alive; then, suddenly, they seemed to focus themselves into a vision, which rose before her perfect in detail, as a thing witnessed by the bodily eye—no uncommon experience of Miss Wolfstone when her dramatic self was awake. For a few moments the vision lingered, its outlines unblurred by any doubts of its reality; then vanished as suddenly as it had come.

A thing to be made a note of! In an instant her memorandum book was out, and these lines were jotted down:

"Funeral in Smokeover Cemetery—man burying his wife — dark afternoon in midwinter — fog, drizzle, cold—surrounding tombstones described—piled earth by graveside (blue clay? bones and bits of old coffin furniture sticking out?)—cemetery chaplain—Church of England service—"pains of eternal death"—undertaker's men slip in wet clay and drop coffin on chaplain's foot—chaplain swears—conversation of mourners before and after—and of undertakers' men in public-house."

Miss Wolfstone, holding the book before her and with her pen in her mouth, looked at what she had written. "I wonder," she reflected, "if any manager would put that on the stage, or the public stand it. Might, if it were part of a bigger thing. The Pessimist would probably cite it as an instance of putrefaction in Modern Art—'debased realism' and all the rest. After all, the Gravedigger Scene in *Hamlet* is pretty strong meat. Archaic, of course. But it wasn't archaic when Shakespeare wrote it."

However, she would hear that lecture about the tombstones at five o'clock; it was sure to have points. She knew the Pessimist and admired him—"a sharp threshing instrument with teeth." But now to the Christmas Play.

It had for title "Who is my Neighbour?" and was to be described as "an old Morality Play in a new dress." The plot turned on the adventures of Three Wise Men who embark on a systematic exploration of the world for the purpose of discovering who their "neighbour" really is. As they journey from place to place they pass the time on the road in constructing elaborate programmes of the "good" they will do to their "neighbour" when they find him. At each halting place they meet some fellow traveller whom one of the Three declares to be the "neighbour" they are looking for. But the others not agreeing, they fall into an argument, which develops into a quarrel and an interchange of blows, the relationship of the Three growing more and more acrimonious the further the search is prolonged. At length, after endless quarrels and unneighbourly treatment of one another, the Three Wise Men discover to their immense surprise that each has been "neighbour" to the other two all the time, and that they would have done far better to stay at home and respect each other's landmarks.

The scene on which Miss Wolfstone was now working was that in which the Three Wise Men come to blows for the last time over the question "Who is my neighbour?" The idea to be developed was that the quarrels between them had to reach the extreme limit of bitterness before the discovery could be made that each was neighbour to the others; this was now to emerge like a flame of spontaneous combustion as they knocked their heads together in a last and desperate scrimmage. In all this she had her eye on something in the Hegelian philosophy, with which she was not unacquainted; she was also thinking of the war and its lessons; but her main problem at the moment was to contrive the scene in a form which could be acted by the three graceful girls, who played the Wise Men, without undue violence on the one hand and without sacrifice of essential humour on the other.

To this, then, she addressed herself, concentrating her mind on the problem before her and making a great effort to pick up the thread and recapture the spirit in which she had left off last night. But soon she found, to her great annoyance, that the vein was completely dried up. Her brain seemed paralyzed at the point where the spirit needed its assistance for invention, creation, expression; paralyzed at that point, but intensely active at others. Nothing to the purpose would come. Every expression she jotted down was unnatural; every line had to be blotted out, and the next attempt would only yield something worse. A stagnant and melancholy atmosphere, in which creation was impossible, seemed to surround her; and the springs of laughter, essential for the vitalizing of the scene, refused to flow.

The truth was that she could not wrench her mind away from the dark track into which it had been forced by her recent graveyard meditations. These acted as an inhibition. Do what she would, the miserable scenes her imagination had conjured up, hovering in the background of the mind, gave their tone to all the rest and kept her thoughts on the level of unhappy things; where, by a subtle association, they passed rapidly from one calamity to another, but always alighting at last, for some reason she could not explain, on the image of Mr. Hooker and his troubles. She thought of his gloomy home; of his bereavements; of his loneliness; of the skeleton in his cupboard; of his racked and agitated conscience; of the insoluble problem he was battling with; of the shock and the horror of the accident on the line. Then she remembered his piteous consent to receive the advice of the Ethical Society and the desperation such an act implied, and the cold comfort he would get from the advice. She had written to him herself. What good had she done? She wondered. Perhaps it was a foolish act.

There was something in common between Miss Wolfstone and the millionaire. Like him she came of a Puritan ancestry, and was aware that, in spite of all the changes her mind had undergone, the old habit of looking for a "lead" and trusting to fugitive intuitions was still strong within her. She had often observed the same thing in him. When, for example, he had startled the Society by his grotesque proposal about Rumbelow, she divined at once how the idea had originated. It had burst upon him in the night watches, and, suddenly reverting to type, he had accepted it with the uncritical obstinacy of a mystic. She had done the same thing herself a thousand times, sometimes with unfortunate results, but not always—no, not *always* by any means!

And there was another link, perhaps deeper. Mr. Hooker's moral philosophy, as another Voice has told, had for its bedrock a certain maxim or Great

Principle—"So live that by affirming your own personality you may help others to affirm theirs." This maxim, reiterated by Mr. Hooker a thousand times, was the lode star of his conduct and the theme on which his ethical propaganda, his lectures and speeches were variations. To the members of the Society it formed the centre of an endless and inconclusive argument, and when Professors came down from Oxford with the latest pronouncement of philosophical culture, they seldom failed to point out that the Great Principle was nothing new, a mere restatement of an old formula of Kant, and open to grave objection on logical grounds. It was noted, however, that Miss Wolfstone made no contribution to these exercises, but remained consistently silent whenever the Great Principle was in question. She was meditating on its dramatic possibilities.

One night, walking home with Mr. Hooker after a meeting, as she often did, she said to him, "Mr. Hooker, I believe in your Principle. That is, I believe in it not as a thing to be argued about, but as a thing to be *tried*. It's the best working philosophy I know of, provided always you limit the field of its application to a scope you can manage. I have tried it myself within limits, and I want to tell you that it works admirably—yes, delightfully. Before I have done I mean to make it the driving power in the life of my school. I do it all by indirection, chiefly by means of the plays I write for the girls and make them act. I never mention the Principle itself, though I shall when I have got it fully at work. The girls fall into it unconsciously; so do the teachers. In the course of time it will become the basis of education everywhere, the source of a spiritual revival, beginning in the schools. Dear Mr. Hooker"—she often addressed him thus—"I can't measure what I owe you for fixing that idea in my mind. It is such a sound thing; so different from all the rotten contentiousness of our Society! It was the first clear point of departure, the first authentic finger-post, that I found at a time when I was completely lost in life. I owe it to you. Thank you a thousand times. Good-night."

Thinking of these things and weighed down by a sense of failure, Miss Wolfstone laid her manuscript aside, realizing that by no effort could she produce another line that day. Very slowly she opened a drawer, placed the manuscript inside, and, with the same slow movement, closed the drawer, musing deeply all the time.

She looked at her watch; it was half-past four. Should she go to the Pessimist's lecture—or join the girls in the gymnasium? True, she had had enough of Smokeover Cemetery for that afternoon. Still, the Pessimist was always worth hearing; and then the speeches afterwards—they would certainly be amusing!

A few minutes later Miss Wolfstone found herself in one of the crowded trams. Among the passengers she noticed several members of the Ethical Society—the Champion of the Simple Life, the designer of women's frocks, the dentist and two spiritualists—these last in close conversation—all on their way to the lecture.

Presently a schoolboy in a dripping macintosh got in, and seeing Miss Wolfstone at the further end forced his way through the standing passengers until he was in front of her. It was Billie Smith, the would-be pirate, a close friend of the headmistress.

"Where are you going, Billie?" she asked.

"I'm going to the lecture. Father said I might. He doesn't believe in cemeteries. He and Mother are going to be cremated. It's better fun than being buried—don't you think so, Miss Wolfstone? Father's always talking about cemeteries, and he wants Ted and me to grow up to hate them. I heard him tell Mother so. But we haven't quite made up our minds. Ted can't come to the lecture—he's got a sore throat. I want to see the pictures. They're sure to be ripping."

"I hate cemeteries as much as your father does," said Miss Wolfstone. "I've seen one this afternoon, and it was a very nasty place.

"Then I think *I* shall hate them, too," said Billie. "You know, I *mean to*, Miss Wolfstone. But, oh, I say, there's something to tell you! Father says Mr. Hooker doesn't know what to do with all his money. Ted and I have got a plan!"

And without a pause he reeled off the great scheme of buried treasure.

"It's a bully plan, Billie," said Miss Wolfstone. "You'll take me with you on the pirate ship, won't you?"

"Rather!" cried Billie. "You shall be head stewardess.—No, you shall be nurse to the wounded. We're sure to have lots of wounded, Miss Wolfstone. And—oh, I say—if we get wrecked, you shall save my life—no, Ted's life—same as you saved Mr. Rumbelow's when you were torpedoed."

"I'd rather be nurse, if you don't mind, Billie. And I suppose you'll give me a share of the treasure."

"Rather! How much would you like?"

"I shall want a million at least."

"Oh, I say, that's a lot! It won't leave much for the others."

"I won't go for less, Billie, especially if I have to save Ted's life. But are you two going to be pirates *always?*"

"Oh, no, only for a bit. When we've finished being pirates we are going to be doctors.—Oh, I say, do you know what a boy said in form this morning? Old Baines asked him for an example of the Ablative Absolute—not in Latin, in English—and what do you think he said? 'Cæsar, having finished being sick, pursued the Gauls.' Wasn't it fun?"

"And it was a wrong example too, Billie. So when you and Ted have finished being pirates you are going to pursue your patients. Is that it?"

"We're going to make them better," said Billie.

"How are you going to do it?"

"Promise you won't tell anybody!"

"Yes."

"Well, we are going to invent a *medicine* that will put all the bad people to sleep for the rest of their lives—so that they can't do any more harm and—you know—so that they can't have any children."

Billie said all this in a whisper and hesitated a little over the last sentence, as though he were dimly conscious that the topic was rather an indelicate one to broach to a lady.

"So you are a Eugenist, Billie?"

"Father's one. He's always talking about that—when he isn't talking about cemeteries."

"Does he talk to Ted and you about it?"

"No, not exactly. But, you know, we *listen* sometimes." And Billie blushed to the roots of his hair.

"But when you have invented your medicine, how are you going to find out who the bad people are?"

"Oh, the policeman will do that! Every policeman is to have a bottle of our medicine in his pocket, and when he catches a bad person he'll give him a dose. We'll give one to Mr. Rumbelow. We heard Father say that the police ought to give him a sleeping draught. That's what gave us the idea."

"But suppose the bad people get hold of your medicine and give it to the good ones?"

"The policeman wouldn't let them," said Billie. "The policemen are all good."

"Ah, but you know, Billie, the bad people would hire bad policemen—new ones."

"The beasts!" said Billie. "We didn't think of that. But I know! We shall have to keep the medicine *locked up!*"

"I think you will," said Miss Wolfstone. "And mind you get a good lock, and a good policeman to stand guard over it."

Hereupon the designer of women's frocks burst into loud laughter. Billie, who had incautiously raised his voice at the last sentences, gave the listener a glance of wrath and mentally put him down as one of the first to whom the lethal draught should be administered. Then, resuming his whisper, he turned to Miss Wolfstone and went off on another tack.

"Oh, Miss Wolfstone," he said, "do you know what happened this afternoon? I was just going to tell you when you began about the pirates. Father heard it from a man who was there, and said to Mother if that didn't prove cremation what did? It happened at Mrs. Hooker's funeral. The clergyman was quite tipsy, and swore like anything, and some of the men barged into him with the coffin, and there was a regular fight. Wasn't it awful?"

At that moment the car stopped in front of the Hall where the Pessimist was to lecture, and the passengers began to alight. Miss Wolfstone, who was very pale, kept her seat.

"You're coming too," said Billie, as he prepared to follow the others.

"No, not to-night, Billie."

Billie's countenance fell.

"Oh, *do!*" he cried. "If you don't come I shan't enjoy the lecture one bit. And then we can go home together and talk about the policeman. And see," he added, pulling something out of his pocket, "I've got a box of chocolates. Ripping ones!"

"No, I'm too tired. Besides, I've been in Smokeover Cemetery once already to-day, and between you and me, Billie, I can't stand any more. Goodnight, dear!"

On returning to the High School, Miss Wolfstone went straight to her study, took out her memorandum book, copied what she had written in the afternoon, and in a parallel column wrote down word for word the story she had heard from Billie.

CHAPTER TWO

Miss Wolfstone Proves Herself an Adventuress

WHILE Miss Wolfstone and Billie Smith were discoursing in the manner aforesaid of buried treasure, eugenics, the disposal of the dead and the suppression of the wicked, Mr. Hooker, as the Legend has told, was being confirmed, by a strange series of events, in a certain irrevocable determination. In consequence of which a tall gentleman with a keen face and masterful hands, a black bag open at his side, might have been seen next day in a first-class carriage on the line to Smokeover. This was Mr. Polycarp, the lawyer, summoned by the millionaire to receive instructions in respect of his new Will.

Mr. Polycarp was far from being enchanted with the prospect before him. For some time past evidence had been accumulating which, in Mr. Polycarp's judgment, confirmed the embarrassing conclusion that his client's mind was becoming unhinged. For example, among the documents in the black bag was the letter, written by Hooker many weeks before, which had first aroused the lawyer's suspicions. Mr. Polycarp took it out and read it over again. "My dear Polycarp," it ran, "I have been trying to think out the matter of making my Will in philosophical terms. The difficulties it presents may

MISS WOLFSTONE AN ADVENTURESS

recall to you the discussions we had in the old days when we studied Moral Science together at Trinity. What precisely is the philosophical significance of *making one's Will?* I take it that a man's Will should be the affirmation of his personality after he is dead. But how can a man continue to affirm his personality when he is not there to conduct the operation, and when he is no longer conscious of what he is doing? Unfortunately the philosophers give us no help; what they have to say refers to the wills of living men; not a word about the wills of dead ones. One may read all that has been written on the Will by the greatest thinkers of ancient and modern times without receiving one hint or plain word of direction as to how a Will should be *made*. Most of these thinkers appear to have been poor, or relatively so. Had they been millionaires, I venture to think that their views would have been different; at least they would not have overlooked the problem I have now to solve. Nevertheless, my principles require me to make a *Good* Will, in the sense in which Kant uses the term. You will understand the governing idea on which I desire you to act, when I say that my intention is to devote the whole of my disposable property to *financing the Moral Ideal*."

"How the devil that is to be done God only knows," said Polycarp, as he replaced the letter in the bag.

But the letter was now ancient history, and worse had happened since. There was the endowment of the nurse, an act out of all proportion; and, if rumour spoke true, there was another woman hovering on the horizon. Would it not be better, Mr. Polycarp asked himself, to wash his hands of the whole business? Perhaps; but millionaire clients were not to be picked up every day, and old friendship counted for something. At least he might protect Hooker from the wolves and the sharks, of whom many were sure to be on the prowl.

A few hours later the lawyer and the doctor who had accompanied Mr. Hooker to the cemetery were dining together in the room where the latter had eaten his melancholy breakfast, Mr. Hooker having submitted to the order that he was to see no one else that day. When the cloth was removed Polycarp said:

"You probably know what has brought me here, doctor. It's a most difficult and perplexing proposition. To begin with, I doubt if Mr. Hooker is mentally in a fit condition to make his Will."

"To be candid," said the doctor, "the case is beyond the reach of my practice."

"Same here!" said the lawyer, remembering the letter he had read in the train.

"On general grounds," the doctor continued, "I should say without hesitation that Hooker is the victim of delusions. At the same time there is reason to think that the delusions saved his life. It was touch-and-go for a long time until something happened, the nature of which I have not been able to find out. The nurse lied about it. But various indications have led me to think that a sudden change occurred in his brain."

"Pathological?"

"Only a specialist could tell you that. Speaking at

a venture I should say yes. His manner and conversation at the funeral were most extraordinary. He seemed utterly oblivious of what was going on, which was fortunate in the circumstances, and poured out a lot of incomprehensible stuff about the unreality of it all."

And the doctor repeated what he could remember, which was not very much, of Hooker's metaphysical remarks in the cemetery.

"Highly significant," said Polycarp. "But it's a pity you cannot speak more definitely. A distinct medical opinion one way or the other would be of the greatest value to me at the present moment."

Here the doctor meditated for a few moments. Finally he decided to say nothing about the snubbing he had received from the millionaire.

"You should call in a specialist," he said.

"That is precisely what I wish to do. The difficulty is to manage Hooker. A suggestion from us that his mind is unhinged might unhinge it still further."

"I doubt it," said the doctor. "He knows what we think. In fact, he said as much this morning. I believe he would assent at once to the specialist."

"Whom do you recommend?"

"Timbertree, unquestionably."

"I know him," said the lawyer.

"*Do* you?" said the doctor, pouring out his fourth glass of port. "Then you know the biggest blackguard and the biggest genius in the medical profession."

The conversation now branched off to the merits and demerits of Sir William Timbertree, Baronet.

It was garnished with lurid and amazing stories, and was going from bad to worse when a servant entered the room.

"Mr. Hooker wishes to see the doctor," he said.

The doctor left the room. Returning after ten minutes he resumed his seat at the table, drank another glass of port and said:

"That's all right. There's telepathy in this house, Mr. Polycarp; the old boy has anticipated us. Insists on being certified by a specialist before he makes his Will. Timbertree is to be summoned to-morrow morning. What do you make of *that*?"

"Bad sign. Shows that he's doubtful about himself. When a man doesn't know whether he's drunk or sober, he's always drunk."

"Then pass the decanter. Thanks. But I say, Mr. Polycarp, what are your ideas on telepathy?"

"None at all. I leave it to the fools and to the women."

"You shouldn't. You lawyers ought to cross-examine it. I'm not a psychic myself—not a bit of it. But I'll tell you a curious thing. Of course my practice takes me into a lot of houses. And I never enter a house without feeling on the instant that it is either a bad place or a good one. If it's bad there's sure to be trouble. If it's good I generally pull the patient through."

"Which sort is the house we are in at the present moment?"

"Bad—damned bad—except for this port. But where do you imagine Hooker has been this afternoon?"

"Where?"

"At Rumbelow's."

"Phew! That's the very mischief!"

"Didn't I say this was a bad house? Full of demons. I can smell 'em. But wait till you've seen My Lady. She's a sorceress."

"I have been dreading this all along," said Polycarp, whose potations had been more moderate than those of his companion. "The only hope now is that Timbertree will certify him as insane."

"Telepathy again!" cried the doctor. "I was thinking the same thing. I say, Mr. Polycarp, you ought to study telepathy."

"Change the subject."

"All right! Buried Treasure—let's talk about that. I'll tell you a story. One day when Hooker was ill they showed me into the library. There was a heap of letters on a table; I read 'em—mean thing, but I did it. They came from a crowd of imbeciles in the Ethical Society advising Hooker what to do with his money—and there was one from a schoolboy. It split me in two! He advised Hooker to bury his money on a desert island and have it hunted for by pirates. What do you think of *that?*"

"I think," said Mr. Polycarp, "that Hooker will probably end by following the schoolboy's advice. But bedtime, doctor! We shall have a busy day tomorrow."

"All right; but finish the bottle first. And there was another letter from Miss Wolfstone."

"What!"

"Miss Wolfstone. Able woman. And a damn cunning letter. She's after the millions. And she's in with the Rumbelows. Saved his life when the

Germans torpedoed 'em. The devils! Swims like a fish."

"Tell me more about this to-morrow morning. Good-night."

"Good-night, Mr. Polycarp. Good-night, sir. I'm glad you are going to sleep in this house. Bad place. I'm not a believer in ghosts, but I don't like 'em—no, I don't like 'em! And look here, Mr. Polycarp, I'll give you a tip—a damn good tip! If you've any spare cash at the bank, put it on Joy Lady. Hooker's backing her for twenty thousand."

Sir William Timbertree arrived next day. A man not more than fifty, of the middle height, broadly and coarsely built, except for his hands, and with a fresh complexion eloquent of Sunday golf. The son of a bricklayer, he had worked his way to the head of his profession with the momentum of a steam roller, winning all the medical and surgical degrees the University of London has to offer, and astonishing the experts with the ruthless daring of his surgical feats. He had been decorated by half the scientific academies of Europe, and his consulting room was a museum of orders and gold medals, which he loved to display. In the hall of his house in Harley Street there hung an immense portrait of him by a leading painter, in which he was represented as a jolly demon in the act of delivering a lecture, with a human brain on a table beside him. His presence was compact of vigour, rapidity and animation; his address blunt, decisive and overwhelming. He spoke with a Cockney accent, dropped his "h's," and there were other traces of his lowly origin which he was at no pains to disguise. Most of his adjectives were prefixed by "damned" or, preferably, by another expletive which has not yet found its way into polite literature. People said that he combined the instincts of a street Arab, the manners of an ostler and the science of a master mind. In the medical profession he was familiarly known as "Bill."

After hearing the main features of the case from the family doctor, and a few words from Polycarp on the legal side, Sir William lost no time in getting to business. For two hours he was closeted with Mr. Hooker.

On returning to the library, where the lawyer was smoking a cigar, he said:

"You're in a 'ole, Polycarp. He's super-sane."

"Which means, I suppose, that he's *in*sane," said Polycarp.

"Yes, and no. Sanity's a mean between two extremes—idiocy at one end, genius at the other. But you can't treat 'em by the same methods. He's told me the whole story. The queerest old fandingo you ever heard. His head's chock full of Plato and Christianity."

"I never heard him mention either," said Polycarp.

"P'raps not; but that's the name of his disease."

"A religious delusion, then?"

"'Alf-and-'alf. The devil's been gettin' at him from the other side."

"What devil?"

"A woman, of course; or rather, women. But no tomfoolery. A thought-out thing. He believes that his money is safest in the hands of a woman, and means to leave it all to that play-writing schoolmistress in Smokeover."

"What can be done?"

"Nothing, but let him have his way. Unless you give him his head he'll buck you out of the saddle. Repression would be fatal; he would be a raving lunatic to-morrow morning. For the rest, see Miss Wolfstone and square things with her as best you can. Use your lawyer's wits."

Before Polycarp could interfere Sir William had rung the bell, and the butler entering:

"Send the car immediately to fetch Miss Wolfstone," he said; "and say that Mr. Polycarp and Sir William Timbertree want to see her."

"Isn't that unwise?" said Polycarp, when the man had gone. "The servants will talk."

"They're talking already. I've interviewed most of them—and a precious set of rascals they are. Unless you can 'andle Miss Wolfstone, you're done!"

"I wish you had left me to summon Miss Wolfstone at the proper time. But it's too late now. Are you prepared to certify that Hooker is of 'sound mind'?"

"What else? Check him, and you drive him mad. I wouldn't do it for a million. My duty is to the patient, and I'm not going to risk him to make business for a lot of—lawyers. Go to his room; make his Will exactly as he wishes; don't thwart him in anything. Otherwise you take the consequences and —you won't like them. Look 'ere, Polycarp. 'Ooker's on the brink of an explosion—no kid about

MISS WOLFSTONE AN ADVENTURESS

that! Miss Wolfstone's the safety valve. You want to sit on it. You'll be blown up!"

"The worst that could happen," said Polycarp, "is that his fortune would go to an Ethical Society—that is, assuming he leaves his old Will unrevoked."

"You're not reckoning with *me!*" said Timbertree. "You don't seem to be aware that I'm master of the situation. Make his Will as I tell you, and I attest it before leaving the house. Swerve a hair's-breadth from my orders and I'm a witness on the other side."

"What other side?"

"The other side that I shall make."

"Do you know Miss Wolfstone, then?"

"Bah!" cried Timbertree. "What do I care about Miss Wolfstone or Miss Anybody-else? Let him leave his money where he will. What's that to me? I'm here to save 'Ooker—and he's a great old boy. Thwart him, and you bring on a crisis. Humour him, and he'll come to his senses in six months. Then you can make a new start."

"Suppose he dies in the meantime?"

"Barring accidents, he won't And what if he does? He's super-sane, I tell you. Knows what he's doing better than the tom-fools that make their wills in your office. I tell you what, Polycarp, the world's ruled more than it knows by the wills of dead men. And damned bad wills most of them are."

"Except from a lawyer's point of view," said Polycarp.

"Of course," said Timbertree. "But who knows better than you what tosh it all is? A man tryin' to keep his hold on his money after he's dead! Can't be done! Who but a fool would think it could?"

Mr. Polycarp smiled.

"Of course," Sir William continued, "if you didn't like 'Ooker's games you should have headed him off when he *began*. Why didn't you put the stopper on when he made his first Will? What the hell can an Ethical Society do with two millions—what but quarrel among 'emselves? You should have frightened him. Why didn't you call me in then? In two minutes I could have made him quiet as a lamb."

"I doubt if you could," said Polycarp. "He's as obstinate as a mule. An ordinary Christian, Timbertree, one can manage, but a millionaire with a conscience is the very devil."

"We could have called it 'religious delusion,'" said Timbertree. "It's the same with conscience as with everything else. Too much, and you're mad. Too little, and you're a beast. But talking of religious delusions reminds me of a case I was treating last week. An able man, physicist and all that. Well, thirty years ago he said a prayer, and made up his mind never to say another. It all turned on that. The prayer was—this is how he put it to me—'O Lord, I expect you to look after all my interests for the rest of my life, and believing that you're a gentleman and that you won't forget, I'm never going to worry you again.' Well, he lost his three sons in the war, same as 'Ooker, and went clean off his chump. He's written a book called *The Great Forgetter*, proving that God has no memory, and that unless you keep on reminding Him of what you want Him to do for you, He forgets it all and does nothing. He thinks he committed a crime when he made up his mind not to worry God—sin against the Holy Ghost and all that, and he's written this book to square himself on the Judgment Day. Scripture texts by the bucketful! The first thing he said to me was, 'Pray without ceasing—pray *without ceasing*, Sir William.' And argument!. My snakes, he'd argue the head off the Lord Chief Justice."

"Do you never pray yourself?" asked Mr. Polycarp.

"You know I do! *Everybody* knows I do! When I'm going to perform an operation. Only then. Would you like to hear how it started, Polycarp? All right. Well, my old mother—she used to take in washin'—I tell you she was proud of *me*, my boy! Of course I made the old lady comfortable when the shekels began to come in. Bought her a nice little 'ouse on Blackheath, with a good servant to wait on her, and a gramophone to recite poetry; had it specially made for her, records and all; paid first rate actors to spout the stuff into the machine—I'll tell you about that in a minute. Well, every Sunday afternoon I used to spend at Blackheath with my old mother. And what do you think we talked about? *My operations!* She knew every one of 'em by heart! And could remember 'em years afterwards. My hat! what a woman doctor she'd have made! And the poetry! Fond of it—I should just think she *was*—she could reel it off by the yard! Tip-top stuff, too, Shakespeare and Browning and all that! Knew the difference between the real thing and the confectionery—by God! What do you think of *that*, my hearty, for an old washerwoman? Nobody would believe it—but then, there's lots of things in this world that nobody would believe, as you know well, Johnnie Polycarp. Oh, she was a great woman, was my mother, and be damned to her good old soul! Used to say that my operations were poems—reminded her of William Blake, 'Tiger, tiger, burning bright'—you know it?"

"Yes, I know it," said Mr. Polycarp. "But what has all this to do with your prayers?"

"I'm coming to that. What are you in such a hurry for? I'm not gassin'. I'm getting the instruments ready. Well, first I'd tell the old gal about my operations; then she'd recite her poetry, and after that we had a bit of religion. And every time she kissed me good-bye on Sunday afternoon she said the same thing. 'Bill,' she said, 'Bill, my treasure, never touch the knife without first going down on your knees.' I promised her I would—and I've kept my word—and mean to! Mark that, you sceptical old ignoramus! And if you want my candid opinion, I'll give it you! I owe my success more to what my old mother taught me than to anything else in this world—more than to anything else, I tell you!"

Several times Sir William repeated the words "more than to anything else." And Mr. Polycarp observed that the prominent eyes of the great alienist had become moist.

"We live in a queer world," he said.

"We do," said Sir William, "and here's Miss

Wolfstone to make it queerer still. I hear the car in the drive."

A minute later Miss Wolfstone entered the room.

The doctor and the lawyer, standing on either side of the fireplace, turned swift glances of inquiry upon the newcomer, which she steadily returned. It was a pity that a Recorder of Emotional Disturbance was not in the room. The needle would have trembled twice; first, rather violently, for Sir William Timbertree; then more faintly, for Mr. Polycarp. And each was instantly aware that he had met his match—and perhaps something more. "Candour," thought Mr. Polycarp, "is a more formidable antagonist than cunning. And there it is."

Not taking the chair that was offered her, but placing one for herself at the end of the table, she sat down, her arms resting on the table and hands clasped in front. The men also drew up chairs, and a glance from Timbertree signalled to Polycarp that it was for him to begin.

"Miss Wolfstone," he began, "the circumstances necessitating this interview, which we thank you for granting so promptly, are these. Mr. Hooker is in danger of a mental breakdown. In spite of his unfitness for so doing, he is determined to make a new Will; and Sir William has decided that any attempt to thwart him in this matter will be followed by the gravest consequences. In that event his wealth, which you know is enormous, will be disposed of under his old Will and pass to the Society for Ethical Culture. Do you know any of his motives for wishing to alter this bequest?"

"I can imagine them," she answered; "but why do you ask me?"

"Because under the new Will he proposes to make you will become his heiress."

The two men looked to see the effect of this bombshell. She did not move, and except for a bright smile there was no change in her expression.

"I expected this," she said, "or something like it; I am not unprepared. But the matter is of little importance—I mean, to me personally. A Will made under these conditions is invalid, and I do not see how you, Mr. Polycarp, can be a party to making it."

"You state the difficulty with precision," said Polycarp. "But the alternative to making this Will is that Mr. Hooker's mind will give way."

"I will do anything to prevent that," she said quietly; "he is one of my dearest friends."

"In that case we must ask you to help us, and trust to your discretion in carrying through a somewhat anomalous transaction."

"That will interest me," she replied, "and I shall enjoy being trusted."

"But may I ask why you expected Mr. Hooker to do this?"

"He allowed me, along with some others, to advise him about the disposal of his money; and intending quite otherwise, I wrote him a letter which I now see would have precisely this effect on a man of his temper and ideals, especially if he were forced to make a sudden decision. And I have other reasons, which may be summed up by saying that between him and me there is a strong link of personal sympathy."

"Do you regret writing the letter?"

"Not in the least."

"I wish you would show us your mind more plainly," said Sir William, speaking with a more pronounced Cockney accent than usual. " 'Ow does this news affect you in general?"

"Much as I should be affected by a proposal of marriage from Giant Despair," was the quick response. At which both men laughed, Sir William immoderately.

"I suppose, Miss Wolfstone, you would refuse the Giant," said Polycarp. "Are you going to refuse the millions?"

"I am not going to run away. What do you advise, Sir William?" she asked.

"The fact is," said Sir William in a confidential tone, "the fact is, we are between the devil and the deep sea."

"The deep sea for me," said Miss Wolfstone in the same quiet tone. "I can swim."

"You look as though you could," replied Sir William in his loud voice. "You look as though you could swim the channel! But to come to the point. Miss Wolfstone, Mr. 'Ooker wants to see you. He'll 'ave to see you. Repression at this stage would be fatal. No kid about it at all! And, what's more, you'll 'ave to fall in with his wishes to the letter. There's no choice between that and a crisis. Don't argue with him. Don't say you'd rather not. Don't try the Giant Despair stunt. Give in all round. Say you're pleased. That clears the way for the next few years, and then you and he can come to what arrangement you like. If he dies in the meantime, which is not likely, then it's a lawyer's job—not my affair; you and Mr. Polycarp and several more will all be swimmin' in the deep sea together; and some of you will get drowned. But my duty is to Mr. 'Ooker."

"Do you agree to this, Mr. Polycarp?" asked Miss Wolfstone.

"I do. At the same time I must point out that it places you in a difficult position."

"You mean," she replied, "that I shall be compromised—that nobody will ever believe that I had any other motive than to obtain possession of Mr. Hooker's wealth, and that people will suspect me of employing the means—well, the means that women always employ—to obtain my end?"

"Precisely."

"And that litigation may follow."

"Not if I can avoid it."

"And that if it does you yourself will be compromised along with me."

"Possibly."

"And you, Sir William?"

"Write me off," said Timbertree. "I do my duty to the patient, and don't care a damn—excuse me—what happens afterwards. My orders are given. And the sooner they are carried out the better."

"Very well, then," said Miss Wolfstone. "I consent on one condition. It is that the Will—the document—be placed in my keeping."

The lawyer looked at the doctor.

"It's up to you to answer that," said Timbertree. "Not my job."

"Miss Wolfstone," said Polycarp, "the whole

situation is in your hands. I raise no objection to your keeping the Will, provided Mr. Hooker gives his consent."

"That finishes it," said Timbertree. "Miss Wolfstone, I shall 'ave the pleasure of showin' you to Mr. 'Ooker's room."

"Wait a moment," said Polycarp. "I have a question to ask, Miss Wolfstone, which you will answer or not at your discretion. But under the circumstances I think you will find it a right and proper question for me to ask. Assuming you become possessed of this immense fortune, have you any plan, any formed idea, as to what you would do with it?"

"Yes," she answered. "But I was about to speak of something else. I shall not see Mr. Hooker, either alone or otherwise. Perhaps you will be kind enough to tell him what I have said. I leave the rest entirely in your hands."

Sir William Timbertree's red face turned crimson. Banging his fist on the table he cried out:

"I say you *must* see him, and you *shall!*"

"At that point the deciding voice is mine," she answered. "I am sorry to disobey you, Sir William, but at this moment I am not acting under your orders."

And without the least trace of ill humour or affected triumph she made her adieux and passed out of the room.

The steam-roller, brought to a sudden standstill, looked a derelict, and it was some time before it showed any sign of renewed activity.

"Well," it snorted at last, "that's a corker and no mistake!"

"She's not a conspirator," said Polycarp, who seemed to have some difficulty in restraining his mirth.

"She's a *thoroughbred!*" said the steam-roller.

At which Mr. Polycarp could restrain himself no longer. When it was over he said:

"She took you down, Timbertree. But remember it was your doing and not mine that she was sent for."

"She did. And I like her all the better for it. Look 'ere, Polycarp. If trouble comes of this—and when it does, it will be your turn to look a fool—you'll find me on the same side with that woman."

"All right; I shall not forget it. But give me an opinion. Is the woman an adventuress?"

"Yes: and one of the right sort, too! 'Ooker knows what he's doin'. Didn't I tell you so? What better thing could he have done? Answer me that, Mr. Lawyer. You mark my word—if she gets his money she'll set things 'umming."

"I'm inclined to agree," said Polycarp. "At all events one great danger has been averted."

CHAPTER THREE

And Embarks Forthwith on a Dangerous Adventure

TWO days afterwards Miss Wolfstone was in her study, still struggling with the last scenes of her Christmas Play, and with less hope than ever of moulding them to her liking; for, somehow, the driving power was gone. She was interrupted by a gentle tap on the door, and bidding the visitor enter Billie Smith appeared on the threshold.

"Oh, Miss Wolfstone," he cried, "we couldn't play that game!"

"What game, Billie, and who couldn't play it?"

"The medicine-game. Every half-holiday Ted and I and five other boys from our school play our plans in Mr. Hooker's big field—not the one with the bull in it, but that other one where the wood is; *you* know! Father says that unless you can *play* your plans they are not good ones. The pirates played well, but the medicine wouldn't play at all."

"Ah! I thought you would get into difficulties with that medicine. What was the trouble?"

"We couldn't keep the medicine *locked up*. The bad people got it every time and gave it to the good ones. Ted and I played the bad ones."

"Do you know, Billie, I saw Mr. Rumbelow the other day, and told him that you meant to give him a dose!"

"Oh, we've altered that," cried Billie. "We are going to have Mr. Rumbelow on the other side. He's good."

"How have you found that out?"

"Because you wouldn't have saved his life if he had been bad. You'd have saved somebody else and let him drown. Besides, we heard Father say he isn't as bad as he's painted. But what did Mr. Rumbelow say?"

"He said he thought you were a rather promising boy, and that he'd like to play the medicine-game with you. And he said there was a man in his office who had a secret for keeping all kinds of medicine locked up where bad people couldn't get at them."

"Do you think he'd tell it to us?"

"No, I don't. It's a very great secret. If I were you I should try another game."

"Can you think of one?"

Miss Wolfstone reflected for a few moments.

"Well, Billie, what do you say to the League of Nations? You can get your father to tell you all about it. Let me see—there are seven of you. Yes, just right. Each of you can be one of the Great Powers."

"Splendid!" said Billie. "I'll be England and Ted shall be France. But who's to be Germany?"

"You will have to draw lots for that."

"The person that gets Germany will be in a beastly temper, and won't play fair," said Billie.

"That will only make it more life-like. And, mark my word, Billie, unless you get 'Germany' out of his beastly temper he will win the game."

"Then I'll have to be Germany myself," said

A DANGEROUS ADVENTURE

Billie. "The other fellows would never understand that."

"Good—and come and tell me all about it afterwards. But get along now. I'm very busy."

As Billie was going Miss Wolfstone called after him:

"There's one thing I forgot to say, dear. Mind you don't play the League of Nations in the field where the bull is!"

"Oh, we'll not do that! We played 'the Union of the Churches' in that field, and the bull chased us all over the place."

"Who put it into your heads to play 'the Union of the Churches'?"

"There was a man gave a lecture on it at our school."

When he was gone Miss Wolfstone, by way of restoring the interrupted sequence of thought and of calming her merriment, found it necessary to light a cigarette. But the effect of the nicotine was not exactly what she desired. As the toxin worked, her mind, instead of recovering the lost thread, broke out into a new direction altogether. She began by wondering how the boys would play the game she had suggested, and from that she passed to asking how she would play it herself. For a moment her thought centred on the *bull*. She knew well enough what she had meant by her warning to Billie. But then the thought was in the background of her mind and only clear enough to prompt a jest; now it rushed into the foreground and became full of interest and significance, and began to multiply itself into a whole family of thoughts. Little by little there rose before her the vague outlines of a dramatic situation, with the world for a stage and the nations for actors, and behind them all an untamed and brutal force with which in the last resort they must all do battle together—the bull.

And the war! With millions of others she had been swept into the conflict, had seen its horrors on their darkest side, had felt in her body the shock of its catastrophes. There was one view of it that had never left her, that seemed to sum up all that she had read in books or experienced in her own person—the impression of a vast inundation of forces which outmatched human powers of control and made a mock of all who pretended to control them, out of hand from first to last, submitting here or there to the directing touch of exceptionally brave or able men, but, as a whole, undirected by wit or will, forcing its own way forward, imposing confusion on its would-be masters, and ending at last in an issue which none had foreseen and none could claim the credit for having brought about.

Then thought, still keeping the same structure, contracted its area. This problem of the millionaire's, in which her own life was becoming entangled, what was it but the characteristic problem of a well-meaning civilization suddenly endowed with enormous wealth which, it had neither the moral nor the intellectual powers to handle aright? All the personifications were present. Herself to begin with, and the men and women with whom catastrophes had brought her into contact: Hooker, Rumbelow, My Lady, Polycarp, Timbertree, the members of the Ethical Society, were they not all living embodiments of the elemental powers which make history through their impact upon one another? She had no need to go far for materials. They were all under her hand. But could she make use of them? She remembered the saying of the critic that no woman had ever been a great dramatist. But such generalizations have different effects on different minds. To say that no woman has ever done this or that may discourage the timid, but to a woman of high mettle it is an incentive to break the rule by doing for the first time what has never been done before. So it acted on Margaret Wolfstone. Within an hour of Billie's departure a new vision of her life's work had formed itself in the high heavens, and her will was engaged to attempt it—at what risk of disastrous failure she well knew.

And what of the work that was already hers, the work of education, which she had taken up not as a profession, but as a mission, and found so delightful, so full of romance and unexplored possibilities, so rich in human relationships, so amenable to the Great Principle of Hooker and to the Great Motto of Rumbelow? Would she be renouncing it? By no means. Might not the method which had raised the teaching of the Smokeover High School for Girls to a higher level of efficiency than that of any similar school in the kingdom be extended to a wider field and developed into an instrument of education for the whole community? Might not the drama be the appointed means for revealing to the public mind the inner significance of the appalling crisis through which the world had just passed, and which the economists and the moralists and the political philosophers and the Ethical Societies and the Churches, with their effete and ineffective methods, had wholly failed to disentangle and express.

It was a daring, extravagant dream, and none but an adventuress would have entertained it. But entertain it she did. Here was a possible use for Mr. Hooker's millions, whether they remained his or whether they became hers. Most assuredly she would tell him about it forthwith. And she would tell Rumbelow. She would engage the interest of both of them to her scheme—a new application for the Great Principle and the Great Motto! The last especially came back to her mind, and she repeated it aloud several times. She remembered the first occasion she had heard it from the lips of the bookmaker. She was supporting him in the water, and with infinite difficulty had drawn a life-belt over his head and fixed it under his arms, when Rumbelow, his teeth chattering with the cold, managed to articulate before they drew him on board, "Ideal aims, businesslike methods and sportsmanlike principles." Well, she was in deep waters again, and the Motto gave her comfort as she measured herself against her task.

When the Christmas Play was produced in due course by the girls of the High School it had a cold reception from the critics. The first two acts, they said, were up to the level of previous plays and were in Miss Wolfstone's usual style, full of high spirits, fun and idealism. But in the last act there was an unaccountable falling off, as though the writer were unequal to the crisis her imagination had developed. The dialogue, which had been easy and natural up to that point, seemed to halt, the action became uncertain, the characters lost their distinctiveness, the conclusion was hurried and unconvincing. Miss Wolfstone acknowledged the truth of these criticisms. "I knew," she said, "that I was out for a duck! But the girls were waiting to rehearse and the thing had to go on. I shall do better next time."

Now there was in the city of Smokeover a certain newspaper called *The Tracker*, which appeared every week. It subsisted in large measure on scraps of carrion picked up in the servants' halls of the neighbourhood, and made a handsome living for its owners by appealing to the meanest recesses of human nature. In the art of spitting venom while pretending to do something else it had developed an ingenuity that would have done credit to the Serpent of Eden after it had been turned into a toad. In actions for libel *The Tracker* rejoiced; they were excellent advertisements and increased the circulation far out of proportion to the damages the proprietors had to pay. There were thousands of men and women and boys and girls in Smokeover who may be said to have been brought up on *The Tracker*; they read it through from cover to cover every week, and they real little else. So much at least they owed to the benevolent system under which they had been taught to read at the public expense.

To Miss Wolfstone and her Christmas Play *The Tracker* devoted a whole column of innuendo, dividing it up into paragraphs with three asterisks at the end of each, and challenging an action for libel in every one. *The Tracker* wanted to know what truth there was in the rumour that of late she had become a frequent visitor in the houses of "our two leading millionaires." It was known of course that she had saved the life of one of them, an act of gallantry which might form the beginning of a sensational novel. But the case of the other was not so clear, unless it might be assumed that Miss Wolfstone had entered his sick-room in the capacity of nurse, which *The Tracker* understood she had abandoned on accepting her present position. Now that the invalid was completely recovered, and happily in a position to enjoy the modest profit he had made out of the war, it was to be presumed that he would no longer need the professional attendance of Miss Wolfstone. *The Tracker* would like to know whether her attendance up to date had been gratuitous or whether there had been a fee—and if so, how much? If the other millionaire would prefer to have these questions addressed to him, *The Tracker* would have no objection to make the change. Perhaps one or the other of them would explain to the public whether these things had any connexion with the remarkable fit of absence of mind in which "our gifted headmistress" appeared to have written the concluding portion of her Christmas Play? And a copy of the paper, with the passage marked in blue pencil, was sent to every member of the Council of the High School for Girls.

The professional scandalmongers were joined by a host of amateurs. Perhaps through the ministrations of key-hole listeners in Mr. Hooker's domestic establishment, perhaps through the indiscretions of the port-drinking doctor, enough spicy material was soon forthcoming to provide the tongue of gossip with a tempting theme. Miss Wolfstone was one of those women whose fate it is to be as much hated, among their own sex, by whose who know them through description and report, as they are beloved by those who know them through personal contact. Speaking generally, the women of Smokeover were none too well disposed to the headmistress; not because they doubted her high gifts, but because they were forced to acknowledge them, a state of things which is even more dangerous to a good reputation among women than it is among men. This was the soil into which the insane root of calumny first struck its fibres. There were stories about her "goings-on" with the wounded officers while in charge of the hospital in France—a laugh with one, a jest with another, a gesture with a third, a cigarette smoked with a fourth—which stories, being raked together, were woven into a coherent whole by venomous imaginations. The fact that she had saved the bookmaker's life was emphasized and added to the rest; and the vilest interpretation was put upon it by shrugged shoulders, pursed-up lips and averted eyes. Then a rumour got abroad that she had been asked to resign by the Ethical Society, and that Rumbelow was in some way connected with it; at which Virtue pulled its longest face. And who had not observed the change in her manner, her look of preoccupation as she walked the streets, the frequency with which she would pass acquaintances without noticing them—plain proofs of a guilty mind? On all these grounds Miss Wolfstone's reputation was open to assault, and what more delightful occupation for little minds and evil tongues than to assault it? Not that the purveyors of the garbage viewed their own actions in this light. On the contrary, they believed themselves to have "ideal aims." Heaven knows they had "businesslike methods." But for want of "the sportsmanlike principle" their virtue became vice.

Once started the slander had to run its course. It grew and multiplied and spawned by all the modes of growth and reproduction known to the student of low organisms, sometimes by fission like a polyp, sometimes by endless extension like a tapeworm. For a time Margaret Wolfstone was the most talked-of woman in Smokeover. The kindest thing her detractors could find to say was to call her an adventuress of the most dangerous type—the keyhole listeners in Mr. Hooker's house could prove that!

Yet unkindness was not always safe, especially if that one-armed officer happened to be within hearing; Miss Wolfstone's friends, though few, were not to be tampered with! One night there was a dreadful scene in the Conservative Club, when a local Member of Parliament, having spoken a little too loudly, learnt from the shattering blow that fell on his lying mouth that one arm can sometimes strike with the strength of two. Yes, you had to be careful. The one-armed officer struck, indeed, for Miss Wolfstone's honour, but it may be doubted if he served her cause. For when men fight about a woman, the presumption generally is that she is

A DANGEROUS ADVENTURE

no better than she ought to be. This, at all events, was the interpretation which the evil minds of Smokeover put upon the gallant officer's well-meant intervention.

And now history quickened her slow paces, and things began to move. *The Tracker* was instantly on the scent, hopes of an action for libel running high in the editor's noble breast. This gentleman, who had studied the art of journalism in America, wrote the article with his own hand. "Great Fight for a Schoolmistress between a Member of Parliament and a Lieutenant-General"—such was the fascinating headline. *The Tracker* began by reminding its readers of the function it had long fulfilled as guardian of the public morals of Smokeover; "nor shall we shrink from doing our duty on the present occasion, painful as it is to our personal feelings, dangerous as it may be to our private interests." Then followed a string of pompous imbecilities in the style of Mr. Podsnap which meant, in form, that *The Tracker* was actuated by the purest motives; in substance, that it was going to do a dirty trick. After which it got to business. With a fine sense of historical analogy, *The Tracker* pointed out that this was the second Great Fight which had stirred the moral indignation of the Smokeover public within the space of a month. The first had taken place on a solemn occasion in the cemetery, of which, it would be remembered, *The Tracker* had secured the earliest authentic information, with the result that a clergyman, unworthy of his cloth, had been dismissed from his post. *The Tracker* was far from suggesting that the two Fights were connected, though the lady who figured so prominently in the second, and *had a careless habit of leaving her note-books lying about,* was in all probability not unacquainted with the facts of the first. Then followed a description of the scene in the Conservative Club, and the article wound up by proclaiming in language of great dignity that the whole incident was an eloquent sign of the times. It proved among other things that the spirit of romance, which the war had done so much to stimulate in the gentler sex, was beginning to invade our system of High School education, whether to the moral advantage of the daughters of Smokeover their parents would now be in a position to judge.

The parents were not slow in acting upon the hint. A few of the most "particular" removed their daughters from the High School at once. Then, one by one, the less "particular" began to follow their example; at first giving a term's notice with no reason assigned; then notice with the reasons dimly hinted; then no notice with the reasons boldly stated. Matters looked serious. The Treasurer, who had been in high jinks since Miss Wolfstone took command, began to tremble for his balance sheet; the shareholders were alarmed; the Council was gravely perturbed. A special meeting was summoned to consider the crisis.

It has already been noted, as a characteristic of Miss Wolfstone's relations with others, that her friends were devoted and her enemies implacable. On the present occasion devoted friends were not wanting, of whom the radical lawyer of the Ethical Society was the chief. The enemy presented his case in splashes, which, when taken singly, were lurid enough, but, when pieced together, yielded no coherent or intelligible picture. The lawyer had no difficulty in tearing it to shreds, and for the moment the enemy seemed not only discomfited but ashamed of himself.

But, alas! the moment came when the "sound political sense," for which the public life of Smokeover is famous, reared its portentous head amid the confusion and began to assert itself. A gentleman of irreproachable life, with a marked tendency to begin and end all his arguments with negative propositions, got upon his feet. He declared that the question before them was not one of persons, but one of "principles" and of "*policy*"—and from the emphasis with which the last word was spoken one might have guessed that something mean was about to be born. They must not concentrate too much attention on Miss Wolfstone as an individual. Perhaps Miss Wolfstone was a slandered woman; for his part he was not prepared to say she was not. But he would not answer for the public. The meeting must take a broader view. They had the interests of the school to consider. They had the susceptibilities of the parent to consider. They had their own responsibilities to the public to consider. They had the moral effect on the girls to consider. The mere fact that Miss Wolfstone was an object of suspicion, that mud was being thrown at her, was enough to condemn the "policy" of her friends. Their attitude was, no doubt, generous, but it was not practical. It was essential that the character of the headmistress of a school like this should be—etc., etc. In short, he begged to move that Miss Wolfstone's services be not retained.

Professor Pawkins rose in support of the last speaker. He said he had never believed in Miss Wolfstone's methods of education. From the first he had condemned them as flashy and unsound. He was only too familiar with her play-acting methods of dealing with morality; she had introduced them at the Ethical Society, with disastrous results on the minds of several of the members. Introduced among girls, especially among adolescent girls, he had no hesitation in saying that their effect would be poisonous. He believed that Miss Wolfstone's influence was altogether bad. He had always predicted that the recent prosperity of the school would collapse, and he was glad the collapse had come before further mischief had been done. There was another circumstance to which he desired to call their attention, and he was astounded that it had not been remarked upon before. The incident of her saving the life of Rumbelow, a highly doubtful service to humanity, had surrounded her personality with a false glamour, and he was sorry to find that several members had evidently been influenced by it in her favour. But what were the facts? He himself had made careful inquiries into the circumstances of that incident and he had been fortunate enough to get the evidence of an eyewitness. The ship was sinking by the starboard side, on which she had been torpedoed, and on that side over thirty wounded officers were struggling in the water. Rumbelow, by some chance, had been blown into the water on the other side. Miss Wolfstone had been left on deck. What did she do? According to his informant she ran along the starboard side, coldly inspecting the crowd of drowning men as though she were looking for somebody, and paying not the slightest heed to their appalling cries for help. Then she clambered to the other side, and seeing Rumbelow, instantly dived into the sea and saved him—a man who, in the judgment of all right-thinking persons, was one of the greatest villains of modern times. What trust could they place in the moral instincts of a woman who could make a selection like that? He seconded the resolution.

Miss Wolfstone's friends continued to fight; they fought to the last ditch, but the pettyfoggers were too many for them. That fatal tendency of corporate bodies, by which the best is driven down to compromise with the worst until agreement is reached on the vulgar, carried the day. "Policy" triumphed; the resolution was passed.

When Margaret Wolfstone learnt her fate she knew, of course, that her reputation was besmirched, that her career as a teacher of girls was ruined, that her dismissal would set the seal of truth upon slander and never be forgotten as long as she lived. To say that all this caused her no pain would be far from the truth. She was deeply hurt, but without indignation, without dismay and without pity of herself as a tragic personality. She belonged to that high race of mortals to whom pain is a right to be embraced rather than a terror to be run away from.

Far more vivid than her sense of wrong was her

consciousness of unexhausted powers. In the vision of a great achievement yet to be accomplished, the strife of which she was centre lost much of its importance and some of its reality. She had a mighty instrument in her hand which she was learning to use, and with which she had so far only played. So that, if there was one sense in which she cared, there was another in which she hardly cared at all. The real world for her at that moment was that in which her imagination was at work; the half real that where her honour was being attacked. She had refused to take the step, which some of her friends had urged upon her, of voluntarily resigning. She was not the woman to take herself or her fellows or the half-reality called Smokeover too seriously, and her bright laugh broke out more than once.

Nevertheless there were some painful scenes. One occurred in the big schoolroom when she took leave of the remaining girls. High School girls are not given to making riots, but they came near to making one that day. There was another in her private room when the assistants came to bid her good-bye. They were all leaving, they said. One, a dark-eyed Frenchwoman, stayed behind when the others were gone and passionately flung herself into Miss Wolfstone's arms. Then for the first and only time she broke down and the two women mingled their tears.

A week later she was in Rumbelow's Castle leaning over the terrace and looking out on a sunny landscape bounded by blue hills. My Lady was seated

A DANGEROUS ADVENTURE

by her side, her lustrous eyes watching her companion.

"I am wondering," said Miss Wolfstone, "why I came to grief so completely in the last act of my Christmas Play."

"Dearest Margaret——" My Lady began. But she said no more. The rest of the reply was a smile, which flashed across her face like a message from a hidden world.

Thus ended the Legend of Margaret Wolfstone.
And now the Author began to observe a certain similarity in all these endings. Wondering what this might mean, he resolved to try the Communicator with questions—a risky experiment, as all clairaudients know.

"What message from the hidden world," he asked, "did My Lady's smile convey?"

"Wait and see," said the retreating Voice.

"When shall I learn," shouted the Author—for the Voice was now a great way off—"when shall I learn what Mr. Hooker did with his millions?"

"To-night."

Then the cock crew, the sun came up, and the Author, keenly expectant, went his way. The next night's Entertainment answered his questions.

PART FOUR
The Legend of Professor Ripplemark

CHAPTER ONE

The Emergence of Professor Ripplemark

THOUGH Mr. Hooker had been forbidden by his doctor to take any part in business or public life for three months, he nevertheless managed to keep himself closely informed of the events which ended in the dismissal of Margaret Wolfstone. So deep was his concern in the issue that he did not hesitate to break orders, writing urgent letters in defence of the accused to the members of the Council and to others. Under ordinary circumstances these letters would have carried weight. But as it was, his intervention, like that of the one-armed officer, did Miss Wolfstone more harm than good. For, just as her reputation for womanly virtue was under a cloud, so was his for male judgment and sound common sense. Rumour now reported him under the influence of women, and under treatment by a mental specialist. Moreover, his partiality for Miss Wolfstone was known. In addition to all which Mr. Hooker was now in high disfavour with the Ethical Society, which was strongly represented on the Council, and especially with Professor Pawkins, who frankly represented him as insane. For these reasons it would have been better for Miss Wolfstone if Mr. Hooker had said nothing.

Mr. Hooker was one of the gentlest spirits that

ever drew the breath of life. His toleration as a friend, his leniency as a magistrate, were known to all men. For the weakness of mortal flesh, for the rebellions and escapades of the natural man, he had no condemnation. When he sat upon the bench the heart of the poacher leaped for joy; he would shed tears, instead of passing judgment over the servant girl or the munition worker charged with concealing a birth; and it is hardly too much to say that the "drunks and disorderlies" loved him. He had a horror of prisons and of the prison system, and put an interpretation on the delinquencies of police-court offenders that made it easier for them to sin no more. But if turpitude stalked abroad or hypocrisy showed its double face, a sword would flash out and the wicked would tremble for his soul. When such things confronted Mr. Hooker his moral indignation was terrible to see. His eyes gleamed lightnings, his massive brows were clouded with thunderstorms, and he became as one into whose hands it were a fearful thing to fall.

When the circumstances of Miss Wolfstone's dismissal were reported to him he rose up, therefore, like a man of wrath, invective poured from his lips and his very servants quailed in his presence. "When the boss opened his letters this morning," said the butler, "blest if I didn't think the Day of Judgment had come full clap." Chafing under his restraints nothing could prevent him using his pen. Like the editor of *The Tracker*, but for different reasons, Mr. Hooker would have welcomed an action for libel. To the members of the Ethical Society who had taken part in the dismissal he wrote in terms which must have suggested, even to their emancipated minds, that the Day of Judgment was a reality. For the first time they learnt to their immense surprise of his original intention to make the Society his residuary legatee; they learnt also that he regarded them as men of inverted conscience, and that they had forfeited both his respect and his fortune. "Your action in attacking Miss Wolfstone," he wrote to Professor Pawkins, "especially the construction you placed on her motive for saving Rumbelow, reveals a mind whose moral structure I shrink from contemplating. Let the day perish in which such a deed was done!"

To Miss Wolfstone he wrote:

"My dear Margaret,
"*Moriturus te salutat*. To-day I have received from the Directors of my Firm a long letter, full of tergiversation and false reasons, which mean, when reduced to plain terms, that I am to be excluded henceforth from all active participation in business on the ground that I am regarded as insane. It is a new link between us. We are both outcasts; you as a wicked woman, I as an imbecile. But, *sursum corda!*

"The circumstances of your dismissal have almost turned me into a hater of my kind. I had not deemed it possible that human nature could clothe itself in such infamy. But I have my consolations. When I think of you and of Rumbelow and of My Lady I know that the ultimates are secure. Were I worthy of such high company I would say, 'Let us form a League of Outcasts and front the world together.'

"I have just been studying, after a lapse of thirty years, the life and sayings of the founder of Christianity. What a splendid creation he was! How he would have lashed Pawkins! And what a tragedy that a spirit so exalted should find himself in a world like this! They ought to have sent him to another and a better planet. Do read his parable of the wicked husbandmen. It is your story as well as His—the story of the everlasting conspiracy of the base against the noble. But nothing can break them! They rise again after three days. So will you.

"One thing greatly comforts me. More and more I am learning the insignificance of that end of life where these vile things are done. The very people who do them, the Pawkins' and the rest, are gibbering ghosts. They are not *real*, Margaret, and that is what we mean when we call them humbugs. Treat them as phantasmal, as incapable of knowing what they do, and find your real world in the great achievements that are awaiting you.

"I need not bid you be afraid for nothing. But remember that in whatever you attempt, whether in education, as I hope, or in literature, which is nearly the same thing, the whole of my resources are behind you. Affirm your personality in your own way and trust me to back you. It will be the joy of my declining years, a kindness done by you to me beyond the reach of my gratitude to repay."

Not many days afterwards, as Mr. Hooker was eating his solitary breakfast and reading *The Times*

PROFESSOR RIPPLEMARK EMERGES

Literary Supplement at the same time, his eye was caught by the following, among the "preliminary notices" of books that had just appeared:

"*The Moral Will: a Treatise on Ethical Psychology. By Maurice Ripplemark, LL.D., Regius Professor of Virtue in the University of Oxford.* This book, which we intend to review at length later on, reveals on a first survey matter of the deepest interest. The author's name alone carries great weight. And the circumstance that Professor Ripplemark was awarded the V.C. for a deed of exceptional gallantry at the battle of the Somme will no doubt increase his circle of readers. We know of no other work in philosophy the author of which could write the letters LL.D. and V.C. at the end of his name."

Mr. Hooker immediately wrote down the name of the book on a slip of paper and said, handing it to Robert the butler:

"Give this paper to Jenkins and tell him to take the small car into town at once and get that book for me at Quin's."

The man took the slip and made his way to the garage, where the chauffeur was washing the cars.

"You've got to scoot," said Robert. "He wants that book from Quin's. Flash of lightnin'," he says.

"Damn his books!" replied the chauffeur. "That's the fourth time he's sent me to Quin's this week. What book does he want now?"

"I dunno. You can see for yourself. It's on that paper."

The chauffeur glanced at the slip:

"Blest if the old joss isn't goin' to make another Will!" he said.

"I could ha' told you that," answered Robert. "Polycarp was here the other day, and that clipper schoolmistress as was fired for 'anky-panky with the orficers. I 'eard all about '*er* when I was in the 'ospital at Boolong. There's a game on, my boy."

Mr. Jenkins did not deign to notice this last remark. In his universe there was "a game on" everywhere. That one should be going on in Mr. Hooker's house gave it, in his eyes, no significance out of the ordinary. So he returned to the former point.

"It's a new sort o' Will he's going to make this time. Look at that, Robert! 'The Moral Will.' See what he's up to?"

"'The Moral Will'—what sort of a Will's that, Jenk?"

"Oh," said the chauffeur, "it means 'orspitals and the Life Boat and the Railway Orphanage, and a tight 'and on the women, and all that. I always knew he'd do something silly with that —— conscience of his. When a bloke's got a conscience, I'm not takin' any, I tell you that! They're a tricky lot. Don't trust 'em; that's my advice. I know 'em!" And he flung a bucket of water at the wheels of the car.

"Does a Moral Will mean anythink for *us?*" asked Robert.

"A bit," said Jenkins, in a tone of contempt. "They don't leave *much* to the servants in Moral Wills—at least not as a rule. It all goes to Charities. Give *me* a real gentleman's will, that's what I say! Why, there was Lord Timbertree—brother to that red-faced doctor as come here—all them Timbertrees was born in the gutter—made his money in bottled stout, he did, and rare good stuff it was, and many a glass of it I've had, and I wouldn't mind blowin' the froth off one at this minute—died of good living, he did, so they said—well, did you see his Will in the paper last week? Two thousand to his 'ousekeeper; five hundred apiece to every servant as 'ad been with him seven years—and ten thousand to the lady's maid! Put that in your pipe, Mr. Robert, and smoke it! And then you'll know what a real gentleman's Will ought to be like."

"I'll give you a tip, Jenk," said the other. "If you want him to leave *you* anythink, don't tell him what you won on the St. Leger."

"And don't *you* tell him," retorted Jenkins, "what *you* won on that little sweepstake you got up last week in the 'all."

"Look here!" said the discomfited Robert. "I'll bet you three to one in quids that I'll find out in a fortnight if he's going to leave anythink to *us*."

"How are you goin' to do that?"

"Easy. When he reads a book, he always marks the bits he likes in pencil. See him do it 'undreds o' times. I'll look 'em over in *The Moral Will* before he comes down in the morning. And if I can't find out that way, I know another. 'Ave you never 'eard him talkin' to himself? Three to one on it, Jenk, and no kid!"

"Get out!" said Jenkins as he mounted the car. "We'll not know who's won till he's dead, you big son of a blunderbuss! I'm not goin' to wait till then.

A bet like that isn't worth a blow of my 'orn! You go and learn what bettin' is." And he drove off, with the order for *The Moral Will* in his waistcoat pocket.

Mr. Hooker's manner of reading a book was intense, methodical and conscientious. He sat upright before his desk, disdaining arm-chairs, a large ivory paper knife in his left hand, a gold pencil in his right and the sober spirit of his Quaker ancestry in control of every feature in his face. As he read he would beat time with the paper knife, holding it like a conductor's baton. Now and then he would lean back in his chair, resting the point of the paper knife on a particular passage in the text, turning his head slightly, with a keen sidelong glance fixed on the words indicated by the knife. After which he would lean over his book and, with the tip of his tongue between his lips, draw a firm line at the side of the important passage, perhaps adding a note, in a very fine hand, on the margin. His sense of duty, always apparent, was never more active than when he was thus engaged. He held it a stern obligation to pay the closest attention to the written word, and would often comment on the scampering slap-dash method of reading, now so common, as one of the peculiar immoralities of the present age. Especially when a book of philosophy was in question. On these occasions his insistence on "the rigour of the game" was as uncompromising as Mrs. Battle's.

For several days we see Mr. Hooker thus, immersed in the study of *The Moral Will*, his mind steeled against all other preoccupations and his five

PROFESSOR RIPPLEMARK EMERGES

senses almost out of commission. Many sounds are in the air, some sweet, some shrill, some sonorous; but he hears them not. The great clock made by his grandfather, with "Thomas Hooker, Smokeover," printed in beautiful old letters on the dial, ticks in the corner; the canary sings in its cage; the peacocks cry on the terrace; the wind sighs in the great cedars; the cocks crow on the Home Farm; the watch dog barks by the stable door. Mr. Hooker pays no heed. Every sense, every faculty, is absorbed in *The Moral Will*.

But when, through the open window, there comes the whirr of the mowing machine on the tennis lawn below, where now, alas! no tennis is played, we observe that the swaying of the paper knife suddenly stops and that Mr. Hooker looks up and listens. What is he thinking? He is thinking of three tall boys in white flannels who, till the last syllable of Time has been recorded, will play tennis no more. Then Mr. Hooker resumes the study of *The Moral Will*, and some minutes elapse before the ivory knife recovers its even sway.

Had Mr. Hooker read Professor Ripplemark's work before the evil days came upon him he would have been first astonished, then impatient, then angry, and perhaps, in one of those fits of indignation to which his high nature was prone, would have flung the volume into the flames. But a man who has been salted with fire will endure many things that the unsalted cannot away with, and may even be indulgent to originality in a moralist. Certainly this book was original enough to ruin the reputation of any philosopher. It was lively at those points where most thinkers are tiresome; it was daring where they are overcautious. Where they walk, it ran, where they trot on asses, it soared on eagles' wings, where they drive a hearse, it drove a fiery chariot behind the coursers of the sun. It abounded in the work of the imagination; there were pages which only needed the transposition of a few words to become blank verse; there were Great Presences which stalked through the book like Titans on the mountain tops; there were battles and strange adventures and tales of discovery; and the chapter on Death, which ended the book, was like the close of a great symphony.

Professor Ripplemark laid it down that the Moral Will was the private possession of no man, but a copartnership of reciprocally interacting personalities. Of course everybody had heard that before. But the way in which the Professor dealt with his "copartnership of reciprocally interacting personalities" was certainly new. He said its form might be compared with that of a Business Incorporation, a *Trust* in the real sense of the word, with a competent Directorate to manage its affairs; and he quoted the saying "Make to yourselves friends of the mammon of unrighteousness, that, when ye fail, they may receive you into everlasting habitations."

When Mr. Hooker came to the chapter on "The Board of Directors" the point of his ivory paper knife was on the page at every line.

The ideal Board of Directors for moral enterprise in a world such as ours, said the Professor, should be composed of six persons: (1) A Business Expert—

with all the sciences at his elbow; (2) An Artist—preferably in the realms of literature; (3) A Moralist of the Old School; (4) An Enthusiast for Education; (5) A Seer; (6) A Gentleman of Sporting Instincts.

These are the elements to constitute a Moral Will at the point which the history of civilization has now reached. They actually exist, in abundance, in modern society. But they meet at no Common Board and transact no common business; they act singly; and for that reason they are ineffective and the Moral Will does not arise. Each by himself is a failure. The Moralist of the Old School, by himself, is a dotard. The Business Expert, by himself, is a rascal. The Artist, by himself, is a decadent. The Enthusiast for Education, by himself, teaches nonsense. The Seer, by himself, is a humbug. The Gentleman of Sporting Instincts, by himself, is a swindler. The value of each Director depends on the other Directors who sit with him at the Board.

Very curious, too, was the Professor's treatment of the various "interactions" going on at his Board. At first the Moralist of the Old School and the Gentleman of Sporting Instincts had immense difficulty in understanding one another. But the problem was tackled, and at last each, under the influence of the other, became so transfigured that he hardly knew himself. So with all the others. The Artist and the Business Expert thought they could never agree; but they did; and then the pair of them set to work on the Moralist and the Gentleman, and there was a further transfiguration of all four of them. So on till all the possible combinations were exhausted and the whole Board was finally transfigured into the reality of the Moral Will.

Among the passages in Ripplemark's work which Mr. Hooker scored with his gold pencil was one of some length, against which he had written several marks of exclamation and a marginal note of strong approval. It ran as follows:

"Along with the desire for an *ordered* existence, which is one of the chief objects of the Moral Will, there are powerful tendencies in human nature working in a contrary direction. The *risks* and *uncertainties* of life are not uncongenial to the mind of man, which at this point, as at many others, shows signs of adaptation to a world of sudden and unexpected vicissitudes. The prevalence of the gambling habit in all ages, and its diffusion among all classes of society, indicates that risk may itself become an object of desire apart from any contingent prospect of gain. On this account it is to be doubted whether mankind would be satisfied with an assured and orderly existence, even if it could be achieved. For example, careful observers have noted the fact that, whenever economic changes raise wages to a level which assures the workers against want, an outbreak of gambling immediately follows. And, in general, assured conditions of well-being are precisely those which men seem most willing to stake on the issue of uncertain events. A fixed sum is more easily used as a gambling counter than one which is fluid and uncertain. A thing may be too precious to risk; but, again, it may be just precious enough to be worth risking for its double. Hence there is truth in the saying that a society where a modest well-being was guaranteed to everyone would be a paradise for the bookmakers. . . . Until this tendency to prefer the uncertain to the certain is eliminated from human nature—of which there seems little prospect—no system of distributing wealth is likely to give stable results. It would always be at the mercy of experts in the science of probability. The estimation of what are called chances has indeed a scientific basis, but it seems also to demand a power akin to that of genius in the artist. There is nothing in which men differ more widely than in the degree of this power they severally possess; whence it is easy to imagine a state of society otherwise well ordered in which the men who possess this power in the highest degree would be completely masters of the situation. . . . This possibility has not been sufficiently considered by those who maintain that the social problem will be solved when present forms of exploitation are abolished. Much more dangerous forms of exploitation are possible than any which revolutionary Socialism is now seeking to overthrow. The gambling tendencies of mankind are the easiest to exploit; and men who are capable of exploiting them will never be difficult to find. Conceivably these men might make themselves masters of the world."

Mr. Hooker sat spellbound. What was the origin of this passage? What could have suggested a line of thought so unusual in a Regius Professor of Virtue? Mr. Hooker's suspicions were awakened. Could it be that Rumbelow, in his many wanderings round the world, had come into contact with Ripplemark? Could it be that the bookmaker had opened the Professor's mind at this point, by showing him some actual instance of the obstinacy of the gambling habit, such as he himself had witnessed on the night of the railway accident? Why, of course! Had not both men served in the war? And had not Miss Wolfstone told him that Ripplemark had passed through her hospital at Boulogne? As Mr. Hooker fixed his eyes on the startling passage the bold eyes of Rumbelow seemed to be looking at him from the page.

For a long time Mr. Hooker sat pondering this passage and reading it over and over again. At last he determined to probe the matter to the bottom. He would send a telegram to Professor Ripplemark, asking him for an interview in Oxford on the earliest convenient opportunity.

Next morning he was up betimes, and had no sooner finished his breakfast than the book was again in his hand. Turning up the critical passage he was greatly annoyed to see on the margin the brownish imprint of a large and very dirty thumb, almost obliterating one of his finely written notes.

Now, if there was any small thing in this world that could rouse the well-governed passions of the millionaire, it was the sight of a blot or a defilement on the pages of his books. He violently rang the bell, and the butler appeared.

"Did you wash yourself this morning, sir?" said the stern voice of his master.

"Yes, sir," said the trembling menial.

"Then perhaps you will explain how you came to put your dirty fingers on *The Moral Will.*"

"Never touched the book, sir."

"How do you know that I am talking about a *book?*"

"See the name on the back, sir. It's not me, sir. It must have been one of the maids as dusts the room."

Mr. Hooker held up the incriminating evidence before the pale face of Robert.

"These," he said, "are not the thumb marks of a woman. Besides, they show signs of tobacco juice. Your own fingers are deeply stained with it at this moment. You smoke too many cigarettes. You have not washed yourself this morning, sir. You have told me two lies in the space of half a minute. Tell me no more!"

Mr. Hooker was quite capable of decisive language when morality was in question. The butler said nothing, and his face was that of a sheep.

"And now," Mr. Hooker went on, "I wish to know why you are interested in *The Moral Will.* Your finger marks are all over the book."

"Well, sir," said Robert in a hurried voice, "I'll tell you the honest truth. It's all along of Mr. Jenkins, sir. Mr. Jenkins has been savin' his wages ever since he come into your service, sir; and somebody's been tellin' him he ought to make his will. He's been worried about it, bein', as you know, sir, a very partickler man. 'Robert,' he says to me, 'I want to make a *good* will, a will as'll show people when I'm dead that I've been a moral man.' Well, sir, you'll remember as 'ow you give Mr. Jenkins the name of the book on a piece of paper to take to Quin's. When he come home he says to me, 'Robert,' he says, 'I believe that book would help *me*. It's about a Moral Will. Take a dip into it whenever you can and see if you can find out anything that would show a man, as wants to leave a hunblemished character behind him, how to do his duty?' And that, sir, is a full and truthful explanation of my conduct, sir. A man has feelin's, sir, especially towards his fellow-servants, sir."

For some moments Mr. Hooker looked the butler steadily in the face. Then, in a quiet but terrible voice:

"You have been lying," he said.

"Sir——" said the butler.

"You are about to lie again," replied Mr. Hooker.

"Then," said the man, changing his voice to a snarl, "you can take a month's warning on the spot."

Without another word the butler slunk out of the room. Mr. Hooker rang the bell that connected the library with the garage. Presently the chauffeur entered.

"Jenkins," said Mr. Hooker, "take the small car to Quin's immediately and get me another copy of *The Moral Will*. And take this copy to the back premises, soak it in petrol and set it on fire."

There are some men who are most offended by the large-scale evils of the world—by the spectacle of festering slums and of multitudes that are as sheep without a shepherd, by fields of battle soaked in blood, by streets thronged with prostitutes, by the prisons where Society, in the name of right, perpetrates a stupid and enormous wrong. There are others who stumble most heavily when their feet strike upon minor treacheries, upon meanness in the grain. Mr. Hooker was one of these.

When the chauffeur was gone he sank into a chair and showed the countenance of a man in despair, of a victim to black thoughts and to dangerous exaggerations. Had a pessimist entered the room at that moment and expounded the vanity of all ideals, the futility of all gospels, the illusoriness of human progress in general, he would have found the millionaire a sympathetic hearer.

"What difference does it make," he was asking himself, "to a man like Robert, and to the immense multitudes of which he is a sample, whether Professor Ripplemark defines the Moral Will as 'a copartnership of reciprocally interacting personalities,' or as anything else you please? What difference would it make to him—to them—if Ripplemark had put a 'not' into his definition? Or if all the philosophers and moralists in the world were to revise their systems and to put 'nots' into every sentence where they don't exist, and delete them from every sentence where they do? No difference whatsoever. He and his like are as little affected by these things as if they happened on the other side of the moon. Yet they are the very people who need affecting. The 'great ideas' have been in the world for thousands of years, 'leavening the mass,' 'filtering down into the common mind,' and all the rest of it. By this time, one would think, they ought to have reached Robert the butler. They have not. The thing he represents remains untouched and impregnable, a mass of immovable ignorance, of blind habit, and a greater factor in the life of the world than all the philosophies of life. And what hope is there that the next 'great idea'—Ripplemark's or Rumbelow's or anybody's—will fare better than its predecessors? How little do the teachers of mankind realize their impotence to move the world! How exaggerated their hopes! How false their expectations! How ready they are to swallow the foolish tributes that are paid to their importance—to believe, for example, that the whole planet trembles every time one of *them* is let loose upon its surface! The stupid flood pursues its course, never changing its direction, while they, like children, sail their toy ships in the quiet backwaters and think they are battle-fleets destined to conquer the universe. So it has been from the beginning. So it will be to the end! What a farce! Nay, what a tragedy!"

A look of pain passed over Mr. Hooker's features. For his thoughts had taken another turn, more precise in its self-accusation.

"For two years," they went on, "I have had that despicable rascal in my service and been in personal contact with him every day. And I, all the time, have been vapouring about moral ideals, the progress of humanity, the perfectibility of man and what not other nonsense, oblivious that the 'humanity' which needs reforming was standing behind my chair with a napkin on its arm—and a lie in its heart—it and I as remote from one another as if we had been living on two different planets, with forty million miles of space between us! Where in the world is there a greater fool, a greater humbug, than I have been and still am? And to this humbug, to this fool, has now fallen the problem of administering one of the greatest fortunes of modern times. What likelihood is there that I shall end otherwise than by making myself a spectacle to the gods?"

And Mr. Hooker laughed in the bitterness of his heart.

Then, suddenly, he bethought him of Miss Wolfstone's play—*Who is My Neighbour?*—a typewritten copy of which was lying on the table at his side. He took it up and, for the third time, read it through from beginning to end.

When he had finished you would have seen that a change for the better had taken place in Mr. Hooker's countenance. It had lost its look of anger and of pain.

"How true that is!" he said aloud. "And yet how feeble the ending of the play. I wonder why? There is something incomplete in that woman's life."

He was still wondering why, when a servant entered the room and handed him a parcel tied up in brown paper. He carefully untied the string—for it was a rule with the millionaire never to cut a string that could be untied—took out a clean copy of *The Moral Will* by Professor Ripplemark, and after glancing at the title page, which seemed to interest him, laid it gently on the top of Miss Wolfstone's play, already deposited on the table by his side. Then he leaned back in his chair, clasped his hands behind his head, and resumed his meditations.

Suddenly, as though a bright thought had struck him, he jumped up, went to his bookcase, took down *Who's Who,* and turned up the name of Maurice Ripplemark, LL.D., V.C. In five minutes Mr.

Hooker had learnt by heart all that *Who's Who* had to tell him about the gallant Professor—his parentage, his birthplace, his age, his family connexions, his University honours, and his favourite recreation, which, said the authority, was "flying." As Mr. Hooker closed the book he took a deep breath and uttered an exclamation. "Ha!" he cried. And he repeated "Ha!" again and again, each "Ha!" with a deeper breath and a more emphatic note.

At the last exclamation Mr. Hooker crossed the room with a rapid step towards the great window of his library, and standing there in his favourite attitude, hands behind his back, looked out. For the first time he noticed a thing of which till that moment he had been completely oblivious. The weather was changed. The sullen clouds which had smothered Smokeover for so many days had dispersed, the sun shone, a soft wind blew, and a thrush, thinking that spring was come, sang lustily from a neighbouring tree. And Mr. Hooker, in the exuberance of the moment, gave utterance to an expression he seldom used:

"Thank God!"

The truth is that there had just come to Mr. Hooker one of the cogent inspirations of his life, with a plan of action and a resolution in its train. Or shall we say that a knot had suddenly untied itself, of which his recent untying of the string round *The Moral Will* had been a kind of symbol or premonition, arranged for their own amusement by the Invisible Powers?

For some time afterwards you might have seen the millionaire pacing his library, a liberated and rejoicing man, his features aglow with the look of exaltation they had not worn since he discovered the Unreal End of Things in the Smokeover Cemetery.

"I must get further information at once," he says aloud. "I must consult Rumbelow and My Lady."

He goes to his telephone, takes the instrument in his hand, pauses for a moment to reflect, and then, quickly replacing it, rings off.

"No," he says, "the emotional disturbance would be too great. I must find a mediator—Mr. Hotblack, of course!"

He seizes the telephone again. "Will Mr. Hotblack dine with him, alone, in this house, to-night?" Mr. Hotblack will be delighted.

CHAPTER TWO

Mr. Hooker Verifies an Intuition

IT was nine o'clock in the evening; the millionaire and his guest, both in spotless evening dress, which Mr. Hooker seemed the more accustomed to wearing, had finished their meal; the cloth was removed, and two pot-bellied decanters of cut-glass, one containing excellent port, the other incomparable madeira, were placed on the shining mahogany. Each was offered to Mr. Hotblack in turn and declined by the cautious psychologist. Mr. Hooker then replaced the stoppers and pushed the decanters to a safe distance. Whereupon both gentlemen filled their glasses with water.

No sooner had the black-visaged butler relieved them of his unwelcome presence, than Mr. Hotblack, after looking round the room to assure himself that they were alone, opened the conversation as follows:

"I understand, sir, that your interview with Sir William Timbertree was satisfactory."

"Entirely so," replied Mr. Hooker. "And more than satisfactory. I believe that I have found a new friend in Sir William—a valuable acquisition to a man whose friends are not numerous. We spent two hours in close conversation. I discovered that Sir William, beneath an exterior which some people would find offensive, and which I confess tried me at

AN INTUITION VERIFIED

moments, has many fine qualities. In particular, he revealed himself as a man of deep filial piety—which I strongly suspect, Mr. Hotblack, is the source of that mystical element which you rightly mentioned as one of his peculiarities. He told me of his relations with his mother, who appears to have been a remarkable woman—one of the many remarkable women the world knows nothing of—though again I must confess that some of the epithets he applied to her were quite astounding. But I have no doubt that Sir William, who is a master in his own business, introduced this topic with a purpose."

Here Mr. Hotblack slowly nodded his head several times, with the air of a man thoroughly familiar with the purpose in question.

"After that," Mr. Hooker continued, "Sir William and I diverged to other topics. As you may imagine, he was not long in finding a way to his favourite theme, to which you referred at our last meeting—the tendency of the group mind to deteriorate into imbecility, a tendency which increases, so he said, in proportion to the largeness of the group. Sir William, I found, is an advocate of the small group as against the large one. In this also we were in complete accord. About my own condition he said nothing at all until he was in the act of leaving the room. He then paused for a moment at the door, and after asking me if I ever played golf on Sundays, told me in effect—I am sorry to say his actual words are quite unquotable—that he would give the people who had raised the question of my sanity a piece of his mind. In the same breath he asked me for his cheque, which our interesting conversation had unfortunately caused me to forget."

Mr. Hotblack was not insensible to the humour of Mr. Hooker's narrative, and at the end could not restrain himself from one of those violent bursts of laughter which are held by purists to indicate a certain want of good breeding.

"In spite of Sir William's boisterous manners," Mr. Hooker proceeded, "he impressed me as a thinker and a humanist. Our conversation had led us on to the affairs of the world at large. Speaking of the 'Great Powers,' as they are called, Sir William insisted that all of them betray symptoms which admit of a clear pathological definition. The malady indicated is an acute *megalomania*. Each of them, he said, exhibits the symptoms in a form peculiar to itself; while the lesser units contract it from the greater by imitation, or unconscious mimicry, some of the worst cases arising in this way. Six forms of national megalomania can be identified in Europe, and a seventh in America, all derivatives from a common type, but developing regional or endemic variations, according to race, climate or other conditions. The diagnosis is best established by a study of the foreign policies of the Powers affected, the signs of mental alienation being much more marked on this field than in domestic affairs. The difficulty, however, is not with the diagnosis, which is simple, but with the treatment. The nature of this malady, it appears, is to reinforce itself by association and contiguity among the patients. It is therefore essential to keep them apart from one another; the consequence of bringing them together being that they egg one another on, until at last their mania breaks out into criminal insanity—of which Sir William gave several examples from the recent history of Europe. Unfortunately no means can be found for isolating the Powers, great or small, which have contracted the disease, the tendency of the times being all the other way; this it is that renders effective treatment extraordinarily difficult. The difficulty reaches its height in the imitative outbreaks of the malady among the smaller units, which are sometimes disguised under claims for self-determination. Sir William wound up by pointing out the distinction between national megalomania and patriotism. Megalomania is patriotism in the state of degeneration and incipient decay, or, more simply, patriotism gone mad. He thinks that the degeneration of the one thing into the other has come about through the enormous growth in the magnitude of modern States."

"The Chief has a saying to the same effect," said Mr. Hotblack: " 'Power drives nations mad.' "

"I found Sir William an ardent advocate of international *co-operation*," Mr. Hooker went on, "but utterly sceptical as to international *government*. He regards the project as an attempt to set up democracy in a madhouse."

"As a compact between *Powers* it can be nothing else," said Mr. Hotblack, "a mere arrangement for pooling the toxin which maddens them all. But that is not the only conception of the League of Nations. Mr. Rumbelow has another. A world which cannot be organized on the basis of power may yet be organized in other ways. But proceed, sir, if you please. Sir William's opinions on this matter are of profound interest to a psychologist."

"He regards the world of international politics as a Bedlam, in which the sane elements dance to the tunes played by the megalomaniacs," said Mr. Hooker. "His contempt for the corporate intelligence of States is almost boundless. Of course he instanced the war as the outstanding proof. But beyond that he mentioned a long list of 'symptoms,' as he called them, all pointing to criminal insanity in States. One thing struck me with peculiar force. In the course of his attack on the group-mind he brought up the question of prisons—institutions, Mr. Hotblack, which I have long held in the utmost abhorrence. He declared with great vehemence that the crimes which States commit against their subjects in prisons outweigh all the crimes for which the law-breakers are punished."

"As a psychologist I support him," interposed Mr. Hotblack. "I should not be surprised to learn, sir, that in speaking of prisons Sir William used the word 'hell' with considerable emphasis."

"He did," replied Mr. Hooker, "but I have not thought it necessary to quote his expletives."

"In this instance," said Mr. Hotblack, "the word was more than an expletive. Has it ever occurred to you, sir, that our prison-system has received its ultimate sanction from the idea of an eternal prison, where a lawyer's God torments the souls of his rebellious subjects for ever and ever? I should like to have your opinion on that point."

"I have not the least doubt," replied Mr. Hooker, "that hell and prison are connected institu-

AN INTUITION VERIFIED

.tions. Which is derived from which is difficult to say. I take them as variant expressions of the same idea—twin diabolisms, one might call them. But you have just used a phrase, Mr. Hotblack, which arrests me. You spoke of a 'lawyer's God.' What exactly do you mean by that?"

"I mean," said the psychologist, "the Deity whose attributes are suggested in 'God save the King,' which accurately represents the popular conception of the Divine Nature, as it exists not in this country alone but in all countries which have contracted the megalomania referred to by Sir William Timbertree. This conception of God had its origin in military necessities, and was subsequently elaborated by pact-making conquistadors, to consolidate their conquests and to prepare for new ones—a soldier's child and a lawyer's nursling. In the broad outlines of its structure the whole theology of the West reveals the lawyer's mind, Hebraic or Roman as the case may be, completing the work of the military conqueror. The religious mind has had far less to do with these things than is commonly supposed. Instead of originating its own theology, the religious mind has had to adapt itself as best it could, and always at a great loss, to forms of thought laid down for it by the lawyers of conquering states. Had Western civilization devoted its energies to Beauty and Joy, instead of to Power and Wealth, not one of the creeds would be in existence; men would have thought more nobly of God and of the universe, and would have dealt more kindly one with another. I may remind you, sir, that Moses, from whom Western theology takes its rise, was a lawyer and a conqueror. Beauty and Joy were not on his programme. His daring raid into Palestine, and the appalling atrocities perpetrated by his lieutenant on the inhabitants of the Promised Land, have furnished a model which men of blood and iron have never been slow to imitate; while the Being who directed these butcheries, and sometimes finished them off with his own hands, remains to this day identified in the popular imagination with the Creator and Lawgiver of the universe. In spite of the Greek infusion, which has been considerable, religion, ethics, law and international polity are still dominated by ideas appropriate to the conquest of the Canaanites. What wonder, sir, that 'man's inhumanity to man makes countless millions mourn?' What hope for goodwill among men so long as these stupid and wicked survivals are integral parts of the popular religion?"

"Sir William said much the same thing," replied Mr. Hooker, "though, of course, he phrased it differently. In touching upon my own problem he urged me, above all things, 'to beware of the lawyers,' using language which vividly recalled to my mind some passages of the New Testament I have recently been studying. In spite of the abominable adjective which he invariably placed before his noun, I could not help perceiving that Sir William's attitude towards legalism was essentially the same with that of my Quaker ancestors. The Quakers have never submitted to the censorship of the legal mind."

"Nor will Mr. Rumbelow," added Mr. Hotblack. "The Chief, sir, is no enemy of the law, but

AN INTUITION VERIFIED

he is determined to keep the legalists in their proper place."

"I gathered so much from our last interview," said the millionaire.

"Our last interview," said Mr. Hotblack, "has produced interesting results in several directions. You have told me of one. Permit me to tell you of another. In consequence of a trifling mistake on the part of the listeners who tried to overhear our conversation at the Club, the news was spread about Smokeover that you were backing Joy Lady, a runner in the Grand National, for twenty thousand pounds. Before nightfall all the betting men in the Club, and hundreds of others, were backing the horse of that name for all they were worth, and some for more than they were worth. She lost the race, which nobody in his senses expected her to win. You may imagine the rest. The only consolation Smokeover has is that you, sir, have lost twenty thousand pounds to Rumbelow, Stallybrass & Corker—that, in short, we have thoroughly taken you in."

"It is the first time," said Mr. Hooker with a smile, "that I have known the work of a great poet lead either to a financial disaster or to a scandal. Coleridge can hardly have foreseen that this would result from his fine verses."

"In the regions psychology has to study," replied the other, "my wonder never ceases at the extraordinary combinations of cause and effect that are brought about by what look like the merest accidents. The tricks that are played upon what is called 'the fixed system of natural law' by the reactions upon it of the human mind are, indeed, a perpetual marvel to me. No one who has studied them can doubt for a moment that a sportsmanlike principle is at work in the very constitution of things—a principle, sir, not incapable of playing a practical joke on those who deserve it. Nature—and nature in the proper sense must always include the reactions of the human mind—abhors mechanism. In the last resort, I am convinced, we are dealing with a consummate artist, or, which is the same thing, with a sportsman. There is a subtle and hidden beauty, sir, in these strange concatenations. For my own part I have little doubt that the trifling incident we are now discussing is nothing else than an interlude of comedy, introduced by a master hand into the drama of events. Or shall we say a scherzo, or a weird and lovely dance, breaking and yet maintaining the movement of a majestic symphony? In contemplating these wonderful combinations, Mr. Hooker, I am often reminded of the way an affluent musician plays with his theme, evoking an endless chain of astonishing variations from half a dozen notes."

Here Mr. Hotblack paused, and, with an accuracy of tone which showed that he was no mean musician, hummed and boomed the variations of Beethoven's Sonata in A flat, indicating the time by a gentle movement of his uplifted hand.

Then, quite suddenly, but without any violence of transition, his humming ran on into articulate speech, as though the theme of the sonata and the remarks that followed were all of one piece:

"Indeed, I have become convinced that the whole

entanglement—the seeming entanglement—in which you are now involved, those problems of yours which are moving to their solution in time with the march of events, the strange experiences through which you have recently passed, and the surprising variations of outlook to which they have led—I am convinced, sir, that all this, regarded synoptically, *has a musical structure*. You may wonder what has led me to this conclusion. I will tell you. Acting under Mr. Rumbelow's orders I have given a close professional study to your adventures—if I may so call them—both as a whole and in detail, and have discovered at many points unmistakable signs of orchestration. Mark my words, Mr. Hooker; the end of all this will be *music!* I do not anticipate that you will achieve the regeneration of humanity by any panacea, or set scheme designed for the purpose, which, after all, would only provide a new field of operation for the very evils it sought to cure. But I do anticipate a work of art, a deed that cannot be repeated, a thing of beauty and a joy for ever."

"Mr. Hotblack," said the millionaire, who had followed this flight of fancy with evident pleasure, "I am beginning to suspect that in substance your philosophy is my own. Quite lately I, too, have been led to think that Beauty plays a larger part in determining the actual course of the world than most of our thinkers are aware of—though I must make an exception of Professor Ripplemark. At all events you have introduced incidentally one of the chief topics on which I desire to consult you. You have reminded me of problems still remaining on my hands. Well, sir, I am fully resolved that the disposition of the wealth for which I am responsible shall not be left to the mercy of mechanical methods."

"There is no harm in mechanical methods," interposed Mr. Hotblack, "provided the application of them is entrusted to sportsmanlike hands. Indeed, sir, they are essential."

"I am beginning to understand your dialect," said Mr. Hooker. "It is an interesting experiment in the use of language—a field in which experiment is much to be commended. In the meantime will you be good enough to tell me whether you are familiar —whether the Firm is familiar—with the phrase 'a copartnership of reciprocally interacting personalities'?"

"We are thoroughly familiar with it," said Mr. Hotblack, "though of course it is not the kind of language we employ in the conduct of business. The phrase was coined by Professor Ripplemark. It occurs in *The Moral Will*, a remarkable work, of which Mr. Rumbelow has distributed a hundred copies among the leading members of the Firm. The whole book, sir, supports the combination we have been discussing—the creativeness of the sportsmanlike principle wedded to the efficiency of the mechanical method."

"In which combination," said Mr. Hooker, "everything turns on the individual characters of the interacting personalities."

"Call them sportsmen," interrupted Mr. Hotblack.

"The name is of no consequence."

AN INTUITION VERIFIED

"Pardon me, sir, the name is of great consequence. But please to go on."

"Well, then, the position is this. The wealth at my disposition is far too great to be administered by any single individual. On those terms the problem is frankly insoluble. Everything points to a division of responsibility. This mass of wealth must be broken up, not into a heap of unrelated fragments by giving it to this and that—the usual practice—but by putting it under diversity of administration. A community of wills must be constituted, each of which shall so affirm itself as to help forward the self-affirmation of the others, working for ends that are different, but yet related in the unity of the spirit."

"And in the bond of peace," added Mr. Hotblack. "I understand you perfectly, sir, though, if you will again pardon me, the Firm would render your meaning with less circumlocution. In plain speech, the members of your community must be persons who love one another."

"You anticipate my thought," continued the millionaire. "Mr. Hotblack, I need hardly explain to you, as a psychologist, that in my present position I am an epitome of civilization, the summary of a world which has suddenly grown rich and has yet to learn what riches are for. Moreover, I am not the rightful owner of what I possess. It is full of evil possibilities I cannot control. Any lawyer, any parson, any economist, any vulgar plutocrat, any tub-thumping agitator at a street corner, could tell me what to do with it. But their ways of disposing of wealth are the mere makeshifts of the universal ignorance. Nor can I restore it to those to whom it originally belonged, for the simple reason that they are not to be found. Smokeover has no more right to it than I have. If I give it to the State I give it to the chief waster of the common substance; the State will only have so much more at its disposal when it makes the next war. If I give it to beggars I merely support and countenance the evil conditions of which my present position is the outcome. If I give it to the Ethical Society, morality, like religion, will become professional, institutional, an affair of vested interests and appointments, and so lose the little influence it might otherwise have. If I endow my own opinions, they will degenerate in the hands of the men I have bribed to teach them. At all points I am confronted with an unmanageable task. Human nature was not meant for wealth on this scale; it is a power far too great to be lodged in the hands of any man, even the wisest."

"I am glad to hear," interposed Mr. Hotblack, "that you have no intention of handing your fortune over to the State. There has been a rumour in Smokeover to that effect."

"The State," replied Mr. Hooker, "is in a position analogous to my own, handling wealth on a scale which it lacks intelligence to cope with, and setting its subjects a most pernicious example in the spending of it—the very type of a dangerous multi-millionaire. Sir William Timbertree referred to this as a crowning instance of the ignorance of the group mind. It astounds me, Mr. Hotblack, to hear the agitators demanding that I should surrender my

AN INTUITION VERIFIED

fortune to the State. But how are the eyes of the public to be opened?"

"Education, sir! education!" said Mr. Hotblack, taking time to consider his answer and pronouncing the words with great emphasis. "But we have a long furrow to plough."

"I observe," replied Mr. Hooker, "that you said 'we.' Has the Firm any interest in education?"

"It has become the ruling passion of Mr. Rumbelow's life, as it has always been that of My Lady's. He regards the present movement for education as the most fascinating and promising gamble on which the human race has ever embarked."

"We have come to my second point sooner than I expected," said Mr. Hooker, referring to a notebook. "Mr. Hotblack, I have long been meditating on these lines. But this morning an incident occurred in this household—it was connected with the man who has been waiting on us at table—which brought my thoughts to a sudden focus. My mind is now irrevocably made up. I shall devote my fortune, for the time it remains at my disposal, to the cause of education."

"Good!" cried Mr. Hotblack.

"But I shall do it in my own way."

"Good again!"

"I shall work through a copartnership of reciprocally interacting personalities."

"Better than ever."

"My plan is to form a community of three."

"A well-chosen number, sir! When communities are composed of more than three persons, or five at most, the psychological conditions are apt to deteriorate. Three is an awkward number in affairs of the heart but the best for effective co-operation. Yes, the best number for a company of gentleman adventurers. But see to it, sir, that all three are sportsmen at heart! Everything else turns upon that."

"We have reached the critical question," said Mr. Hooker, drawing his chair close to the psychologist. "We mentioned just now the name of Professor Ripplemark. Mr. Rumbelow knows him? Speak low, sir."

"Mr. Rumbelow is in touch with all that is most adventurous in the mind of the age. He knows Professor Ripplemark well."

"Ha!" said Mr. Hooker; then with a glance round the room, "I am not altogether easy in my mind, Mr. Hotblack. There may be listeners about. Come further from the door; we are too near the keyhole. The names I am about to mention must not be overheard, nor supposed to be the names of horses. A profound secrecy is essential. This is no time for the Invisible Powers to amuse themselves."

The two now shifted their position, drew up their chairs in close proximity to one another at either side of a small round table, and with bent brows and eager faces attacked the crisis of their discussion; but in tones so subdued that the Immortals who report these dialogues could hear no more than the stray ejaculations, or rather explosions, in which the pent-up enthusiasm of Mr. Hotblack found relief.

AN INTUITION VERIFIED

It was abundantly evident that Mr. Hooker's plans had the warm approval of the psychologist. Towards the end he had some difficulty in restraining himself. Finally, when a gesture from Mr. Hooker indicated that the matter was concluded, he sprang from his seat, grasped the millionaire by the hand and threw caution to the winds.

"Let me congratulate you again, sir," he cried; "let me congratulate you in the name of the Firm on the most brilliant conception that ever originated in the mind of a millionaire! A stroke of genius, sir! A work of art in the true sense of the term! I would not have believed that any mind save one was capable of creating such a masterpiece—so daring in motive, so farseeing in aim, so harmonious in design. Worthy of the Chief himself, sir, and what more can I say? You have caught the very spirit of the Firm! You are establishing a new point of contact with the invisible world! Your action will reverberate through the ages! Your name will be linked with the Chief's!"

Mr. Hotblack said more in the same strain, until at last, with a scarcely perceptible transition and as though he could find no other mode of expressing himself, he wound up his rhapsody by reciting, once more, the lines which had brought disaster to the racing fraternity of Smokeover.

Mr. Hotblack's enthusiasm had ended on a note so high that for some minutes Mr. Hooker, who was deeply moved, found it impossible to resume the conversation. He had no alternative but to wait until he had himself under control, and until Mr. Hotblack, who had been pacing the room during his recitation like a man possessed, had subsided into a chair. At last he ventured to say:

"I can tell you an interesting fact regarding the poem you have just recited. I learnt it from Sir William Timbertree. The poem was a favourite with his mother. She repeated it constantly on her deathbed, and died with the last lines on her lips."

"I am aware of it," replied Mr. Hotblack. "A fact of profound psychological significance, and one, I assure you, that has not been overlooked by the Department of the Firm over which I have the honour to preside. Mr. Hooker, I have no right to obtrude my own affairs on your notice, but I can hardly refrain at the moment from divulging a domestic detail. I have left instructions sir, with Mrs. Hotblack, who will probably survive me, that those lines are to be inscribed on my tomb. They will strike a new note in Smokeover Cemetery."

Here Mr. Hotblack, who was trembling with excitement, frankly broke down. Then, with an effort, and as though excusing himself, he went on:

"You must understand, sir, that the service on which I am engaged is hardly compatible with a long life. Psychology, to a man who .kes it in earnest, is an exhausting vocation—the most important but the most neglected of all the sciences, despised and rejected by the powers that pretend to rule the world. Yes, sir, it is an uphill fight. But no matter! I serve a great master, and am willing that nothing should be remembered of me save the spirit in which I served him. It has been the spirit of joy, sir—the spirit in which I have faced the odds of this world, and hope, with Sir William Timber-

AN INTUITION VERIFIED

tree's mother, to face the odds of the next. Those lines express it."

At this unexpected self-revelation Mr. Hooker was visibly affected, and he, too, had some emotion to suppress.

"I perceive, Mr. Hotblack," he said, "that you are guided by a star."

"I am, sir; and it shines on My Lady's forehead."

"I have seen it," said the millionaire in a solemn voice.

There was another pause, broken at last by Mr. Hooker.

"I have to thank you," he said, "for giving me to-night the information that makes me sure of my ground."

At these words Mr. Hotblack's countenance resumed its businesslike expression.

"One thing only remains," he replied. "The Firm must immediately compute the odds on the success of what you propose to undertake. The necessary data are all in my office and they shall be passed on to the relevant Departments to-morrow. But I must warn you, Mr. Hooker"—and here his tone became exceedingly grave—"*that the odds may turn out against you.*"

"That will not affect my resolution in the smallest degree."

"Nor the value of what you propose."

"Nor the value of what I propose," repeated Mr. Hooker. Then, changing his tone: "And now, Mr. Hotblack, our business being at an end I suggest that you and I drink a glass of wine together."

A moment later the psychologist and the millionaire were pledging each other in a draught of incomparable madeira.

As they deposited their empty glasses the distant clock of Smokeover Cathedral struck twelve.

Next morning Mr. Hooker was in Oxford.

CHAPTER THREE

Professor Ripplemark is put to the Question

IT has been said, by an earlier Voice, that Mr. Hooker's interesting problems had penetrated to the Common Rooms of our ancient Universities, where they had been provocative of much discussion, grave and gay. The Regius Professor of Virtue was, of course, well abreast of the controversy. He had propounded several methods for extricating Mr. Hooker from his difficulties, which, to say the least of them, were somewhat unusual in the circumstances; and more than once he had startled the audience in the Common Room by asserting that the problem was, in essence, "a sporting proposition." To which his argumentative colleagues had immediately replied by challenging him to define his terms.

Now Professor Maurice Ripplemark was notoriously careless in the definition of terms, a failing which nearly caused the Regius Professorship to go to his opponent, a gentleman seventy-three years of age, famous the world over as a master of Definition.

And this indeed would have happened had not one of Ripplemark's supporters, a fervent disciple of Aristotle, put in a powerful plea, enforced by quotations from the original Greek, in which he argued that *Valour* was an essential qualification in a Professor of *Virtue*, and that no moralist was fitted to hold such a position, least of all among the young men (and the young women) of Oxford, unless he had shown evidence of a strong nerve, a stout heart, a clear head, an iron will and a complete disregard for his personal safety—as Ripplemark had, and as the septuagenarian had not. This argument, which profoundly impressed the august powers responsible for the appointment, carried the day.

But Ripplemark had not been long in office before he began to give evidence of his failing. When the Hooker question came up, the language he flung about the University was so loose and vague as almost to constitute an academic scandal. Again and again the attempt was made to force from him a precise statement of what he meant by "a sporting proposition." This he obstinately refused to give, asserting that the phrase represented an ultimate and self-evident category of thought, which might explain other things but could not itself be explained. And he would always end by expressing some surprise that the University of Oxford, of all institutions in the world, could have any doubts as to the meaning of the phrase—a remark which gave some offence.

It was clearly needful to bring the Professor to book on this matter. So the University Contention Club, whose rule it was to discuss a practical problem once in seven years, invited him to read a paper on the subject in a lecture room of one of the Colleges, under the title: "What ought Mr. Hooker to do with his millions?"

Ripplemark recognized the sportsmanlike character of the invitation and responded in kind by immediate consent. Whereupon the wits of the Club, of whom there were several, began sharpening their swords and preparing their impromptus; and there was every prospect of a very lively debate.

And so, at the very moment when Mr. Hooker was in the act of ordering his thumb-marked copy of *The Moral Will* to be soaked in petrol and burned with fire, the author of the book was engaged in composing a discourse upon Mr. Hooker, and he was still so engaged when the millionaire's telegram arrived proposing an interview. With this also Ripplemark closed at once. He was naturally startled by the coincidence. But his experience in the war had taught him not to be greatly surprised at anything. However, a surprise was in store for him.

Mr. Hooker, who had recently been learning to be interested in persons as well as in principles, spent some time on the journey to Oxford in trying to form a mental image of the kind of man Ripplemark might be. So far he had nothing to go upon except *The Moral Will* and the particulars in *Who's Who*. Neither was sufficient for clear vision. There were several chapters in *The Moral Will* which were not incompatible with a seasoned maturity; but there were others that betrayed the love of danger that goes with the inexperience of youth. So Mr. Hooker's visualizations were confused. Now he would see before him a very lively young gentleman; now a prematurely old one; the first would vanish on his remembering that Ripplemark was Regius Professor of Virtue; the second on his remembering that he was a "V.C." There was nothing for it but to wait for objective evidence.

Professor Ripplemark received the millionaire in his college rooms. The man whom Hooker saw before him might be thirty-five years of age. He was erect without being stiff, his head finely poised on a muscular neck. He wore an air of cheerful vitality which—as a cynic once said of him—would have been more befitting in a Professor of Vice. Intense activity was bespoken at every point of his lithe figure; thought sat upon a clear brow; the eye was large and liquid as a poet's. At a glance you saw the high temper of the man, and thought, perhaps, of a glittering blade wrought of the finest Damascus steel. You saw also that Ripplemark was wise; but wise rather after the manner of the serpent, with its fatal spring, than of the owl with its dismal profundity and melancholy flight. That a man so débonnaire and radiant, so formidable and yet so attractive, should profess Virtue by a King's command, would have seemed natural to a Greek of the time of Alcibiades, or perhaps to an Englishman in the merry days of Charles II; but to the men of this generation, born under the grey, it was something of a portent and an astonishment. Can you wonder, then, that Mr. Hooker, in spite of his firm faith in a connexion between Virtue and Happiness, gave a slight start of surprise at his first vision of the Regius Professor?

"You are Professor Ripplemark — Professor *Maurice* Ripplemark?" he asked, the thought suddenly occurring that possibly there might be two of them.

THE PROFESSOR QUESTIONED

The Professor smiled. "I see, sir," he said, "you expected Virtue to have a more venerable representative. But the Universities have changed greatly since the war. The ring of octogenarians is being broken up, and there is less intolerance towards young men. Virtue, also, is less dismal that it was, and there is a dare-devil element even in education."

"I congratulate you," said Mr. Hooker, "on your appointment, which I hear was vigorously contested. I congratulate the University. I congratulate the nation. And I congratulate the King. You have made a fine beginning, Professor. And you have begun at the right end—the Moral Will. The essential thing in philosophy—is it not?—is to get the right opening, to know where to begin. I hope you are going to follow it up."

Ripplemark said to himself: "So he is not going to be a bore after all." Then aloud:

"I wrote that book, Mr. Hooker, before the war —save for one chapter. But I have learnt much since then. And, as you say, I must follow it up. But I perceive you are a student of philosophy."

"Yes," answered Hooker, "I am what some people call a tainted philosopher. A philosopher tainted with business, and now still more deeply tainted with money. There are those who think I know nothing about business; you will probably think that I know less about philosophy. Meanwhile the world calls me a profiteer. Not an easy position."

"An interesting combination," said Ripplemark. "And one with great possibilities."

"I am glad you see that," said Hooker, speaking with great eagerness. "You interpret my own thought. By the way—forgive me for asking—do you know anything about business?"

"Hardly in your sense. Of course I have read Political Economy. But I have no experience in the handling of money on a large scale, which is a defect in a Professor of Virtue. The moral problems of our time, sir, turn on the handling of money more than on anything else. Say what they will, money is the raw material, so to speak, with which the Moral Will has to deal. But in business you have the advantage of me."

"Let us look into that," said Hooker. "Naturally you have had no business training in the ordinary sense. But you have served in the war. You know the importance of organization, discipline, exactitude, scientific method."

Ripplemark wondered what he was driving at. He was silent for a few moments, reflecting that he would test the millionaire with generalities and make sure of his ground before getting further involved.

"Oh yes," he said, "of course I was in the war—did my bit like the rest of us. And I learnt a good many things that will prove useful in my profession. For example——"

"In what branch of the Service were you?" interrupted Hooker.

"I was in the infantry to begin with, and then transferred to the Flying Corps."

"Ha!" cried the other, going off at a tangent. "I had a son in the Flying Corps. He was killed." And he began to give particulars. Did Professor Ripplemark happen to have met his son? No.

"Naturally," Hooker went on, "I feel an interest

THE PROFESSOR QUESTIONED

in all flying men. I hope you won't mind my saying that it forms a link between you and me."

"You are extremely kind to say so. The link holds reciprocally. The father of a flying man who was killed—well, my own father is living, and I, too, happen to be alive."

Here there was a slight emotional disturbance on the part of Mr. Hooker, which brought the conversation to a pause. Ripplemark, breaking the silence at a venture, began to talk disconnectedly.

"Flying, Mr. Hooker, is no bad training for a philosopher. It's good for your psychology, helps you to see things in perspective, accustoms you to the unexpected, teaches you the meaning of decision —and a lot more besides. For example: your valuation of the planet is quite different when you are 15,000 feet above from what it is when you are on the surface. It might almost be said to alter your sense of relative values. A man should fly, sir, before he graduates in philosophy. Or failing that, let him study astronomy. Astronomy achieves the same result in another form—a powerful solvent of limitations and a terrible corrector of human pride—'just dreadful,' as Carlyle said."

"You said just now," broke in Hooker, "that *The Moral Will* was written before the war. Do you still stand by it?"

"Yes; but only as an introduction to the subject. I emphasized that. As you said, the book needs to be followed up."

"It is the following up that I am interested in," replied Mr. Hooker, "and I will return to that in a moment. In the meantime I would ask a question.

That chapter in which you say that a man's will, though not *private*, is yet *all his own*—your experience in the Flying Corps has not altered that?"

"On the contrary; that is precisely what flying has confirmed. If a man wants to discover whether or no he has a will of his own, let him fly, Mr. Hooker; let him fly over the German lines with a hostile squadron in pursuit of him. You can understand, sir, that you are then in a position where you can't consult anybody: neither your lawyer, nor your doctor, nor your father confessor, nor your commander-in-chief. Of course you may consult God. Some do. But consulting God is only another name for reinforcing your own independence. You act on your own initiative and take your risk. And there you have the meaning of life focussed to a point. Life, Mr. Hooker, consists in the facing of risks. I said that in my book."

"That," replied Hooker, "is a view of life which has only recently appealed to me. Perhaps I have something important yet to learn about it. By the way, do you possess an aeroplane at the present time?"

"No; but I can always get the use of one."

"Then I wish," said Hooker with a smile, "that one day you would take me for a flight."

Professor Ripplemark seemed amused. "I wonder," he thought, "if that is what he has been driving at all the time. However, I will put him off."

"You are taking more risks than you know, Mr. Hooker," he said. "But I am afraid the experiment would not be satisfactory. To make it complete you ought to take *me* for a flight, not I you. And then

THE PROFESSOR QUESTIONED

—over the German lines, and with a hostile squadron in pursuit. We could hardly reproduce that."

"I am not so sure," said the millionaire. "Before the talk is over you may find, Professor, that I am taking *you* for a flight, a pretty dangerous one, too; certainly at a great altitude and with a horde of little minds in pursuit of us. But you must understand that I am a lonely man—isolated from others by circumstances which you can imagine—and such men are subject to strange fancies. But leave that aside and let us come to the object of my visit. Do you happen by any chance to be acquainted with my friend, Mr. Arthur Rumbelow?"

"I know him well," said Ripplemark, "and I honour him as one of the greatest of men. We were together in the same hospital in France, and I count the accident that threw us together the most fortunate event of my life. But I am surprised, sir, to hear you call him your friend."

Paying no heed to the last words Hooker went on:

"Were you with him in the hospital ship that was torpedoed?"

"I was."

"Were you an eyewitness of the saving of his life?"

Ripplemark sprang to his feet.

"Then you know Margaret Wolfstone!" he cried.

"Calmly," said Hooker; "tell me what you saw."

"He and I were thrown out on the same side of the ship; both of us were drowning; I called to her for help; she saw me and heard me, but she went after him and left me to my chances."

"And the inference?" asked Hooker, in a fierce tone.

"She is one of the noblest of women!" cried Ripplemark.

Mr. Hooker's expression softened immediately.

"And you know what has happened to her?" he asked.

"A work of hell!" said Ripplemark. "Mr. Hooker, if you have any sympathy with the people who attacked her, may I ask you to end this interview at once."

"I have none," said Hooker. "Professor Ripplemark, there is here an extraordinary convergence of different minds. Your own and mine move to the same point. Your book revealed it and your words confirm it. Miss Wolfstone is my dearest and most trusted friend. Were I to die to-morrow she would be my heiress."

"Good God!"

Ripplemark stood aghast, and Hooker perceiving the shock his words had produced, wished he could recall them. For a few moments both men were at a loss for speech.

"Mr. Hooker," said Ripplemark, "you have brought me evil tidings—evil, at least, to this extent, that they place *me* in a very difficult position."

A light began to dawn upon Hooker's mind, more perhaps from the tone of Ripplemark's voice than from the words themselves. But he was not sure. He resolved to test the ground.

"You mean," he said, "that Margaret Wolfstone, as what she was, is one person: Margaret Wolfstone, as my heiress, another?"

THE PROFESSOR QUESTIONED

"I mean percisely that," said Ripplemark.

Mr. Hooker needed no further assurance. Doubt gone, he plunged ahead.

"You have said, Professor Ripplemark, that what I last told you places you in a difficult position. Will you allow me to be the means of your extrication?"

Here Ripplemark, for some reason the other could not divine, broke into a hearty peal of laughter.

"Pardon me, Mr. Hooker," he said, "the situation is most extraordinary. At the moment of your entering this room I was engaged in an attempt to extricate *you* from a difficulty. And now you are proposing to extricate *me* from one of my own which, if it is not presumptuous to say so, is almost as great as any of yours."

"You are speaking in riddles," said Hooker; "I must ask you to solve them."

Ripplemark then told him what had happened: of the challenge he had received as Regius Professor to take up the much-talked-of problem; of the debate that was due in a few days.

When the recital was over the two men were in high spirits and for the next five minutes there was enough laughter on both sides to make the conversation quite incoherent. When things had settled down Hooker said:

"It is an unexpected opportunity for each of us to illustrate your doctrine of 'reciprocally interacting personalities.' I give you a free hand to extricate me from my difficulties as best you can. And now, seriously, will you allow me to extricate you from yours in my own way?"

"That depends on how you propose to do it."

"Listen, then. You spoke just now, Professor, of taking sudden decisions. Are you prepared to take one now?"

"Yes. But I should like to see first where we are going to alight."

"You must hear a long story first; but you will find it useful in the preparation of your paper. The disposition of my wealth during my lifetime has still to be determined. Were it not for the friends I have discovered it would be an intolerable burden. I had a wife; sorrow broke her; she is dead. My three sons were killed. I am, save for my friends, alone."

He went on at some length. Very rapidly, but omitting nothing that was relevant, he told the story of his life, bringing it down to the very moment when he found himself face to face with Ripplemark. When he had done he said, without waiting for any comment on his story,

"And now, Professor Ripplemark, for the precise mode in which I propose to extricate you from your difficulty. Will you go into *business* with me, into partnership, giving up your Professorship for that purpose if it should be found necessary?"

"Certainly not!" said Ripplemark, with a look of amusement on his face. "Nothing would induce me to take such a step. You have told me a profoundly moving story, Mr. Hooker, but this that you propose is no way out of your difficulties nor out of mine. I know nothing of business."

For a moment Ripplemark thought, as so many others had done, that the millionaire was beside him—

self. But Hooker gave him no time to indulge his doubts.

"You refuse to go into business with *me*," he said. "Then will you go into business with *me and Miss Wolfstone?*"

"That I will," cried Ripplemark, "if you can show me how it is to be done! *What* business? What will you make, what goods will you sell, and who will buy them?"

"In the Kingdom of Ends," said Hooker, "they neither buy nor sell; but, by Heaven, they do business!"

"That savours of Rumbelow," said Ripplemark, "and it is profoundly true. But it is you who now speak in riddles. Resolve them, Mr. Hooker."

"Have you not written in your book," said Hooker, "that there comes a point in the history of every philosophical system when it must either be translated into action or dismissed as false? I ask you to go into partnership with me and with Miss Wolfstone on the very lines indicated in your own book."

"I confess, Mr. Hooker," the other said, "that your main idea—that of translating the Moral Will from a book theory into a social force—appeals to me strongly. But the form you have given it is novel and bewildering—something of a bombshell to an academic mind. In this University we study the Moral Will for the purpose of passing examinations, obtaining Professorships and scoring off one another in argument. Ours to *understand* the Moral Will or write books about it, not to *make* it."

Since the manifestation of Dr. Jekyll and Mr.

Hyde the phenomenon of dual personality surprises nobody. Let no sceptic bark therefore when he learns that at this moment there were *three* persons in the room. There was Hooker, the millionaire; there was Ripplemark, LL.D.; and there was Ripplemark, V.C.

It was Ripplemark LL.D. who had made the last remark. It was Ripplemark V.C. who made the next, and the next after that.

"And yet the Moral Will ought to be created as well as talked about. Show me how to do it, Mr. Hooker. This 'business' you speak of—what is it? Tell me plainly."

Then, as though a sudden inspiration had come to him, he cried out in a voice of enthusiasm:

"Is it Education?"

"How can it be anything else," said Hooker, "since Margaret Wolfstone is one of the partners?"

"Go on, sir! Go on!" cried Ripplemark.

"Miss Wolfstone will be in Oxford next week."

"I know it! For the Educational Conference. We insisted on asking her as a protest against the action of those villains. And that play she has begun to write will be a big thing, Mr. Hooker!"

"I'm going to back it—the first deliberate gamble of my life. But a moral gamble, if ever there was such a thing."

"There are thousands of them!" cried Ripplemark. "A hundred to one on Margaret Wolfstone! I'm glad you've taken it on, sir! The Moral Will Handicap and Margaret Wolfstone the favourite!"

THE PROFESSOR QUESTIONED

"You speak a strange language for a Professor of Virtue," said Hooker.

"Metaphors," said Ripplemark, checking himself. "The truth is, my mind is rather full of the subject just now. As you know, the love of gambling is a tremendous force in modern civilization. I am investigating its relations to the Moral Will, and I assure you that the results are of profound interest. I hope to deal with it fully in my forthcoming book. But don't be alarmed, sir. Remember that by your own confession you have been gambling yourself."

Here Mr. Hooker began to smile at his own thoughts. He was thinking of the report recently spread about Smokeover that he was backing "Joy Lady" for twenty thousand pounds. And he remembered Mr. Hotblack's comments on the incident. He was about to mention the coincidence when he suddenly recollected that "Joy Lady" had lost the race, and feeling that this would spoil the story, he resolved to say nothing about it.

"Yes," he said, still smiling, "it's hardly an expression I should have used to the Society of Ethical Culture. But I see we understand one another. And now to the matter in hand. Clearly before we go further Miss Wolfstone must be consulted. You consent to meet her?"

"Certainly," said the V. C.

"Well, then, this day week we three will meet in my private room at the Mitre Hotel."

"An admirable proposition."

"Then let me prepare you for the broad outlines of what is coming. You and Miss Wolfstone will have before you a business proposition, in the sense in which business is done in the Kingdom of Ends. You understand me?"

"Perfectly."

"Assuming that you and Miss Wolfstone consent, you will become my partners on a footing of equality. My fortune will be divided into three equal parts, and each of us will have the free disposition of his own. We form a community of three with mutual loyalty as the only law of our relations. Think that out in the light of what you have written in *The Moral Will.*"

And with that Mr. Hooker rose quickly from his seat, grasped the Regius Professor by the hand and said "Good-bye."

The Professor flung himself down in his armchair and lit his pipe: Ripplemark LL.D. astounded and incredulous; Ripplemark V. C. alert, eager and believing; and the two fell into hot debate. Meanwhile Hooker, passing through the quad, was murmuring in half-audible tones: "Complications certainly. But that will only strengthen the alliance."

CHAPTER FOUR

Professor Ripplemark is Extricated from a Difficulty

THE proceedings at the Conference on Educational Reform were reported at no great length in the daily press. Half a column *per diem* was all the editors could spare, the bulk of their space being required for international politics, the state of the markets and the debates in Parliament. But it may well be doubted whether this distribution of space showed a true sense of relative values. Had a Victor Hugo been present, first to follow the proceedings of the Conference on Education, and then to spend a week in attending the debates in Parliament, he would probably have said, in the words of the priest of *Notre Dame,* "*ceci tuera cela.*"

The men and women who attended the Conference were in earnest; most of them were persons of great ability; idealists, full of enthusiasm, of hope and of faith. Among them were the great pundits of educational theory gathered from all parts of the world, for the Conference was international, a true League of Nations, though called by another name. There were Professors from the Universities and a crowd of teachers, of both sexes, from public, private, secondary, elementary and technical schools. Youth and age were here fellow-workmen; male and female were one soul. The note of a great revival was in the air and only the spiritually dead could fail to hear it.

On the day preceding the Conference Miss Wolfstone, who had taken lodgings in the north of Oxford, found a letter from Mr. Hooker awaiting her on the breakfast table. She read as follows:

"My dear Margaret,

"Like 'the Three Wise Men' in your Christmas Play I have spent much of my life in a vain search for 'my neighbour.' Recently I have found him, or rather I have found *four*. First I found you, the nearest of them all; then I found Rumbelow and My Lady; and within the last few days I have found Professor Ripplemark. All four I can honestly claim to love as I love myself; and, to tell the truth, I love myself not a little. I wish all five of us could meet at once and proceed to do to each other as each would that the others should do to him —neglecting the rest of the world for the time being. But since that is impossible at the moment I propose a Council of Three—you, Professor Ripplemark and myself. We have business to transact in the Kingdom of Ends. Will you join us, dear friend, in my private room at the Mitre Hotel next Thursday? We three can then knock our heads together according to the Hegelian formula, Thesis, Antithesis and Synthesis. Which is which we must leave to be determined by the course of events. The situation should appeal to your dramatic instincts."

For some minutes after reading this letter Miss Wolfstone stood quite still, a bright light in her eyes, thinking rapidly. She looked at her watch:

EXTRICATED FROM ONE DIFFICULTY

it was half-past seven. Leaving the breakfast untouched she put on her hat and went out. Half an hour's walk brought her to Mr. Blackwell the bookseller's shop, where the boy was just opening the door; nobody else was about.

"I want *The Moral Will*, by Maurice Ripplemark," she said.

The boy, astonished by so early a customer and bewildered by a proposition outside "his station and its duties," went searching among the shelves. "What did you say was the name of the book, Miss?" he cried from the other end of the shop.

"*The Moral Will.*"

The boy went on searching, and presently took down a second-hand copy of *Jones on the Making of a Will*, as the nearest thing he could find. But when he came back to offer it to his customer she was gone. She had found *The Moral Will* for herself and left the money on the counter.

All day she sat close in her room reading the book, oblivious for the time being of the Conference on Educational Reform. She read on for hours, never flagging. She read on into the small hours of the next morning. When she had done she closed the book with the single exclamation "Good!" Then she wrote a brief note to Mr. Hooker, accepting the appointment and adding this remark only:

"In all these things I cannot help thinking that you and I and the rest of our 'neighbours' have fallen under a spell, and that Billie Smith is the wizard. Or is it Plato? In either event the important thing is, as Socrates says, that the just should act upon it."

At the session of the Conference which took place

next day it had been arranged that Miss Wolfstone was to speak. The subject was "Democracy and Education." No sooner had her name been called by the Chairman than the whole audience rose to its feet and cheered tumultuously for three minutes. The audience had its reasons for that. When it was over, Hooker, who was seated next to Ripplemark, turned to his companion with tears streaming down his face and said:

"These people are my people, Professor. The Lord do so to me and more also if aught save death shall part between them and me!"

The summary of Miss Wolfstone's speech as reported next morning in the *Times* ran thus:

"The mission of democracy is to enthrone education as the supreme business of mankind, and to place all the other interests of society in their proper order beneath it. When democracy has accomplished this task its mission will be fulfilled, and it will give way to a mightier than itself. The form of education is aristocratic. Education presupposes the eternal difference between wisdom and folly, between ignorance and knowledge, between the good and the very good, in the last resort the difference between the best and the worst. That spells aristocracy—the aristocracy that is rooted in the constitution of the world and in the nature of the human mind. Aristocracy, impossible as a form of government, is a necessary principle of education, the one and only solution of the problem of *power*, which a thousand political experiments have not yet solved, and which, indeed, is insoluble on political ground.

EXTRICATED FROM ONE DIFFICULTY

Education can never be carried on by a plebiscite of the taught. The wisdom of the teacher cannot be ruled by the vote of the pupil."

As Miss Wolfstone descended from the platform an oldish man, with a lean figure, unmistakably a hard-worked schoolmaster, rose suddenly to his feet near the middle of the Hall. He was a stutterer and, labouring as he was under great excitement, found himself unable to articulate a word. For many seconds—to those who watched him it seemed an age—he stood mouthing, writhing, gesticulating, and finally sobbing in the agony of his speechlessness—a grotesque but terrible apparition. At last the pent-up energy released itself in a great shout, which burst out of him all in a moment, and rang like a trumpet in every corner of the building. "For God's sake, sir, ask that lady to go on!" But the next speaker had already been called and the oratory resumed its course.

After the meeting it was observed that Miss Wolfstone made her way to the stutterer and they two went out together.

The place of meeting for "the Council of Three" was in a room overlooking the Oxford High Street.

Miss Wolfstone, arriving five minutes before the time, found the room empty. So she stood at the window, looking at the stream of bicycles passing up and down the street and thinking how like they were to shoals of fishes swimming in opposite directions.

Suddenly two cyclists, an undergraduate and a girl, collided at the corner of the street opposite, and went sprawling in the roadway on the top of their machines. A third cyclist immediately ran into the heap, and for a moment it seemed as if the double current would pile itself up into a mountain of protruding wheels and struggling humanity.

Miss Wolfstone was out into the street in a flash; only to find that it was all over, everybody apologizing to everybody else and offering to pay damages, while a policeman, note-book in hand, stood benevolently by with no occupation. A girl undergraduate, leaning on a twisted bicycle, her feet entangled in the ruins of a skirt and one side of her face plastered with mud, was assuring an apologetic youth of the same denomination, whose nose was bleeding profusely, that 'it didn't matter in the least.' A butcher's boy, in the best of humour, was extracting a large beefsteak from the middle of the débris, while a middle-aged gentleman in cap and gown, who had been rolled in a mess of smashed eggs, was receiving expert advice from an old lady as to the best method of treating his clothes. In a few moments the crumpled bicycles, the hats and hat-pins, the provisions, the note-books, the spectacles, the fountain pens were collected and distributed to their rightful owners, the entanglement dissolved, the traffic went on as before, and it was as though such a thing had never been.

When Mr. Hooker and Professor Ripplemark entered the room they were astonished to find Miss Wolfstone in the last stages of a violent fit of laughter. She told them what had happened, and then said, turning to Ripplemark:

"If only we could introduce the spirit of that

EXTRICATED FROM ONE DIFFICULTY

girl with the muddy face into the conduct of great affairs, the problem of your 'Moral Will' would soon solve itself."

"Till then there is not much prospect of its being solved at all," he answered. "I agree with you that the Moral Will ought not to take itself too seriously. It can afford to be jolly at times."

"One might almost define it as the will-to-be-jolly," she said; "at least that is the way your undergraduates seem to take it. I had no idea that the spirit of Mark Tapley was so potent in this place."

"I must introduce you," said Ripplemark, "to a select few of our pessimistic dons. I assure you that when some of us discuss the signs of the times all the dogs in the parish begin to howl."

"That explains something that has been puzzling me," said Miss Wolfstone. "Last night, as I was passing your college, I heard the most appalling howls. I thought you must be waking a corpse. Dogs didn't occur to me at the moment. But doubtless you and your pessimistic friends were discussing the signs of the times and the dogs of the parish were making the chorus."

"It was a bump supper," said Ripplemark. "We were giving vent to the high spirits of the 'Moral Will.'"

"Were *you* howling?"

"I was; but in a manner not out of keeping, I trust, with my position."

"So that the principle of your howling might be law universal to all howlers."

"Pardon me—only to howling Professors of

Virtue. Your conception of universality, Miss Wolfstone, is defective."

So they went on: Hooker a silent listener, but well pleased.

Presently they found themselves seated at a square table in the middle of the room; Miss Wolfstone choosing the seat opposite the window, Hooker and Ripplemark at either end.

"And now," said Miss Wolfstone, "let us begin our story from the Arabian Nights. Mr. Hooker is the good Genie, and we the two Poor Fishermen."

"Or rather," said Hooker, "you are two Islands in which I propose to bury my treasure."

At which figure of speech Professor Ripplemark looked puzzled, but said nevertheless:

"Islands are united by the bottom of the sea."

Mr. Hooker now composed his features to a look of the utmost seriousness, yet not so successfully but that a close observer—and there were two in the room—might have seen the faintest trace of a smile flitting from moment to moment about the corners of his sensitive mouth. He also assumed the tone in which he had been wont, in former times, to deliver his annual address to the Ethical Society. But neither was that altogether successful.

"Let us quit the realms of fancy and get to business," he said. "Miss Wolfstone knows that for many years I have tried to govern my actions by a simple rule—'So live that in affirming your own personality you may help others to affirm theirs.' It has affinity to your own doctrine, Professor Ripplemark, as expounded in *The Moral Will*. By a slight change of terms, which would be appropriate

EXTRICATED FROM ONE DIFFICULTY

under certain conditions, we may read the rule thus: 'So live, that in extricating yourself from your own difficulties you may help other people to extricate themselves from theirs.' Now, I happen to be, as you know well, in a great difficulty over the disposition of my wealth, at least for the rest of my lifetime. I have also learnt that Professor Ripplemark is in a great difficulty of another kind"—here the smile could no longer be restrained—"and I have thought out a method of applying my principle to precisely these conditions. I propose to hand over immediately to each of you, with your consent, a third portion of my total wealth, retaining the remaining third in my own hands, and to do this without any conditions whatsoever, leaving you both entirely free to affirm your own personalities in your own ways. I have various other motives, of which I will state only one. My total fortune is far too great for any man to deal with. On general grounds it ought to be broken up into much smaller portions than those which I propose to hand over to you. But the problem of breaking it up into its ultimate units is, of course, only another name for the problem of dealing with it in general. No man is good enough or wise enough to break up a fortune of three millions—for that is what it now amounts to—without incurring responsibilities which he cannot sustain. I propose therefore to proceed by stages, choosing in the first instance two persons, in whom I have complete confidence, to act with me in the process of breaking up, or, if you will, spending these millions. You are the two persons I have chosen, not I assure you without full knowledge of the grounds on which I was acting. In this way the breaking up process will be carried out, according to the principles of Professor Ripplemark's philosophy, by a group of 'reciprocally interacting personalities'—in other words, by a Moral Will. When each of you receives the million you can break it up still further in any manner you choose. The matter merely awaits your consent."

When Mr. Hooker had finished his stiff oration, Miss Wolfstone turned a look of entreaty upon Ripplemark. The entreaty was, "For Heaven's sake, speak first! I am utterly at a loss." Ripplemark himself was in straits no less dire, but Miss Wolfstone's look gave him a subtle joy and put him on his mettle.

"Mr. Hooker," he said, "for some time past I have been scandalizing the University, and jeopardizing my reputation, by maintaining that your problem was essentially a sporting proposition. You have proved it by what you have just said. If I receive your gift I shall regard my own problem exactly as I now regard yours—as a sporting proposition. You must realize that, sir, before going any further."

"I realized that," said Hooker, "on reading your *Moral Will*. It is one of my strongest reasons for making the present proposal. I have learnt from sources which I leave you to imagine, that a sportsmanlike principle is essential to the highest spiritual achievement. But by way of testing whether we are really in accord and understand one another, let me ask if either of you knows precisely how you would apply this wealth?"

EXTRICATED FROM ONE DIFFICULTY

"Yes," said Miss Wolfstone, "I should devote it to the promotion of individual lovingkindness in infinite ways. Forgive me for speaking first, Professor Ripplemark."

"It is your right," he answered.

"But what would *you* do?" she asked.

"I am waiting for you," said the Professor in a low voice.

She turned her clear eyes full upon him and seemed to question his face. "I see," she said, "you want me to explain myself. Well, what are called the big things don't primarily interest me. I love the little ones, and have longed all my life, ever since I was a child, for power and money to look after them. If Mr. Hooker will give me money for that purpose, I will take it, without hesitation, without shame."

"But do you know *how* you would do all these little things?" asked Ripplemark.

"No and yes. No, in the sense that I should have no plan, scheme, theory or fixed idea. Yes, in the sense that I should begin with the first that came, and let the field extend and the items multiply as they would, taking them one by one, and sure that as each one came another would immediately follow. Through the little things I should learn the secrets of the big ones, and perhaps, at the last, might venture to touch some of them, very gently. For example, I should begin with that stutterer who stood up at the Conference the other day—you both saw him—as the one readiest to hand. By the way, I never met a stutterer who was a fool; have you, Professor Ripplemark? No. Well, that man is not a fool. Oh, by no means—but I mustn't talk about him now. I only mean that he is as good a point of departure as any other. I should start with him, and just go about doing what I could, taking my own line with every one, without reference to the Society for this or to the League for that."

"But are you sure," said Ripplemark, "that you would not do more harm than good?"

"Can you tell me of any rule or formula that will guarantee me against doing more harm than good?"

"The best that I know of," said Ripplemark, "is in the thirteenth chapter of First Corinthians. And there are many others. But I can't tell you how to apply any one of them."

"Aye, there's the rub!" cried Miss Wolfstone. "Given the opportunity, I should begin with the applications, and then you, Professor Ripplemark, might deduce the principle of my action when I had done. History first, philosophy afterwards, as you say in your book."

"But do I understand you to mean," said Mr. Hooker, who had been listening with knitted brows, "that you intend to desert the Great Causes of Humanity?"

"That *is* the Great Cause of Humanity," she cried, "in the infinite wonder of its minute particulars! There is no other. All others are of minor importance."

While she was speaking Ripplemark was leaning forward on the table, his hands extended in front of him, and clasped together, his bright eyes gleaming with thought.

EXTRICATED FROM ONE DIFFICULTY

"It seems," he said quietly, "that you attach no importance to the Universality of the Moral Will."

"I take it from the other end," she said. "You expect me to be interested in the Universal Will. I expect the Universal Will to be interested in me. Here I am; if it exists, let it use me. Neither you nor I can apply it. If we try to, we make fools of ourselves. But if it is what it claims to be, let it apply itself. Has the Universal no will of its own? Meanwhile my business is with the stutterer. I know what to do and mean to do it. No doubt the principles are there, and when the thing is done, but not till then, we'll find out what they are. It will be interesting, and perhaps amusing, too."

"I doubt," said Mr. Hooker, speaking in the dry tones of Ethical controversy, "whether you would know quite so clearly what to do with the stutterer if the Great Principles had never been enunciated."

"Be it so," said Miss Wolfstone. "The Great Principles have been enunciated ten thousand times. We are not going to gain much by enunciating them once more. They are here, let them work in whom they will, and meanwhile, instead of talking about them, which only weakens them, let us give them a chance to reveal themselves in action."

"Wait a moment," said Ripplemark; "you are going too fast, Miss Wolfstone, even for a flying man. Don't be so severe on the Principles. You have just stated one of the best known of them all —that of individual lovingkindness."

"There are two kinds of Principles," she answered, "those that can be applied and those that cannot. Mine can."

"Do you mind naming one that cannot?" said Ripplemark.

"The love of Humanity."

"Oh!" cried Mr. Hooker.

"Mr. Hooker," she said, "do *you* love Humanity?"

"Not as much as I ought," answered the millionaire.

"And do *you*, Professor?"

"No," said Ripplemark, "I don't. I have no love to throw away on abstractions."

"Neither does Mr. Hooker. He's far too good a man. He loves his neighbour; and that is the only sort of 'Humanity' that any of us can love."

"And who is our neighbour?" said Ripplemark.

"The one who is *nearest*. The one who comes *next*. The one who lives next door. The one whose landmark is in the next field to yours. Not the generalized anybody, but the particular somebody. The one you understand and call by his first name, not the one you don't understand and call an inhabitant of Kamskatka. In all honesty, does any one of us three *love* the Kamskatkans?"

"I know very well that I don't," said Ripplemark. "I am under no illusions about that." Mr. Hooker was silent.

"You will go too fast," Ripplemark went on, though his manner seemed to say that he wanted to go faster than anybody. "Consider this, Miss Wolfstone. If you begin to pick out the individuals you love, you discover at the same time how many individuals you hate."

"And that is precisely what people hide from

themselves by all these windy phrases. They daren't face their own hard-heartedness. Their soft-headedness to the 'many' makes them hard-hearted to the 'one.' Oh!" she cried, "I loathe it all! So violent, so stupid, so insincere! It ends in nothing but speech-making and iniquity. Let us three get out of that fog."

She spoke with passion, and her voice trembled. Ripplemark was still keeping himself in hand.

"Miss Wolfstone," he said, "I want to ask you a thing. You are writing a drama—you told me so. Has this any connexion with what you have been saying just now?"

"Of course!" she answered. "Why has the world come to its present anarchy? Simply because we have all been playing with ideas we don't understand, tampering with forces we can't control, befogging ourselves with vast generalizations that mean nothing, pretending to care for things to which we are really indifferent, professing to love 'Humanity' or the 'State,' while we despise the man who lives next door—and all the time neglecting the only thing that counts, the only thing your Moral Will can control, the love of our neighbour—the man who comes next, the man whose bicycle runs into yours and sends you sprawling into the middle of the road! That girl with the muddy face! She was immortal, Mr. Hooker! She deserves to be remembered to the end of the world!"

"The sportsmanlike principle once more," said Ripplemark.

"And the thirteenth chapter of First Corinthians," said Miss Wolfstone.

"They are the same. But are we not talking in the air?"

"And where else should an airman be more at home?" she flashed back.

All three joined in the laugh. Mr. Hooker was the first to collect himself.

"Before we proceed further," he said, "I am going to test your reactions. This morning I have received two letters giving me advice—I receive such letters every day. The first assures me that it does not matter what I do with the millions provided my *motives* are good. What do you think of that?"

"Your responsibilities are far too momentous to be covered by imbecilities of that kind," said Ripplemark.

"They are mere verbiage," said Miss Wolfstone.

"Good," replied Hooker. "And now for the other letter. The writer urges me to sell all that I have and give to the poor."

"The writer of that is not sincere," said Miss Wolfstone. "Had he been honest he would have spent his pennies on bread for the poor and not on a postage stamp."

"He would deny it," said Ripplemark. "But his arguments to prove himself sincere would be his crowning insincerity."

"Then I think we may proceed," said Hooker. "In an arrangement of this kind the essentials are secure from the moment the parties have perfect confidence in one another."

"Still," said Ripplemark, "we are not yet on a business-like footing. Forgive me, Miss Wolfstone,

EXTRICATED FROM ONE DIFFICULTY

if I play the cross-examiner again. I asked you a moment ago *how* you meant to do these things. May I ask now *where* you mean to do them?"

"I have a profession," she answered; "and unless I am mistaken, Professor Ripplemark, it is the same as your own. We are both school-teachers."

Ripplemark sprang to his feet.

"That is the deciding word!" he said. "Mr. Hooker, there are two men in me. One would live a life of argumentative futility. The other would act immediately—would begin, with Miss Wolfstone, upon the one who comes next. The last is my deciding self. I accept your offer."

"Is he no more than your *deciding* self?" interrupted Miss Wolfstone. "Because, if he is no more than that, *I* shall refuse."

"I think he is more," said Ripplemark. "He is the man who does not love Humanity, but does love his neighbour."

"That will do," she said, turning to Mr. Hooker; "Professor Ripplemark's answer is mine."

Mr. Hooker leant back in his chair, his benignant face beaming with smiles. His quick intelligence had perceived from the first that the speech between these two was gradually becoming the vehicle of an invisible drama. He saw that the crisis was at hand. Miss Wolfstone looked steadily towards the window as before, and Ripplemark watched her.

"The matter is settled," said Hooker. "The necessary arrangements will be made at once. And now I shall withdraw and leave you two to argue your differences between yourselves."

Without waiting for a word of thanks the old

millionaire shook hands with the young ones and was gone.

Miss Wolfstone now rose and went to the window, looking out upon the scene of the recent accident. Ripplemark remained where he was.

Presently he said: "Would you mind repeating your definition of one's neighbour?"

His manner in saying this was that of a Professor catechizing a pupil. She saw the mockery, but answered quite gravely:

"The man who comes next."

"But what if the next-comer happens to be not a man but a woman?"

"Then the difficulty will be reciprocal. The woman will have met a man."

"And supposing that these two suddenly discover that they do not love, but hate?" said the Professor.

"Then one of them must immediately leave the room," said Miss Wolfstone.

Instantly he crossed to where she was standing.

"I am not going to leave the room," he said.

"Neither am I," she answered.

It was done; and that, too, in full view of whatever observers there may have been at the opposite window.

In this manner Professor Maurice Ripplemark was extricated from his difficulty.

CHAPTER FIVE

And Forthwith Finds Himself in Another

BEFORE Mr. Hooker's problem is forgotten it is to be hoped that some careful student of civilization will collect and classify the enormous multitude of divergent or contradictory answers that were given to it, in the period of its ascendancy, by different sections of the public, and by different individuals in each. Many would rattle off an answer in five seconds; some in terms of champagne and packs of hounds; some in terms of Revivals at home and Missions abroad. Very often the answers thus given would be accompanied with an air of immense wisdom in reserve, as who should say, "Give *me* the millions and I'll just show you what to do with them." But of the thousands who treated the question in this airy fashion there was hardly one but broke down hopelessly when cross-examined by the representatives of contradictory views. After the debate had been roaring for months, the solution was no nearer than at the beginning; nay, like the Irish question, it was further off. Never has there been a greater confusion since the reign of Chaos and old Night.

The University of Oxford was no exception. There was observable, indeed, a certain tendency to the superficial agreement that the millions would be well bestowed on the University; in which particular Oxford resembled the various Hospitals, Charities, Churches, "Movements" and Societies which submitted their needs to Mr. Hooker. But though Oxford was, in a manner of speaking, agreed on this point, you had only to raise the question, "What would the University do with the millions if it got them?" to raise a Babel of voices, each seeking to drown the rest. It is perhaps as well that Mr. Hooker did not bestow them on the University. Had he done so, that ancient institution might have been rent by internal dissensions.

What would Ripplemark say to the Contention Club? When it became known that the Regius Professor would deliver himself, the question flew to all lips; and when the news leaked out that Mr. Hooker himself had been in Oxford, expectation rose to bursting pitch.

If the University knew nothing of what the Professor would say, the Professor himself knew no more. He was in a great perplexity. It is an annoying feature in the constitution of the universe that a turn in the march of events which extricates us from one difficulty often implicates us in another— an experience familiar to lovers, philosophers and statesmen. Thus it happened to the Regius Professor of Virtue. On the one hand Mr. Hooker's anomalous conduct had brought his relations with Margaret Wolfstone to a most triumphant issue; on the other it had created new complications in his relations with the world, with the University, and, not least, with the Contention Club. He was under an engagement to offer the Club a *de jure* solution of Mr. Hooker's problem; and this solution was due to be presented on the day following that on which Mr. Hooker had achieved a *de facto* solution for himself. Strictly speaking, therefore, Mr. Hooker's problem no longer existed—at least in its original form. Moreover, Professor Ripplemark had himself become an accomplice, a confederate, or active partner, to the solution, on terms in easy accord with the adventurous elements of his personal character, but not so easy to reconcile with his official position.

How, under these circumstances, was he to act? He had only a few hours to make up his mind. As he paced up and down his room on the morning of the critical day, he paused once or twice to reflect on the perversity of things and on the paradoxes of philosophy. Mr. Hooker, in solving his own problem, had created another for Professor Ripplemark—that was the perversity of things. Mr. Hooker, in affirming his own personality, had made it extremely difficult for the Regius Professor of Virtue to affirm his without getting into hot water—that was the paradox of philosophy. But the Professor had no time to indulge in these general speculations: he could only make a note of them for future reflection. Anyone who had seen the expression on his face, as he threw himself down in a chair and lit his pipe, would have realized that his gift for rapid decision was being put to the test, and that the test was exceptionally severe. There was certainly no time to lose.

At all costs his engagement to the Club, complicated though it was by an engagement of a very different kind, must be fulfilled; the alternative was unthinkable. But how, with any show of honesty, could he treat the question before the House as though his interest in it were purely philosophic? How could he treat it as open when, in reality, it was closed? How could he avoid revealing the facts? And how could he reveal them without making himself, Mr. Hooker and—worst of all—Miss Wolfstone at least ridiculous? What version of the facts could he present which would be intelligible to academic minds? To be sure, he might appeal to their sporting instincts, which, he well knew, were strong, easily aroused and closely related to their conception of Virtue. But even so the risks were enormous. An ill-chosen word, an untimely gesture, might ruin everything.

What helped Professor Ripplemark most at this juncture was not, it must be confessed, his philosophy, but the memory of his past achievements. As he pondered the crisis before him he was reminded, suddenly and vividly, of certain glorious moments during his service in the Flying Corps. He recalled in particular how once, when the visibility was as bad as it could be, he had delivered his squadron, by a bold and decisive stroke, from a hopeless entanglement in the upper air, for which service an enthusiastic Commander-in-Chief had recommended him for the V.C. At these memories the spirits of the Regius Professor, which had been somewhat depressed on a first review of his difficulties, rose high; and his resolution was instantly taken. It displaced another, half formed, which was less worthy of him.

Some days before his first interview with Mr.

AND FINDS HIMSELF IN ANOTHER

Hooker the Professor had sketched the main lines of his coming discourse, and there, on the table before him, lay the rough notes he had then made. On glancing through them he observed, with no little pleasure, that his own *de jure* solution of the Hooker problem was identical in principle with the *de facto* solution achieved by the millionaire himself. The following were some of the points noted down for elaboration:

Ripplemark had resolved to inform the Club that the problem was insoluble on logical grounds; that the data for solving it did not exist in the present imperfect state of our social knowledge; that the whole discussion of it was infected by prevailing ignorance as to the right uses of wealth; that this ignorance was shared by the poor with the rich, by Labour with Capital, by Oxford with Smokeover, by the individual with the State; and that, in consequence, anyone who pretended to give a scientific solution was a quack.

For the same reason Ripplemark absolutely rejected the solution, so freely offered by agitators and others, that the millionaire ought to restore his wealth to the community. If he did so, he would restore it to an owner whose incompetence to deal with it was only greater than his own. The community had no valid claim to Mr. Hooker's millions. It had often been said that his fortune had been created by the labour of his fellow men. It were truer to say that it had been created by the errors of his fellow men. Without the connivance of social folly on an enormous scale such a fortune would never have come into existence. The agitators were always proclaiming that Mr. Hooker owed his wealth, not to his own exertions, but to "society." Yes, but he owed it to what was *worst* in society: to its blindness, its stupidity, its limited intelligence, its barbaric passions, its national greeds and to the monstrous delusions which dominated the international situation. That being so, the notion that "society" had a claim to Mr. Hooker's millions seemed to him preposterous, unless the principle were allowed that fools were always to be guaranteed against the fruits of their folly. Let it be granted that Mr. Hooker did not know what to do with his money. But did "society"? Did the community? Did the State? Did the Government? They had only to examine the budget of any great State to find examples, by the hundred, of the misapplication of wealth in its most stupid and flagitious forms. It were more to the point if Mr. Hooker were to use his millions for *chastising* the community for the ignorance and crime which had thrust him into his present position.

The only solution which he could offer as satisfactory would take a *dramatic* rather than a logical form. It might appeal to the artist, but would offend the doctrinaire—the type of solution which convinces nobody when set out on paper, but convinces everybody when it becomes an accomplished fact. Fortunately the universe they were living in did not condemn men to inaction till they could find a logical way out of their difficulties. Otherwise the most beneficent deeds of history would never have been done. The structure of the universe was on the side of those who had the courage to attempt

AND FINDS HIMSELF IN ANOTHER

dramatic solutions of problems that were otherwise insoluble. It favoured the heroic virtues; and he hoped that Mr. Hooker would solve his problem on heroic lines. Had he the means of doing so, he would advise the millionaire, on grounds of dramatic justice, *to devote the whole of his fortune to attacking the very ignorance which created it. Yes, he would urge Mr. Hooker to give his money back to "society,"—not, however, in the form of doles or ransom, but in the form of a smashing blow. He would implore him to give back by hitting back; to strike with all the force that three millions sterling could put into his arm; and to strike at the most dangerous feature in society—to wit, its ignorance.*

These metaphors were the proper mode to express his final conclusion, which was *that Mr. Hooker should place his millions at the service of Education.* But now he would tell them what he meant by Education—for on that point, he imagined, there was some difference of opinion.

Such were the notes of the Address with which the Regius Professor of Virtue had originally intended to enlighten the members of the Contention Club. Glancing through them on the morning of the great day, his first impulse had been to adhere to his original plan, and to say nothing of what had happened. But here his conscience smote him sharply. It would be a merry prank, no doubt, to keep his secret up his sleeve; but would it be fair, would it be straight? Above all, would it be playing the game? *Absit!* With a swift and angry movement the Professor of Virtue rolled his sheet of notes into a ball and flung them into the fire. He would do a cleaner and bolder thing—a thing for which the candid soul of Margaret Wolfstone would give him praise, as it would give him blame for the other—appalling thought! He would tell the Club that Mr. Hooker's problem was solved; he would tell them that he himself was an active partner in the solution; he would tell them exactly how and on what terms. And let the consequences be what they might!

This matter disposed of, the Professor of Virtue felt himself relieved of a burden and of a menace to his moral integrity. He would make no further preparations for his Address, but trust to the inspiration of the moment to tell a plain, straightforward tale. His self-confidence was equal to that. It is not to be denied that he took a secret pleasure in contemplating the surprise he had in store for the redoubtable Contenders, and laughed to himself as he thought of the wits of the Club, whose premeditated impromptus would be put out of commission. He looked forward to an interesting evening.

His mind was now free to admit another topic, which, if truth must be told, had been knocking loudly for admittance during the whole of the foregoing meditations. What the topic was his actions immediately revealed. From a drawer at his side he took out his bank-book, added up the figures, and found that he had an available balance of £300. This sum the Professor of Virtue resolved to devote, in its entirety and with no delay, to the purchase of an engagement ring for Margaret Wolfstone, without pausing to ask himself a single question about "the right uses of wealth." His next act was to consult Bradshaw and his watch. Yes, there was time to do it. He could catch the one o'clock train to London, make his purchase, and be back by 8:30 for the meeting of the Contention Club. And, then, when the meeting was over, he would present the ring to its destined owner, who was still in Oxford and sure to be wide awake, though the hour would be midnight, and somewhat late for a Professor of Virtue to be entertaining his mistress. Whereupon the prospect for the day became more interesting than ever. "This day," he reflected, "is going to be wonderful." He was not mistaken.

Meanwhile the coming debate was being talked of as one of the greatest sporting events in the history of the University. All day the colleges were tense with expectation; books were thrown aside, games played half-heartedly, lectures given absent-mindedly, and poured forth to deaf ears. Not only in the University but outside bets were being made right and left on the chances of Ripplemark giving a definite answer to his problem. Rumour declared that Rumbelow, Stallybrass & Corker were telegraphing the odds all over the country. At six o'clock in the evening they were reported as 7 to 1 against Ripplemark.

Half an hour before proceedings were due to begin the room was packed to suffocation. Not only did the audience fill all the seats, they sat on the tables and under them, on the floor, on the windowsills, on the bookcases. Some, by an art which is the secret of the Oxford undergraduate, had attached themselves, high up, to the walls, where they had the appearance of hanging from the picture-hooks like pieces of tapestry. One had perched himself immediately behind a bust of Cardinal Newman, and seemed to be sitting astride of that distinguished head, as indeed he partly was. Had Superstition been present it would have read this as a dark omen. But the Contention Club was not superstitious. It was open-minded and highly critical. It expected the Regius Professor to be original in his handling of the question, but it would meet him with the tolerant incredulity which befits a great University in the presence of new ideas.

The audience watched the clock. As the hands reached 8.30 conversation subsided, and all eyes turned towards the door by which the speaker of the evening was to enter. It remained closed. At 8.35 it was partly opened by the Chairman, who thrust his head into the room, glanced round as though he were looking for somebody, and then withdrew. At 8.40 there were signs of impatience and cries of "Hurry up!" At 8.45 the Chairman, followed by the Secretary and Treasurer, entered and took their places. But there was no Ripplemark. The Chairman began to explain. He was afraid there had been a miscarriage. Professor Ripplemark was not to be found. He had left Oxford at one o'clock and had not been seen since. A fresh relay of searchers had been sent out, and he proposed that the meeting should await their return. If the new searchers had no success, the meeting must consider what it would do. The matter was mysterious; the more so as Professor Ripplemark was known to them all as a man of meticulous punctuality in keeping an engagement.

AND FINDS HIMSELF IN ANOTHER

He had barely said the last words when a young man appeared from behind and thrust a telegram into his hand. The young man whispered to the officials. He was saying that the telegram had arrived at the Chairman's private address after his departure for the meeting, which had been early, and that its importance had only just been discovered.

From the expression on the Chairman's face the audience guessed the worst. A moment later they learnt from his lips that hope must be abandoned. "Accident; deeply regret impossible to keep engagement; no cause for alarm." So ran the fatal words of the message read by the Chairman. What he did not read, however, was the name of the office in London from which the telegram had been despatched. This, in spite of Ripplemark's assurance to the contrary, alarmed him greatly.

For a moment the whole audience was aghast, as though it had been just missed by a thunderbolt. A groan of disappointment followed, which broke up and dispersed itself into a buzz of conversation; as on a racecourse when the favourite is not at the starting post, or as in a crowded theatre when the manager announces that a great actor's part will be taken by an understudy. What could it mean? Had Ripplemark's courage failed him at the last moment? Had stage-fright attacked him? Had he run away? These suggestions, made by a gentleman who had not served in the Flying Corps, and would not have won the V.C. if he had, were dismissed as abominable. But what then? No one could answer. The data were so scanty that even the acutest minds of the

Club could hardly frame an intelligible question, or challenge a definition of terms.

But the spirit of Contention is not easily baulked. No sooner had the shock subsided than proposals arose from all sides for a makeshift debate. Speeches were waiting for delivery, and the gentlemen who had prepared impromptus would not lightly throw them away. In consequence of all which the Chairman presently announced, amid loud applause, that he himself would step into the breach and open the discussion.

The Chairman, who was a prominent member of the Fabian Society, did his best. His discourse was a creditable but rather dull exercise on the thesis so decisively rejected by Professor Ripplemark in his original draft—namely, that Mr. Hooker ought to restore his millions to the community whose labour had created them, and that, if he failed to do so of his freewill, the "State" must compel him to disgorge.

The result of this opening was that the discussion immediately took the form of a battle royal between the Individualists and the Socialists, following in the main the lines of an argument on which Contention has been sharpening its faculties for half a century, and which has every prospect of performing the function of grindstone until it ends, as many great controversies have ended, by being forgotten.

Midnight was approaching and asphyxiation had almost done its worst, when the last speaker got upon his feet; and with him there came a diversion. He was an undergraduate, and, by the look of him, a formidable one, with the profile of Mephistopheles

AND FINDS HIMSELF IN ANOTHER

and a full face of the most charming innocence—an anomalous young gentleman whom his tutors knew not how to handle; for apparently he did no work, though he managed to win every University prize he attempted, at once the shame and the glory of his college; which complication was further complicated by the fact that he was the heir to a peerage, and a rising poet into the bargain. Speaking with a slight stammer and a pronounced lisp the undergraduate announced his regret that the discussion so far had been left to the dons, and submitted that the time had come for the less important section of the University to make itself heard. He did not believe in the State, and regarded with contempt any argument which invoked it to solve the question before the House. The State was the apotheosis of the general incompetence, the vulgar mind writ large, a god made by fools in their own image. It was devoid of Beauty, and therefore of real value. It was high time that this idol shared the fate of all the false gods, that, namely, of being laughed out of existence. Authority, whether in Church or State, had lost all claim to be taken seriously. It had ceased even to be fraudulent, and become simply absurd. Laughter, not revolution, was the solvent of the problem of Power; and the world was merely waiting for a new Voltaire or a new Cervantes to raise the chorus of derision in which all the big wigs would vanish for ever. For his part he could never look upon any holder of power decked out in his robes of office without an impulse to burst out laughing, cut a caper and stand on his head. The only truthful portraits of power-holders he had ever seen were the cartoons in *Punch:* those, for example, where they were represented as wooden figures in Noah's Ark, looking forth distressfully on the surrounding flood. The private memoirs of great personages, of which so many had recently been published, were sufficient proofs that the entire performance in which these puppets took part was a mockery. As the eyes of the public were gradually opened, by these means, to what went on behind the seats of the mighty, the whole apparatus of power would collapse, to the accompaniment of the universal mirth; while the revolutionaries, who were just as ridiculous as the funny automata whose robes of office they were trying to steal, would find themselves without an occupation. The only sphere where power had a real meaning to-day was the army, in which he had recently served. As everybody knew, whose eyes were in his head, the modern State was constructed on a military model. It was a camouflaged army; a vast fighting machine painted to look like a factory; or, if they liked, a Big Bertha hidden in a Foreign Office. The theories which derived the State from the family, or any other pacific group, were pure nonsense. It was derived from the army, and the way in which this patent fact was hushed up by political philosophers, who would lose their jobs if they told the truth, was a public scandal. As for Mr. Hooker and his like, they were the nightbirds who followed in the wake of the host, always at a safe distance, and enriched themselves by stripping the dead on the battlefields, and emptying the pockets of the wounded, whose throats they had cut—like the ghouls described in

AND FINDS HIMSELF IN ANOTHER

Les Misérables. They should be shot at sight. He congratulated posterity on the new aristocracy of battlefield robbers founded during the war; their children had a fair chance of ruling the world for the next hundred years, and, if the House cared to look into the matter, they would find that many aristocracies had originated in the same manner. His own family was a notable example.

He was proceeding to enlarge on the history of his family, and had got so far as to sketch the character of his great-grandfather, who was a bosom friend of George IV, when the Chairman called him to order for the irrelevance of his remarks, and the hour being late, declared the proceedings at an end.

So the meeting broke up, leaving Mr. Hooker's problem exactly where it had been when the proceedings began.

In the meantime other telegrams had been received, and the air was thick with the most alarming rumours as to the cause of Ripplemark's absence. It was said that the Vice-Chancellor, attended by a cortège of Heads of Houses and Doctors of Divinity, had taken the midnight train to London on a mission of rescue. This rumour, with others of yet darker import, met the members of the Contention Club as they dispersed to their homes through the otherwise silent streets. For the time being, interest in Mr. Hooker's problem was submerged in compassion for the miserable plight in which the Regius Professor was reported to be, and in speculation as to its probable results.

Now, there is a well-known tendency in ancient universities which brings all important discussions to a dramatic climax in the question of "appointments." So it was in the present instance. The last question the members of the Contention Club asked one another before saying "good-night" was—"*Who will succeed Ripplemark?*"

But what had happened?

Following Professor Ripplemark from the moment when he left Oxford on his fascinating errand, we behold him, about four o'clock of the afternoon, standing in front of a jeweller's window in Bond Street, London. This is a new adventure, and Ripplemark is not very sure of his powers to bring the same to a successful issue. He will inspect the shop window before going in.

There are many rings in the window, and the Professor lingers in front of them, unable to make up his mind. Then he walks up the street, comes back to the shop window and lingers again. This time two other gentlemen, very fashionably dressed, are also looking into the window, apparently in the same state of mind as himself. The street is crowded with passers-by, and a large shining motor is waiting opposite the shop door.

The two gentlemen are discussing an aigrette of diamonds displayed in the window. Presently one of them says to the other: "Why the devil don't they put the prices on these things?" Then, turning to Ripplemark, "I wonder if you, sir, have any idea what that thing is worth." Ripplemark says that he hasn't the ghost of an idea. At the same moment two other gentlemen draw up, and begin inspecting this and that. And there is a buzz of conversation round the shop window, in the course of which one of the gentlemen proposes to the other three that they should all dine together at the Carlton Club.

Ripplemark now detaches himself from the group to enter the shop, but pauses for a moment to make way for a lady in sables, who is passing out of the door on her way to the shining motor, a small satchel tightly clasped in her hand.

At the same instant a violent shock from behind flings Ripplemark full against the lady, who would be knocked down, were it not that two of the gentlemen are now on the other side, gallantly supporting her. For three seconds, no more, the six figures form a bunch; there is just time for the lady to give a scream, and Ripplemark finds himself standing by her side alone.

"You've snatched my satchel," she gasps; "you passed it on to the other men!" And with that she becomes speechless and faint.

A powerful chauffeur has his grip on Ripplemark's collar; a crowd is gathering; a whistle is blown; two policemen are hurrying up. Ripplemark wrenches himself free from the chauffeur; but the two policemen have him; the lady says, "Yes, I am sure that's the man," and almost before he knows what has happened the author of *The Moral Will* is in a taxicab, with a police officer on either side of him, on his way to Bow Street Station.

On the way to the station Ripplemark says not a word, recovering from the shock and collecting his wits. At the station he says quietly that a mistake has been made, informs the police who he is, produces his card. He explains why he was waiting outside the shop. All which information the police receive with due professional reserve.

Meanwhile, in another room, the lady in sables is stating that she can swear to the man; that she saw him watching her when she entered the shop; that it was he and no other who flung himself upon her; that she felt his hand on hers as it was holding the satchel; that she saw the satchel pass from him to another; that it contained pearls worth £3,000. The chauffeur corroborates. He saw Ripplemark waiting—a long time; he saw the others come up to him; he saw them all in earnest conversation; he did not see the satchel snatched; but the man, when he collared him, made violent efforts to escape.

The police express intelligent hesitations. But this only makes the lady more indignant. She will not yield a hair's-breadth. She is a great personage, and this is not the first time her jewels have been stolen. What did the police do for her last year when the burglars ransacked her dressing-room? Nothing! But now they have caught the thief red-handed and they shall not let him go! She has no doubt it is the same man, the dressing-room burglar —someone familiar with her movements. She insists on charging him with stealing her pearls—value £3,000. And the long and short of it is that the Regius Professor of Virtue must face the charge to-morrow morning, and be kept under lock and key meanwhile. Yes, he may send telegrams: But these things have taken time.

So Ripplemark spent the night in the cells, leaving the Oxford Contenders to solve Mr. Hooker's problem as best they could. And a most miserable

AND FINDS HIMSELF IN ANOTHER

night it was. Insects attacked his body and gloomy thoughts possessed his mind. But a stout heart, a sound philosophy and a clean conscience carried him through. And from time to time his thoughts would go back to a magnificent ring, blazing with sapphires and diamonds, which he had seen in the shop window. Margaret would have to wait a little longer, but, by heaven, she should have that ring! This thought gave him great consolation.

Next morning he was of course discharged. *A priori* improbability overwhelmed the evidence of the senses, which was dead against him. But his extrication was not altogether easy. The evidence of the lady, of the chauffeur and of some passers-by was positive and consistent, and yielded nothing under cross-examination. The wearer of sables was furious at the magistrate's decision and made a scene, in course of which she did not hesitate to tell the magistrate what she thought of the intelligence of the Court; for she was a woman of fiery spirit and fluent speech. She remains convinced to this day that Ripplemark was the thief, and has imparted that conviction to many of her friends. Nor was the public fully satisfied. There were biting comments in the gutter press. "If the accused had been a man of the people instead of belonging to a protected class," etc. etc.

That Oxford could be anything but loyal to its Regius Professor, in these distressing circumstances, would of course be inconceivable. All the sporting instincts of the University rallied to his side. None the less, with his reputation for "Bolshevism," which he had recently acquired for no reason in particular, and with the rumours that began to fly about of his relations with Hooker, not to speak of his other peculiarities, the opinion gained ground that his resignation would not be an altogether untoward event. Outside Oxford the feeling was that "policy" imperatively demanded a new Regius Professor of Virtue, one, preferably, whom no wearer of sables suspected of stealing her pearls. And there was another person who, for reasons quite different, had no doubt about the matter, and did not hesitate to say so. "Dearest," wrote Margaret Wolfstone, "you must resign. I shall love you all the more when――" But the rest shall be silence.

Professor Ripplemark was long in doubt as to his course of action. For once, the V.C. and the LL.D. were evenly matched, and pulled in opposite directions. The V.C. said, "Stick to your guns." The LL.D. said, "Resign."

Meanwhile Mr. Hotblack, the psychologist, was working overtime. His private room was at all hours of the day the least disturbed in the Office of Rumbelow, Stallybrass & Corker; but when the staff had gone home and the premises were closed, it was one of the quietest nooks in the universe. Here, night after night, you might see him immersed in the profoundest studies, but always punctually suspending his labours when the great clock of Smokeover Cathedral, made by Mr. Hooker's father, boomed out the last stroke of twelve.

What was he doing?

Acting under Mr. Rumbelow's orders he was engaged in translating the brutal treatment which Fate

AND FINDS HIMSELF IN ANOTHER

had just inflicted on a Professor of Virtue into terms of a spiritual experience.

To say that Mr. Hotblack found his task an easy one would be doing injustice to his great talent as a psychologist. His grasp of the science was sufficiently comprehensive to reveal the difficulty of the problem before him. But he did not despair. He remembered how the accident on the railway, after resisting all the solvents he had applied to it, had suddenly yielded a spiritual meaning at a moment when he least expected it. Still he was perplexed.

One night, when the eagerness of his countenance and the rapidity of his work seemed to indicate that he was on the track of a solution, he took down his telephone and rang up the Chief.

"I am glad to report, sir," said Mr. Hotblack through the instrument, "that the signs of a musical structure are beginning to disclose themselves. At the same time there can be no doubt that Professor Ripplemark's mishap has struck a discord, the exact relation of which to the underlying theme I have yet to discover. The data for a solution will not be complete until the question of his resignation has been finally determined. In my judgment it is important that this question should be settled in concert by all the parties concerned in bringing about the present situation. They should all meet face to face. If I may venture to make the suggestion, I submit to you and My Lady that such a meeting be arranged without delay in your own house."

In consequence of this suggestion Mr. Hotblack, attired in the evening dress he wore so seldom, found himself some days later at the dining-table of his

Chief, Professor Ripplemark and Miss Wolfstone on either side of him, and in front My Lady, Mr. Rumbelow and Mr. Hooker. For the table was round.

"Has it occurred to you, Professor," asked Mr. Hotblack, while dinner was in progress, "that the Board of Directors outlined in your *Moral Will* is in actual being at this moment, and is holding its first meeting round this table?"

"It has," replied Ripplemark. "And it strikes me as passing strange that the first business the Board should have to transact is the question of my resignation as a Professor of Virtue."

"A sure sign of *orchestration*," whispered Mr. Hotblack. "I attach the greatest importance to it. This, sir, is the beginning of great developments. I feel the moment full of promise. It will lead on, sir, to the most beautiful variations!"

Here Mr. Hotblack, forgetting for the moment where he was, began to hum the theme of one of his favourite sonatas; but checked himself immediately.

Then the conversation became general, but so entangled that even the Immortals cannot report it correctly. Moreover, My Lady, overjoyed at the impending union of Ripplemark and Miss Wolfstone, would constantly raise the level of the discussion to heights of Beauty remote from its starting point, and introduce remarks which it is not lawful to repeat. But Mr. Hotblack lost not a word of what she said.

Towards the end attempts were made to sum up, and the conditions became easier for the reporters.

"Unquestionably," Mr. Hooker was heard to

AND FINDS HIMSELF IN ANOTHER

say, "the University of Oxford will have greater freedom to affirm its personality in its own way if Ripplemark affirms his by resigning the Professorship."

To which Mr. Rumbelow added:

"My dear Ripplemark, the loyalty which Oxford has shown to you is magnificent. It fills me with admiration for the University and with hope for the future of civilization. I intend to set aside a large sum of money for the purpose of sending young men to Oxford. But sportsmanlike principles forbid us to put too great a strain on the loyalty of our friends, especially when their loyalty to us is itself the highest expression of sportsmanship. You must resign."

"And then," said Miss Wolfstone, "our League of Outcasts will become an accomplished fact."

At which Mr. Hotblack, unable as usual to restrain himself at a critical moment, jumped to his feet and cried:

"Ladies and gentlemen, the proof of orchestration is now complete!"

So Ripplemark resigned. He was the first Regius Professor of Virtue in the University of Oxford. And the last.

PART FIVE

The Legend of the League

CHAPTER ONE

A Den of Thieves

"I SUPPOSE," said Ripplemark, "that the ultimate ground of the alliance between you and me lies in the fact that both of us are engaged in 'speculation'—you as a gambler, and I as a Professor of Virtue."

"You mean as an ex-Professor," said Rumbelow. "Don't forget that you have won a new reputation as a Stealer of Pearls. From the world's point of view both of us are thieves."

"Yes," said Ripplemark; "and when the time comes for us to be crucified I wonder whom the world will find to crucify between us."

At this remark the two men paused in their walk and leant over the balustrade, gazing in silence into the blue distance, where the first signs of a storm were gathering on the horizon. It was an evening in late September. They had been walking up and down the terrace of Rumbelow's Castle, awaiting the other members of the party. Margaret and Hooker had gone out into the park to meet My Lady, returning from the Sanctuary, where, at that hour of the day, she was always engaged in private devotion.

Presently Rumbelow said:

"We are a den of thieves, Ripplemark. Thief is

the mildest of the terms *The Tracker* is now applying to Margaret. Hooker has been called a thief ever since he made his fortune. As to My Lady, she, of course, is the arch-thief of the gang."

"That makes five crosses," said Ripplemark. "It will be a bloody spectacle. And I see now who will be in the middle. When the women acquired their rights they forgot that they were acquiring the right to be crucified along with the rest of their new privileges."

"They have enjoyed it a long time," said Rumbelow, "but not officially. They make good victims. But what in the name of heaven has started us on this Via Dolorosa?"

"It was the cloud on the horizon. Unless My Lady makes haste with her devotions the tempest will overtake her.—But tell me, Rumbelow, what is to be the next speculation of the Firm?"

"The League of Nations," answered the bookmaker. "Our agents have been pursuing inquiries all over the world, and the Department of Foreign Information has been at work night and day."

"And what are the odds on the League?"

"Zero. Nothing doing. No race. No odds to be declared. We have declined to put the speculation on our books unless the data can be radically altered."

"What are the data?"

"Hopeless at present. Twenty-seven different countries have been canvassed by skilled investigators and the result is the same in every case."

"What is it?"

"Briefly this. Each of the twenty-seven is eager to have world-authority imposed on the other

A DEN OF THIEVES

twenty-six, but not one of them is willing to have world-authority imposed upon itself. A complete deadlock, of course. The horses won't start, the jockeys are all on strike, and every prospect of a riot on the course. So we've written it off—*for the present.*"

"You were right," said Ripplemark. "My own speculations have been moving on lines that converge to the same result. The League of Nations in its present form is a league of those who want to govern but object to being governed—the universal formula of human nature. It is the *reductio ad absurdum* of the fatal problem of power, round which the history of civilization has moved in a vicious circle for five thousand years, and which has never been solved and never can be, for the simple reason that men are not made either for exercising power over their fellows, or for submitting to it when it is exercised over them by others. It demoralizes the rulers and turns the ruled into rebels. The problem of power has never advanced one hair's-breadth beyond the point where Plato left it, and he left it only half solved. He, as you know, attacked the question of breeding men who are fit to exercise power over others. But what on earth is gained by doing that, unless at the same time you breed another class who are willing to submit to the power exercised by the first? This is the crux of the whole matter, and the rock on which the League of Nations is splitting at the present moment. And sooner or later civilization itself will split on the same rock, unless somebody can find a way round."

"I strongly suspect," said Rumbelow, "that the

origin of this delusion about power, which infects the whole of our civilization, lies in ideas about the government of the universe. My experience as a gambler has convinced me that the universe is not *governed* at all.—Not that I am any more of an unbeliever than you are. My religion is My Lady's, or at least an echo of it, and she, as you know, worships the Holy Spirit; I have no doubt she is engaged in conversation with it at the present moment. Well, as I said, the universe is clearly not *governed*. A year's experience in our Office would convince any sane man that the relation of the Spirit to the world is that of a lover to his beloved, or of a creative artist to a wild mass of unpromising material out of which he is perpetually evoking, by a divine and loving art, the most surprising and beautiful combinations—anything but the relation of a power-loving potentate to his subjects, which is the very last thing that should be thought of in such a connexion. It passes my comprehension, Ripplemark, to understand how the idea of power should have become the dominant idea of religion, as it plainly is in the religion of the West—though not, I think, in that of the East."

"You have put your finger on the root of the evil," said Ripplemark, "and it is another point on which our respective types of speculation converge. As to the origin of the fiction of power, I am inclined to think that the Western world took it over from the old Hebrew religion, whose God was a fighting potentate—"a man of war," "the Lord of Hosts"— who has since been made into the ally of all the self-righteous bullies in the world. Hence the belief with which the Western mind is, one might almost say, besotted, that the relation of the Spirit to the universe is that of *ruling* it, which of course would be appropriate if the universe were a military organization, but not otherwise. The belief was born and nurtured in the atmosphere of war, and is plainly related to the needs of war-making states. The truth is, my dear Rumbelow, that the philosophy of the West, and the morality derived from it, are militaristic through and through. It all starts from the conception of a cosmic commander-in-chief, ruling the universe under a system of iron law, appropriate to an army but altogether opposed to humane relationships; and from thence the idea has been carried down through the whole range of our institutions, society itself being constructed upon it, with the result that war, domestic and foreign, never ends. A fool can see how it affects morality. When a man hears that he has been made in the image of God he inevitably thinks of himself as a little potentate and begins to bully his neighbours. Was there ever such an imbecility? This was precisely the point at which Christ and the most enlightened of his apostles attacked the military religion of his day, and of course they crucified him for his pains—as they will crucify you and me when they catch us. For, mark you, my friend—the moment the Scribes and Pharisees of our day learn what we are after, it will be denounced as subversive of all morality."

"They will have to reckon with Rumbelow, Stallybrass & Corker," said the bookmaker, "and we shall not prove so easy to catch. The Firm did not exist in the days of Christ and his apostles. And that makes all the difference. But this 'way round' that you spoke of. Does it exist?"

"I believe it does," said Ripplemark. "You know the constitution of my University."

"It is admirable," said Rumbelow, "and almost identical with the constitution of our Firm."

"Well, there you have the two ideas of 'teaching' and 'ruling.' But observe, Rumbelow, the order in which they stand. 'Teaching' is primary, 'ruling' is secondary. That is to say, we teach, not in order to bolster up a system of University discipline, but we apply discipline only so far as is needed to promote the ends of teaching. How does that strike you as a model for the constitution of human society in general?"

"Unquestionably the true model," said Rumbelow; "government a department of education instead of education a department of government. I know your formula. A thoroughly sportsmanlike arrangement."

"And yet," said the ex-Professor, "when I mooted the idea in our sporting University the Dons were amazed, I was called a Bolshevist and the hint given me that I ought to resign. But let that pass, and grasp the principle—that the function of the best towards what is not the best is, not to *rule*, but to *teach* it; the superiority of one man or group over others conferring no right to order inferiors about, but an obligation to raise them to its own level. That is what Margaret meant when she spoke of aristocracy as the true form of education."

"I wish Margaret had used another term," said

A DEN OF THIEVES

Rumbelow. "I am afraid 'aristocracy' will frighten the Labour Party, who are rapidly moving towards the Firm. And it may cause difficulties in America, where we are establishing a new branch. But go on."

"Assuming, then, that the supremacy of the best consists precisely in its determination to raise what is not the best to its own level, instead of keeping it down in a position of stereotyped inferiority, the conception of power passes at once into that of education. This now becomes the basis of all human relations. The power basis is abolished, and power takes its place as a subsidiary interest of mankind, destined to become less and less important in proportion as the major end is attained. From that point the evolution of man breaks out in a new direction. It has, in fact, already begun. A new interest in education has burst out simultaneously all over the world, one of the unexpected results of the war. Every day it becomes more clamant, and my belief is that it only needs businesslike handling to end the malignant reign of power and to become the dominant concern of the human race."

"Businesslike handling, and sportsmen to handle it," said Rumbelow.

"Precisely. But can you supply them?"

"We can!" cried Rumbelow. "Listen to this, Ripplemark. Our agents—in twenty-seven countries, remember—have sent in Reports which indicate, without exception, that the world is on the eve of a spiritual revolution, of the same nature as the Revival of Learning in the fifteenth century, but on an immensely greater scale and on far higher ground. At the same time they show that tremendous opposition is gathering. The holders of power all over the world, so say the Reports, are getting alarmed, and when they see what is coming they will fight to the last ditch. But again they will have to reckon with Rumbelow, Stallybrass & Corker. You will understand that the mere fact of the Firm selecting a candidate for favour makes a difference to the candidate's chance of winning— a point often overlooked by persons who are ignorant of gambling. Know then, Ripplemark, that the Schoolmaster is our selection! We are going to back that horse against the whole field! We are going to back it with all the influence, the skill, the organization and the resources of the Firm!"

"That is the best news I have heard since I came back from the war," said Ripplemark. "I thank God anew that I was not killed, and am alive to see this day! I have often despaired. The forces against us are such that nothing can overcome them save a league of all the venturesome spirits in the world. But even so it will be a gamble against tremendous odds."

"The Firm is prepared to undertake it none the less," said Rumbelow. "We shall make it the greatest sporting event of the ages. We shall mobilize behind it the sporting instincts of all nations. As you say, the gamble is at long odds. But believe me, that when the preparations of the Firm are completed the odds will come out very different from what they are now. Of course we shall need your help—the help of a mind which knows what Education really is. And Margaret's for the same reason. Both of you must join the new Board.

A DEN OF THIEVES

We shall mobilize the sporting women as well as the men—a vital point. Hooker is completely converted and will be a tower of strength with his Quaker mind. And My Lady—the heart and soul of the enterprise, the link between us and the invisible world! By heaven, here she comes! And just in time."

At this moment three figures were seen hurrying across the park.

Rumbelow and Ripplemark, leaning over the parapet that bounded the terrace on that side, and pursuing their conversation, had forgotten the black cloud that was slowly coming up against the wind. But now great drops were beginning to fall, and the three figures had barely gained the terrace before a flash of lightning shot across the darkened landscape, a peal of thunder shattered the sky and the fountains of the great deep were opened overhead.

They were now within doors, and My Lady, fresh from her devotions, was in high spirits. Margaret and Ripplemark were in the window-seat, watching the storm. The other three were gathered round the fire. The spirit of joy was in the room, in harmony with the frolic of the Titans that was going on outside.

"I have been quarrelling with Mr. Hooker!" cried My Lady.

"About what?" asked Rumbelow.

"He has been asking my forgiveness!"

"For having introduced himself, in a style so original on the night of the accident?"

"How immensely stupid you are!" said My Lady. "Mr. Hooker and I made that up long ago."

And without more ado she rose up from her place, placed a low stool beside Mr. Hooker's chair and sat down at his feet, resting her head against his arm—a thing very beautiful to see, and not lost upon those who saw it.

"And now," said Rumbelow, "that matter being settled and all parties, including myself, fully satisfied with the terms of reconciliation, perhaps you will tell us for what else Mr. Hooker has been seeking forgiveness."

"I will save My Lady from answering," said Hooker. "I have been asking her forgiveness for talking too much about myself the last time we met. And I ask it again."

"All honest men are interested in themselves," said Rumbelow.

"So I told him," answered My Lady. "And we are never more dishonest than when we try to conceal it."

"Beware!" cried Rumbelow. "You are launching My Lady on her favourite theme. She is a most dangerous metaphysician, Mr. Hooker, and in a moment more she will lead us into the wilderness, and we shall be lost in mazes where even Ripplemark cannot find us."

"It will be no new experience to me," said Hooker. "Let My Lady go on."

"I often think," she continued, "that nothing so clearly reveals the interest we take in ourselves as the language we use about escaping from ourselves. The sage who desires to be absorbed in the infinite always imagines himself standing by and enjoying the spectacle of his own absorption. His interest in himself takes that form. It strikes me as rather flamboyant."

" 'Tis a form that flatters his vanity," said Rumbelow. "Being absorbed in the infinite is the equivalent with these gentlemen of being raised to the House of Lords. If they were really humble they would be content to be absorbed into the common clay."

"You are hatefully cynical," said My Lady. "Will you never learn, Arthur, to be charitable to philosophers? Theirs is the most tragic of all occupations. Their desire to be absorbed in the infinite is a sign of it. Who knows it better than the Stealer of Pearls in the window-seat yonder?"

"You remind me, dearest," said Rumbelow, "that the first time we met I thought the infinite was absorbed in *you*. I was convinced of it!"

"I have the same impression now," said Hooker with emphasis. "And I have had it before in the presence of things less lovely."

The tone of solemn ardour in which Hooker spoke seemed for an instant to plunge the joyous current into a silent pool. But My Lady passed it off with a laugh and the merry waters went babbling on.

"Oh," she cried, "that is nothing out of the common! The infinite is absorbed in everybody. How else would any human being be really lovable? The same with everything that has a trace of beauty in its composition—the edges of the clouds, the gradations of colour in the wing of a bird, the song of brooks, the veining of leaves and the small things that lie about us in millions. But seriously, O Stealer of Pearls, don't you think that the advice philosophers give us to get rid of our finite selves may become an affectation?"

"Most easily," answered Ripplemark, who, with Margaret, had now joined the group. "But I hope you will never get rid of yours."

"I shall never try," laughed My Lady, "since the very act of trying would only make me a shallower egotist than I am. Anyone who is interested in his finite self to the point of wanting to get rid of it must have an outrageous sense of his own importance. Perhaps you have noticed, O Thief, that when a man talks of being absorbed in the infinite it is always his own absorption that attracts him and not that of anybody else."

"Which proves how easily such men deceive themselves," said Ripplemark. "If they were as selfless as they imagine they would be indifferent who was absorbed so long as somebody was. But they always want to be absorbed *themselves*, and, as you say, they imagine themselves present to see what is going on. Indeed, My Lady, I regard this doctrine as the supreme expression of human egotism. I have heard of a man who actually set about it, and kept a book in which he recorded day by day his progress towards absorption in the infinite. I think he had been converted to Buddhism. One day, reading through what he had written in the book, he was so appalled by the egotism it disclosed that he fell down in a swoon."

"He should have done that at the first and so saved himself all the trouble," said Rumbelow.

A DEN OF THIEVES

"Then you agree with me," said My Lady, "that all our philosophy has its roots in the interest we take in ourselves."

"It is an affectation to pretend otherwise," said Ripplemark; "and the interest in ourselves deepens at every stage of our reflection."

"I think it *rises*," said My Lady. "But tell me, Mr. Hooker, do tell me what *your* philosophy is. I have long been eager to know it."

"It centres," said the millionaire, "on a simple practical rule. 'So live that in affirming your own self, you may help others to affirm theirs.'"

"We must have that in the Firm!" cried Rumbelow with great vehemence. "We must have that in the Firm, Mr. Hooker! Do you mind repeating it?"

Hooker repeated his formula. Rumbelow wrote it down in a pocket-book, and gazed at the words, deep in thought.

"I shall place that in the hands of our experts to-morrow," he said. "It must be harnessed to the businesslike method! It breathes the very spirit of the Firm! What do you say, dearest?"

"It is the motto of the Firm in other language," said My Lady.

"With immense scope for the sportsmanlike principle!" cried Rumbelow. "Immense! And the ideal aim is manifest. All that it needs is the businesslike method."

"The businesslike method will be understood," answered Hooker; "but whenever you mention your 'sportsmanlike principle' the world will be mystified and bewildered. It will strike a jarring note in vulgar minds. They will find it a discord, an impurity, an adulteration. They will say it has no place in the realm of the Good."

"It belongs to the realm of the Beautiful, where all great enterprises are born and nurtured," said My Lady. "It is another name for the high romance of the spirit. It marks the point where Law turns into Love, and the prose of life becomes poetry, and the music begins. Without it, Mr. Hooker, your own philosophy would have no power and no radiance. It would wither for lack of light and joy, as all bare moralities have withered and will wither to the end of time."

"Did I not say she was a dangerous metaphysician?" broke in Rumbelow.

"One of the most dangerous I have ever met," said Ripplemark.

"It seems to me," Hooker continued, "that your principle might be otherwise named. 'Sportsmanlike' breaks the connexion."

"On the contrary," said Rumbelow, "it is a bridge between time and eternity. Of all the forces that sway the life of man, the sporting instinct is the easiest transformed into its spiritual equivalents."

"At least," said Hooker, "I can bear testimony that it saved my life."

"And mine," said Rumbelow, with a glance at Margaret.

"But it left me to drown," said Ripplemark.

"It died on Calvary," said Margaret.

"But rose again the third day," said My Lady.

"Amen!" said Mr. Hooker.

He spoke this word in a low and solemn tone.

A DEN OF THIEVES

Barely had it passed his lips when a flash of forked lightning ripped across the sky, leapt into the darkening room and revealed the faces of the five to one another. Then the rain lashed and beat upon the window-panes, and a peal of thunder, bursting immediately overhead, shook the great house to its foundations.

Suddenly all became still and Rumbelow pursued his theme.

"When the sporting instinct is absent, Mr. Hooker, moral principles are invariably perverted into instruments of iniquity. Witness the attack upon Margaret. Witness the present relations of states and governments. Their meanness and inhumanity to one another are execrable; and each in turn justifies injustice in the name of a perverted moral principle. Your own maxim, good as it is, would be unsafe in the hands of any man who was not a sportsman at heart."

"I have often reflected," said Hooker, "how easily bad men might capture my rule, twist it to their own ends, and use it as a cover for the vilest misdeeds."

"All the highest truths are exposed to the same danger. The sportsmanlike principle is their only protection," said Ripplemark.

"They share it with life in general," said Rumbelow. "Unless our courage can face the risk of being in the wrong we shall never find ourselves in the right. Every great principle gambles with the risks of its misapplication: and for that reason every moral enterprise turns out to be a sporting proposition. There, Mr. Hooker, is the philosophy of the

Firm in a nutshell. You will observe that it is complementary to your own."

"I must admit," said Hooker, "that the only person I have known who took my principle seriously is the woman who has just gone back to the window-seat. To all the rest it was a mere theme for discussion. Whether they agreed with it or not, and with most of them it was a point of honour not to agree, it made no perceptible difference to their daily lives."

"Be thankful it was no worse," said Rumbelow. "If the devil had heard of your Principle he would have adopted it at once and used it to make hell more efficient."

"Silence!" cried My Lady. "We have had enough cynicism for to-day. Mr. Hooker, you are not the first propounder of great truths who has had a woman for his chief disciple. Yours will not betray you."

"Yes, dearest," said Rumbelow; "you have your Jaels, but Judas is a peculiar product of the male denomination."

At the mention of this name Mr. Hooker winced, and looking at his watch declared that it was time to dress for dinner. He left the room.

"What has happened to Mr. Hooker?" asked Rumbelow, when he was gone.

"His wounds ache," said Margaret.

CHAPTER TWO

"Les Beaux Esprits s'entendent"

BILLIE SMITH, eldest son to the Professor of History in the University of Smokeover, was lying outstretched in his bed, a much damaged and disillusioned pacifist. His wounds were a black eye, a torn scalp, a dislocated thumb and a broken arm. By his bedside sat Margaret, *née* Wolfstone.

"Father has forbidden us to play the League of Nations any more," said Billie. "He says it's a dangerous game. And he's cross with you for putting us up to it."

"I'm very sorry, Billie. But tell me how it happened."

"It all ended in a regular set-to," said Billie.

"But who began it?"

"Ted. He took Germany after all. I took England. We settled it beforehand that Ted was to begin by repenting. But he was in the beastliest temper you ever saw because he had to be Germany, and wouldn't repent, and began hitting everybody. And America took his side, and then Japan hit America on the nose."

"And who gave you that dreadful black eye?"

"America. But I gave America one back!"

"And how did you get your broken arm?"

"Oh, the bull did that!"

"The bull! I thought he was in the next field—the one where you played the Union of the Churches."

"He was, but he got into ours. He saw us scrapping, and Father says it excited him, and so he broke through the hedge and charged bang into the middle of us, before we saw he was coming."

"Did Ted get hurt?"

"Not much; only his new suit was spoilt. The bull got his horn through the—under his jacket, and mother's been mending his trousers ever since. She says it's just *ruined*. And it cost Father ever such a lot."

"We must ask Mr. Hooker to have that bull chained up."

"I wish he would. You won't catch me playing in those fields again while he's about! I say, Miss Wolfstone—oh, I'm so sorry, I quite forgot that——"

"Call me Margaret, Billie," she said.

"All right, that'll be jolly. But I say, why does the bull always charge us when we're playing at being friends?"

"That's because you're only *playing*, Billie. If you really meant it he wouldn't charge you."

"I don't understand that," said Billie.

Not long afterwards Margaret had important business with Mr. Rumbelow in his private office. The business done, she took occasion to report to him the foregoing conversation with Billie.

"It throws an interesting light on our problem," said Rumbelow. "The bull is going to be our difficulty. I shall set Hotblack to study his mind. But

"LES BEAUX ESPRITS"

one thing is clear, Margaret. We must have that boy in the Firm. He has in him the making of a great sportsman. I shall approach his father at once."

"I think," said Margaret, "that with little difficulty we could get the father as well. He is by far the most humane and sensible of that group, and, as you know, an accomplished historian. We are weak on the historical side, Arthur, and there is not a doubt that Professor Smith would be a great acquisition to the Firm."

As other Voices have told, there is nothing more interesting to the candid mind than the strange linkage of causes and effects by which great events are brought about in this vast imbroglio which plain men call Life, and philosophers Experience. One would have thought that in the whole realm of Moral Being no two institutions could stand further apart from one another than the Firm of Mr. Rumbelow and the Smokeover Branch of the Society for Ethical Culture. None the less it had been ordained by the Contrivers of Sport that Billie Smith was to act as a link, or point of contact, between the two. Through his friendship with Margaret he won the admiring notice of Mr. Rumbelow, who became forthwith Billie's hero, not least on the ground of his amazing talent in the invention of new games, of which Billie was swift to take advantage. The result was that Billie and his companions transferred their scene of operations from Mr. Hooker's field to Mr. Rumbelow's park, where there was no bull, and where My Lady and Margaret and three very sympathetic gentlemen would sometimes watch the games from the terrace. From this point no great distance had to be traversed before Professor and Mrs. Smith found themselves guests at Mr. Rumbelow's dinner table, and in the presence of that radiant being whose beauty was only another name for her goodness. Next, by a series of steps which can be easily imagined, Professor Smith resigned the Chair of History in the University of Smokeover and became chief manager of the Historical Department of Mr. Rumbelow's Firm, at a salary of £2,000 a year, and on the understanding that a stool in the office should be kept vacant for Billie on the completion of his Oxford course, which Mr. Rumbelow insisted upon his taking in due time.

Then began that strange process of absorption, which is still astonishing the inhabitants of Smokeover and making a mock of all the prophets who have ever appeared in that forward-looking city. To begin with, all that was alive in the Ethical Society, and there was a good deal, was gradually absorbed into Mr. Rumbelow's Firm. Lucrative and congenial employment was found for the two agitators, for the spiritualists, for the designer of women's frocks and for Mr. Whistlefield, the champion of the Simple Life. Nor was this all. To capture the Ethical Society was to capture a position commanding the University and the Council of the High School for Girls. Professor Smith was a member of all three bodies, and there were other similar pluralists. Hence it was that the public became gradually accustomed to professorial secessions in the direction already taken by Professor Smith. In due

"LES BEAUX ESPRITS"

course Professor Giles, the psychologist, and Professor Marchbanks, the economist, both followed the example of the historian, and the talk now is that, if this kind of thing goes on much longer, Mr. Rumbelow's Firm will itself become the headquarters of the University of Smokeover, though in a transfigured form, and under a new motto—that, namely, of "ideal aims, businesslike methods and sportsmanlike principles."

But what had happened in Mr. Rumbelow's Firm to render possible such startling changes?

At the great banquet which had marked the reopening of his business after the war Mr. Rumbelow had promised the transfiguration of the Firm—transfiguration without sacrifice of historical continuity. And he had kept his word.

To put the least thing first, the name of the Firm had been changed. It was no longer "Rumbelow, Stallybrass & Corker," but "Rumbelow, Hooker & Ripplemark."

But this was nothing to the inner transfiguration which had been accomplished by the fusion of minds, or, as Ripplemark would say, through the gathering together of "reciprocally interacting personalities."

The most remarkable instance of fusion was that which had taken place between the speculative ideas of Ripplemark and the sportsmanlike temperament of Mr. Rumbelow. Ripplemark had imported into the mind of the Firm the whole system of philosophy which he had set forth in *The Moral Will*, not displacing the philosophy of Rumbelow but assimilating it as nourishment—a true syncretism. After consultation with My Lady, who was fully in accord with him, Ripplemark insisted that the first business to be transacted by the new syndicate, or Board of Directors, should be precisely that which he had outlined in *The Moral Will*—the business, namely, of establishing a fraternal community among the nations of mankind.

The Seven Mighty Men were then summoned before the Board and informed by Rumbelow of the business in hand. He told them that the first draft of the enterprise would be left in their hands. In seeking their model, he said, they were on no account to copy the features of any existing government or state. They were to look rather to the type of structure represented by a University—they were, indeed, to contrive a world-wide University, or teaching institution, as the first form in which the common interests of mankind might be correlated and organized.

"In carrying out this commission," said Mr. Rumbelow, "you will remember that the word 'policy' is not to appear. The Board has decided that the idea connoted by this word is the mother of meanness. From this time onwards it is discharged from the vocabulary of the Firm. . . ."

"It is the intention of the Firm," he went on, "to send mankind to school in whole communities, from the old men to the children. You will therefore deal with the nations first, as independent units and as members of a common organism, the Board having decided that it is idle to attack the reign of ignorance elsewhere until it has been attacked on international ground. From that high ground we shall work downwards and inwards, tracking ignorance to its remotest lairs and pursuing it to the utmost bounds of the shadow of death.

"You will base your work on the principle that man's primary need is to be redeemed from his ignorance. You will then proceed to correlate this conception with Mr. Hooker's philosophy; that is to say, you will devise for each nation in turn a form of education by which it may learn so to affirm its own personality as to help other nations to affirm theirs. Having formulated your ideas in language intelligible to all human beings you will pass on your results, first, to our Propaganda Department for world-wide transmission, then, to the Mathematical Laboratory, when the odds on success will be immediately computed.

"Meanwhile our other Departments will be overhauling every branch and variety of education in its relation to the true end of man. The results, as they come in, will be placed in your hands, and you will at once proceed to co-ordinate them with your international constructions, making such modifications as you may deem necessary to secure the utmost unity of the spirit with the utmost diversity of operation in the progress of the human race. And mark this especially: your conception of Progress is to be governed throughout by the Motto of the Firm.

"The preliminary odds in favour of success have been reported from the Mathematical Laboratory as 2 to 1. Encouraging as these odds are, they indicate that we are far from the limit of absolute certainty. The risk of bankruptcy and ruin has to be faced.

"Any intervals of leisure you may find, during

office hours, you will employ in meditating upon this contingency and in taking counsel with one another. In the event of our overthrow, under the impact of brutal and unintelligent forces, the Board will look to the Seven Mighty Men to do their duty at the head of the Staff. We shall then all perish together, as sportsmen should; the pageant will be ended, the book of the Firm will be drowned and not a wrack will be left behind.

"Finally you will bear in mind that the question of our success in the visible world is regarded by the Board as of little importance. It is only at the Unreal End of Things, to which Smokeover and all its villainies belong, that defeat can overtake an enterprise such as ours. Viewed from the Real World, in which the Firm has laid its foundations, our overthrow in the realm of shadows would be our victory in the realm of substance, provided always that in the moment of our downfall we quit ourselves like sportsmen, thereby revealing to the world the eternal dwelling-place of our designs."

On receiving these instructions the Seven Mighty Men said through their spokesman, "We understand"; bowed low to My Lady and retired from the Board Room. They were not in the habit of making speeches.

The next step was to overhaul the entire machinery of the Firm, to examine each one of its endless ramifications, with a view to introducing such changes in detail as the new enterprise might require, so that, when the hour was ripe, this immense complex of interacting forces might be turned on, in its businesslike majesty and irresistible momentum, to the work

"LES BEAUX ESPRITS"

in hand. Finally, the cloud of telegraph wires overhead was minutely inspected, a thousand new ones were added, and orders given for the erection of a wireless apparatus that would command half the world.

All being reported in perfect order the Head Mathematical Expert was called into the Board Room, where a long conversation took place between him and Mr. Rumbelow in the technical language of betting. The upshot was that the Expert undertook to report the odds, hour by hour, on each important step undertaken by the Board.

"The Board," said the Expert, "will be interested to learn that, though the Department has not yet completed its calculations, we have been able to arrive at a more accurate estimate of our chances. On the data now before us the Department gives the odds on the whole enterprise as 3 to 1 in favour of success. I state these figures under reserve. They are subject to revision according to the march of events."

"Remember," said Rumbelow, in dismissing him, "that you are responsible for maintaining the historical continuity of the Firm."

"Such were the inner transfigurations. The touch which gave them their final form was the touch of Maurice Ripplemark, author of *The Moral Will*, ex-airman, ex-Professor of Virtue, LL.D. and V.C. To him more than to any other, always excepting the paramount influence of My Lady, may be attributed the process of absorption by which the Smokeover Branch of the Society for Ethical Culture lost its finite self in the larger whole of that nefarious undertaking which, a few months before, it had petitioned both Houses of Parliament to suppress. Hence, also, that growing desire on the part of the local University to co-operate with the Firm; hence that growing ambition in all its Professors to be transferred to the world-wide form of the Service which Rumbelow, Hooker & Ripplemark were busy in creating. To surround the undertaking with the University atmosphere was indeed no small part of Ripplemark's contribution to the operations of the Firm, a result which might never have been achieved but for his accession to the Board. He himself was thoroughly at home; more at home, he would often say, in his Smokeover office, where the Moral Will was being acted, than in his Oxford lecture room, where he used to discuss its implications. Indeed he would thank God that he had gone into business, and with especial fervency when Margaret was working by his side. At these monents a new vision of relative values would break forth within him. He could hardly resist the belief that he was again flying at a great altitude, the mountains beneath him no bigger than mole hills and Smokeover a mere smudge on the surface of the earth. Yet all this time the lady in the sable coat was firmly persuaded that Ripplemark had stolen her pearls.

Each of the Directors placed the whole of his capital in the Firm. Rumbelow's stake was vastly in excess of the equal portions brought in by the other millionaires. But this made no difference, save that the bookmaker was voted to the Chair as the greatest Master of them all in things appertaining to the Sportsmanship of the Spirit.

"LES BEAUX ESPRITS"

Every meeting of the Board brought the Five together in a deeper loyalty to one another. It was observable, too, that as they came to know each other better a kind of telepathy grew up between them, so that all five would frequently come to the Board with the same proposition on their lips. Nay, it sometimes happened that the Five, on sitting down to the table, would simultaneously anticipate the odds for the day before they had been reported by the Head Mathematical Expert, which seems to suggest that telepathy was at work through the entire Office. Margaret was the first of the Five to notice this strange phenomenon. But she kept these things in her heart.

She, in the meantime, worked steadily at her Play, the hope of the Firm being that by next Christmas, or by the next after that, it might be produced in the Hall of Silence by the greatest actors of the day, and all Smokeover invited to the performance. At first she had found the theme quite unmanageable, the scene of action too undefined, the time data too elusive, the forces at work too vast and amorphous to submit to any kind of concrete personification. For many weeks Margaret was buffeted in deep waters, now swept by violent currents out to sea, now caught in whirlpools, now driven towards the black rocks where dead men's bones lay whitening in the sun, swimming strongly, but doubting if she would ever make the land. Then, as before, her vision contracted. Why not dramatize the History of the Firm itself, the clash of forces out of which it had emerged, the interactions of its personalities, and of all the Invisible Powers, dæmonic and divine, which had guided its destinies—thereby holding the mirror up to civilization itself? From the moment she shaped it thus, the Play seemed to grow and exfoliate by an irresistible impulse from within, so that she suffered no further check, save now and then, when the forces her art would control seemed to get out of hand and to rush onward with a will of their own towards a tragic issue. At these moments she would remember that the odds in favour of success were only 3 to 1. Then a dark foreboding would overcast her and she would lay down her pen.

Mr. Hooker never misses a meeting of the Board. But the ineluctable years are beginning to tell. The stout old Puritan has fought his last battle against principalities and powers. His work is done. Sometimes he forgets the question on the table and seems to be conscious of nothing save My Lady's presence. Sometimes he fails to answer when spoken to, lost in the satisfaction of remembering that he has kept the faith. Or again, at the end of a long sitting, he will grow weary with the technicalities of business, fall into a slumber and dream. He sees his wife running forward to meet him with her arms extended. He sees his sons playing tennis in the clouds. Or he is aboard the Ship of Great Souls; winds that make no ripple on the sea are driving it forward; My Lady is at the helm; Billie Smith in the crow's-nest has just sighted land. Then a sound, faint at first but coming nearer, breaks out from all points of the compass; and the pirates, suspending their labours, gather together and listen. It is the music and dancing of an immortal world.

"LES BEAUX ESPRITS"

The Voice had no more to say, and the Author knew that the Legends of Smokeover were at an end. He knew it because, as the last word was spoken, the sequence was immediately taken up by the music and dancing which Mr. Hooker was hearing in his dreams. The sound lasted for a moment only; but the Author recognized the climax. So, turning his back on the Bridge and on the River of Forgetfulness, he placed his heavy manuscript under his arm and fared forward into the Smokeover streets, where the patter of ten thousand feet betokened that Man was going forth to his work and to his labour until the evening.

As he hurried to his hotel, where his absence all night had given rise to some alarm, he was accosted by a schoolboy, who said, in the most musical voice imaginable:

"If you please, sir, would you mind telling me the time."

Moved by a sudden impulse the Author asked the boy his name, and learnt that it was Billie. He then took out his watch; but there was no need to tell Billie the time. For at that moment the great clock of Smokeover Cathedral, which was immediately overhead, struck the hour; and the deep tones of the last stroke were still booming in the air when suddenly there broke out an indescribable din of syrens, hooters and steam-whistles, of bolts shot back, of iron shutters thrown up, of massive gates turning on their hinges, of doors opened, and of multitudes thronging in.. The day's work had begun.